LET THE GAMES BEGIN!

"That which is begun may be ended, by death or by default. There is no dishonor in default, nor is death necessary. He is the winner who is left standing at the end of the contest."

Braldt and Batta Flor rose to their feet and began to circle, arms held apart from their bodies, eyes probing, searching for the first sign of weakness.

The lupebeast made his first move, a lightning slash that was finished before Braldt even sensed the movement, leaving a welter of crimson stripes across his belly. Braldt wiped the blood, feeling the rough scar tissue bequeathed to him by Batta Flor.

Once again they began to circle, only this time, Braldt was careful to keep a greater distance between himself and his opponent.

Braldt slipped in close behind Batta Flor and brought his hands up in front of the lupebeast's arms and linked his hands behind the creature's neck, exerting a steady downward pressure. But the deadly hold did not even phase his opponent.

Batta Flor turned to face Braldt and gathered him up in an embrace, hugging him tightly to his chest.

Braldt felt his feet leave the ground, saw Batta Flor's face whirl beneath him, heard a bone snap in his arm and knew that his death was fast approaching...

THE
HUNTER

THE

HUNTER

BY
ROSE ESTES

POPULAR LIBRARY

An Imprint of Warner Books, Inc.

A Warner Communications Company

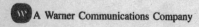

This book is dedicated
to the memory of
Joe Orlowski,
Master gamer, fellow dreamer
and a fine friend.

THE
HUNTER

1

The chase had gone on too long. It seemed to Braldt that the lupebeats were growing craftier and more difficult to kill in recent years. Braldt had been tracking this one—from the depth and spread of its tracks a large, heavy male—for five dawnings and six moonsets, ever since he had discovered what was left of the kill.

Braldt closed his eyes briefly as though to shut out the sight of what would be fixed forever in his memory. No amount of blinking would erase the memory of that bright splash of dark blood staining the smooth sandstone upon which the torn bodies lay, the bodies of Hafnor and Solstead, his two elderly friends whose habit it was to sit on the rocks during the heat of the morning, absorbing the welcome warmth into their brittle bones. Their presence would be missed at the Council meetings, but Braldt knew that he would miss Artallo far more.

Braldt clenched his jaw and squinted down at the tracks, now merely faint imprints in the red dirt. He was determined that he would not lose them, and that he would have revenge on the beast who had robbed him of Artallo's friendship with one scything sweep of its immense curving incisors.

There had been little left of the bodies, the flesh gnawed from the bones, even that of the skull, and the bones themselves had been ground between powerful molars and cracked to extract the last bit of sweet, white marrow. Artallo had been granted leave following the morning's exercises and he had been seen in the company of the two older men as they left the camp. Solstead had been his grandfather.

3

There had been little left but the torn and blood-drenched robes. There had also been the ring that held the robe at the shoulder, the ring that Braldt had given to Artallo when he had passed the last of the tests and joined the warrior ranks. Even the ring, which now rested on Braldt's third finger, bore the deep imprint of the lupebeast's teeth.

Braldt had been sent for as soon as the bodies were discovered, but he had been alerted by the outcry and the wailings of the crowd and had arrived on his own. Little remained other than the torn and blooded robes and broken bones. What clues there might have been had been destroyed by the footprints of those who had discovered the scene.

Braldt had ordered the horrified onlookers away and had studied what was left, trying to harden his mind against the grief that threatened to overwhelm him.

Artallo had been the very best of the young men. The best that Braldt had ever seen. His reflexes were sharper and quicker than others and his strength a match for that of Braldt himself. They had shared an uncommon meeting of minds; to look into Artallo's eyes was like peering into his own soul.

Braldt had watched the younger man's progress over the years and guided his training, hoping that when he passed the final tests he would be allowed to have the youngster at his side. It would be good to be two, rather than one. But now, that hope was gone.

Braldt shook himself back to the present and stared around him, studying the harsh terrain. The tracks of the beast had headed due south following the kill and had never deviated in the days that followed. He had followed those tracks though the undulating plains that were home to his clan. The land had grown sere and the vegetation sparse as they passed the Guardian Stones that marked the boundary of their lands, the point beyond which no man might venture without risking the vengeance of the gods. The land had given way to the soft red dust of the lifeless desert basin. Only the slavers ventured here, perhaps beneath the notice of the gods, and, in such cases as this, the warrior protectors.

Still the tracks continued on, the creature who made them always staying far enough ahead to remain unseen. Now the clinging sands gave way to rougher terrain, the beginnings of the saw-toothed mountains that rose sharply in the distance. The imprint of the beast's toes could be clearly seen as the hated creature dug in for greater purchase. Here, the four long claws had punctured the soil and here was a scraped rock as the beast scrambled up the face of a small outcrop.

Artallo had been sharp of hearing and swift and strong, with short sword and dagger at his waist, yet the sword had been sheathed and the dagger still in its waist loop when Braldt had examined the bloody remains. So swift and so cunning was the lupebeast, Artallo had had no time to protect himself or his two elderly companions.

Braldt did not intend to meet that same fate.

The rocks rose up on either side of him now and were drawing close, forming a narrow defile, a perfect place of ambush for predators. Braldt caught the scent of water borne through the rocky channel by a short-lived burst of cool air. The floor of the cut had been deeply grooved by the passage of those seeking water. There was no doubt in Braldt's mind that it was a site well known by predators and victims alike, the precious water an irresistible lodestone drawing them in, the gauntlet of predators the price to be paid.

The sun beat down on Braldt's head and shoulders from its zenith. It was the time that predators and victims alike were lying up in whatever bits of shade could be found, waiting for the cool shadows of evening. Dawn and dusk were the prime times for danger, and there was always the night. It seemed likely that the lupebeast's lair was somewhere among the rocky crags that abounded in these rugged outcroppings. Braldt did not think that the lupebeast would be seeking food, for its belly was still heavy with meat, but still, there was always an abundance of creatures on the prowl and the lupebeast was not the only danger to be considered.

Turning aside from the narrow passage, Braldt sheathed his dagger and sought for finger- and toeholds in the smooth rock face. He would not go meekly into that defile like another meat animal going to slaughter; he would take to the rocks himself, for was he too not a dangerous predator?

Climbing the face of the rock proved more difficult than Braldt had anticipated, and he cursed the nimble agility of the beast that put his own abilities to shame. When measured from the nose to the base of its tail, an adult lupebeast stood at least six heads taller than a full-grown human male. Its two long, curved incisors were considered its most dangerous aspects, but Braldt also had great respect for the double rows of sharply ridged molars that lined its jaws and were capable of cracking a man's skull as though it were no more than an eggshell. Its teeth curved backward, which had the effect of setting them like fish hooks once they had fastened on flesh. They could be removed, but only at great cost. The mouth of a lupebeast was a filthy thing, with bits of rotting meat caught between the teeth themselves, and the slightest bite always produced a festering infection that frequently maimed even if it did not kill.

The beast had the odd habit of walking upright when it suited its needs. Others, more superstitious than Braldt, whispered that lupebeasts were the ghosts of warriors who had dishonored themselves in battle and were forced to wander the world in animal form until they themselves were killed. Braldt had always been careful not to show his disdain for such thinking, for it did not do to insult one's comrades, but the lupebeast did not need such animistic baggage to make it more fearful; it was a worthy opponent, all on its own.

Grunting with exertion, Braldt dug his fingertips into a thin hairline crack and pulled himself up, scrabbling for a foothold. Inch by torturous inch, he crawled up the sheer face of the rock, cursing the lupebeast every step of the way. His body dripping with sweat, muscles corded with effort, he dragged himself over the edge of the precipice and found himself to be slightly more than two man heights above the narrow trail. The rocky plateau was marked by the imprint of claws, silent testament to the predators who made it their stalking ground. Here they would lie in wait, choosing their victims as they passed below and setting up the hunt that would so often end in death.

Plucking his dagger from its waist loop and drawing his short sword as well, Braldt began to stalk the lupebeast. The victim would become the hunter.

The rock was smooth and gave no hint to the passage of the lupebeast, nor could Braldt be sure that the scrapes he had seen were those of the creature he sought. But he could not allow doubts to assail him now. The beast had headed directly for this place and here he would be found.

Braldt crouched behind an upswept pinnacle, one of the many fanciful designs that the cutting winds had sculptured out of the soft red rock, and studied the landscape before him, his keen eyes of so startling a shade of blue picking out the sites that a lupebeast might choose for its lair.

The rock was like a red ocean, frozen in midmove, undulating surfaces here, sharp peaks of waves there, and deep swells and hollows in between. Possible hiding places were legion with gold and yellow and amber striations in the rock melding with dark shadows and real sinkholes, confusing the eye still further. The place would be a nightmarish deathscape for those who did not know its secrets.

Braldt isolated two likely lair sites, although he did not anticipate being so fortunate as to find his quarry so easily, and plotted his course across the treacherous terrain, knowing that any number of other beasts could be lying up in the shadows, waiting out the worst of the heat before the onset of dusk.

Keeping low to the ground, Braldt slunk toward the two dark openings in a craggy outcrop and did his best to present no clear glimpse of himself. Briefly, he entertained the thought of waiting until nightfall, but then discarded the idea. If darkness was beneficial to him, it would aid the night creatures even more. Best to make his move now when the day's heat had them slumbering in their chambers.

A sharp hiss at his side drew his immediate attention and revealed a red-banded rock viper coiled and ready to strike, its tiny, hate-filled eyes glittering like bits of black crystal. Braldt's hand shot out and seized the snake immediately behind its head, immobilizing it, its mouth gaping wide and the hot sunlight shimmering on the clear drops of fluid that clung to the tips of the five fangs. Knowing that even a single drop could fell him on the spot were it to touch his skin, Braldt snapped the snake's neck with his thumb and dropped it to the ground with distaste. He wanted to hack it to bits with his sword, yet he knew that he could little afford the telltale sound.

Silently he crept on, alert now for the red-banded rock viper as well as its many deadly relations. Another pinnacle loomed up before him and its shadow sheltered a sleeping merebear surrounded by the bones and hooves and bits of fur from its last meal.

Braldt slipped past the creature, willing to permit it to live in order to accomplish his task. He was not deceived by the childlike posture of the beast, twisted in its sleep with hind paws and rounded belly upturned, its head turned to the side, and its muzzle wrapped in its forepaws. Its soft dense fur and short stature gave it the appearance of a cuddly child toy, but Braldt knew that even though the pads and toes of the paws were pink and babyish, the retractable claws were sharp enough to sever his head from his shoulders, and should it be awakened, there would be nothing cuddly in the red death rage that would fill its eyes. The merebear was a fierce and relentless predator and Braldt was glad that it was not his quarry.

Two omnicats, slinky bodies twined around each other, peered at him over a ledge to his left and then withdrew hastily, spotted ears plastered flat against their broad flat skulls, hissing hatefully as their amber eyes narrowed to slits. And then they were gone with only a white tufted flick of a tail to show where they had been.

Braldt reached the mouth of the first cave that was

taller and wider than he had originally realized. The stink of the carrion cat hung heavy on the hot air and Braldt knew that no other creature would share its quarters. A great accumulation of its offal was strewn before the opening, a disgusting but effective boundary marker to its territorial claim. Mixed in the dung itself and everywhere in between were the grisly remains of past meals, everything from beetles to bullocks. Carrion cats would and did eat anything that moved.

The second opening, some distance away and upwind from the carrion cat, gave no clue as to its occupant, but Braldt was not so foolish as to enter in order to learn its identity.

He quartered the area, hoping to pick up some tracks or a scat, even loose bits of fur, anything that might tell him what lay inside the dark opening. Finally, on the sharp rocks that formed the irregular opening, he found bits of black fur that clung to both sides as well as the uppermost curve of the rock that was a full arm's length above his head.

Braldt backed off swiftly, knowing that the cave housed one of the most dangerous of all beasts, the dread nightshadow, said to be a cross between a cat and some larger beast, but none knew for certain for no one had ever lived through a nightshadow attack and returned to tell the tale.

The sun was falling swiftly off to his right and shadows were creeping over the rock, precursors of the darkness that was soon to follow, and the lupebeast still eluded him. The cold, calculating portion of his mind told him to retreat and to do so quickly before the denizens of the rock wakened for their evening's hunt. But the hot flame of rage that had fed his desire for revenge since discovering Artallo's body argued otherwise. He knew that if he left off now, he would never find the lupebeast, and it would merely vanish and Artallo's death would be unavenged.

Braldt did not possess Solstead's calm logic, nor Hafnor's ability to separate out everything that was not important, leaving only the kernel of the matter. Braldt was first and foremost a hunter, a killer, a warrior, and faced with the

wisdom of retreat, he chose otherwise, preferring to die
rather than relinquish his revenge.

He used the shadows to his advantage, slinking from
one dark patch to another, disturbing a meandering rock
vole that peered at him vaguely with minuscule eyes, rising
up on its hind legs to wave hairless pink paws at him while
scenting the air with its long, sensitive probing nose. Scenting
danger at last, it dropped to all fours and hurried away,
waddling comically and squealing softly to itself.

Braldt smiled, imagining the tale it would tell its mate,
then chided himself for not killing the vole. Small as it was
it would have provided a mouthful of energy. But the small,
dim voles and their earthen cousins had provided him with
many moments of cheer when he was young and alone with
little cause to smile and he could not bring himself to harm
them. They had far too many other enemies who were
willing to feed on their soft defenseless bodies for him to
add himself to their numbers.

The ledge had been rising steadily underfoot and now it
rose up before him, suddenly steep and unscalable, and
swept toward the edge of the precipice. He was left with
nowhere to go except back the way he had come, or across
the defile, if he could make the leap.

Braldt had no wish to return, for the plateau would be
thick with animals wakening and ready for the hunt. It did
not seem that he could scale the ledge, for exposed to the
constant wash of the winds, it was smooth and unbroken
without handholds or footholds. Nor did it seem that he
could cross the defile for it was more than two man lengths
wide at this point, certainly farther than he could jump.

As he was pondering the problem, the red orb of the
sun fell behind the shoulder of the ledge; the shadows
lengthened and darkness descended with the finality of
death.

Blinking to adjust his eyes and take in what little light
was available, Braldt backed up against the ledge, knowing
that .it would provide the only protection available. The
ledge was too high to permit an animal to drop down upon
him. If he could edge as close as possible to the precipice he

could only be approached from the front and the right, narrowing the odds somewhat. But as his fingers felt their way along the rock, the rock fell away suddenly several paces short of the edge of the plateau.

Braldt whirled, wondering if his eyes had been tricked by the shadows, had missed the opening of a cave where some creature might even now be waiting to spring. There was no cave. What there was, what Braldt's eyes had failed to find, was a slender trail that led along the edge of the precipice, flanked on one side by the steep rising cliff and on the other side by empty air. The trail was narrow, but it was wide enough for a lupebeast . . . and wide enough for Braldt to follow.

2

The ledge rose steadily beneath Braldt's feet. As warm as it was during the day, the temperature fell swiftly when the sun went down, and the cold night air came out of the north and swept around him, cutting through his thin blue robes and chilling him to the bone. Worse than the cold, the wind ushered his scent before him, announcing his presence to any who might lurk in the darkness.

The smell of water was stronger now, reminding Braldt of his own hunger and thirst. It had been two days since he had last eaten, and that had been a small ground squirrel eaten raw. His only moisture had been that which he was able to extract from the bitter, oily leaves of the ciba, a skeletal, thorny bush that grew in the dry red desert sands. But he put the thought from him, knowing that he could drink his fill after the lupebeast had been found. For now he concentrated on keeping his footing. The edge of the trail crumbled beneath his weight and the darkness of the defile yawned, waiting for his first and last misstep.

Then, suddenly, the cliff fell away beneath his fingers and there was nothing before him but cold, empty darkness. Fighting down the panic, his questing fingers sought the solid comfort of the rock and found it curving away at a sharp angle to his left. The trail itself had ended for there was nothing but empty space beyond. Clinging to the rock and pressing his back hard against the cliff, he peered around the abrupt corner and saw that the trail resumed on the far side. Starlight and the rising crescent of moon revealed a fresh scar where a large section of rock had broken away carrying the trail with it.

Braldt inched backward until he reached a relatively

wide spot. He turned so that he faced inward toward the cliff and then retraced his steps. It would be tricky, but if he could retain his footing and straddle the open space, perhaps he could gain the other side.

His fingers seized a bit of rock that seemed firmly bedded in the cliff, and placing all his weight on his left foot, he moved his right foot out over the broken trail, searching blindly for the other side, and found nothing. Sharp, stinging sweat dripped into his eyes and his stomach fluttered nervously. A rock stinger skittered toward him, head down, death-dealing tail coiled above its back, defying gravity. Braldt bared his teeth in hatred and flicked the creature away before it could inflict its painful sting. But where there was one, there would be more. Determined, Braldt moved to the very edge of the chasm and shifted his weight to the right, clinging to the rock by his fingertips as his feet desperately sought secure footing. Rock crumbled and fell beneath the weight of his foot and then held just as his numbed fingers could hold no more.

He flattened himself against the rock and breathed deeply, feeling the cold night air rasp painfully against his dry throat, wishing that he could somehow quench his thirst. The smell of water hung heavy in the air, tormenting him. Lifting his head, he saw by the light of the swiftly rising moon that he was in a natural amphitheater, circled on all sides by steep walls of rock. At the base of the rock lay a large and black pool, which seeped from the rock itself and contained an image of the rising moon. More important for his purposes was a dark opening, a cleft in the rock, just ahead that could be the lair of the crafty lupebeast, for they were most cautious where they denned. Having no wish to meet the beast on the narrow ledge, Braldt crept forward on silent feet, once more gripping his weapons and trusting his footing to the gods.

The cleft opened into the face of the cliff and disappeared into utter darkness, giving no clue as to its inhabitant. A rush of fetid air swept overhead, swirling about his head like a strong current, filling his nostrils with the stench of rotten meat and his head with shrill, piercing whistles. Bloodwings!

Braldt crouched low, waving his short sword above his head, but he hideous things were gone, sweeping into the night in search of larger prey whom they would settle on and drain of their life's blood, overwhelming the victim by the sheer weight of their numbers.

Braldt watched them go with a shudder, knowing that he had been lucky, then turned his attention back to the cave, wondering if it was home to more than the bloodwings. The moon, rising majestically on its course, chose that moment to illuminate the mouth of the cave, revealing bloodwing droppings and numerous tracks imprinted in the dust, tracks of the lupebeast whom he had been seeking. Braldt raised his face to the Moon Mother and let her benedictions shine down upon him, knowing that she could safeguard him with her blessed presence only so long as he was within her radiant sight.

Glancing upward one last time, taking courage from the silver-white globe that was his god, Braldt crept through the narrow opening and paused, allowing his eyes to become adjusted to the darkness within. To his surprise he found that the cave was larger than he had anticipated, spreading away before him in all directions with a multitude of ledges and nooks that would provide comfortable dens to a score of more lupebeasts. The cave itself was well lit, for the brightness of the Moon Mother filtered down through numerous long cracks that dimpled the surface of the low roof, and he nodded to himself, comforted by this omen that his god was with him. The roof was obviously unstable and at some point in the near future, it would fall, but with any luck, the lupebeast would have no further need for its shelter.

A long, low, rumbling growl filled the cavern, raising the short hairs on the back of his neck and turning him toward the sound. Braldt saw not one but five pairs of green eyes glowing at him out of the darkness! Crouching low, crossing the sword and dagger before him, he tensed for the attack, wondering bitterly how it was that he had failed to consider that the den might be shared by more than one beast.

There was no more time for thinking for the beast was upon him, springing out of the darkness and landing behind him rather than before him at the mercy of his weapons.

Braldt whirled and raised his sword as the beast sprang forward, paws extended, hoping to pin him to the ground. Braldt slipped to the side and lunged forward, trying to end the battle quickly for its companions would undoubtedly join the battle soon, dragging him down by sheer numbers. The lupebeast leaped aside as soon as it touched down, easily evading Braldt's charge.

Braldt and the beast circled, eyes locked upon each other, searching for a weakness. Braldt feinted left and the lupebeast countered, malevolent intelligence glinting in its eyes. It almost seemed as though the animal was laughing at him, toying with him before the audience of others who had not joined the fray but lay watching from a ledge like spectators at the games.

The lupebeast darted forward and slashed at Braldt's leg. Braldt sliced downward, but the beast was already gone, circling behind him and then dashing in to rip at the other leg before trotting away contemptuously with its back to him as though he offered no danger at all. Braldt felt the blood pouring down his legs, the pain burning hot along the edges. He knew that this battle could not be won by strength or power, but by cunning.

Crying aloud as though he had been grievously wounded, Braldt allowed the dagger to clatter to the ground and then, clutching his leg, curled up in a pathetic fetal bundle, whimpering and whining in pain.

The lupebeast circled suspiciously, sniffing the air as though sniffing out his intent for surely it had known that he was not seriously injured. Closer and closer it came, head extended, sniffing at him, almost touching him and then retreating to stare in puzzlement. Braldt shrieked loudly each time the beast drew near and made no move to reach for his dagger that lay in plain view. This at last seemed to convince the lupebeast. It gathered itself and sprang forward, striking Braldt full force. But Braldt was prepared this time and rolled onto his back, stabbing upward with his sword, stabbing upward with all his might between the legs of the beast, grim satisfaction filling his heart as he felt the blade pierce the thick sternum and penetrate the hard, fibrous muscle of the heart itself.

Hideous shrieks erupted from the mouth of the beast as it flung itself backward in agony, its efforts serving only to impale itself farther on the blade. Mortally wounded, it slavered and bit at its body, rending its own flesh in an attempt to rid itself of the offending blade. Hot blood pulsed down upon Braldt with every beat of the dying heart, and he held the sword with grim pleasure, savoring each convulsion and utterance of pain, unaware that his lips were drawn back, bared in a grimace of a smile.

And then it was done, with a final tormented shudder. The beast hung heavy and unmoving on the blade. Braldt flung it from him and scrambled to his feet, scooping the dagger from the ground, ready for the others that would surely come now. Blood poured down his body, drenching his robes, blood of the lupebeast and blood of his own from a score of long furrows inflicted by the dying creature's claws. His legs shook with tremors of nervous shock as his body reacted to the great surge of adrenaline that had carried him through the initial attack. He fought it off, waving the blade before him, waiting for the next attack, wondering whether they would come at him one at a time or all in a rush. They did neither. The green eyes still glowed from the ledge, but now there were nervous blinks as well as low whines of uncertainty.

There was something odd about the sound. Blade outstretched cautiously before him, Braldt approached the ledge. In the dim light that filtered in through the cracks, he saw what he had not seen before, the five sets of glowing eyes belonged to a litter of pups, lupebeast pups. As he advanced toward them they began to whimper and whine, shifting nervously from paw to paw, sensing that something was amiss.

He dispatched four of the cubs swiftly, avoiding their snarling, snapping jaws, which, despite their young age, were still capable of inflicting painful bites. But the fifth pup made no effort to avoid him and stared up into his eyes calmly with quiet resolve. It would not follow its littermates into death crying and cringing. With the courage of a warrior it held its eyes even with his own as he raised his weapon and brought it down with a clang, turning the blade aside and striking the ledge at the last moment.

Something in the young eyes held him, spoke to him in a language beyond speech. He could not kill the pup. Braldt was filled with confusion that he did not understand. How could he allow a lupebeast pup to live? It was unthinkable. And yet there was something about the eyes...

Braldt cocked his head to one side and studied the pup, and it cocked its head and stared back. It might have been a trick of the light, but it seemed that the pup's eyes glinted with humor and one corner of its lips tilted up with the hint of a grin so familiar that it nearly stopped Braldt's heart.

Artallo! Could it be? It was said that lupebeasts were dishonored warriors born again. But Artallo had never dishonored himself or his rank. Could it be that the spirit of his friend had somehow found its way into this small creature's body?

Braldt turned his back on the animal, his thoughts raging inside his head. He raised his dagger once but lowered it immediately, knowing that he would be unable to kill the creature. Disgust and anger pulsed within him as he crossed to the carcass and withdrew his sword, wiping the gore from the blade on the beast's flanks. Only then did he take note of the heavy dugs and realize that he had slain a nursing female. He wondered briefly what the cubs had eaten while the shebeast had been away from the lair, for she had been gone for more than six moonsets. But the thought vanished when he saw that the pup had crawled down from the ledge and was sitting at his feet staring up at him expectantly.

Braldt was shaken, his mind filled with conflicting thoughts. A silent voice urged him to take the pup and return with it, but another voice argued that the pup was a dangerous enemy and commanded him to kill it immediately.

Braldt turned from the pup's bright eyes and staggered

toward the entrance, scarcely aware of the blood running down his legs or the numerous other wounds that he had sustained. The cool night air licked at his skin, bringing with it the clean scent of water, and he hurried forward, unthinking.

Suddenly the light was blotted from view and a great weight struck him full in the chest carrying him backward into the cave, toppling him from his feet. He struck the ground heavily, the air forced from his lungs, and rolled to the side, more from habit and training than from cogent thought. Only when he heard the deep, rumbling growl did he realize that he had been attacked by a second lupebeast.

Braldt reacted swiftly, bringing up his hands and seizing the beast's neck, desperately attempting to keep its jaws from finding his own throat. The hot stink of its breath came full upon his face, all but gagging him with its foulness. Thick, clotted growls of fury came from the creature's jaws and ropes of foamy drool looped across his face and neck. Flinging himself to one side, Braldt sought to throw the animal from himself in order to reach his sword, but the animal found its footing and dove forward, jaws snapping, seizing his upper shoulder in its teeth.

Braldt felt the teeth sink through the heavy muscles and scrape the very bone itself. The pain was akin to being immersed in fire. Now the lupebeast was scrambling for a foothold and jerking him backward like some recalcitrant bit of dead meat. Braldt all but fainted from the pain. Darkness swept over him and explosions of red cartwheeled before his eyes as the taste of coppery bile filled his throat. Each time the beast tugged at his arm, the darkness came closer.

The pain had him now, totally engulfing his mind from his body in a way that he did not understand. While his body was being mauled by the beast, his mind dealt with the problem. At least one, if not both, of the great curved incisors had penetrated his shoulder, as well as both rows of teeth at the front of the jaw. Those teeth pointed inward and back, which meant that they could not release their grip as long as his weight pulled against them. Therefore, so long as he was held by the beast's jaws, it could not bite him elsewhere. In a manner of speaking, while it held him, it was helpless to defend itself.

The logic of his thoughts progressed slowly through his numbed mind. Reaching across his body, under the throat of the lupebeast, Braldt drew his knife from its sheath and, forcing his arm to move, raised the blade. Things seemed to move in slow motion, taking two or even three times the span of time that they would take in real life. Slowly, inexorably, the knife came up, up, up, and then, at last, pierced the outstretched throat of the lupebeast, severing it, slicing through one, then both of the great arteries that lay on either side of the neck. Soon the beast ceased to growl, its voice box ruptured, and shook its head from side to side, jerking Braldt and his rag-doll body with it as it raged against the pain, feeling its life slipping away.

The darkness came then and carried Braldt away on waves of blackness, its peaks tinged with crimson, and blessedly he allowed himself to slip beneath the surface into nothingness.

It was that same pain that brought him back, depositing him on the shores of consciousness like some bit of storm-tossed jetsam. His shoulder was still anchored between the jaws of the dead beast, ripped and torn into a gruesome mess of shredded flesh. The dead eyes of the beast stared into his own and a carrion fly crawled across the unblinking surface.

The air was thick with humming fat, blue-bodied flies. They swarmed in a solid mat over the clotted blood of the beast's wounds, as well as his own. He could feel them moving, burrowing into his torn flesh to feed and lay their eggs that would be cemented in place by a mixture of mucus and feces. Disgust welled up in him, and bringing up his free arm, he tried to dislodge the lupebeast's jaws.

At the first move, the carrion flies rose up in a buzzing metallic-hued swarm, then settled again to continue gorging on the blood. He felt them squash beneath his palm as he beat upon the dead beast. The pain threatened to overcome him again, but he bit down on his lip, bringing fresh pain that held the darkness at bay. He pushed and pried at the jaws, at the clenched teeth, but they would not loosen their grip, held in place firmly by the rictus of death.

Braldt felt around on the hard stony ground and found his knife. Slowly, and with great deliberation, holding the pain back by sheer willpower, he hacked at the lupebeast's muzzle, chipping away at the bone until he severed the upper jaw completely. Only then was he able to remove the terrible teeth from his flesh. The pain was so great that again he was forced to give in to it and the darkness curled over him once more.

The flies were crawling inside his mouth and exploring his nostrils when he wakened, and he spat them out like stones and staggered out from beneath the corpse of the lupebeast, which was beginning to swell and stink with putrefaction.

His legs shook with weakness and he knew they would not carry him down the narrow, treacherous trail. The air was thick with the stink of the dead lupebeasts and the clouds of flies. Braldt moved back into the cool shadows of the cave, realizing that it was midday and dimly wondering how long he had lain unconscious. The passage of time did not matter, thirst and fever would kill him if he did not find some way of assuaging both.

He could barely feel the rough ground beneath his feet; it almost seemed as though he were floating, bumping along beneath the ceiling, his feet a thousand leagues below. He looked down and nearly toppled over, so great was the distance to his toes. His arm was caked with blood and dirt and hung useless at his side, unfeeling. But his tongue, ah, his tongue was swelled to thrice its normal size and filled his mouth like a rock. A very dry rock.

Braldt heard a whimper and turned to look for the source and then realized that it was he, himself. Something soft and warm brushed against his leg and he tottered back and forth for several steps and then looked down. The lupebeast pup, the one he had not slain, regarded him curiously and then trotted off, stopping and turning to look back at him as though commanding him to follow.

Braldt stared dumbly at the animal. "Is that you,

'Tallo?" he mumbled. "Have you come back as a 'beast'? Shouldn'ta died. Maybe I'll die too. Both be beasts then. Hate flies, don' wanna live ina cave with flies though. Hafta find another cave without flies . . ." Overcome by fever and the poison that raged through his body, Braldt staggered after the tiny pup as it led him deeper and deeper into the darkness of the cave. Finally, when he felt he could go no farther, he heard the sound of water, a steady drip, drip, drip echoing in the darkness.

His feet, so unreliable and unfeeling, took him unnervingly to the source of the sound, a broad, shallow pool of water carved into the rock by a steady seepage from above. He collapsed then, falling heavily on his ravaged arm, the pain hitting him like a solid blow to the belly. He inched his way forward, nudging into the pool like a turtle forsaking the land, and let the cool water lave his hot skin, filling his mouth with the precious liquid, feeling it slide down his parched throat and salve his burning flesh. He slithered farther into the water, allowing it to bathe his fearsome wound and cool his fevered body.

Braldt lay there until he began to shiver and then crawled back out onto the floor of the cave. The pup sat beside his head, staring down at him with wide, serious eyes. He had not seen it come, it simply appeared. He wondered if he had killed it and forgotten and now it too was a spirit. He wondered if he too were dead; if both of them were ghosts. Braldt closed his eyes against the solemn regard of the pup, for he had no answers to its questions or even his own.

When he opened his eyes again, the cave was in darkness, and it occurred to him that he had slept and that it was night again for the second or perhaps even the third time since he had killed the shebeast. He was still fevered and thirsty as well. He dragged himself back to the pool to drink again and felt a warm weight pressing against his side. Looking down, he discovered the lupebeast pup, no spirit and real enough from the feel of it, snuggled against him, rolled in a tight, furry ball. He drank and then, drawing the small creature to him, slept again.

His sleep was filled with images. Artallo was there, sitting by his side, warming him with his presence, talking to him earnestly, trying to tell him something of importance. Something that he knew was the most important thing in the world, something that would solve all the problems he would ever have, give him all the knowledge he would ever need. Try as he might, though, he could not hear anything that Artallo said. His mouth moved but there was no sound. He strained to see, and then Artallo sprouted tall ears, lupebeast ears that rose high above his head. His face elongated and became a lupebeast muzzle, long and narrow and filled with rows of sharp teeth. His eyes were no longer blue but amber-colored. Yellow. And even as Braldt watched, the face of his friend became that of the pup, watching him with quiet concern. And then the lupebeast that was Artallo spoke to him and told him to sleep without dreams, to heal without hurt, and then the light faded and took the strange images away.

■

Light streamed in from above, shining directly in Braldt's eyes. His body was one enormous throbbing ache and he could not remember the last time he had eaten. He turned his head toward the water and saw the pup sitting beside his head, just as he had in the dream. He no longer thought that he was a spirit, nor the pup either, for it was obvious that they were both alive. No spirit could hurt as much as he did. But whether the pup contained the spirit of Artallo was another matter and one that could wait for another day. For now, it was enough that he was alive and he would do his best to see that he . . . or, rather, they remained so.

3

Braldt felt his way back toward the cave opening, his only thought being to somehow make his way down the narrow trail and find something to put in his empty belly. His legs were shaky and his body weak, but he knew that it must be done or he would die. He reached for his weapons with his good hand, only to realize that he still held the jaw of the lupebeast in his hand. He stared at it in the dim light, seeing the long, curved incisors and the double rows of teeth still stained with his blood, and nodded to himself, thinking that it would serve as a trophy as well as a reminder of the nearness of death. He tucked the jawbone into the folds of his robes and found his dagger still in its loop. His short sword was nowhere to be found and he could not remember when he had it last. He hoped that it was not back at the pool for his legs were without the strength to carry him there and back again. He could only hope that it would be found at the side of the slain he-beast.

As Braldt drew near the cavern where he had killed the lupebeasts, the pup stopped abruptly, its large ears stiffly erect, the piebald-colored fur on its back rising in ridged spikes. A low growl emerged from between its teeth, a poor imitation of its parents, but a growl nonetheless.

Braldt studied the pup, wondering what would cause such a reaction, then, because his head was feeling very heavy and his vision blurring with every step, he decided that it was nothing more than bad memories. After all, the pup had seen its entire family slain. Under the circumstances a growl was not inappropriate.

The pup stood stiff-legged and growled continuously, seemingly unwilling to advance farther. Braldt brushed past the pup, anxious to find his sword and be gone from the place. The pup would follow or not as it liked. When he looked back, the pup was following, although he still growled and his little tail, whip thin and without the plume-like brush that would distinguish it as an adult, swept back and forth like a nervous tic.

Braldt could see the entrance to the cave now, the brilliant midday sun pouring in through the opening, bathing the stony ground with its harsh, hot light. He hurried forward, anxious to feel the hot sun on his body, realizing that he was chilled to the bone by the cold darkness of the cave.

As he drew closer, his eyes fixed on the sunlight, Braldt suddenly became aware of a sound that he had been hearing for some time. It was a curious shrill, chittering sound, almost like quarrelsome children arguing in high-pitched voices. Braldt moved farther into the cavern, shaking his head in irritation and willing his eyes to stop playing tricks. The entire floor of the cavern appeared to be undulating.

Braldt made his way toward the body of the he-beast so that he could reclaim his sword, for he was certain that that was where it would be found, but as he advanced, the entire floor seemed to explode, rising up around him in screaming, flapping hysteria! Braldt could hear the pup barking wildly as he flung his arm across his face to protect his eyes, realizing too late what he had done. Bloodwings! Thousands of them were feasting on the rotting carcasses of the slain lupebeasts and he had waded into the midst of them!

He could feel them flapping against his bare skin, attempting to settle so that they might suck his blood with their long, sharp-edged hollow fangs, replacing what they withdrew with a pale fluid that deadened the flesh around the wound. Harmless in small doses, the pale fluid could kill if the bites were numerous enough.

Braldt attempted to cover his head and shoulders with his robes, but his injured arm still hung heavy and useless at his side, and as the robe came over his head, he could feel the wings of two of the hideous creatures flapping against his neck and chest, trapped inside the folds of the fabric!

Then he was bitten on the thigh and again on his calf and he felt the cold wings with their tiny clinging claws gripping him tightly as they siphoned the blood from his body. More and more bloodwings clung to him as he flung himself from side to side, beating at their soft bodies, plucking them from his flesh, and throwing them aside. They scented fresh blood now, and for every bloodwing he dispatched, two and three more took its place. He could hear the pup howling now, a low, keening sound that only served to intensify the horror.

Braldt threw himself to the ground and felt the soft bodies smash beneath his weight, heard the sharp crack of fragile wing bones, and the shrill screams. Over and over he rolled, crushing the bloodwings beneath him, ignoring the pain of his shoulder and the dizziness that threatened to overcome him. Somehow, he was aware that the pup was close by, its jaws snapping and crunching an accompaniment to his passage.

He then came up hard against the body of the male lupebeast, stinking and rotting, filling his nostrils with the stench of decay. His hand reached out and swept over the ground, searching, searching, no longer attempting to beat off the screaming maelstrom of bloodwings who settled upon it, until at last he found what he was searching for. He rose up with a scream and plunged the blade of the sword up into the low, earthen ceiling time and again until he was rewarded by a cascade of dirt and stones that swept down upon him, stripping the bloodwings from his body. He struck out again and again, widening the hole, allowing the bright sunlight to pour in, creating havoc.

Once begun, the low roof, already weakened by the numerous cracks that crisscrossed its surface, collapsed in upon itself, burying the bodies of the lupebeasts and the coven of bloodwings. A few escaped, but these made no attempt to attack and quickly departed, seeking safer, darker quarters.

The earth stirred at Braldt's feet and the pup's nose emerged, caked with dirt, quickly followed by the rest of its head and shoulders. It sneezed once, twice, and then stared up at Braldt with bright eyes as though wondering what came next. For all his pain, Braldt was forced to laugh, for the young animal, hated lupebeast though it might be, had the heart of a warrior.

"Come, little one, it is time we left this place, you and I, our bellies are empty and I have had my fill of bloodwings and death." Gripping the pup by the scruff of its neck, Braldt fitted it into the drape of his robe and began to search for a way out.

Much of the roof was unstable and came down as soon as Braldt placed any weight on it, tumbling to the floor of the cavern, burying it still deeper. But at last he found an area that was composed of rock and did not give under his weight. He could not pull himself up with one hand for he was too weak, but he piled rocks one on top of the other until he was able to climb out of the ruins of the cavern and rest on the hot, sun-drenched plateau. The pup slipped out of his robes and lay flat beside him, its head lowered, ears flattened against its broad skull, and the bright intelligent eyes, darting nervously in all directions, filled with fear. The pup panted heavily, from fright rather than heat, but made no attempt to leave Braldt's side.

"First time you've been outside," Braldt said, laying his palm atop the pup's head. "No wonder you're frightened. It's a scary place, little one, and if you're going to make your way in it, you'll have to grow up fast and tough . . . just like I did. It starts now and we'd best be on our way before something else tries to kill us. Stay close and you'll be fine."

Braldt struggled to his feet and set off with the pup hugging his heels. Sometimes it pressed too close and all but tripped Braldt, whining fearfully and hugging the ground with its belly, casting wide, frightened eyes about in all directions. It occurred to Braldt that the small creature was absolutely terrified by the wide stretch of blue sky and the burning white orb that hung above them, for all of its young life had been lived in near darkness. The hot rock was surely scorching its tender paws that had none of the thick, callused protection it would develop in later years. Taking pity on the small animal, Braldt lifted it up and placed it inside his robes again where it immediately settled and was still.

"I wish it were that simple for me," Braldt said to himself as he patted the trembling pup. "Food and shelter. Got to have food and shelter and then deal with this arm, if I don't want to lose it."

Strangely enough, the bloodwings had done him a favor, for sensing the fresh blood, they had gone straight for his wounded shoulder. They had robbed him of his blood and they had replaced it with their own fluid that was intended to dull the senses of their sleeping victims, but in his case served to deaden the pain, enabling him to travel. Braldt didn't know how long it would last or if it would have any lasting effects, but he welcomed even the temporary relief from pain.

And then suddenly a path appeared beneath his feet, a deep indentation in the soft red rock that led straight to the edge of the precipice and then slipped over. Braldt wondered if a section of rock had broken off here as well, but as he drew closer he saw that the trail descended the face of the cliff at a steep but passable incline that terminated at one end of the stony amphitheater. There was a large pool of water, deep enough to withstand the worst of droughts, as well as several stands of small trees, thick grasses, and tall reeds, and a variety of weedy foliage.

There were still the predators to be considered, none of which he cared to meet with the scent of blood hanging heavy about him. But the small oasis offered all that he needed to heal himself: water, shelter, and the promise of food. Home and safety lay six moonsets distant and between them lay seventy leagues of danger and harsh, inhospitable terrain. To travel in his condition was an open invitation to death.

His decision made, Braldt descended the face of the cliff.

■

Ten moonsets later, well fed and rested, recovering from the worst of his wounds, Braldt and the pup, whom he had chosen to call Beast, left the spring and set out for home. The jawbone of the he-beast had been stripped of flesh and polished by an accommodating colony of fire beetles. It now hung from a thong around his neck. The shiny new pink skin of his shoulder contrasted sharply with the dark, coppery tan of his body, and while it too would darken with time, it would always bear the scars inflicted by the lupebeast.

Braldt was not concerned with the color of his skin, nor the scars, merely pleased that the arm had suffered no permanent damage and would still be able to wield a weapon. This had caused him a good deal of concern during his recuperation for he had trained since youth to be a fighter and a protector of his tribe and he could envision no other life.

He had been right in his assessment of the spring for he had found all the medicinal herbs needed to treat his wounds. Wild animals and birds had come to the springs at dawn and at dusk in great numbers, braving the gauntlet of predators, and if some of their numbers fell, they were not missed in the multitudes that depended on the steady source of sweet water that flowed even in the hot time.

Trees and reeds had provided shelter as well as firewood and the fire burning brightly all night long held the predators safely at bay. Carefully placed snares had provided fat birds to roast over the fire and a well-thrown rock had brought down a small desert deer.

He had not forgotten to offer homage to Mother Moon and he sang her praises and offered her homage each night as she rose majestically over the edge of the plateau by burning bits of flesh to show his gratitude for watching over him and sparing his life. Beast had added his own quavering tones to his, an eerie combination, but somehow fitting for both had lived despite the odds against them.

Braldt and Beast had come to know each other better. The pup had accepted him into his world and looked to him for direction, but there was a fierce burning light that shone from deep within his amber eyes and Braldt knew that for all his apparent loyalty, this would never be a tame dog to do his master's bidding.

There seemed to be little need for words between the two of them, the pup needing only to look at Braldt to know what was expected. They had begun to work as a team, the pup rushing forth barking wildly and scaring the prey within throwing range. The technique was not perfect for the pup was filled with all the erratic enthusiasm of youth, but Braldt could see that with his obvious intelligence, the rough edges would soon be honed away.

The pup's presence and his intelligence touched something deep inside Braldt, something that only Artallo had come close to touching. Others, more knowledgeable and sensitive to their own needs, would have called it friendship.

As they made their way across the empty Forbidden Lands, back toward the tribal state, Braldt allowed his thoughts to reach forward and wonder how Beast would be welcomed. It was a foolish question for even though lupebeasts were the sworn enemy of his tribe and all others, Braldt could have brought a raging merebear into the middle of the city and gotten away with it. He was the chosen favorite of the chief.

Braldt grinned as he thought back on some of the pranks he had played in his own erratic youth and remembered how Chief Auslic had tried to keep his face grim and unsmiling while issuing a reprimand. Carn, his younger half-brother and Auslic's own nephew, had seldom gotten off so lightly with his misdemeanors. Braldt himself had been adopted by Carn's family soon after he was found in the desert beside the bodies of his parents.

They had been strangers, unknown to the tribe, different from them in every way. The dead man and woman had been fair of skin, their eyes as blue as the distant sea, and their hair as white as the sun that burned in the sky. Braldt grew up in their image with high, broad cheekbones, straight nose, and wide, flat brow—all flat planes and hard, sharp edges, so unlike the features of his adopted tribe.

His body developed differently as well. Although he and Carn were nearly the same age, Carn had the slender, wiry build so common to the tribe as well as dark eyes and skin and curly brown hair. Carn's strength lay in his endurance and his burning hatred of failure, and he practiced long hours on the hard-packed earth of the training ring, drilling over and over the proscribed movements of sword and dagger. Equally long days were spent with bow and arrow.

Braldt grew taller and broader than Carn, taller by a full head and a good deal heavier. His bulk was not excess flesh, however, for he was solidly muscled and the smaller, thinner Duroni could only look at him and marvel. He was their champion and the pride of the tribe.

For him the long arduous hours of practice were unnecessary, for the moves came as naturally as though they had been born a part of him like the knowledge of breathing and walking, and while he practiced alongside Carn and the others, it was for him a joy, a pleasure to be indulged rather than a chore. In the end, he outstripped them and all that his mentors could teach him. He knew more than his teachers and ventured into unexplored areas of expertise on his own. He developed a method of training that allowed him to practice alone, to compete against himself, for the others were unable to keep up with him and to attempt to do so was to show them their shortcomings. So he practiced alone, and even though they admired him and praised him and boasted of his prowess, a distance had sprung up between himself and his former playmates. He could call none of them friend. Except for Auslic.

Lines of worry creased Braldt's forehead as he thought of Auslic, for while he was still chief in every meaning of the word, he was by far the oldest member of the tribe and had grown noticeably frail. Braldt knew that the deaths of Hafnor and Solstead would be harsh blows, for they had been Auslic's oldest friends and strongest supporters in the Council, that body of men who governed the tribe. With their deaths, Auslic's power would be greatly diminished.

Braldt pondered the problem as his legs rose and fell tirelessly. Auslic was old, it was true, but still the best qualified to govern the tribe. Over the years he had dealt with rival tribes who had sought to rob them of their rich farms and grazing lands and their ample water rights as well as the constant onslaughts of the primitive beastmen, the karks, those strange creatures. They were neither man nor animal but something in between with their manlike features, clever hands, and shaggy, powerful bodies.

He often wondered if it would be possible to speak to them, to communicate, but there had never been an opportunity. Whenever they met, which was but seldom, it was in battle. Little was known of the karks for they came out of the east, out of the Spirit Land, lands that were forbidden to enter, even to such as Braldt. But the karks came and went with impunity and the priests said that they were unclean and not loved by the gods and that the gods were offended by their presence and much honor fell to those who killed them. Braldt had killed many of the karks who fought bravely and died with eyes filled with hatred, and yet, still, despite the assurance of the priests, Braldt wondered...

He also helped to defend the tribe against the periodic raids of the slavers who traveled in darkness and secrecy, slipping in whenever possible to steal children or breeding-age women or strong, able men and disappearing swiftly, leaving little or no trail to follow. But such matters were routine and little affected the working of the city, and under Auslic's long rule the clan had grown and prospered. It was hard to remember a time when Auslic had not ruled. For many, he was the heart of the tribe itself.

But others, Carn among them, whispered that Auslic had ruled too long and should give way to a younger more vigorous leader, by which they meant themselves.

Braldt could imagine no chief other than Auslic and he had taken it upon himself to remain at the old man's side whenever possible, lending him strength by his presence. For him it was a silent statement that not all the young men wished him to be gone. Auslic, while never commenting on his presence, seemed to enjoy having him at his side and made a place for him at the Council, beside his chair of state, which earned Braldt many a dark look from Carn and his followers. Braldt had not thought to speak to Auslic before leaving to seek out the lupebeast, never realizing that the deed would take him so far nor keep him away so long.

His concern for Auslic and what might be happening in

his absence drove him on long after his lungs and muscles burned with fatigue and begged for respite. The pup had fallen behind that first day, whining piteously before the sun had even reached its peak in the hot white roof of the sky, and Braldt had been forced to carry him in his robes, further adding to his exhaustion as he ran on through the long hot day and into the night.

The leading edge of the sun was dimpling the horizon, tinging the pale grey mists with pinkish hues, when Braldt passed the great standing Guardian Stone that marked the southernmost boundary of the Duroni lands. He had run throughout the night, without cease, taking advantage of the absence of the burning sun that scorched the lands during the day, and his body throbbed with exhaustion.

Beast stirred within his robes and chirped softly. Braldt slowed and came to rest against the intricately carved face of the Guardian Stone. No man knew the meaning of the carvings that marked its face, not even Auslic for they were ancient beyond memory.

In places, the stone was worn as smooth as a baby's cheek, the stark runes all but obliterated. But when viewed from an angle, the outlines of a manlike being could be seen underlying the carving, stern, blank eyes staring forward into the hot empty desert lands as though standing silent guard against unseen invaders. Braldt had often been found at the foot of the stone in the early days, staring upward at the cold, chiseled stone, for he imagined that he saw something of his own features in that hard rock, and it was just beyond the stone that he and his dead parents had been discovered.

He had stared at the runes over the years, trying to decipher their meaning, hoping that in some way they would explain his own mysterious origins, but understanding continued to elude him, and eventually he had come to accept the futility of his actions. But the stone still drew him, for it was a tenuous link with his unknown past, and he felt none of the fear that it engendered in the rest of the tribe, and to it he returned in times of trouble or loneliness.

The feel of the rough stone under his hand was comforting

and he stood there, breathing deeply, body slicked with sweat, watching the sun burn its way through the mist barrier, as he had done so many times in the past. Beast had wandered away to squat in puppy fashion behind the stone and suddenly came bounding stiff-legged back toward Braldt, ears and eyes focused on the stone, tail standing straight up, his sharp yips breaking the dawn's sweet silence.

Instantly alert, Braldt drew his short sword and gestured to Beast to be quiet. The pup fell back behind Braldt, growling low in his throat, willing to relinquish the lead, but unable to still his voice.

Braldt crept forward, wondering what manner of creature Beast had flushed out of hiding, perhaps a desert cat or a rock lion, both of whom occasionally ventured into Duroni lands in search of a fatted bullock or a careless herdsman.

Braldt skirted the edge of the great stone and leaped out into the open, dropping his sword and staring in some confusion at the figure of the girl who crouched there, spear and sword gripped tightly in her own small hands, staring up at him with equal surprise.

"Keri?" Braldt said in amazement as he recognized his adopted sister. "What are you doing here?"

"Waiting for you. Hoping that you would come this way if you came at all."

Her voice faltered as she looked at the terrible scar that swathed his shoulder and the numerous wounds that marked his body, then down at the pup who had not ceased his growling despite the fact that Braldt had made no attempt to kill her.

"Well, so you have found me," Braldt said impatiently, his heart hammering in his chest. "What is wrong?"

"Auslic," the girl replied in a stammer, dragging her eyes away from Beast. "He is failing. I do not know if he still lives for it was four moonsets ago that he took to his bed. The full Council is gathering and Carn says that Auslic will die, although Father says no. I took him a bowl of Mother's broth, and when none were listening, he bid me to find you. I dared not venture into the Forbidden Lands by myself and I could but pray that the Guardian Stone and the Moon Mother would protect me and that you would return by this same path.''

Keri's bright brown eyes were filled with defiance and the old anger that she had not been born a boy. Braldt knew what it cost her to admit that she had been afraid to enter the empty lands by herself, for throughout her young life Keri had competed with Carn and Braldt and had often bested Carn even though he was older by fully eight moon turns. She had never ceased to resent her mother's insistence that she don long skirts when she reached the turning age and was always willing to slip away with bow and arrow and spear when she should have been learning to cook and mend and tend to household chores. Braldt admired her fierce nature, so like his own, and felt his heart quicken at the risk she had taken in remaining alone in this isolated and dangerous place waiting for him to return. He doubted that even Carn would have had the courage to do so.

''What happened,'' he asked as he began to pace swiftly toward the city.

''I don't know. He fell silent when he learned of Hafnor's and Solstead's deaths and he had no interest in his food, even though Mother prepared all his favorites to tempt him and the priests lay their hands upon him. Since then he has not moved but sits in his chair and looks before him, seeing nothing.''

Keri glanced back at her sleeping bundle and her small pile of possessions and then at Braldt's back as he drew swiftly away from her and shook her head impatiently as she hurried to catch up with Beast darting in to snap at her heels.

''I knew it. I should never have gone,'' Braldt muttered, blaming himself for Auslic's collapse.

''How could you not go, it is your . . . ow! Braldt, call off your monster, it keeps biting at my ankles! Why have you brought this thing back with you? Ow! Stop!'' She turned to swat at Beast and he surged forward and snapped at her fingers.

''Beast,'' Braldt said with a grunt as he swept the pup

up and slipped him inside his robes. Immediately the pup's head emerged from the confining robes and kept Keri in constant view, growling as though to let her know that Braldt was under his protection. "He is with me, now."

"So, it would seem," Keri mumbled with displeasure, glaring at the upturned lip and glistening incisors, as she wiped the smear of blood from her fingertips. "I thought the idea was to kill the lupebeasts, not tame them."

Braldt did not reply, saving his energy for the distance yet to be covered and whatever he might find when he arrived.

4

The Guardian Stone stood a full day's travel from the center of the city as did all the stones that ringed the perimeter. In all, there were two hundred and forty Guardian Stones, as many stones as there were moonsets in a full turning, and Braldt had visited all of them during the long years of his youth as he passed through one station and then another of his initiation into adulthood.

All boys began together in one raw lump, undistinguished from one another, having only their age, five, in common. They were taken from their parents then and reared in communal buildings by the priests and the men who did their bidding, who would decide their futures.

The priests were silent, never speaking, their features hidden away behind voluminous folds of dark material that swathed them from head to toe. Even their hands were covered by gloves. A large silver plate, an image of Mother Moon, hung in the center of their black robes, not a necklet or even woven into the heavy material, but seemingly fitted directly into their bodies. This emblem was matched by a smaller image on the palm of their right hand.

Every boy wondered what the priests really looked like beneath the concealing folds of their robes and whether they disrobed at night, but none dared to implement any of the plans that were brewed under the blankets in hushed whispers. There was something mysterious and frightening about the priests, despite the fact that they were Mother Moon's emissaries, something that could not be defined. But as one grew older, the boys who were now men laughed at the memory of their younger selves and tried to convince themselves that their fears had been nothing more than the overactive imagination of youth. Braldt did not join in that laughter.

The priests going about their business wrapped in eerie silence, in robes of black and midnight blue, had decided their lives, directing them first into classes where the basics of knowledge and religion were pounded into them. Those who showed quick minds and aptitude were separated from their classmates and advanced to higher classes where they were taught all that their minds could hold of mathematics, geography, religion, history, and philosophy. Those few who excelled were divided yet again and given to the appropriate teachers.

Those who advanced no further than the first level completed their limited education and were then trained to become the farmers and herdsmen and menial laborers of the tribe. There was no onus in these chores for they were necessary, the basis of the wealth upon which the clan depended for their daily sustenance. But neither was there glory.

Others became teachers themselves or were slated to join the ranks of bureaucrats who functioned, mostly unseen, in the myriad of chores needed to maintain tribal affairs. A few were chosen to become acolytes to the priests, and while their parents accepted the rare honor with a glad face, in private they wept for they knew that their sons would be sent to the Temple of the Moon and when and if they were seen again, they too would be wrapped in dark robes of silence.

All boys, even those destined to become priests and scholars, were required to learn the rudiments of battle. But, as with education, those who excelled advanced on to other stations where they were taught all that they could learn. Those few who were the very best, such as Braldt and Carn and a handful of others, would become the protectors, the very backbone of the city-state, sworn to keep it from danger at the cost of their own lives if necessary.

Only a very few of these boys survived the keen scrutiny and winnowing process of the teachers and priests and went on to form the elite cadre of those who were deemed superior in both mind and body. From these precious few would come the future leaders and Council members of the tribe. Braldt could count himself among those few, as could Carn and four others. Those who had gone before them had already taken their places in the Council or other positions of responsibility.

Braldt had thought little of his future role in the affairs of the clan for he was content with his life as he knew it. Auslic's friendship warmed him and fulfilled his need for human companionship, and the duties that took him off into the desolate far reaches of their lands satisfied his need for action as well as solitude. But if Keri's words were true, his world was about to crumble.

Braldt himself had no desire for a higher station and dreaded the day when he would be charged to take his place on the Council, for he had no liking for the incessant yammer of voices arguing matters that for him held little interest. Nor could he picture the clan without Auslic at its head. But all men must pass in their time, even Auslic.

Braldt knew that the title of chief would never pass to him for he was an outsider even though he had spent his life among the Duroni. If Auslic should die, the title would undoubtedly be passed to Carn. Braldt shook off the feeling of dread that accompanied this thought, trying to think of Carn's good points, trying to convince himself that all would be well.

Carn was the obvious choice. He was a direct descendant of Auslic. He was intelligent, of that there was no doubt; his bright eyes spoke eloquently of the brilliance that lurked behind them, the sharp, cutting wit and barbed words that flew straight to their mark defeating any reply. Nor was he short of courage and his skill with sword and dagger were well known.

But there was something dark that lurked in Carn, some hidden anger that rose to the surface under stress and unleased sudden rages that he could not always control. Carn had once killed a man during such a rage, over an imagined slight, and only his unfeigned grief and his father's influence and several circles of silver had managed to sweep the matter under the table.

These thoughts and more filled Braldt's exhausted mind as he drove himself over the last remaining distance into the outskirts of the city. Beast had long ago given himself over to sleep for it was impossible to keep up and Braldt had kept him firmly wrapped inside the sling of his robes. Keri had fallen behind early in the day and though he would have welcomed her presence, he could not afford the delay of waiting for her or matching his strides to those of her own. She had been sent to find him and she would understand his actions. He hoped.

The open rangeland where the beasts of burden and those who provided meal and drink roamed had long been left behind, their keepers, many of whom were old friends, had raised their spears in greeting as he passed. The long, straight rows of the farmlands had appeared then, the abundant crops of hot time having been gathered in and the pale green shoots of cool time just emerging from the dark soil. Now there appeared the long, low rows of barracks that housed the young boys, serving as their homes and their schools as they grew, determining their futures and the course of their lives.

The red sandstone circle that was the ring rose up before him, blotting out the sight of the newly risen moon. Braldt could picture the rows upon rows of stone seats that circled the hard-packed earth that lay at the center. The ring. The place where they played, studied, worked, trained, and ultimately fought, pitting themselves against their teachers, one another, and then warriors from other tribes and, occasionally, fierce animals, all for the glory of the Moon Mother. Or so the priests would have them believe. Braldt had his doubts.

The red sandstone cubes and high-walled circles that were home to the clan came next, the size and number of their cubes and circles dictated by the size of the family that dwelled within. Some families, blessed with numerous offspring and extended marriages, took up entire blocks with their enclaves. Other families, such as Carn's, were quite small, composed of but four members: Carn; his father, Otius; his mother, Jos; Keri; and Braldt. Each had his or her own cube for sleeping and there was a central cube for the purpose of eating and family matters, but they had no need for their own circular courtyard for they entertained no one but themselves and to Otius's great sorrow, no grandchildren clung to his fingers or bounced upon his knee.

The inner city with its labyrinth of buildings lay beyond the warren of dwellings, filled with the offices of those who ran the city-state and all their hundreds of minions forever scurrying thither and yon like demented rabbits. Braldt took little notice of them for the thought of them numbed his mind. Not for a heartbeat could he bear to imagine their dull, confined lives. All of his attention was focused on the circular building that rose beyond the conclave of the bureaucrats, and was constructed of shining black stone. It rose three times the height of any other building in the city and surpassed even the ring in size. Only the Temple of the Moon was larger, more imposing. But here was the heart of the city, here was the Council chambers, the place where the full Council convened and where Auslic ruled.

Braldt passed through the tall, narrow silver doors crowned by the emblem of the full moon, flanked on either side by a trail of stars. This image was engraved upon the metal doors as well as the breast plates of the guards who stood watch on either side, acknowledging Braldt's presence by the fact that they made no move to stop him from entering.

He passed swiftly through the empty corridors lit only by silvery orbs of light attached to the walls at regular intervals, priest fire as it was called, and found only in the Council building and the Temple and the priest's own quarters; homes and offices were lit by tapers and torches.

Cold black stone surrounded him and gleamed underfoot, unrelieved except for silvery metal insets of the moon in all its phases placed high on the walls, surrounded as always by the stars who offered their attendance in the frieze as well as in nature. The silvery metal, like the shining black stone, was an unknown substance, its source a mystery except, perhaps, to the priests who, of course, had no comment.

Braldt could hear the murmur of voices rising and falling as he hurried through the empty halls flanked on either side by the dark shining stone, but he could not make out the words.

Finally, he came to the central arena, the place where all corridors led. Here, as in the ring, were row upon row of seats carved out of the ebon rock descending, rather than rising, where the members of the full Council sat, each representing his own family group. Petitioners and penitents sat as well, waiting the pleasure of the court to beg for some personal favor or the sentence for some indiscretion.

Now, the rows were filled to overflowing with the members of the full Council, each draped in the robes that designated their status. Crimson red robes for the bureaucrats and green for the merchants and moneylenders, brown for the landholders and pale green for the tillers of the soil. The black robes of the priests were much in evidence, as were the silver robes of their acolytes. And blue of course for the warriors such as Braldt. These last were clustered around the foot of the steps that rose from the very center of the circle, the steps that rose to the highest position of power in all the land, the black stone throne crested by a full moon rising and occupied by the High Chief of all the Duroni. Auslic the Wise.

As Braldt hurried forward, descending the steps two and three at a time, unmindful of the murmur that arose at his passage, the raised circle of fingers invoking the protection of the Mother Moon against the sight of Beast who now trailed at Braldt's heels, growling and snarling in all directions. The band of worry that had gripped his chest since hearing Keri's words loosened. He had arrived in time. Auslic still lived. Wasting no time for the bended knee and slow progression that was the accepted procedure for approaching the High Chief, Braldt took the steps to the throne with the same haste that he had descended, sinking to his knees at Auslic's feet, equally unmindful of the gasps of horror that accompanied this total lack of propriety.

Auslic raised his head slowly and looked down upon the young man whom he had come to think of as his son, and his tired eyes filled with gladness. One side of his face twitched with the beginning of a smile, a greeting, and he stirred in his chair. The other side of his face remained frozen, unmoving, dragged down and stiff as though carved from stone. His right hand reached out tremulously to seize Braldt's own, but his left arm and the hand that wore the great crystal moon ring of his office dangled uselessly at his side.

"... said you were dead," came the voice, a mere whisper of sound, a thread that held no semblance to the hearty, gruff bass that was his normal tone. "... said they had found your bones in the empty lands ... lupebeasts."

Braldt enfolded Auslic's hand in his own and pressed it to his chest so that the man might feel the beating of his heart. "I am no spirit, Father. Braldt the Hunter still lives. They were mistaken, as you can see, and I have avenged the deaths of those taken by the lupebeast."

"... showed me your ring ..." muttered Auslic and using the fingers of his right hand pried open the tight grip of the left hand to reveal Braldt's own emblem ring, that which usually held his own blue robes at the shoulder, the ring which had mysteriously vanished from his room more than a fortnight ago. Braldt had wondered at its absence and had assumed that he had lost it, although such a thing seemed unlikely. Its appearance now, under such strange circumstances, was peculiar, suspicious in nature, and Braldt stared about him at the cluster of upturned faces, wondering who, if any among them, had cause to wish him ill, then shook the thought from him and turned his attention back to Auslic for that was all that really mattered.

"How do you fare, Father? Why are you in this place? Let me take you to your bed where you may rest more easily and heal yourself."

"Now you are here ... not enough time ... Carn ... tribe ... much to say ... I will send you word ... you will understand and forgive me ..." Auslic held Braldt's hand in a tight, almost painful grip and uttered his words in a fierce whisper intended for Braldt's ears alone although there were many who crowded near. Braldt brought his ear close to Auslic's lips to catch the slightest word, but even so, the words were disjointed and were more a puzzle than an explanation. ". . . stand up," Auslic said clearly, his eyes blazing with determination, and Braldt hurried to obey, feeling the strange stiff flesh and slack muscles move beneath his hands as he raised and steadied Auslic.

"By right of the Moon Mother, I, Auslic the Wise, of the royal House of the Moon, declare Braldt the Hunter to be my heir and take my place as the High Chief of the Duroni!" Struggling, he drew his ring off his finger and placed it on Braldt's. Next, he slid the heavy silver chain up over his head from which dangled the face of Mother Moon herself, a diadem of crystal stars crowning her silvery head, and hung it around Braldt's neck as well.

These words and actions, even more electrifying than the startling sight of their chief standing erect when he had seemed so close to death only heartbeats before, shot through the crowd like a lightning bolt, bringing them to their feet—clerks, Councilman, and priests alike to stare at the outsider who had usurped the most powerful seat in all the land.

Their roars of protest drowned Auslic's voice, although it could not undo the words or the deeds, for it was Auslic's right and his right alone to name his successor. So loud was their outcry that none of them noticed when Auslic slumped against Braldt and fell senseless into his arms.

▪

The healers had gathered at Auslic's bedside, as well as the highest ranking members of the full Council, and a complement of black-robed priests, all doing their best to edge Braldt away. But Braldt stood like a rock by Auslic's side, refusing to be moved, keeping a sharp eye on all who approached, and trusting none of them.

Those gathered in Auslic's chambers came together and formed groups, odd combinations of men who had much to lose and would forge whatever alliances deemed necessary to prevent unwelcome change. And despite their

many differences none of them had any doubt that Braldt as
High Chief would bring about great changes in their lives
for he was outspoken in his criticism of the system by which
the city-state operated and the widespread practice of graft
and corruption that greased the wheels.

A small group approached Braldt as he hovered next to
Auslic's side, Beast growling ominously at his feet. Braldt
allowed them to come within ten paces and then raised his
hand to indicate that they should go no farther. Beast's
growls and twitching lip added further weight to his wishes.

Braldt eyed the group with disfavor, noting Envelius, a
healer who enjoyed more success than failure among his
patients, Ypren, a wigged and furred merchant who controlled much of the inter-state commerce with other tribes,
and Antiqus, a highly respected elder member of the full
Council. Envelius raised his hand, palm up, invoking the
benediction and protection of the Moon Mother, before he
spoke as though to give his words religious significance.

"Glorious Son, we welcome your return and are glad
that the rumor of your death was no more than false words.
We could only wish that the occasion were happier and that
you had found our glorious leader in full health and posses-
sion of all his faculties instead of sick onto death and
uttering foolish words in his delirium. We can only imagine
what he might have meant had he not been so ill, his words
misunderstood . . ."

Braldt stepped forward, his eyes narrowing, Beast
keeping pace, the tenor of his growls becoming more fierce
and his eyes glowing yellow. Envelius fell back, his words
shriveling on his tongue as his hand darted to his throat.

"What Envelius means to say . . ." Ypren said in tones
which fell on Braldt's ear like the harsh clamor of winter
birds.

"I know what Envelius meant to say and I know what
you will try to say as well. All of you! You may save your
voices and eat your words for I obey no man but my master,
my father, Auslic the Wise who has commanded me. I have
no wish to take on this office, but if it is his wish that I do
so, it shall be done and nothing you say will stop it. It is his

right to choose his successor and he has done so. Only he can say otherwise. Take yourselves away and leave us in peace. You are not welcome in this house and I bid you to go.''

Braldt's eyes were ringed red with exhaustion and sorrow clung to him like a robe, but none gathered in Auslic's chambers doubted that he would kill them if they failed to obey him. One by one they filed from the room, glancing furtively over their shoulders to make certain that none were lagging behind, in order to forge a secret deal.

Finally, the last of them passed through the door and only then did Braldt sheath his sword and bar the door from within. Otius and his wife, a shy, gentle woman by the name of Jos, emerged from one of the inner rooms, Jos bearing a steaming kettle of fragrant broth. Keri and Carn were there as well, Keri's exhaustion obvious in the lines at the corners of her mouth and the fine coating of dust that lay thick in the folds of her clothing. Braldt was glad to see them and opened his mouth to speak, but was stopped by the look of naked hatred that distorted Carn's features.

''Well, 'brother,' so you've got what you've wanted all these years, may you rot and die before it brings you pleasure!''

''Carn!'' Jos said in horror, her hand raised to her own lips as though she could scarcely believe what she was hearing. ''Why do you speak so to your brother? Are you mad?''

''I am not mad, Mother, and this is no brother of my flesh. Do you doubt my sanity? Can you not see that it has always been his plan to take the place that is rightfully mine? He has worked his way into Auslic's heart from the very first. Always there when the old man wanted someone to listen to his stories. Always there when there were errands to be run. Yes, Father, no, Father, toadying up to him in order to rob me of my birthright. Can you not see what he has done? Has he fooled you as well?''

Carn's voice was low-pitched and conversational in tone, but each word was formed in hatred and laced with the bitterness of gall. His eyes shone bright with rage.

Braldt was stunned, the malevolence of Carn's words

striking him like a blow and robbing him of words to reply. Carn was his brother! He above all men should know that he had no desire to sit as High Chief! The allegation was terrible in itself, but the depth of Carn's obvious hatred was far worse. How long had he felt this way? How could Braldt who prided himself on being observant have failed to notice?

Otius spoke then, placing himself between the two men he had raised as sons, loving both with equal measure, and tried to calm Carn, but Carn would not listen and continued to spit abuse at Braldt and his parents as well.

Keri pushed her way into the fray, shoving Carn hard with both hands thrust upon his chest. "You are stupid, Carn. Do you know? You're stupid. Always have been and always will be. Can't you see that Braldt has no interest in being chief? All he wants, all he's ever wanted, was to be free to wander wherever he will. You're imagining things, seeing plots where there are none, putting your own desires in his mind. Can't you see that he had nothing to do with this? Auslic likes him, that's all. You had the same opportunity, you could have spent time with him, he's your uncle, too. But you were always too busy, the old man was too boring if I remember your words. So do not blame Braldt for your own shortcomings."

Two bright spots formed high on Carn's cheekbones, burning there like firespots, and Braldt stared at them, wishing that none of this was happening, wishing that he could erase the words and deeds that had transpired, yet knowing in his heart that whatever happened, nothing could ever be the same again.

"At least I am not in love with him," Carn said, spitting the words out like arrows that seemed to pierce Keri's heart for she staggered back as though she had been struck. "For all the good it has done you, little sister, for he has no more interest in you than a rock."

Keri covered her face with her hands and rushed blindly from the room, her mother calling her name and following after her.

"That's enough, Carn, say no more." Otius sank down

upon a low bench, watching his son with saddened eyes. Carn turned on him swiftly, ready to spew more poisonous words, but Otius silenced him with a look for there was much of his brother's regal bearing about him when he chose to use it. "Every man writes the book of his own life, my son, and if the story does not go as you wish it, you have no one to blame but yourself."

"But Braldt . . ."

". . . did nothing but love your uncle and all of us, yourself included, as his own flesh. His only fault being that his love and his caring are of a better quality than your own. I have often thought, may the Moon Mother forgive me, that you love no one so much as you love yourself. Braldt has received no more than he deserves and he brings much honor to our House. I ask you to swallow your words. This is a time for prayers and reflection, there is no room for anger or ambition. Come to your senses, lad, that is your uncle lying there, have you no feelings for him?"

Carn stared at his father, his face flushing darkly, then growing strangely pale. A pulse throbbed at his temple, the only sign of the emotion that raged within.

"I care. More than you will ever know. But believe me when I say that Braldt is no brother to me, no son to you, and will always be what he is . . . an outsider. And I promise you that I will die before I see him become High Chief, on this you have my word."

5

Braldt and Carn stared at each other, rediscovering old familiar features and reinterpreting them in different ways, taking each other's measure. Beast, sensing the hostility that lay heavy on the air, intensified his throaty growls and slunk forward, inching his way toward Carn on his belly, looking no less dangerous for all his obvious youth.

The door to the outside swung open without the customary announcement stating the caller's name and the name of the person he had come to see. Such an abrupt entry was both rude and offensive to custom, but it served to distract Carn and Braldt from an open confrontation that seemed inevitable.

Braldt turned his eyes away from Carn and silenced Beast with a hacking motion as he studied the old man who had entered the room accompanied by Attruk, High Priest of the Temple of the Moon. Braldt, who had no love for the priests who governed and guided the tribe through every facet of its existence, averted his eyes from Attruk, whom he had seen no more than twice in his lifetime. The High Priest spent all of his time locked away in the highest tower of the shining black Temple. There were as many opinions of how he spent his time as there were stars in the sky, but no one knew for certain. Braldt did not care.

He did care for the old man who accompanied the priest, an ancient healer, perhaps even older than Auslic himself, a man named Tarn who had never shown him anything but kindness since his earliest days. At times, Braldt had felt the weight of the old man's eyes upon him and looked up to discover a look of pity in the old, rheumy eyes. The look had vanished as quickly as a cloud drifting

48

across the moon, leaving Braldt none the wiser. But Tarn was a staunch friend of Auslic's and Braldt was glad for his presence.

"Greetings, good sir, father priest, I bid you both welcome to this House. I can only wish that it were under happier circumstances." Otius took Tarn's frail hand in his own and led the ancient healer to a cushioned bench. To the priest he nodded, for no man was allowed to touch a priest. The priest nodded silently in return, his features hidden completely by the enveloping folds of the heavy black cowl. He took his place beside the healer, standing there like a dark shadow. A feeling of heavy watchfulness fell upon the room and even Beast kept silent and huddled at Braldt's feet.

Tarn took a cup of Jos's steaming broth with a grateful smile. She offered the tray to the priest who stared through her without even acknowledging her presence and she hurried away gladly, while chiding herself for feeling afraid.

Tarn swallowed the last drop of the rich broth and carefully placed the cup to one side. Looking up, he stared at Otius, Carn, and Braldt each in their turn, studying their faces. Otius raised his head and met the old man's gaze and then faltered and turned aside; Carn flushed darkly and stared at the floor angrily. Only Braldt was able to look into the old man's eyes, and this time he saw many things, the glimmer of hope, the warmth of caring, and a deep sadness tinged with unmistakable overtones of pity. This, all in an instant. Yet the look had been open and frank, with no hint of dissembling. The old man had meant for him to see his true feelings.

"Good sir, master healer, is there anything . . ."

Tarn held up a wrinkled hand to silence Otius, the flesh mottled with age and thin as a butterfly's wing, his eyes still fixed on Braldt. He beckoned him with a single crooked finger. Braldt, with Beast at his heels, walked forward.

The old man looked down then and smiled at the lupebeast pup, chucking it under the chin and earning himself a guttural rumble of pleasure as Beast curled himself into a ball on top of the old man's feet. Braldt was astounded for the pup had never granted him such liberties.

"You have no wish to become High Chief." It was not a question, but a statement of fact.

"No, old father, I have no wish to be anything other than what I am," Braldt replied honestly. Behind him, he heard Carn snort in disbelief.

"There is a chance that Auslic's life can be saved, spared from that dark river that will take him to the Great Moon Mother and his eternal rest. But it is only a chance at best and will require much courage."

Braldt stared at the old man, wondering at his words. Wondering if it were really true. If the old one could truly save Auslic, why was he wasting time talking when he could be working his magic?

His confusion must have been apparent for Tarn smiled again, the sadness openly visible for all to read. "No magic spells will work this wonder, my young friend, for that which ails Auslic is a failure of the body and not the spirit and cannot be cured by words alone. It is a thing that is required, a rare and precious object that will be most difficult to obtain."

"Tell me where I may find this thing and I will bring it to you," Braldt replied without hesitation.

Tarn smiled sadly and shook his head as though he had never doubted Braldt's response. "And you, Carn, are you willing as well?"

Carn pushed past Braldt, jostling him with his shoulder and placing himself directly in front of Tarn. "Of course, old one. Is Auslic not of my blood?" Turning, Carn smiled at Braldt, a smile that held no warmth but only the promise of hard times to come. "Braldt and I will do this thing together, whatever it may be."

Tarn appeared to take no notice of the unspoken hostility that hung thick in the air, although Braldt thought it unlikely that it had gone unnoticed.

"I too will go." Otius joined Braldt and Carn, his hand closed upon the hilt of his sword that had not been drawn for anything other than ceremonial purposes since Carn's own youth.

The priest raised his gloved hand and placed it flat upon his chest, directly atop the large metal emblem of the Moon Mother fixed in the center of his chest. A moment of silence followed this gesture. Then the priest raised his hand and made a cutting, dismissive sign and Otius fell back a step, his face pale and drawn.

"This is a journey for young men, my friend," Tarn said kindly, softening the priest's harsh gesture with his words. "You are needed here beside your brother to lend him your strength and the desire to live. The journey is dangerous and the way fraught with unusual peril, but the object we seek is the only chance we have to save your brother's life, elsewise I would not even consider it."

"I am not afraid, old man. Tell me what it is that you wish and I will do it. Nor do I need another to dog my steps. I will travel faster and return more swiftly if I am alone," Carn said boldly, ignoring Braldt as though he did not exist.

"This is no competition, Carn. The dangers are real enough and no single person could hope to accomplish the deed on his own. If you are to go at all, you will do as I say and swear upon the honor of your House that you will obey me!"

Never had Tarn spoken so sharply, with such authority, and Braldt as well as Carn hesitated only a heartbeat before nodding their assent.

"Sit then," Tarn said in a tired voice, looking to Jos for another cup of broth, "for the tale is long and not quickly told.

"As you know from your teachings, our world was born of the moon and is composed primarily of red stone, sandstone, and hardrock. Here and there if we are lucky, we find deposits of rose and white and gold crystal that many of us wear in honor of the Mother Moon who birthed us.

"She gave us this fertile land to feed and nurture us

and gave us the gods and the priests who decipher their will so that we might know how to live and give her honor.''

The old man paused for a moment to sip at his cup of broth and Braldt thought of the hundred and one gods whose rules governed their existence. There was a god for everything one did. There was a god of the earth who governed the times of sowing and reaping. A god of war who decreed when the tribe's boundaries had been violated and a war party should be sent to avenge the incursion. There was even a god of love whose approval was required before unions could be blessed. And it was the priests alone who deciphered the gods' wishes, the people had little or no voice in their own destiny. Dissension, what little there was, was most often stifled, for the priests dealt harshly with those who opposed them.

"She has blessed us in many ways," continued Tarn, "and in return requires only that we obey her. Without her love and guidance, we would be no more than the karks, lowly animals in form and deed. Of all the world, we are the most blessed, and everything beyond our borders must live without that same blessing. I know that young blood runs hot and impatient and sometimes chafes beneath the constraints of rules they cannot understand, but you must realize that without rules, this clan, this city, this world, could not exist. Beyond our boundaries is a world without rules, a world that is not governed by Mother Moon's love.''

"We know all of that," Carn said impatiently. "What has that to do with us?''

Tarn smiled up at Carn, a smile meant more for himself than Carn. "Everything, my impatient young friend, for it is beyond our borders that this quest will take you.''

Carn started visibly and then stared at the old man to see if perhaps he was joking or playing him for a fool, for few men were allowed to venture beyond the Guardian Stones. To do so without permission was to die, struck down by a thunderbolt out of the sky, the gods' messenger of death.

Braldt said nothing and wondered what it was that they

would be seeking. Although he himself had been given permission to venture beyond the stones, he had done so rarely and then only in pursuit of raiding karks or predators. His pulse quickened at the thought of traveling within the Forbidden Lands and he cast his thoughts over that barren ground, the empty desert and the sere mountainous regions that lay beyond.

"That which you seek lies two score dawnings to the east." Braldt's head came up sharply, his eyes searching and holding those of Tarn's, stunned and yet wanting to hope, to believe the truth of the old man's words. A single sharp intake of breath from Carn as well as a brief choked cry from Jos told him that the others shared his disbelief, for no man, not even Braldt, was allowed to enter those Forbidden Lands that was the home of the gods and certain death to mere mortals.

Tarn met Braldt's silent inquiry with a level gaze.

"Why . . . why do the gods wish such a thing?" Jos asked tearfully as Otius patted her on the back and held her close, attempting to calm her. "Is it not enough that the gods are taking Auslic from us, must they have my sons as well?"

"Dry your tears, Mother, the gods do not ask for us so that they may place us on the Great River, they have a need for us and require our services. We will do this thing and save uncle's life, and when we return, you may boast that your son is favored by the gods!"

But Jos was not comforted by Carn's bold words and buried her face in her husband's shoulder and sobbed.

Braldt reached out and squeezed her shoulder gently, then turned again to the old man.

"We have the gods' permission to enter the Forbidden Lands?" he asked.

The old man nodded.

"What is this thing we seek and how will we find it?"

The priest rose then and stood before Braldt and Carn, his flowing robes obliterating the old man like a storm cloud covers the sun. He raised his hands before him and Braldt shivered, knowing what was to come. Stifling an impulse to glance at Carn, he lowered his head.

The priest placed his hands atop Carn's and Braldt's bowed heads and silence, broken only by Jos's muffled weeping, filled the room.

A tingling came over Braldt with the first touch of the priest's palm. It was not unpleasant, nor was there any pain, rather a sense of invasion as though something were searching through his mind like flipping the pages of a book. Although he had never experienced the priest's touch, he had heard it described and was prepared, blanking out all thought, thinking of nothing, filling his mind with the image of the floor beneath his feet. He could not have explained why he did such a thing, nor had he spent any time contemplating such an action, for never had he imagined that it would be necessary.

The sensation of probing ceased, withdrew, and was replaced by a vision. Braldt recognized the easternmost border of tribal lands, saw the immense stone that gazed implacably outward, keeping watch, holding the savages at bay. Then he was speeding over the land that was verdant and green, with lush grasses and immense ancient trees. Tiny streams and wide rushing rivers crisscrossed the land, nurturing the abundant plant life, animals grazing on the thick grasses, their numbers vast and untroubled by the thought of man. Predators, their flanks as sleek and well fed as their quarry, lounged beneath trees and sunned themselves on rocks, oblivious and without fear. Nowhere was there evidence of man. If this land was the home of the gods, they did not hunt or farm the land. Did gods eat? The irreverent thought popped into Braldt's head unbidden, but he received no answer and the images continued to fill his mind.

Crossing the broad savannah they entered the foothills of the mountains that were normally but a distant blue smear on the horizon. The river that fed the fertile valley frothed and swept through a narrow gorge carved out of rock, not the familiar red rock that formed the basis of the city, but the shining black rock from which the Council chamber and the Temple of the Moon were constructed.

The vision continued, tracing the course of the river as it plunged down the mountain from the heights above. A brief glimpse showed the peaks of the mountains towering above them, capped with a blanket of whiteness.

Braldt did his best to fix the images in his mind, picking out landmarks that he might recognize again when he and Carn were part of that same landscape. The voyage of the mind continued, ever upward, scaling sheer walls of rock over which the river plunged in foamy plumes of white, heights that no man but only gods could hope to ascend.

Then the scene switched abruptly, showing another river course, this one empty and dry, although it was evident that water had recently filled its banks. This second course diverged from the first and rose in a southerly direction climbing the flank of the mountain and entered the mountain itself beneath a huge overhanging boulder. This boulder seemed to bear the entire weight of the mountain on its back.

Braldt held his breath as his mind's eye swept beneath the boulder, entering a darkness that was not shadow but the course of the riverbed, now empty and dry but for a narrow thread of water that trickled down the middle. Light appeared before them, magically illuminating the way, showing them the subterranean passage that the water had carved from the stone. And then abruptly, the passage ended in a fall of rock so dense that it sealed the course completely, allowing only the merest trickle of water to escape. Back and forth the image roamed, exploring the face of the rockfall, searching for a weak spot, and Braldt understood then what was wanted.

Back they flew, back through the curving dark passage, back into blessed daylight, out from beneath the dark rock, back to the branch of the river that still flowed. Now they climbed again, higher and higher still to dizzying heights so that the land was small and insignificant below them, like a child's toy until they came to a gaping hole in the very peak of the mountain from which the river arose, spewing forth under great pressure to begin its long descent to the land below. The vision explored this new mouth of the great river in infinite detail as though searching for a way to enter. But the river allowed no entrance, not even to the vision.

The image dissolved and then re-formed to show another cavern, this one lit by priest fire that was contained in clear crystal orbs that hung from the black stone ceiling. It was obvious that the cavern had recently been inundated by water. But this was no mere cavern for it was filled with mysterious objects clearly illuminated by the steady glow of the priest fire. Objects that were unlike anything Braldt had ever seen. The vision skimmed over the wondrous contents of the room even though Braldt longed to examine them more closely. But even this brief glimpse was enough to see that great damage had been inflicted upon the place. It was in great disarray. Holes had been breached in smooth surfaces and objects torn from the walls, and the floor was strewn with water-soaked debris.

The vision directed itself at the far end of the cavern where it was possible to see that the river had flowed at one time through a precisely carved channel. Water still eddied at the bottom of this channel, butting up against a landslide of black rock that filled the channel from its lowest point and rose to the roof above, solid and impenetrable. Finding no access, the water had found another exit, punching its way through a wall that had proved weaker than its relentless strength.

Now he beheld a wall that bristled with strange objects and mysterious runes and a variety of blinking lights in all colors of the rainbow. It was confusing and painful to see, for Braldt understood nothing, recognized not a single item that had any reference to his life. The vision fixed on a single object, a handle of some sort, pressed flat against the wall. In his mind the handle seemed to raise of its own will until it was fixed in an upright position in a direction completely opposite the way it had been. The vision repeated itself twice again and then Braldt understood what was wanted. The handle was to be raised upright and he was to do it. The vision repeated itself a third time and a warm glow filled his mind and he knew that he had not been mistaken.

Then the view moved to another wall, this one damaged more heavily, and focused on a square object, white in color with a crimson mark fixed in the exact center, two straight lines, one vertical, one horizontal, crossing in the center. The image fixed itself on the white box and remained there until it faded away.

Braldt blinked and raised his head, looking straight at Attruk but seeing the image of the white box still, knowing that it was the object they would seek; the thing that would save Auslic's life.

6

They left the following morning after being blessed by priests and cried over by Jos. Otius had laid his palm on their heads as well and then walked away, leaning on his walking stick more heavily than was his custom, with head bowed as though he had become an old man overnight.

Before dawn Braldt had wakened, unable to sleep despite his extreme fatigue, and he had crept through the sleeping house and entered Auslic's chambers, needing to feel his presence. Much to his surprise, Auslic lay with his head turned toward the door, awake and alert as though he had been awaiting Braldt's arrival.

Braldt hurried to the bed and knelt beside him. Although his face was still contorted and fixed, it was obvious that Auslic was far from the shores of the River of Death. He looked at Braldt and smiled fondly. "I knew you would come; you have never failed me yet."

"And never will I fail you, Father," Braldt replied. "I must call Jos and your brother, they will rejoice to see you awake and well."

"No!" Auslic whispered harshly, seizing Braldt by the wrist and holding him firmly. "No one must know. I wish others to believe that the River of Death laps at my feet. I will not die this night but neither am I well. This is no great tragedy for I have lived far longer than other men and I will not argue when it is my turn to sail the Great River, but there is something to be done before I take my leave. Something I should have done many turnings ago had I but had the courage." Auslic's face was grave, the downward cast of his features lending his words a grim overtone.

"Tell me what you wish done, Father, and I will do it

58

for you," said Braldt even as he wondered at the thought of Auslic lacking courage, for Auslic possessed more strength of character than anyone Braldt had ever known.

"You are already doing it for me," Auslic said as he shifted uncomfortably on his pallet, struggling into a seated position, "you are going into the Forbidden Lands with the priest's blessing, something I myself was never able to accomplish."

"But why..."

"There are too many questions and too few answers, Braldt. Ask me nothing for I have only my suspicions and if they are correct... Braldt, promise me that you will keep your eyes sharp when you enter these lands. Study things that seem strange and unusual. Do not be swayed by outward appearance, but search for the real meaning of what you see and, most importantly, keep an open mind, free of religion and superstition. Then, return and tell me and me alone of what you have discovered."

"But what am I looking for? What am I to discover? Tell me what I am to seek," Braldt begged for Auslic's words were unsettlingly vague.

"You will know it when you find it," replied Auslic, tiring visibly. "Now, there is another matter we must speak of, one I should have addressed long ago." Fumbling within his robes, he brought his hand forth and held it toward Braldt, his eyes filled with pain.

Braldt took the thing and studied it, seeing only a gold ring, unusual in that it was set with a clear red stone that had an intricate emblem fixed in the heart of its bloodred depths. Braldt had never seen such a ring before, and while it was extremely beautiful and unusual, it was only a ring. Why should a bit of jewelry cause Auslic such pain? Braldt held the ring up to the faint light that seeped into the room and saw delicate runes, identical to those in the Guardian Stones, circling the inner band.

"It was your father's ring. I myself took it from his hand. The woman, your mother, wore a similar ring, only smaller on her finger, but the priests seized it. They sought for this ring, suspecting that it existed, for its mark was deeply graved on your father's finger, but they could not search me without creating an awkward situation. They watched me for a long time, but I hid the ring away and put all thought of it out of my mind, but I do not think that they have forgotten.''

Braldt stared at Auslic, hearing his words, feeling them sink deep within his being as though they were being engraved upon his heart. ''Why, Father, why do you tell me this now, after all these years? Why did you not speak of it sooner?'' Braldt whispered.

''Pure jealousy, I suppose,'' Auslic said wearily. ''In the beginning I told myself that you were too young, that you wouldn't understand. After all, I myself did not understand. And what was there to say, really, only that two strangers appeared outside our boundaries and died in the desert.

''I watched you grow from infant to toddler and always there was that look about you, courage and strength of character even at that young age, and I wished that you were my son. My own wife had died years before and I had no wish to take another. Against the priest's wishes, I took you from the desert and gave you to Otius and Jos to raise and treated you as a nephew, no different from Carn or Keri, but in my heart, I thought of you as the son I never had.

''Then, as you grew older and sought me out, seeming to desire my company rather than that of your young friends, I held back the ring again, telling myself that you were still too young.

''I know myself well enough to admit that I was afraid that you would love that other man more, he who was your natural father, rather than I who had merely loved you. But now, now that the river finally approaches, I know that I cannot keep it from you any longer and can only hope that you will not hate me.''

A thousand questions filled Braldt's mind, thoughts that he had pondered on a thousand sleepless nights throughout his youth. Who had his parents been? Where had they come from? Why had they looked so different? Was there another tribe of people in the world? And if so, where were they and how could he find them. Endless questions to which there had never been any answers. Until now.

But the pain and despair in Auslic's eyes brought him back to the present. "No, Father," he said gently. "I do not hate you. Another man may have sired me, but you are my father."

Auslic's tortured features relaxed at Braldt's words and he sank back on his pillows.

"Do you think that my parents came from the east, from the Forbidden Lands?" Braldt asked.

"I do not know. I do not think so. Be careful . . . son. I could not bear to lose you, and beware of the priests. I do not know what it is that they wish, but I am certain that they are permitting you this journey to fulfill some need of their own rather than concern for my health."

"Do not let the river take you, Father. I will do the priests' bidding and bring back this thing that will help you as well. They have their secrets, and we will have our own."

And now he and Carn sped across the close-cropped rangeland searching the far horizon for the first glimpse of the Guardian Stones that flanked the boundaries of their land. A cold silence had descended between them as soon as they left the small gathering of priests and family members. Braldt could still see Keri's drawn face, her eyes burning with anger and resentment at being left behind. For it was Keri who had always sought out the highest balustrade of the ring and stared off at the distant misty peaks, wondering, dreaming, imagining what the clouds concealed. It had always been her dream to journey beyond the stones, to be the first to unravel the mystery. And now others would go there in her stead.

Braldt had offered her no apology or word of comfort for to have done so would have been an insult. Instead, he offered her Beast for the pup was too young to keep up and too much of a burden to carry. But Keri had barely glanced down at the pup and Beast had canceled all thoughts of leaving him, for he had bared his double rows of fangs and growled deep in his throat. This was no playful puppy sound, but one of sincere threat. He would allow no one to touch him, save Braldt, and would not even accept food from anyone else's hand. Braldt began to realize how much of a responsibility he had taken on, but still, he did not regret sparing the pup's life. There was something special about this one.

The day passed rapidly as Braldt and Carn wordlessly challenged each other by stepping up the pace, defying the other to fall behind. Both men were outfitted in a similar manner, blue robes draped over their chests and caught at the right shoulder by silver insignia rings, loincloths, and short swords and daggers. Each carried a leather pouch slung from their shoulder that contained stout leather shoes that came to just below the knee, warm breeches and a shirt should the weather turn foul, and leather hand gear. Jos had added dried meats and fruits despite their protests that the land would supply their needs, and Otius had added coils of ropes as well as words of advice. Jos had added a vial of healing unguent while praying that none would be needed.

The packs weighed them down but little and Carn being lighter and swift of foot might have taken the lead had Braldt not driven himself harder in order to keep level. As he had forseen, Beast had tired quickly and it had been necessary to place him inside the pouch where he settled contentedly, chewing on a stick of dried meat.

The Guardian Stone came into sight by late afternoon as their shadows stretched out before them, elongated to twice their normal size. A friend named Caltan, whom they had grown up with and attended school with until separated by the priests, hailed them, calling out their names from atop a craggy outcrop that broke through the red skin of the earth. It would have been rudeness itself to have ignored his greeting and Braldt stopped gladly, feeling the ache deep in his muscles and the steady burning in his chest, knowing that such a pace was foolishness, yet unwilling to protest and give Carn the satisfaction. He knew that Carn would be feeling the same aches and would also accept the interruption gladly.

They stretched out beside the fire that Caltan kept

going in the lee of the outcrop and told him of their mission as he listened in wide-eyed wonder. Caltan had busied himself by placing strips of meat to grill before the fire and handed them a gourd of warmed, fermented milk, both staples of his diet and provided by the grazing herds whom he was charged to watch.

"Are you not afraid?" Caltan asked, repositioning a skewer of meat that sputtered and sizzled as a bit of fat caught fire. "There are merebears and omnicats aplenty and lupebeasts too. I know they are there for they creep forth at night and raid the herd. The Guardian does not stop them at all."

"Beasts are beasts," Carn said with a shrug. "One kills them, that is what spears and swords are for."

He pointedly ignored Beast as he said this although Beast was sitting between Braldt's feet and turned his face from one to the other as they spoke. Braldt said nothing.

"But are you not afraid of the karks?" asked Caltan. "They are becoming bolder all the time and show themselves to me even in the daytime. They even killed a spankow two dawnings past, a shebeast who would have birthed soon. They skinned her and left only the hooves and horns in a pile to show me what they had done. They are not afraid of me for they know that I cannot leave the herd to chase them down. And what good would I do, one against so many. They would kill me as well."

Carn and Braldt exchanged glances. This was unexpected news. Karks rarely ventured across the border and seldom killed from the herds. "Why have you not sent word to the city?" demanded Carn.

"I have done so many times!" Caltan exclaimed angrily. "The priests know what is happening here and I am not the only one. It is happening to all the others as well!"

"Are you sure of this?" Carn asked.

"Do you take me for a fool?" Caltan asked quietly. "I know a kark when I see one and they take little care to hide themselves from us. They strut back and forth just out of spear range taunting us with their presence, hoping that we will be foolish enough to chase after them. Genn was killed four moonsets ago. I found what was left of him threaded on a sharpened pole like this bit of meat here and hung out over a fire. His skin was black and charred and his face had been mutilated, but I knew it was Genn.''

Shocked silence followed his words for while the kark were definitely viewed as an enemy to be killed on sight as they would any beast of prey, no one expected them to fight back. It was as though a mere cat had learned to talk. It was unnatural! Caltan had said that the priests knew of the karks' strange behavior and yet there had been no mention of this when they were being briefed; Attruk had given them no hint. Yet why would he keep it a secret? What purpose would it serve, save getting them killed? Carn and Braldt exchanged uneasy glances.

"And then there is the matter of the God Lights. How do you explain that? In the city the lights are not so bright as they are out here on the plains. Here you can see Mother Moon and the stars clearly, like they are within reach of your hand. The God Lights have always burned brightly over the Spirit Mountains, jumping and crackling about the night sky like the flames of a glorious godly flame, blue and green and silver and crimson. But the God Lights are gone now. We have not seen them for more than two turnings. We have asked the priests for an explanation, but we get no answers. What are they saying in the city?''

"They say it is but a phase that will pass,'' Carn replied, tossing another dried pankow chip onto the fire. The three old friends stared into the fire, each thinking his own thoughts, knowing that the God Lights had never vanished within living memory, daring to wonder what it might mean.

The evening passed swiftly and pleasantly as the old friends reminisced about deeds and misdeeds of their childhood, before Caltan donned the brown robes and Carn and Braldt the blue and went their separate ways. As the night lengthened and Mother Moon rose from her bed below the horizon to shed her cool beneficence upon them, they sang her blessings. The crisp night air was filled with a rude cacophony of sounds as a vulgar imitation of the blessed prayer came back to them, accompanied by jeers, blatting noises, and rude taunts.

Beast immediately responded by throwing back his head and loosing a full-fledged howl, his first, an indication of how swiftly he was growing. This broke the eerie pall thrown over them by the karks, and as Caltan admired Beast, Braldt told of the adventure that had resulted in his presence.

As the moon rose higher and higher in the night sky, Caltan grew restless, rising often to climb to the top of the stone that sheltered them and search the dark plains.

"I do not understand it, Jehan, you remember him, Jehan the Quiet, he was two turnings behind us at school? He is my waymate. He should have been here long ago. It is my turn to stand outwatch."

"Perhaps a shebeast is birthing," suggested Carn.

"Perhaps," agreed Caltan but his expression was troubled, and as they settled themselves for the night, drawing close to the fire for its warmth, he climbed atop the outcrop and, gripping his spear tightly, peered out across the darkened plain.

They took their leave of Caltan before the sun had risen, accepting a gourd of fermented milk and a bundle of smoked meat strips to lend them strength. Caltan's eyes were tired and rimmed with red and lines of worry for his waymate, Jehan, had not appeared.

"Look for him along the way and tell him to bring his lazy bones into camp," Caltan joked as they gripped hands in the old secret elaborate style they had invented in school and then, more seriously, flashed the sign of blessing of Mother Moon—thumb and forefinger joined and drawn in a circle above the heart and then drawn out, a way of saying, "May the blessings of the Mother and those of my heart go with you through all your days."

They took their leave then, pacing away swiftly, feeling the cool morning air flow smoothly across their skin, their legs already dampened by the beads of moisture that clung to the grass, moisture that would soon be burned away by the heat of the rising sun.

They made swift progress during the morning hours for the land was smooth and flat, dotted with low-growing shrubs, tufts of tough lanky grass, and the wandering herds of grazing pankows who fed upon them. The animals showed little or no fear of them, drifting apart to permit them to pass among them, their long, twisted horns rattling against one another. Beast began to bark at them and at the first shrill sound, the shaggy beasts bunched together, horns pointing outward, vertical slitted eyes narrowing as they squinted toward the threat with evil thoughts churning in their golden eyes. Slitted hooves pawed the red earth and the pankows tossed their heads and readied themselves for combat.

Braldt scooped up the pup whose body was stiff with excitement and clamped his hand around its muzzle, stifling the sounds while he and Carn removed themselves from the area as swiftly as possible. While pankows were normally docile and certainly none too bright, they could be roused to a murderous level of rage if the herd contained gravid shebeasts or numerous young as did this herd. Their sharp horns and hooves could inflict painful wounds were one stupid enough to be caught unawares.

"Best keep that one muzzled or leave it behind before it gets us killed," Carn said sharply, and there was little that Braldt could say in return for Carn was right. He placed the pup back inside the sling of his robes with a length of smoked meat to keep it busy and the remainder of the morning passed without incident.

As the sun reached its peak in the clear sky, they drew near a thread of smoke that hung in the air, drawing them like a beacon. It had been visible for some time now and although they had not discussed it, there was never any doubt that they would search out the cause. Fire, any fire loose on the plains, could be disastrous at this time of year for the grass and the land itself was dry, waiting the heavy rains of cold time. Fire could sweep across the land as swiftly as a cloud passes over the sun, destroying all life in its path. The pankow, stupid at best, lost all sense of reason during fires and more often than not rushed directly into the flames even after they had been rescued.

The slender line of smoke, pale and thin against the cold sky, grew darker as they drew close and seemed to have its origins in a narrow gully that snaked its way across the plain.

Braldt glanced at Carn and both men gripped their spears and hefted them to their shoulders in a throwing position. Swords filled their other hand. They crept forward, approaching the defile on silent feet for there was a feeling of wrongness about the place. A feeling of watchfulness hung over them as though enemy eyes were upon their backs. But the plain stretched away emptily on all sides and there was no place for anyone to hide unseen.

They smelled it before they found the body. The sickly sweet smell of roasted flesh filled the narrow confines of the ravine and Beast's ears flattened against his skull as a throaty growl emanated from his exposed fangs. Braldt curled his hand around the pup's muzzle and squeezed gently. The pup ceased his noise but demanded to be put down and stalked forward on stiff legs, fur rising along the ridge of his back in stiff clumps.

Braldt and Carn shared the pup's alarm, despite the fact that they had no ridges of fur to raise, and they advanced with extreme caution, their senses telling them that danger lurked close by.

There was another smell, underlying that of roasted flesh, a scent of salty sweat, blood, and something else, closely akin to the rancid, unwashed smell of men in the barracks after a long day's work in the ring.

There were footprints now, deeply trodden in the damp earth for a small trickle of water flowed down the center of the defile. Humanlike prints were mixed in with those of the pankows who, based upon the numerous trails and number of their clover hoofprints, obviously watered here often. The humanlike prints were another matter completely. Beast snuffled over one, his lips pulled back from his teeth, his mouth slightly agape in a comical expression of distaste, but neither Carn nor Braldt were laughing. Beast trod around the print on stiff legs, then sunk to a low slouch, belly nearly touching the ground, and crept forward sniffing the air carefully at every step.

Braldt and Carn did the same, sidestepping the broad footprint with the widely splayed big toe, twice as thick and twice as long as the next six digits. Karks. There was no way of misreading the distinctive prints.

The scent was stronger now, had become a gagging stench, and Beast, rounding a bend in the streambed, let loose with a chorus of shrill, hysterical yips. All hope of silent surprise gone, Carn and Braldt rushed forward, ready to hurl their spears. The sight that confronted them was so unexpected, so hideous, that Carn bent over double and retched, heaving up the contents of his stomach.

It was a man, or what was left of one. Braldt guessed that it was all that remained of Caltan's missing waymate, Jehan.

The body had been fastened to a boulder with long fibrous roots and twists of a crudely made rope. Primitive at best but more than adequate for the job. The fractured ends of bones poked through the charred flesh between ankle and knee, at midthigh, and in several places along the lower arms. The corpse's eyelids had been cut away as had his ears and nose, and his mouth was but a lipless, gaping hole. The body had been mutilated and punctured in numerous places and the genitalia severed completely. And the heart had been cut out of the body.

It was obvious to both of them that the torturous mutilation had taken place before death. It had been burned after death for the body was still held in place by the fibrous ropes, holding it in place over the embers that still smoldered, spewing the black smoke into the air like a beacon, summoning them to the grisly scene.

The thought came to them at the same time and they sprung apart, swords and spears at the ready, looking at the banks above them and to either side, wondering if they had walked into a trap. But there was nothing to be seen or heard, other than Beast's low keening that seemed entirely appropriate.

A search of the area proved that they were alone, the karks had gone. There seemed no doubt that the karks were responsible, for their footprints were everywhere and they had made no effort to conceal their presence.

Braldt and Carn cut the corpse down and wrapped him in his own robe, the russet brown stained red with his own life's blood, and buried him some distance away on the banks of the ravine. They placed the gourd of fermented milk by his side, along with a twist of meat and a dagger, so that he might go into death as a warrior. Then they said the words that would free his spirit to roam the skies with Mother Moon and made the signs over his grave that would speed his spirit on its way, cutting the air between them with their spears so that the spirit would not cling to the life it had once known. And then it was done and there was nothing to do but go on, which they did gladly, leaving the awful sight behind them, though the memory accompanied them as they traveled deeper into the lonely land.

7

They saw the Guardian Stone rising up out of the red earth, solitary and isolated, long before they reached it. The mountains rose in the distance behind it, distorted by watery, wavery images that would disappear as they drew near. The mountains appeared to be close enough to touch, but Braldt knew that they were still many days away.

They reached the stone at midday and stopped for a brief meal. The stone rose above them, looking outward impassively at the mountains, with a forboding expression in its fixed gaze. Once again Braldt was seized by a feeling of discomfort as he looked up at the plinth, for the features on the stone, although flat and distorted, were undeniably those of his own.

"Still think you're one of them, eh, Braldt," Carn drawled, following the direction of Braldt's eyes. Braldt shrugged and turned away, embarrassed that Carn had caught him out so easily.

"I'm surprised that you bother to live among us mere mortals. Must be rather boring for you. How come you don't just fix that thing that's broken and then heal uncle? Why bother coming on this trip at all? Unless you want to give uncle a chance to die while we're gone. That's it, isn't it, Braldt? You're hoping he'll die while we're gone!"

Braldt stared at Carn and bit back the angry words that filled his mind. Carn's face was darkly flushed and his hand opened and closed spasmodically at his sides, a sure sign of the uncontrollable rage that often overtook him, swiftly and without warning. It was useless to try to reason with him at such times for mere words could not appease him.

"I do not want to fight with you, Carn, your words are

foolishness." Braldt turned away and began rummaging in his pouch, looking for a bit of dried meat to feed Beast. Beast growled ominously and Braldt looked over his shoulder and saw Carn framed by the white sun, with a large rock hefted above his head ready to strike.

Carn screamed and brought the rock down with full force, but Braldt threw himself to one side and grabbed Carn's ankles, jerking them out from under him. Grunting and panting with exertion and emotion, the two men grappled on the hot, dusty earth, searching for a hold while attempting to elude being pinned themselves.

Carn's face was close, his dark eyes full of undisguised, bitter hatred. Braldt was deeply shaken for he had not even suspected the depth of his brother's feelings.

Gasping and panting for breath, the two men rolled back and forth on the hot earth, neither able to gain the advantage. Although Braldt was by far the taller and heavier, Carn was lithe and strong and his hate gave him added strength. Suddenly a knife appeared in Carn's hand, its point pricking at Braldt's throat. But then, just as suddenly, he was gone, his weight removed, and he struck out repeatedly, the knife rising and falling as Braldt threw himself forward, catching Carn around the waist and hurling him facefirst onto the ground.

Yapping shrilly, Beast rose up on his hind legs as the adults of his kind were wont to don and skittered sideways, then dropped to all fours and lunged, snapping at Carn, his double rows of teeth already stained with Carn's blood.

Carn rolled sideways, knocking Braldt off, and then rose to his feet brandishing the knife. Braldt cursed and struggled to his feet, but neither Carn nor Beast paid him any attention, each fixed upon the other. A steady stream of blood pulsed from a wound on Carn's ankle and Beast's flank was scored by a long, shallow cut. Neither was hurt badly but Braldt knew that it could get much worse, quickly.

Braldt ripped his robe free and threw it over Beast, enveloping him in its folds, and held the struggling bundle against his chest while backing away from Carn. He backed until he was stopped by the smooth warm surface of the stone.

"Do you hate me so much, brother?"

"That much and more," replied Carn as he sheathed his dagger and looked into Braldt's eyes. The killing rage had dimmed, replaced by something more easily maintained over a long period of time, hatred.

"You are not my brother and never will be. No words will make it so. You are an outsider. You were not born of the Duroni and have no claim to the throne, no matter what Uncle says. He is old, weak, and useless. He grieves that he has no son to take his place and carry on the family name. He has picked you, but by all rights it should have been me, and *would* have been me had you not appeared so mysteriously. And it will still be me, brother," he said, twisting the word and spitting it out like a bitter seed.

"Carn, I have no wish to be chief. You may have the throne and my allegiance as well. I never asked for the honor. I tell you that it is not what I want."

"Oh, and what is it that you do want, brother?"

"I want for things to be the way they were between us. I want you to stop hating me. How can such a thing be? I have no hatred for you! You are right, I am an outsider, that is plain enough to see. But I cannot control what happened when I was but a babe. Am I to be punished and reviled for the events that robbed me of my own parents, my birthright, my own history? Do you not think that I lie awake nights and wonder who my parents were and how they came to be found in the desert, and wonder what killed them?

"Fate or the gods robbed me of my own family and then gave me into the keeping of yours. Would you deny me the right to love and honor them, the only family I have ever known? Do you think it is easy knowing that I am different and do not belong? You *are* my brother, Carn, and even if you hate me, it will not change the way I feel."

Carn stared at Braldt, measuring his words, weighing them, and then he turned away, his back to Braldt. When he turned back, the hardness had left his eyes, or was well masked, and he was no longer the stranger he had become, but Carn the Stalker, brother of Braldt.

"You mean what you say, don't you?" he said in carefully measured tones.

Braldt nodded.

Carn stared down at the ground, lost in thought, and then at his bleeding ankle and the steady stream of blood that soaked into the parched earth.

"Well, if we are not going to kill each other, maybe you can help me with this leg before I bleed to death," he said with a forced grin. "And maybe you can stop that thing from attacking me again."

Braldt looked down at the squirming bundle and wondered whether Carn could truly change so quickly. He wanted to believe that it was so, but how could anyone hate so strongly one minute and then deny it the next? Beast lunged in his arms, trying to free himself. And then there was Beast. Braldt had no idea what the animal would do; he was no tame creature who would do his bidding. It was possible that Beast would forever view Carn as an enemy.

"I don't know what he'll do, I can but try." Placing the robe down on the ground, Braldt held Beast firmly with one hand and stroked him with the other, murmuring in what he hoped was a soothing tone. Beast quieted and Braldt removed the robe.

Beast looked at Braldt as though seeking reassurance and then up at Carn, fixing him with a steady, burning gaze that spoke of enmity that went far beyond his young age, but he made no move toward him. Then he turned his attentions to himself, pointedly ignoring Carn and tenderly licking the raw edges of the long wound. Nor would he allow Braldt to minister to him, trotting some distance away and settling beneath the low-hanging branches of a greasewood bush.

Freed of that concern the two men dealt with Carn's ankle, washing it with some of their precious water, laving it carefully to cleanse it of any bits of dirt that might later fester and cause the leg to sicken. Fortunately, it had been but a glancing slice of the pup's teeth rather than a solid bite, and though it bled copiously, it was shallow and not of a serious nature. Still, it did not do to take any wound lightly and the ankle was liberally smeared with Jos's stinging healing unguent and bound with strips of clean cloth.

Tending to the wound had allowed their emotions to cool further and without referring to the matter again, they turned to the subject of food, deftly avoiding any mention of what had gone before. Strips of dried meat were brought out of their pouches and hard rounds of cheese, washed down with the gourd of sour fermented milk. They ate in silence, neither of them knowing what to say. Beast returned after a time although he would not come close to either man, viewing both with distrust. Carn threw him a bit of meat that Beast ignored.

"I did not know you hated me," Braldt said, staring straight ahead.

"I am tired of hearing your name. I sometimes think that I do not exist. It is as though Auslic and even my father think that the moon itself rises and sets to please you. It's Braldt did this, Braldt did that. My ears grow weary of hearing your name and no one has eyes for anything that I do.

"Last turning, I killed the merebear that was taking the shebeasts, the one that had ventured to the very outskirts of the city, and when we measured it, Father pointed out that you had once slain one that was larger!" The bitterness was obvious in Carn's voice and even though he had not been present or responsible for Otius's comments, he could feel the pain that they had caused.

"I did not know, Carn, nor do I wish it to be so," Braldt replied simply, not knowing what else he could say.

"That only makes it worse."

"Can we still be brothers?"

"I do not see that I have a choice. We have been sent to do this thing together, and our lives may depend upon each other if it is to be done. But afterward, after we return, I make you no promises."

Carn turned to look at Braldt then, and though the

hatred and naked hostility was gone from his eyes, there was no sign of warmth or caring, either.

Braldt nodded slowly, realizing that the promise of temporary neutrality was all that he could hope for at the present time. He repacked his pouch and refastened his robe as he rose to his feet. "Let us do this thing then, and return quickly so that I may speak to Auslic and tell him how I feel. Come, brother. As Jos is wont to say, the sooner begun, a job is done." He extended his hand to Carn. Carn took it reluctantly and then stood to face Braldt, the two of them looking deep into each other's eyes, taking each other's measure. Neither was reassured by what he saw.

8

Braldt began to suspect that they were being followed during the long hours of the afternoon. They had crossed the boundary of the Duroni lands and were now traveling across the softly undulating hills of the Forbidden Lands. The pace was slower than it had been, for Beast would not allow himself to be picked up and he lagged well behind them. Carn's ankle had begun to bleed and the bandage was stained crimson, but he would not stop, shrugging off the wound even though Braldt could see that it was paining him.

He had paused on the crest of a small hill to find the pup, to make sure that he was still with them, when he first caught glimpse of the follower. At first he thought that he had been mistaken, that it was a trick of the light, for it vanished almost immediately and did not reappear. He did not say anything to Carn, preferring to make certain before he spoke, but subsequent sightings proved his suspicions to be correct. And it was no animal.

He could not tell whether the follower was Duroni, but a Duroni would have no reason to hide and the follower was definitely attempting to conceal his presence. He was good, fast and clever, moving from one bit of shelter to another; but Braldt was better.

He wondered if it could be a slaver, one of the roving bands who enslaved and sold those who were vulnerable or too weak to protect themselves. But this one was traveling alone, at least Braldt could detect no sign of more than one, and slavers were rarely found in less than large numbers. A wise precaution in view of their practices.

They made an early camp at Braldt's insistence, stopping beside a small rivulet of water that flowed through the narrow valley through which they were traveling. Carn protested, but it was obvious that his heart was not in it, and he sank to the ground wearily and made no objection when Braldt examined the wound.

It was ugly. The flesh was red and vastly swollen, the ankle appearing like some grotesque, obscene fruit. A pulse throbbed visibly and blood still seeped from the torn flesh. "Why did you not speak?" Braldt demanded angrily. "Are you determined to be brave and silent at the cost of your leg or even your life?" Carn did not reply.

Braldt built a fire quickly and set the gourd of sour milk to warm at its edge. Carn covered his eyes with the back of his arm and made no sound as Braldt washed the leg and ankle with water from the small stream. Braldt could feel the heat of the flesh beneath his hands and knew that if he could not stop the sickness before it grew, Carn might easily lose his leg. At the very least they would be unable to travel for many days.

Carn had fallen into a deep, exhausted sleep when Braldt slipped out of camp. He had placed both pouches beneath the spread of a large tree, deep in its shadows, and covered them with his robe. It would not fool anyone for long or sustain close scrutiny, but with any luck, it would not be necessary.

He crept out of camp silently, glad for once that the pup was nowhere to be seen, and hid himself beneath a clump of cibas, the acrid stink of their leaves filling his nostrils. He had a clear view of the camp, the burning fire clearly visible as was Carn's sleeping figure and his own crumpled robe. From a distance, it looked quite acceptable. Now, all he had to do was wait.

Darkness closed in quickly, fading from dusty grey to dark in short order as it did every turning when the seasons grew shorter. The fire drew his eyes like a lodestone and he was forced to keep his back turned to it for even a single glance destroyed his night vision. He hoped that his quarry would be drawn to it as well.

With the coming of the Cold Season, much of the

underbrush was dead and the grasses rustled and crackled underfoot. He waited for a long time before he heard the sound he was waiting for, the stealthy advance of one treading carefully through the dry undergrowth. The approach was all but silent but clearly audible to one whose ears were waiting for just such a sound. Braldt had picked his spot with care, placing himself alongside the route he himself would have chosen.

At last his patience was rewarded by the sharp snap of a twig broken underfoot, followed immediately by a long silence where even Braldt found himself holding his breath. The sound was very close. He saw a shadowy figure, no more than a darker bit of shadow, move toward him in a sinuous, silent glide.

He waited until it had passed him and then rose up swiftly bringing the hilt of his sword down hard. His quarry had heard him or sensed his presence at the last moment and begun to turn just as the heavy blow caught him a stunning blow that crumpled him to the ground in a silent heap.

Anxious to learn his identity, Braldt turned the fellow over none too gently. There was a sharp intake of breath and a muffled curse as Braldt recognized his unlikely foe by the wan light of Mother Moon, now rising over the far horizon.

It was Keri.

Angry words leaped into his mind, along with concern, for he might easily have killed her. What was Keri doing here? What game was she playing at? Why, by the name of the blessed Mother and all the gods, had she followed them?

He examined her more closely in the pale light and saw that the blow had landed on the side of her head above her left ear, rather than at the base of her neck. It was swelling quickly and her short hair was wet and sticky with blood. She would have a headache, but she would live (a fact that she might regret by the time he was done with her). Slinging her over his shoulder with all the concern he might have given a sack of pankow feed, he returned to camp.

He dribbled the remainder of the warmed milk down Carn's throat, rinsed the gourd, and filled it with water and a handful of ciba leaves, setting the mess to boil beside the fire. Soon Keri stirred, groaned, and raised herself to a seated position before falling back and groaning even more loudly, pressing her hands to her head.

Braldt waited for her to draw herself upright, without making any attempt to help her, knowing how her head must ache and taking grim satisfaction from the fact.

She stared at him dully, taking in the sight of the camp and her brother lying before the fire with his leg red and swollen.

She stared up at Braldt with a mixture of fear and defiance.

"You aren't sending me back." It was no plea for forgiveness, no graceful attempt to sway him, but a straight-forward attack, blunt and to the point like the girl herself. Angered though he was, Braldt could not help but admire her nerve.

"Don't be stupid. This is no place for you to be, Keri. We don't know what to expect and I don't have time to be worrying about you."

"Why would you have to worry about me?" Keri rose to her feet and faced Braldt defiantly. "I can handle myself just fine. I'm better than most of the boys and can throw a knife as good as any of you and I can run faster and longer than Carn, though it doesn't look as though he's going to be doing any running for a while. I can help take care of him. Between the two of us, we can carry him, you know, make a litter; otherwise you'll have to stay here and that will cost you many dawnings."

Braldt opened his mouth to speak, to tell her that it would never work and that she would return at first light, but before he could utter a single word, Beast began to bark in the shrill puppy voice that signaled alarm. The high-pitched agitated tones carrying an obvious warning. The pup bounded into camp and skittered to a halt before Braldt, his tail erect and pole stiff, the fur standing up all over his back and neck as though it had been rubbed backward by an uncaring hand.

Braldt acted swiftly, kicking dirt over the fire, plunging them into darkness as Beast rose up on his hind legs, now nearly half Braldt's height, and danced on his toes, giving little hopping leaps as he peered intently into the darkness, yipping sharply.

Braldt did not attempt to silence the pup for whatever had caused his alarm had no doubt seen the fire extinguished and knew that they were warned. The pup fell silent of his own volition, whining softly and trotting back and forth nervously.

"What . . . ?"

"Not now," Braldt said, swiftly gathering up their few possessions and thrusting them at Keri. "Take these!" Then he scooped Carn up from where he lay, ignoring his muttered queries, leaped the narrow stream, and trotted off into the darkness without even looking to see if Beast and Keri were following.

Beast appeared beside him almost immediately, and after a moment he could hear Keri following as well. Carn was heavy, a dead weight that he knew he could not carry for long without tiring. He paused to settle his weight more comfortably and to listen, but heard nothing but the sounds of the night, the mournful cry of a night bird and the chittering of insects in the dry grass. Keri appeared silently at his side, asking no questions.

The rising moon was small, a thin sliver of silvery light, in its earliest phase, casting little light on the scene. For a moment, he thought he saw something, a movement, a passage of bodies, but then it was gone and did not reappear.

But Beast showed no diminishment of concern, rising up on his hind legs frequently, peering forth into the darkness with his strange vertically slitted eyes. The pupils opened wide at night, allowing him to see like a cat, and his head moved back and forth while he whimpered and growled low in his throat, his small body trembling, shaking visibly. He had no trouble seeing whatever danger stalked them and from his behavior it was apparent that the danger had not abated.

"I do not know what it is," Braldt said in a soft undertone, whispering directly into Keri's ear. "But he would not behave like this, were there not some very real danger. We must find a place of safety until the dawning.''

Saying was easier than doing for there was little light and they were traveling over unfamiliar ground that rose slowly but constantly beneath their feet. The trees, what few there were, became fewer still. The underbrush thinned and became a mere cushion underfoot. There was no camouflage, nothing to hide them from whatever it was that had alerted Beast. Braldt stopped and looked around, searching for some place where they might take cover that would provide them with safety.

The land rose and fell on all sides in a series of low, smooth-topped mounds like little islands of mud built by a child after the rain, then stranded after the puddle dried. It appeared to be a watershed, a drainage for the larger hills and mountains that rose in the distance. There was no cover, no place to hide. Their only choice was at the base of the mounds; perhaps they could find a cave or lose their pursuers in the myriad of confusing channels.

Braldt signaled to Keri to follow and made his way down the slope in a slithering rush of stones and gravel. Beast preceded them, his tail curled above his back, seemingly more comfortable in the dark gully than he had been on the higher elevations.

It was Keri who found the place they had been seeking. It was a narrow gulch, its mouth solidly plugged with twigs, branches, and leaves. Braldt would have passed it by without thinking, but Keri caught at his arm and brought him back, nodding at the tall mound of debris that rose higher than their heads.

He stopped and studied the mass, seeing its possibilities and nodding in agreement though angered that he had not seen it himself. It was so very obvious, so conspicuous as a hiding place, that it would be overlooked for that very reason.

Braldt placed Carn on the ground and felt his eyes upon his back. But Carn had not been named the Stalker for nothing and had sized up the situation swiftly. There was no need to tell him to keep silent but Beast was another matter.

He danced nervously from one paw to the other, rising up on his hind legs with great frequency and whining softly.

Keri had already begun to dig into the mass, hollowing out a nest into which she thrust their few possessions. Braldt followed her lead, digging out a hole large enough to hold the three of them, and Keri added her efforts to his until the hole was deemed large enough. Dragging his injured leg behind him, Carn struggled into the nest and covered himself with the soft debris. Braldt piled the stuff in front of him until he was satisfied that there was nothing to be seen, nothing unusual to show that the pile had been disturbed. He motioned Keri to go next, but she shook her head stubbornly and nodded to him. He hesitated for a moment and then did as she wanted, knowing that she was right. He settled himself in the waiting hollow and hissed to Beast to join him. The pup would have none of it and would not even meet Braldt's eyes.

Braldt was still trying to call the pup when Keri closed the hole, silencing his efforts. He felt the stuff cover him, cover his face and nostrils, and felt a moment's panic that he stifled. After a moment, he found that he could carefully move within the space. Any abrupt movement caused the entire mass to shift and threatened to expose him, but slow movement enabled him to clear a breathing space as well as a small opening to see. His hands were closed upon sword and dagger and there was nothing left to do but wait.

Beside him there were small cracklings and whisperings of sound as Carn settled himself as well. Keri patted a few handfuls of leaves in place, satisfying herself that all was well, and then burrowed into the face of the mound and settled herself into place with a minimum of noise. There was nothing left to betray their presence other than Beast who snuffled at the wall of debris and whined, then began digging furiously with both paws. Braldt hissed angrily and Beast barked in return, clearly puzzled. His attention was then caught by a sound farther up the gulch and his large ears swiveled forward.

Braldt stifled an impulse to sneeze as well as the desire to scratch, for the clinging stuff was dry and itchy and home to numerous insects and other crawling things. He watched Beast intently. They had not seen or heard anything unusual, nor caught any sign of an enemy, but had fled their camp and hidden themselves away at no more than the pup's say so. For a moment, Braldt wondered if he had been wrong to do so. The pup's reaction could have been caused by anything, a wandering omnicat or a merebear or even an unusual scent carried on the wind, for the pup was relatively young and could easily be mistaken. But Braldt had learned to value the pup's keen nose during their time in the amphitheater when the pup was even younger still. He had not been mistaken then and never had he acted thus except to warn of approaching danger.

Even as he contemplated the possibility that the pup could be mistaken, Beast began to growl fiercely and darted forward, barking wildly, disappearing from Braldt's narrow range of vision. Then he was back, standing on his hind legs, head jutted forward as though straining to see.

A wild cacophony of shrill barks broke out as the pup dropped to all fours, the fur rising all over his body until he appeared to be twice his normal size. He stood his ground, head held low, barking frenziedly. Braldt turned his head to the side, desperate to see what the pup was seeing, wanting to leap out of hiding and wield his sword instead of hiding in a pile of leaves like some cowardly crawler, but caution held him in place for there was more at stake than his own valor.

A spear flew out of the darkness and thunked into the hard-packed earth next to the pup, striking him with its shaft as it fell to the ground. The pup screamed as though he had been blooded and leaped into the air. When his feet touched earth, he was off and running, down the defile, away from the approaching enemy.

Braldt's hands closed on his weapons and he peered forward intently. Could it be slavers this far to the east? Never had he heard of such a thing for even though they were nonbelievers and did not worship Mother Moon, even they honored the borders of the Forbidden Lands; their disbelief lent them no protection and they too could be struck down by the spears of the gods if they ventured beyond the borders.

The mutter of low voices came to Braldt within his leafy cocoon and he stilled all movement, tuning all his senses toward the approaching enemy. But even though he had expected almost anything, he was not prepared for what he saw.

Karks! A party of six males and three females, all carrying spears, crudely made and poorly balanced but spears nonetheless. And even more startling was the fact that they were speaking! No kark had ever been heard to speak! Never had such a thing been suspectcd! Braldt was dumbfounded.

The karks trotted past the hiding place without slowing, although one female, slender and more upright than the others, turned her head and looked directly into Braldt's eyes. He thought he saw a flicker of recognition in those eyes, as though she had seen him clearly, but she made no sound and did not call the others down on him, and they quickly passed out of sight. The sound of their voices, thick and guttural, could be heard long after they were gone, carried back to them by the shape of the gully or the wind. The words were oddly formed and stiff as though spoken by an outsider who had only just learned the language, but still, it was clearly speech.

They were arguing among themselves as to whether or not to continue on for the encampment was behind them and others would be wondering where they had gone. Nor were they entirely certain as to their quarry. Only one or perhaps two of the party had actually seen them; the others were arguing against going on with nothing but a lupebeast to be seen.

And why would a lupebeast be in the company of the Duroni, asked one, suggesting that perhaps the viewer had been mistaken. Since when had a lupebeast learned to build a fire, came the reply, and none too kindly. It seemed that arguments were not limited to civilized people but existed among the karks as well.

The voices faded then as the karks moved farther down

the gully. Still Braldt did not move even though the leafy debris had crept into every crevice of his body and was itching unbearably. There was still the feeling of danger. The mound that was Carn began to shift and Braldt's hand tunneled through the debris and caught hold of Carn's arm and squeezed tight, signaling him to stay.

No sooner had he done so than the karks reappeared on their right, moving silently, without words. Had Carn continued to move or had he emerged, it would have been the death of them. As it was, a few leaves and a small branch slithered off the face of the pile, but drew no notice. From the grim expressions on the karks' heavy features, it appeared that there had been some dissension in their ranks.

As the pack moved past them, the female turned her head once more and stared directly at Braldt, seeking out and holding his eyes. A shock jolted him as he held the contact, unblinking, until she passed from view. There could be no doubt about it! The female kark had known that he was there! And yet she had made no move to betray him! *Why?* How could such a thing be so? Braldt was stunned, his mind reeling under the strange implications, and he wished more than anything that Auslic was there to help him understand what had happened.

They remained in their hiding place for a long time, all of them shaken and fearful, wrapped in their own thoughts. Only when Beast reappeared and sniffed at the wall of concealment before sitting and scratching with an apparent lack of concern, did they venture forth to stand and stare at one another in utter and complete amazement.

9

They continued on throughout the night, making their way even deeper and higher into the hills, supporting Carn between them. The tiny crescent of moon had long since ascended and descended the dark roof of the sky when they came to a final halt in a thick copse of silverwoods. The shimmering leaves, glossy silver on one side, opalescent on the other, shivered and trembled on their fragile stems, perhaps anticipating the not-too-distant moment when they would fall from the branches in a brilliant cascade of glittering light to die on the cold, hard ground. But for now, they clung to the trees like a dense coat, and the constant movement would hide their own, offering some small degree of safety.

There had been no further sign of the karks, nor did Beast give any indication of alarm, trotting behind them with his tail curled over his back or frolicking ahead biting and snapping at shadows. He showed no reticence at their nearness now, and apparently held no grudge toward Carn at whose feet he curled up, wrapping his tail over his nose and going instantly to sleep.

Braldt would have liked nothing more than to emulate the pup for his weariness was bone deep and his thoughts offered him no comfort. But there was Carn's ankle to be dealt with and Keri as well.

Carn leaned against the shaggy bark of an immense, ancient silverwood and grimaced as Braldt rotated the ankle. Braldt studied him intently. "Is it bad?"

"It's bad enough and it'll be stiff for a few dawnings, but don't worry about me, I won't hold you back. If I do, just leave me behind and I'll catch up."

"Don't be a hero, Carn. We can't afford heroes. We must stick together; a man alone would not last long out here."

"I can help," Keri said simply. "You need me. Don't let your pride get in the way of truth, you know that it is so."

Braldt stared at her, trying to find the right words and finding none. They did need her, but it was wrong for her to be with them. It was a man's deed, a thing between men and the gods. It was not fitting for a woman to accompany them on such a sacred mission.

Only men were allowed to attend the inner circles of worship and only men were allowed to become priests and learn the highest mysteries. They themselves had been allowed to enter the Forbidden Lands only on the direct order of the priests, and were spared the deadly bolts of the gods that would have struck them down otherwise. What would the presence of a woman do? Would the gods be angered and kill them all with their fiery bolts? Braldt did not know the answer.

Yet denying Keri's help would be impossible for despite his brave words, Carn would not be able to travel without their assistance and to leave him behind was unthinkable—if the gods did not kill him, the animals or the karks would. Nor could he allow Keri to return alone for it would be even more dangerous for her to travel by herself. Yet he could not risk leaving Carn alone for the time that it took to bring her back. Even if they had had the time.

"We will sleep on this problem. Perhaps the answer will be clear when our minds are less tired. Sleep now and I will keep watch. I will waken you when the sun is at its peak. From now on, we will journey only at night."

Dragging her robe up over her shoulder, Keri settled herself between two roots of a great silverwood, cradled her head on her arm, and was asleep before her body had fitted itself to the contour of the land.

Braldt climbed high into the branches at the edge of the copse and watched as the misty darkness faded into grey only to be tinted by streaks of crimson pink as Sun the

Giver crept slowly over the rim of the Forbidden Lands and warmed the earth with its presence. The leaves of the tree wagged back and forth in constant motion, twisting this way and then that, although Braldt could detect no wind. The effect was hypnotic after a while and Braldt had to fight to shut them out of his consciousness, to keep the rhythm from creeping into his mind.

He concentrated on watching the lower elevations, the way they had come, watching for karks or whatever might come. Already, the Duroni lands were lost in the wavering line of blue that marked the far horizon, although Braldt tried to tell himself that he could still see the tip of the Guardian Stone.

He had traveled farther than most men would go in their entire lifetimes, gone to strange places and seen strange sights, and yet he was loath to leave the Duroni borders behind him this time. Somehow he sensed that when and if he returned, nothing would ever be the same again, and sadness rested on his shoulders like a cloak.

He watched throughout the coolness of the dawning, feeling the dew mist and bead on his chilled flesh, heard the first tentative, sleepy chirps of the birds, and saw a silent herd of split horns browse from bush to bush and disappear as silently as they had arrived.

There were karks, as well. Two bands of them passed beneath him on the lower elevations, trotting swiftly through the complex channels of the water course, spears in hand with no hesitation in their step as though they knew precisely where they were going and were in a hurry to get there. Later, a third party passed not thirty steps from their place of concealment although Braldt did not see them until they appeared on the slope below him. He stiffened and held himself completely still until they were out of sight. He prayed that none of his companions would choose that moment to waken, and none of them did.

The party too was laden with spears and heavy, stone-weighted clubs and ran in a determined line. Braldt stared after them, brow furrowed with thought, and wondered where they were going.

He was grateful when Sun the Giver reached the appointed spot and he was able to waken Keri who opened her eyes, instantly alert at his approach. She listened to his report without comment, taking in the news of the armed karks with an unexpected calmness. Taking a water gourd and a round of hard cheese, she tucked the end of her skirt into the waistband and disappeared into the branches.

Braldt fell into a deep and dreamless sleep, his exhausted body demanding its due. He did not hear Keri when she descended the tree at the end of her watch, nor notice when Carn hoisted himself into position, but slept soundly until nightfall.

Upon waking, he could not think where he was for the sigh of wind in the trees was soothing and reassuring. Beast appeared and snuffled wetly at his face, and then memory returned, rushing back to fill him with alarm. Why had they allowed him to sleep so long? Had they been overcome by karks while he slept? Were they dead? But everything was functioning normally as he could see at a glance. A tiny, smokeless fire had been built within a ring of stones and a gourd was suspended above it filling the air with a pleasing aroma.

Keri was standing beside the ancient tree where she had slept, putting the finishing touches on her outfit. She had disposed of her long, clinging underskirts and ripped the remaining overskirt halfway up the middle both in front and back, then tied the ends around her calves. The result of her efforts was a pair of roomy pants that gave her freedom of movement. The underskirts had been reduced to a narrow bundle that she had tied with strips of leather. She turned to face Braldt, her chin set at a stubborn angle that he knew all too well.

"Everything's been tended to. I watched until dusk and then Carn took over. There've been more karks, lots of them, all armed and heading west."

"Why didn't you wake me?"

"What could you have done, Braldt? Caltan said that reinforcements were coming. They know that the karks are becoming more warlike and have killed the herdsmen. What could we tell them that they don't already know?''

Her reasoning was solid, Braldt mused. And the karks were moving swiftly. There was no way that they could overtake them and bring a warning in time. They had their own mission that was equally, if not more, important.

Carn slithered down the trunk of the tree, landed with a soft grunt, and limped over to where they stood. He drank deeply from the gourd and then passed it to Braldt who found that it contained a thick broth of some sort that flowed into his empty belly and filled it with warmth.

The tiny fire cast more shadow than light upon their features as they crouched beside it to tell Braldt all that had transpired during the long day. It appeared that the karks were on the move, more karks than any of them had known existed, and all of them armed and all of them pointed west. Once again they came to the same conclusion, it was pointless to try to warn the Duroni. The first of the karks had probably reached the border of the Duroni lands by now, and if the guard had not been aware of their presence yet, they soon would be. There was nothing they could do to help the Duroni and they would do well to help themselves. For with so many armed karks roaming the hills, it would be difficult to avoid discovery.

"What do you think they're trying to do?" asked Keri.

"It's a raid," replied Carn. "Stealing pankows as usual."

"But why so many," mused Braldt. "I have never heard of karks traveling in such numbers before. It must be more than just food they are after. And why are they armed? Carn, have you ever heard of them using spears or clubs?"

"Well, once. A herder from the north brought in a broken spear that he said he took from a kark. It was crudely done, like one we might have made as children. The point was stone and poorly chipped and badly balanced as well, but it killed a fully grown ram pankow before the herder killed the kark. Or so he said, though no one believed him at the time."

"It doesn't make sense," said Braldt, still deeply

troubled by the problem. "How could the karks arm themselves and why are they heading for the Duroni?"

"They are not stupid, you know. You talk of them like
they were animals."

Both Carn and Braldt stared at Keri as though she had
gone totally stupid. "What do you mean, of course they are
animals, what do you think they are, Duroni in animal
suits?"

"Animals don't make spears or clubs," Keri answered
her brother patiently. "No, they're not Duroni, but neither
do I think that they are animals, either."

Carn groaned. "C'mon, Keri, don't tell me you're one
of those fools who blather on about how animals have spirits
too and deserve to live in peace. Invite a pankow to break
bread and all that nonsense!"

"I don't know about pankows or other animals," Keri
said evenly, refusing to be riled by her brother's sarcasm.
"But somehow karks are different. They walk on two legs
more often than on four and anyone can see that they're
intelligent, even you."

"Keri, they're covered with hair, long hair all over
their bodies. They're animals pure and simple. Maybe smart
animals, animals who can make spears, but animals just the
same. Lupebeasts walk on two legs. Does that make them
people? C'mon, Keri, don't be dumb. Tell her she's wrong,
Braldt."

"They talked," Braldt said slowly. "We heard them
talk."

"By the name of the Mother!" Carn exclaimed in
disbelief. "Are you saying that you think they're people
too?"

"I don't know what they are," Braldt replied. "But
it's a matter for the priests to decide. What they are does not
concern us except that we must avoid them. Animal or
human, they can kill us, whatever they are, and we must not
let that happen."

Carn was not willing to let the argument go so easily
but Braldt brought the conversation back to their mission.
Scraping the ground clear before the tiny flame, he drew in

the outlines of the mountains that rose behind them, tracing the route that he had spied out that morning.

"The land seems to rise in a series of steps, I'm sure you saw that yourselves. It appears to be wild and heavily wooded, thinning out in the higher elevations. There are numerous waterfalls and I propose that we follow one of them to its source."

"That's all well and good, but how are we to find the mountain we saw in the vision," Carn asked.

"I don't know. Perhaps we will be able to see it once we reach the mountains."

"The priest did not tell us much, or give us much direction."

"No, he didn't. Perhaps he did not know more than he told us."

"But the priests know everything!" Keri cried.

"How, Keri? How would they know?" Braldt looked at her quizzically. "No priest has ever journeyed to these lands, few of them even venture beyond the confines of the city. How would they know?"

"The gods would tell them. Mother Moon would show them the way in their own visions. The priests speak to the gods. They would know!"

"Then why didn't they tell us?" Carn seemed troubled. "Why wouldn't they tell us if they want us to do this thing for them?"

"And why can the gods not do it for themselves?" Braldt murmured more to himself than the others. "If the gods can do anything, why do they need us at all?"

There were no answers to any of their questions and each of them struggled with their own thoughts. To doubt the priests was to doubt the very gods themselves, and to question the gods was to question the very existence of the world they lived in.

10

The land rose steeply before them, the peaks of the distant mountains looming above, higher than anything they had ever seen or imagined. Even though they saw them, it was hard to believe that they really existed and harder still to believe that they were now climbing them.

Beast trotted ahead of them and through his keen senses and warning barks they were able to avoid being seen by additional bands of traveling karks. There were many such bands, composed of equal numbers of males and females and all of them armed.

The sight began to lose its novelty and after a time they were able to detect things that had gone unnoticed earlier. Many of the female karks carried young, nursing at their breasts even as they traveled, spear or club in hand. Many of the creatures wore items of adornment fixed around wrist or ankle or neck. Several of the larger males wore headbands of a sort, twisted bands of leather from which dangled tiny bones, feathers, and bits of ornamental stone. These males, by the very fact of their size alone, they took to be the leaders of the individual bands.

Although they were but animals, albeit smart animals, it was a mistake to take a kark lightly. If they stood upright, which seemed to cause them pain or discomfort, they were taller than the average Duroni although shorter than Braldt. They were covered from head to toe with fur, greenish brown in color and composed of a soft dense undercoat that protected them from the cold and a layer of longer, coarse hair that was impervious to water. Their pelts were much in demand by the Duroni who fashioned them into cloaks and boots and garments to protect them from rain and cold.

But karks did not part with their pelts willingly and were not at all reluctant to use their great strength to protect themselves. In the past, they had been trapped or poisoned, killed from afar, for to venture within reach of their long, powerful limbs was to invite death. It had even been rumored that karks ate the flesh of their enemies, although Braldt had doubts that it was true. So far as he knew, karks ate only plants and insects and the bark of trees. But he did not want to learn the truth firsthand and so they hid whenever Beast warned of their presence.

Mother Moon cast her dim light on them as they traveled and as dawn drew near, she revealed the mouth of a cave where they took shelter for the second day. The mouth of the cave opened to reveal a huge chamber that resonated to their voices.

The light was dim in the outer chamber, and although it showed signs of having been inhabited in the past, there was no trace of recent animal use. The floor was smooth and hard-packed beneath their feet and the roof rose to a high natural arch above their heads. It appeared that a fire had been built in the center of the cave at one time for there was a deep pit that bore the blackened remains of many fires.

They passed through this chamber quickly, entering a wide corridor of sorts that wound through the smooth rock like the vast coils of a stone serpent. The light here was but a shade above total darkness. They sensed other openings and numerous irregular shapes along the walls, but were too exhausted to stop and examine them. There was a peculiar smell in the air, much like rotted leather or old musty clothes, strange, but not unpleasant. Beast growled from time to time, but did not seem overly alarmed.

At last they came to the end of the tunnel and slumped in weariness against the cool walls. The hard-packed earth had given way to soft sand that tugged at their footsteps and now made a soft cushion to lull them into sleep. Being hidden in the heart of the mountain made them feel safe, for it seemed unlikely that they would be found by anyone or anything. Too tired for even the briefest of meals, the three of them wrapped themselves in their cloaks and were soon locked in a deep and dreamless sleep.

Low, rumbling, guttural growls, felt more than heard, brought Braldt back to consciousness. He surfaced slowly, still wrapped in foggy bands of sleep. He closed his hand around Beast's muzzle, feeling the raised lips tremble beneath his palm and the deep rumble continue to vibrate in Beast's throat.

Braldt strained to see, but the corridor was without the merest hint of light and he could see nothing. He felt the ground vibrate beneath him, almost as though it were pulsing with a measured beat, and then he heard it, a long, low, deep, solemn chanting, much like a hymn or a funeral dirge sung on the highest of holy days by the chorus of men at the Temple of the Moon.

Beast began to growl again and Braldt closed his hand more firmly around his muzzle, squeezing tightly and then releasing him, placing his palm on Beast's nose, a sign that he was to stay and remain silent. He wakened Keri and Carn, touching them gently with one hand and placing his palm over their mouths to keep them silent as well. The three of them huddled together, listening to the low chanting that had swelled in volume until it filled the small chamber in which they hid.

The hairs rose up on the back of Braldt's neck as he strained to listen, trying to make out the words, wondering who or what was chanting. He could stand it no longer, placing his hands on Keri's and Carn's shoulders, he pressed them down and told them in whispers what he intended to do. Keri gripped his hand tightly and tried to argue with him, but he slipped loose and crept down the tunnel before she could stop him.

The chanting grew louder still as he worked his way toward the mouth of the corridor and the darkness grew slightly less complete, a dimness that was not light so much as it was the absence of darkness filtered in to light his way. In this twilight he was able to see what his trailing fingers had merely guessed at as they entered the cave; the walls on either side were hollowed out at regular intervals. The holes were four deep, running from the height of the ceiling to a point just above the level of the floor and were large enough and deep enough to have held Braldt easily. They lined the walls on either side in both directions and so far as he could see, they were all empty. A deep sense of unease came over him and he crept forward with great caution, almost certain now of what he would find.

He came to the final bend in the corridor and using the holes like the steps of a ladder climbed up into the uppermost opening and slid his body in so that all that remained exposed was his head. He had thought that he would be able to peer around the final corner, showing nothing but the top of his head, but the angle was too severe and the rock too smooth to grip. He was about to climb down when the light grew much brighter and the sound of the chanting grew louder still. There was no time to climb down from his hiding place and so he did the only thing he could, inching his way to the foot of the hole and curling himself into as small a space as possible. Desperately he hoped that the others had heeded his warning and would stay where he had left them. He also prayed to the gods that Beast would hold his silence.

His prayers were answered for there were no cries of discovery and the chanting and sound of shuffled footsteps ended somewhere close by. He could hear the soft exhalations of breathing and now a cough and what sounded like softly muffled sobs. What had they done? What had they stumbled into and who or what would he see if he dared to look? Braldt ached with desire to raise his head, to peer out of his hiding place, but the light was so very bright, he feared that he would be seen and that was a risk he could not take.

Vision might be denied to him but he was close enough to hear what was being said; he calmed his breathing and strove to understand what he was hearing. The sounds made no sense at first, a constant murmur of meaningless gibberish repeated over and over in a repetitious litany until it droned inside his head like a hive of bees. Only after the sounds had echoed over and over again did they begin to make sense, only then could he begin to assign a meaning to the sounds, decipher the words.

"Oh, Great Master, Giver of Life, Protector of the Weak, accept this body and take its spirit home." There was more, but Braldt could only understand bits and pieces of it for the words were strangely said and ran all together with little or no breaks, and to make it all the more difficult, each speaker seemed to utter the words at their own pace so that no two of them spoke at the same time, their voices all running together, weaving in and out in a most confusing manner. Then, the chanting came to a halt, suddenly and without warning, and in the abrupt silence that followed the soft sobs could be heard clearly.

"Father, we bring you the body of our faithful brother Arba Mintch, killed before his time by the hard ones. We beg you to take his spirit home and give it the peace in death that it fought for so long and bravely in life. Arba Mintch was the bravest of the brave; he fought for the tribe always, defying the hard ones, bringing risk upon himself to spare the others. His mate, Sytha Trubal, is left alone now, to spend her life in sorrow. Please send her comfort and ease her suffering. We beg you to hear our words and come to our aid, or all of our bones shall litter the earth and our spirits will join those of Arba Mintch. Do not desert us in our time of need, Father, but come to us now, we beg of you."

These amazing words, spoken in the same odd, but understandable, inflections, were followed by a loud outcry of sobs as well as individual pleas to the one known as Master or Father. The pain was so intense, the suffering so real, that it was all that Braldt could do to keep himself hidden. No one who spoke so eloquently could be an animal, surely they could speak together. Possibly they were Duroni, although such a thing did not seem possible. And who or what were the "hard ones"?

More words followed as the body was placed inside one of the cubicles on a lower level and somewhere to the side of Braldt's hiding place. There seemed to be a specific form that was followed, one that all were familiar with for the leader, the one with the deep voice, spoke his words that were then echoed by his companions or answered with set responses, all of which seemed to follow a familiar pattern.

The sounds of grief were given open vent now as the ceremony came to an apparent conclusion. That there were women present, there was no doubt, and, from the sound of it, more than a few children. Oldsters, their voices reedy and thin with age, wailed and cried aloud, offering themselves in return for the spirit of the dead Arba Mintch. Braldt felt himself swept up in the depth of their desolation and wished that he could show himself and offer them some solace, but to do so was folly, he could do nothing but hide and listen to their grief.

Then, the sounds that he had most dreaded came to his ears, the sound of Beast barking loudly and in full cry, filling the small corridor with the sound of his alarm. There were sounds of shock and dismay from the mourners and then cries of anger and rage. Torn between the need to remain hidden and the urge to leap from his cubby hole, Braldt listened in horror as Keri and Carn were dragged forth and brought before the gathering.

There were heated demands for their death and cries of hatred broke out on all sides that Carn answered in turn, shouting defiant insults. Keri, except for a single choked cry, said nothing. Beast continued his shrill barking until it too ceased, suddenly and with an ominous finality.

Braldt clenched and unclenched his hands, wondering what to do, knowing now that these were no Duroni, no allies, knowing that he was badly outnumbered and that their only hope was for his presence to go undetected. He could only hope that Keri and Carn would not be killed outright, that somehow he would be given the chance to rescue them.

There were voices, then the speaker, he who had led the prayers and chanting, conferred with his people one at a time, polling them as to their thoughts.

"Crotius," he intoned.

"Death to them as they would deal death to us!" came the reply.

"Ambest."

"Kill the sneaking two-foots!"

"Krantus."

"Death!"

And so it went with none speaking in favor of life and then, just as Braldt was readying himself to leap out of hiding, to try to take the unseen enemy by surprise, another voice spoke out, overwhelming the others, even though it was soft and low-pitched. An uneasy silence fell upon the crowd.

"It must not be so," said the voice. "I, Sytha Trubal, mate of Arba Mintch, say that there will be no more killing."

A fevered outcry answered her words, but she spoke again, silencing them once more.

"Has his death taught us nothing? Will we always be ignorant and be forced to learn the same lessons over and over again? I have said it before and I tell you again, there is no answer in death. We cannot win by striking down the hard ones or even the Duroni. It is wrong and it will gain us nothing. If we strike down a hard one, what do we achieve? We have not done away with it and it will rise again and we will pay with our blood as Arba Mintch paid with his."

"You are wrong, Sytha, you speak with the tongue of a woman," came a harsh reply, interrupting her soft, convincing words. "We have struck down all the hard ones and stopped the great flow. We have stopped them from coming and going and have taken away that which they most want. And now we will strike back at the two-foots for all the pain and suffering they have brought upon us. You are wrong."

"No, Shadath, I am not wrong. You have stopped the hard ones for now, but they will return again and our blood will flow. They are more powerful than we and we cannot win by force alone."

"I do not agree with you. You are a woman and know nothing. What would you have us do with these two-foots? They are here, in our most sacred chambers, what excuse do you offer for their lives?"

"Let them go," the one called Sytha said quietly.

"They can do us no harm. Take their weapons from them and let them go. They will not return."

Amazingly, even though there was much muttering, it seemed to Braldt that the woman's wishes would be honored, not so much because they were in agreement or she had convinced them with her words, but because of the respect they had had for her man. After much argument, it was agreed that Keri and Carn would be released without their weapons and allowed to make their way back to Duroni lands. It was more than Braldt could have hoped for or believed possible. Then, just as the speaker was talking, the gathering erupted in chaos. Yells and screams broke out, angry shouts and, above all, the sound of Carn cursing.

"Dirty karks! Let go of me! Let go!" And then there was the sound of a blow striking bone and flesh and Carn's voice was stilled. Then there was nothing but the sound of Keri weeping amid angry, hostile voices that flowed out of the corridor, out of the chamber that lay beyond, leaving nothing behind but the vibrations of their rage.

11

Braldt could stand it no longer. After the last voice had died away, he slithered out of his hiding place and leaped down, landing softly on the hard-packed earth. A sharp intake of breath was the first indication that he was not alone. Turning swiftly, knife in hand, he found himself looking down on the bowed figure of a female kark who was seated on the ground, her long arms wrapped around her shaggy knees.

The kark made no move to rise, to attack, or even to defend herself, but looked steadily at Braldt with sorrow in her large eyes. Some part of him that was strangely detached noted with surprise that her eyes were green in color and thickly fringed with heavy lashes that would have been the envy of many a Duroni girl. He had no doubt that he was looking at the one called Sytha Trubal, the mate of the deceased Arba Mintch.

Many questions came to his mind, questions that he would very much have liked to have had answered. In fact, he found himself strangely drawn to this creature and at another time would have welcomed the opportunity to speak with her, but now there was no time.

"Where have they taken my friends? What will they do to them?"

The female studied him quietly, wrapped in the same calm dignity that had accompanied her words. "I suppose they will kill them," she said softly, the familiar words falling so oddly from her lips that at first he had trouble comprehending the meaning. It was a thing that his mind could not seem to grasp, as strange and peculiar to him as if

Beast had suddenly begun to talk. But she did talk and he needed her knowledge if he was to save Keri and Carn.

"Where will they go?" he demanded.

"You cannot stop them," she replied. "Their hatred is deep and unreasoning. You are but one small two-foot. What could you do against so many of them?"

He raised his knife in silent answer, a silent threat to her as well, for he was desperate to know what was going to happen.

"Men are the same whether they are two-foots or Madrelli," the female said more to herself than to Braldt, seemingly unafraid of the upraised knife. "You all seem to think that violence and death are the answer to everything."

"I have no wish to harm you," said Braldt, lowering his knife, "but I must help my friends and you must tell me what you know."

"There is nothing that I must do but die in my own good time and now that Arba Mintch is dead, it can be sooner rather than later, it does not matter overly much."

"I am sorry for your loss," Braldt said, finding himself responding to her words much as he would have done to a grieving widow of his own people, for other than her appearance, as time passed, there seemed little difference. "But you must understand that I cannot allow my friends to be killed. You say that you are against killing, well help me then, help me free my friends from your people and prevent their deaths."

"Why should I help you," the female asked, raising her head and looking at Braldt with something like interest in her large, luminous eyes, "after all it was your friends who attacked my people."

"The man is young and impulsive and too quick to act at times, but at heart he is a good man. The girl, his sister, is kind and generous and thinks much as you do about killing. They are my adopted family and neither of them deserves to die. Please help me, Sytha Trubal."

"Arba Mintch would say that I am a fool," Sytha said to herself as tears filled her eyes and trembled on her lower lashes. "He said that there was no strength in compromise and that we would die unless we struck the first blow."

"But Arba Mintch is dead," Braldt said softly, feeling her pain as she closed her eyes at his words, the tears trickling down through the fine bronze fur that covered the high cheekbones on either side of the broad, flat nose.

"Yes, he is dead, struck down by the hard ones even as he broke the last of them and stopped them from their work."

Braldt wondered who and what the hard ones were and what it was they had been working at, for he could think of nothing that would meet that description, but he sensed that Sytha was weakening now and pressed on, regardless of the hurt he was causing her.

"Help me stop the killing, Sytha, help me to help my friends. Perhaps there is a way to save them without bringing death to your people or to mine. If you truly believe what you say, then you will help me."

The kark known as Sytha raised her eyes to his and studied him carefully. "You would do this thing without killing?"

Braldt paused. "If it is possible," he said at last. "Yes."

"They will take them to the rock," Sytha said with a sigh, rising slowly to her feet. She stood quietly, eyes downcast, lost in thought. "I do not think we can get there before them, but perhaps if we hurry, we can stop them. Yes, that is what we must do, if your two legs are equal to the task," she said, looking up at Braldt with a quirk at the corner of her mouth that might have been the beginning of a smile.

"I will keep up," Braldt said gravely. Then, struck by a sudden thought, he turned and gazed around him, finding what he was seeking in the crumpled form of the pup, lying where he had fallen at the base of the far wall. He had expected to find the pup dead and was surprised to see his chest rise and fall. Picking the pup up gently, Braldt placed him inside the drapes of his robe, where he had ridden so often before, and silently commended his fate to the gods. "I am ready," he said.

Sytha made no reply but turned and strode down the corridor, still brightly lit by torches that had been placed in holes in the wall. Following close on her heels, Braldt glanced around him and saw what he had only guessed at before. Each cleanly carved declivity held the earthly remains of a kark, some totally dessicated, their fur and skin brittle and paper-thin, clinging to their bones by habit alone. Others, more recently dead, slowly settling into the sleep of the ages. Beside each body was a small accumulation of articles, small, highly decorated pots containing seeds and nuts, bunches of dried flowers, a polished stone. One small body, obviously that of a child, was wrapped in a soft coverlet and the tiny fist still clutched the carved figure of a doll.

Unwittingly, they had taken shelter in the burial ground of the karks, no small wonder that their discovery had earned them such a violent reaction. Nor could it have been otherwise, thought Braldt, for between kark and Duroni, there had never been anything but enmity. Even now his mind reeled with the thoughts of what he had seen and heard. Karks speaking, burying their dead in a civilized manner, reference to gods that certainly indicated some form of religion and philosophy, and now the lives of Carn and Keri resting in the hands of a kark, whom Braldt would have slain without thinking only a short time before. There was much that he did not understand. When there was time, he and this female, this Sytha Trubal, would talk and he would ask many, many questions.

Once out of the cave it was difficult keeping up with Sytha for she covered the ground twice as quickly as he in a loose, loping sprint that utilized her hands as well as her feet, dropping to all fours when the terrain demanded it. Braldt found himself at a distinct disadvantage, staggering about and falling often on the rough ground, unable to use his hands as Sytha did to stabilize himself, and once he took a painful tumble down a steep slope, rolling over and over, falling atop Beast, and finally crashing to a halt against the bole of a tree, tangled in his robes and the straps of his pouch, smarting from a dozen cuts and bruises. Sytha helped him to his feet without a word, but thereafter her pace was more moderate.

They followed no path or trail that Braldt could discern, first clawed their way up a sheer slope of slippery scree that threatened to bury them at every step, then slid down a nearly perpendicular rock face that removed several layers of Braldt's skin, crossed a swiftly flowing torrent that took his breath away with its icy coldness, and finally made their way to the foot of a massive outcrop of shining black rock, so polished and bright that he could see his own exhausted image gaping back at him.

But Sytha allowed him no time to rest, seizing him by the wrist and pulling him forward. Now he heard it, the sound of voices, angry voices chanting aloud. But this was no religious ceremony, no death dirge, although the result might well be the same, for the voices were chanting, "Death! Death! Death!" over and over and over, growing louder with each intonation, voices that were filled with the sound of rage and hatred rather than sorrow and grief.

His feet found the carved steps that led up the side of the black outcrop, and together they made their way up the incredible stone, struggled over the final crest, and found themselves surrounded on all sides by a furious gathering of karks, all of whom were chanting, "Death! Death! Death!"

His wrist was still firmly gripped by Sytha and as he found himself pulled deeper and deeper into the angry mob, Braldt began to fear that he had allowed himself to be entrapped and that soon he too would join his companions as they faced their deaths.

All around him, karks were becoming aware of his presence. Some few snatched at him with sharp, claw-tipped digits, or tried to strike at him, but his passage was too swift as Sytha made her way through the crowd, the karks parting to allow her to pass, deferring to her even in their rage as though she were royalty. Braldt caught brief glimpses of these attitudes before the expressions turned from quiet deference to rage at the sight of him, and he could but wonder what role Sytha played in this strange society before his thoughts returned to that of his own survival.

And then as the crowd parted before them once again, Braldt saw that they had come to the end of their journey. Before them stood two karks, one taller and bigger than any they had seen before, an elaborate headband fastened around his massive brow, festooned with shells and feathers and bits of the black, shiny rock. Fixed in the center between his jutting brows was the small curl-horned skull of a highland bik-bik, swift of foot and almost impossible to bring down with spear or sling. Bright, intelligent eyes fixed on him and he felt as though his entire self had been judged in that single glance.

Braldt wrenched his eyes away and stared at the second of the karks. This one was old, older even than Auslic from the look of him, for his fur was white and grey and pocked with the mark of ancient scars. He too wore a headband although his was plain and bore no ornament other than a chunk of the shining, black rock, worked in some elaborate design that Braldt's eyes could not identify at the distance. And while the younger kark's gaze had been filled with nothing but hatred, this one looked on him with something akin to sorrow. Holding up a pale and withered hand to silence the angry mob, the old one approached them.

"Sytha Trubal," he said softly, the words somehow conveying the weight of his caring as well as containing the unspoken question.

"Uba Mintch," she replied with respect, bowing her head toward him and gently but powerfully tugging on Braldt's hand so that he too was forced to bow as well or have his arm jerked from its socket. "We have come to speak with you about these two-foots and ask your guidance."

"There is nothing to talk about, nothing at all!" The younger of the two karks thrust himself forward, standing so close to them that they felt the exhalation of his breath and were threatened by his very nearness. Braldt resisted the need to step back, to put space between himself and the kark, and stood straight, doing his best to show no fear. Sytha Trubal stood upright beside him, letting go of his wrist and her hand slipped into his and squeezed it gently as though giving him courage. It also served to let him know that she had not abandoned him and he was shamed for his thoughts.

Sytha stared directly at the young male and did not flinch from his angry gaze. "It is a time for the killing to stop, Batta Flor. Killing accomplishes nothing, leaving only the desire to kill more. I have come to ask counsel of Uba Mintch and only he can deny my request."

"We will talk after we have given the two-foots to the Master. Then, their spirits can join you at the Council Ring. Take this one too!" he cried aloud, gesturing at Braldt. Braldt felt himself seized on either side by rough, powerful hands that began to drag him backward.

"No!" Sytha Trubal spoke the word softly, yet it was enough to stop those who held him, and he could literally feel the weight of their indecision. Sytha drew him toward her, away from their nonresisting grasp, and placed her hand on his shoulder. "This two-foot is mine. He is mine to claim. I take his hand willingly as all may see," and so saying she raised their two joined hands above their heads to the shocked gasps of the crowd. "He is now under my protection. None may harm him. The others are his blood family and as such are mine as well. My roof is theirs now. They are Mintch. They are Madrelli."

The kark known as Batta Flor stared at Sytha Trubal as though unable to believe his ears. Disbelief and pain filled his eyes, which were black and small, and his jaw drooped in what might have been a comic expression, had his distress not been so evident.

"You are sure of this, Sytha Trubal?" the old one asked quietly. "Such a thing has never been done before."

"Well, maybe it is time for such a thing now," Sytha replied, her voice even softer than before, but Braldt, from the short time he had been with her, could sense the fact that even she was shaken by her own actions.

"But, I had thought that you and I . . . Sytha, how can you take a two-foot under your roof, give him your name?" Batta Flor was pleading openly now, the threatening air gone completely, beseeching Sytha to listen. "He has no hair," he said in bewilderment, apropos of absolutely nothing.

"You will always be a welcome guest under my roof, Batta Flor, but it is time for the killing to stop."

"Do you realize what you have done, Sytha Trubal. You have given the keeping of the tribe into the hands of the enemy. You have betrayed us. You have killed us!" A low moan rose behind Braldt as he struggled to comprehend the meaning of what he was hearing. Women began to weep and distressed voices broke out on all sides. Batta Flor stared at Sytha Trubal, begging her silently to take back her words, but even though Braldt felt her hand tremble in his, she did not speak again.

"It is done." Batta Flor spoke in dull, numbed tones, all hope extinguished from his voice. Turning to face the crowd, he raised his arms and spread wide his fingers. The crowd fell silent except for an undertone of frightened crying. "Let it be known that Sytha Trubal, mate of Arba Mintch, High One of the Madrelli, has this day chosen one to share her roof. He and those of his family must pass among us in peace. This is the way of the Madrelli, let no one among us say nay!"

He lowered his arms to the sound of open weeping and, without looked at Sytha Trubal again, turned, his powerful arms hanging loose at his sides, and walked away with head bowed.

Uba Mintch approached them now, his eyes troubled, and stood there silent, pondering.

"Father," Sytha said simply. "There did not seem anything else to do. I could not think of anything that would stop the killing."

Uba Mintch's grey muzzle twisted to one side in an all-but-toothless grin. "Well, you certainly stopped it," he said wryly. "Now, what are you going to do?"

"I—I don't know," she replied, uncertainty entering her voice as she looked up at Braldt with wide eyes as though only just realizing the enormity of her actions.

No longer restrained, Keri and Carn retreated from the

edge of the black rock and hurriedly joined Braldt, looking around them as though they expected to be attacked at any moment.

"What did you say? How did you do that?" Keri cried as she rushed to his side, ignoring Sytha and Uba Mintch as though they did not exist.

"I did nothing, there was nothing I could do," Braldt said, noticing the way that Uba Mintch was forced to step aside to avoid Carn's approach. "It was Sytha Trubal who saved your lives."

Carn and Keri turned and stared at Sytha who did not meet their eyes but stared down at the ground. "What... How?" Keri asked in bewilderment.

The old kark rested on his stick and sighed heavily, the weight of his years bowing him down. "Sytha Trubal was mate to my son. He was High One of the tribe. Upon his death, Sytha Trubal became High One in Waiting because they had no son. She has chosen this one, this two-foot, as her mate. He is now High One of the Madrelli and ruler of our tribe."

12

Carn, Keri, and Braldt stared at Uba Mintch in shock, barely comprehending his words. Braldt had heard the words but took them to mean only that Sytha had extended to him the protection of her home, much as a Duroni would do when hosting a guest. Now, it was apparent that her words had meant much more. He was now her mate, mated to a creature whom he had regarded as an animal only a dawning ago! Had it really been so short a time?

Carn barked out a short laugh accompanied by Keri's cry of dismay as she turned to Braldt in disbelief. "But how . . ."

"Come," interrupted Uba Mintch. "We must talk." He did not stop to see if they would follow, but turned and shuffled away, following the edge of the plateau, seemingly unaware of the fact that the drop was sheer and unbroken, falling thousands of feet to the rocks below. Braldt followed Sytha, who did not even seem to be aware of his presence and walked swiftly, wrapped in her own thoughts.

The massive outflow of shining, black rock sloped sharply downward in a smooth flow, resembling nothing so much as a sheet of black water that had somehow been changed to solid stone. As they made their descent, the shining black flow came to an end, merging with ordinary grey stone and earth.

The kark, or Madrelli, as they called themselves, village came into view then. It lay in a small valley cradled between two towering white-capped peaks, sheltered on three sides by mountainous walls of rock, and approachable only from the edge of the plateau. Braldt admired the clever placement of the village for it seemed all but unassailable by an enemy. A thick ribbon of muddy red water, which could only have had its source in the mountains above, swept through the village, lapping at the uppermost edges of its channel and dividing the village in two.

The village itself and the sixty or more dwellings came as a complete surprise. Braldt would have supposed that karks lived in trees or slept on the ground in grassy nests, but these were no crude nests, but cleverly made buildings constructed entirely of wood and stone. As they entered the village by way of a smooth road made of the shining black stone, all doors and windows were tightly closed, and Braldt had the distinct impression that they were being viewed by many curious eyes.

The main avenue that ran alongside the canal was laid with the black stone as well, carefully fitted stones that provided a smooth and unbroken footing. The dwellings rose to their left and stood slightly above the road and back, allowing for small plots of ground where bright flowers and carefully tended herbs grew in profusion.

The homes themselves were a marvel of the builder's art and even Carn was awestruck at the beauty of their design. Somewhat lower in height than Duroni dwellings, each home was distinct in its design as though reflecting the personality of its builder. Some were constructed entirely of the black, shiny stone, while others were a combination of black and the more common grey. Some builders had chosen to use the trunks of trees rather than stone, and these had been stripped of their bark and with the passage of time had weathered to a pleasant silvery hue. Doors and windows were covered with narrow strips of woven lattice that allowed the movement of air as well as permitting those inside to look out without being seen themselves.

Many of the buildings bore carved runes above their doors, all of them different and indecipherable to Braldt, and while many of the homes were unadorned, an equal number were embellished with carved designs of leaves and flowers that curled around doors and windows or up the sides of blank walls in a cheerful show of exuberance unknown to the dour Duroni.

There were several large buildings in the village, although none as large as the Temple of the Moon or the various schools or the Council chambers of his own city. Braldt found himself wondering at the governing structure of the karks, no, the Madrelli. Considering that they owed them their lives, he would do well to change his thinking, for they were anything but the simple beasts he had thought them to be. That thought jogged his memory and he slipped his hand into his robe and felt Beast stir. Good. He curled his hand around the small one and stroked him gently to let him know that all was well. Beast settled quietly beneath his hand.

Uba Mintch led them over a bridge that was built entirely of worked stone and arched over the ugly red flow. Braldt looked down and wondered at the strange color that fouled the water, for never had he seen such a thing before; water was clear or blue or sometimes brown, but never this dark, ugly shade of red.

The old one stepped off the bridge and led them to one of the largest homes, unusual in that it was twice the size of any other as well as a full two stories in height. It was built entirely of the shining, black stone and its roof was shingled with grey stone tiles. The building itself was unadorned with the single exception of a rune inscribed above the lintel, while two immense silverwoods of great age flanked the double doorway and herbs and flowers had been planted in neat borders.

Uba Mintch paused before the doorstep, a large block of black stone, which had been worn smooth in the middle from the tread of many feet. He looked up at the inscription and touched it gently with the end of his staff before turning to face the others. "This is my home. You are welcome under my roof and safe from harm, so far as we are able to protect you."

Braldt nodded to the old one to show his appreciation. Keri emulated his move, bowing more deeply, and after a moment Carn did so as well, although his obeisance was stiff and almost rude in its brevity.

"Please, sir, what do the runes say?" Keri asked hesitantly.

The old one looked up, his face relaxing in a smile, and he turned to Keri. "It says, 'Protect this house from evil.' Come, enter, we have much to speak of." And with a last look at the sky above, they entered the home of the Madrelli.

The building was completely different from those of the Duroni inside as well as out. Duroni homes consisted of a single large, great room where most family activity took place. Smaller rooms were set aside for individual sleeping places, but these were used for little else and generally held no more than a sleeping mat and a few items of a personal nature.

Madrelli dwellings, if this one could be taken as an example, allotted rooms to each and every member of the household and contained a raised sleeping place piled high with thick, woven coverlets, several strangely shaped chairs, which were much too large for the smaller Duroni, and other pieces of wooden furniture whose meaning was not immediately apparent. Walls were adorned with handworked items that had no function except to please the eye and the stone floors were warmed by hand-woven mats, brightly colored with intricate designs.

Each of them was shown to a room that they were told was theirs for as long as they remained under Uba Mintch's roof. A serving girl, obviously young and more curious than afraid, was instructed to tend to their needs.

Uba Mintch took his leave of them, saying only that they were to rest. It was easy to see that it was Uba Mintch who was tired and needed to refresh himself, but no one voiced an objection, not even Carn.

"If you will join me later, after the sun has passed beneath the twin peaks, we will eat and talk of the things that must be said. Until then I bid you peace." He raised his hand in a benediction and then shuffled slowly down the corridor to his own quarters.

Sytha Trubal showed no sign of wanting to linger and she too hurried after the old man with only a single glance at Braldt, a glance filled with meaning that he did not understand.

Carn waited until both Sytha and Uba Mintch had gone and then turned to Braldt with a wide grin on his face. "Well, what happened between you two, eh? Must have been something special to get us fixed up this good!"

"Carn!" Keri's voice was sharp with disapproval and she looked at Braldt with hurt in her eyes as though waiting for him to deny Carn's words.

"Don't be stupid, Carn. Nothing happened. What do you think? No, don't tell me; do not judge me by your own lack of morals."

"Whatever you say, brother," Carn said in a tone that indicated his disbelief. "When do we leave? Now or later?"

"We do not leave at all. This woman has saved our lives at a considerable risk to her own. It is only fair that we stay and talk, conduct ourselves honorably. There is much to be learned here, many questions that need to be answered. We will not betray them and return their offer of protection with duplicity."

"What are you talking about, Braldt? These aren't people, we don't owe them anything, they're no better than animals!"

Braldt stared at Carn coldly, then turned on his heel and entered the room that had been assigned to him. Hand on the door frame, he turned and spoke in a voice devoid of emotion, his blue eyes blazing in anger. "They have given us their word in honor, a word that I do not intend to betray, and animal or no, one of them has chosen me as mate. Do not cross me, Carn, or you will live only long enough to regret it."

The serving maid entered the room shortly after his exchange with Carn, carrying a bowl of hot, steaming water and several thick towels draped over her arm. She would not look him in the eye but burst into giggles when he thanked her and rushed from the room, hand cupped over her mouth. Braldt could all but imagine the girl regaling a confidant with the story of her terrifying encounter with the horrible two-foot. Only in the retelling, the maid would no doubt have made some brave comment before leaving. He grinned at the thought for it appeared that young maids were the same everywhere.

Braldt took advantage of the hot water and a bar of fragrant floral-scented soap and cleansed himself gladly, luxuriating in the thick, fluffy towel. When his toilet was complete, he investigated the room with interest, taking note of the thick rug that covered the stone floor and the intricate colorful pattern that was woven throughout. Drapes of similar construction hung on either side of the double windows, brightening the room with their colors. Dominating the room was a large bed that stood several feet off the floor and was piled with multiple layers of soft, thick mattresses. It was four times as wide as a Duroni sleeping mat and a good deal shorter. Braldt placed Beast on the soft surface and the pup groaned and curled into a tight ball. Braldt could find no sign of a wound and it would seem that Beast had escaped serious injury.

Braldt sat down beside the pup and immediately sank like a stone in quicksand with the thick comforters wedging him on either side. Beast tumbled into his lap and opening his eyes he snarled at Braldt, leaped nimbly off the bed, and stalked away to the far side of the room. Braldt struggled to extricate himself, wondering how anyone could sleep in such a creation and knowing that he would not.

Beast had settled into one of several strange basketlike objects that dotted the room. Braldt studied them with a grimace, assuming that they were chairs, yet knowing that they would never accommodate his body.

He was studiously avoiding the topic that screamed for his attention, the supposed mating with Sytha Trubal. He was grateful to her for she had undoubtedly saved their lives, but such a thing was impossible. He settled on a broad stone shelf under the window and pondered the problem, trying to find a solution that would permit them to leave with their lives without offending Sytha Trubal or arousing the anger of the tribe.

His thoughts were interrupted by the entry of Keri and

Carn, Carn in the lead, flinging the door wide and entering without a knock or a salutation.

"All right, so they live in houses and sleep on beds and they talk. Someone else probably built the stuff and they killed 'em and took over. The gods only know how they learned to talk, but it doesn't make any difference, they're still animals. We don't owe them anything, Braldt. We've got more important things to do, or have you forgotten Auslic and what we promised the priests?"

"Don't be a fool, Carn, I've forgotten nothing!" Braldt snapped. "I know where my duty lies!"

"Then do it!" Carn replied hotly, closing the distance between them.

"Stop this, it is you who are acting like animals rather than people," Keri cried angrily as she stepped between the two men. "You are both right and there is a way to settle this properly if we but think on it calmly, like civilized people!

"You go sit down there," she said to Carn, pushing him in the direction of the bed, which he avoided, sinking cross-legged to the floor, evidently having had a similar experience with his own bed. "You go over there," she said to Braldt, directing him toward one of the basket chairs, while she herself settled on the window ledge.

"Now," she said, "let's talk." And so they did until the sun had disappeared behind the twin peaks and the room had become grey with dim twilight, but despite their efforts, they had reached no agreement by the time the giggling maid knocked on the door and summoned them to speak with Uba Mintch.

The halls were glowing with a soft light that emanated from steady flames enclosed in transparent globes affixed to the walls. Braldt stared at them in wonder and would have stopped to study them, but was given no opportunity to do so as the maid ushered them down the long hall that opened onto a large room that took up the entire end of the building. At the last moment, Beast had roused from his slumbers and now trotted at Braldt's heels.

Uba Mintch was settled in one of the basket chairs, the

hard surface cushioned by a thick comforter. It fit the shape of his body quite nicely. Across from him, seated in a second chair, was Sytha Trubal who held a smaller version of herself on her lap.

Once they were seated in the same uncomfortable chairs, the maid carried in a tray laden with steaming mugs that she offered to them one at a time, giggling all the while.

Uba Mintch waited until she had left the room before he spoke. "Your health and safekeeping," he murmured as he raised his mug in a solemn toast. They echoed his words with a Duroni toast of their own and then sipped at the steaming brew that was sharply sour on their tongues and somewhat bitter although it warmed their bellies and left a pleasant aftertaste.

"Your presence here among us at this time presents us with somewhat of a dilemma," began Uba Mintch.

"We will gladly take our leave," said Carn, seizing the opportunity to make his wishes known.

"Would that it were so easy," the old one said with a sigh. "Had you not come in such a dramatic manner, there might have been some choice, but arriving as you did, you have left us few alternatives. The wife of my son was forced to claim your friend as a mate and that is not a thing that is done lightly among the Madrelli. I do not know the customs of your people, but Sytha Trubal is our regent, and as her chosen mate, you have now become leader of the tribe. You can scarcely imagine that your presence here will be lightly marked."

"I thank you for this honor, Sytha Trubal, and even more I thank you for the gift of our lives," Braldt said quickly, cutting Carn off before he could speak. "I realize the sacrifice that you have made in order to save us, but you must know that I cannot accept this honor. Your people will never accept me and it would not be right for me to hold a position of such great responsibility. A tribe should be ruled by one of its own."

Sytha Trubal raised her eyes to meet his own and in them he could read her confusion as well as her unhappiness.

"But what can we do . . . I—I do not even know what

you are named," and as the tears gathered and threatened to spill, she looked down and busied herself with the active arm- and leg-waving figure of her daughter.

"I am Braldt, the Hunter, and this one here is my brother, Carn the Stalker, and my sister, Keri, the mischief maker."

Keri shot Braldt a look that he could not decipher and, rising from her chair, crouched beside Sytha and placed her hand hesitantly on Sytha's arm. The two women gazed at each other and a look passed between them that spoke of many things, womanly things that somehow transcended their different races. Without speaking, Sytha picked up the wriggling bundle and handed her to Keri who cradled her expertly, cooing gently and making sounds understandable to infants of any nature. Beast suddenly appeared at her side, studying the infant with interest, his bright eyes watching closely.

"We are puzzled, Uba Mintch," Braldt began in a respectful tone. "You are not what we had imagined you to be. How is it that we have remained ignorant of your true nature. Why is it that we have no knowledge of the fact that you have speech, a cultured way of life equal to our own?"

"Have you given us any opportunity for speech?" Uba Mintch asked softly. "Our encounters are few but violent. Whenever those of your kind meet ours, there is no time for words. The Duroni hunt and trap and kill us like animals for sport or merely for our pelts. There is no thought of speech."

Braldt could only admit that such was indeed the case, but before he could argue the point further, Carn spoke out.

"Look, you can put all the blame on us if it makes you feel better, but you know as well as I do that the violence is not all on our side. What about all the times that your people have attacked the Duroni without warning or reason. What about the herdsman who was tortured and burned to death not two days' march from here. What did he do to deserve that kind of death other than try to protect his herd? Your people are no better than wild animals and the fact that you live in houses and sleep in beds and talk doesn't change that at all!''

Braldt and Keri were stunned by Carn's words and Braldt's hand crept toward his dagger, wondering if Uba Mintch would attack him or summon help. But the old man did nothing but sink farther into the depths of his chair and sigh deeply. Noting Braldt's reaction, he smiled ruefully and nodded his head. ''His words have merit and even though I might not have worded them so baldly, I do not take offense. Sit you down, Carn the Outspoken. Allow me to tell you the story of the Madrelli, and perhaps when all is done, you will understand.''

13

"We have not always been as we are now," began Uba Mintch, his eyes taking on a distant look as though he were remembering other times, other vistas. "Once we were no more than the animals you describe, somewhat intelligent, yet given to fits of violence, we were without words, and we may well have lived in trees or slept in nests on the ground, I cannot say for no records exist from that time, at least no records of our keeping.

"Then, others discovered that we could be trained to do clever things, things that were too difficult or too dangerous for other beings. But our violence and our unwillingness to perform for others made us unsatisfactory for projects of any but those of a short duration.

"But the others had need of our services and being stronger, more intelligent, and more highly advanced, they enslaved us and performed many tests upon those of our tribe. After a time, during which many of our people were sacrificed in the name of their desires and greater knowledge, they devised a way to bring us under control, under their control, a way that would heighten our intelligence as well as make us subservient to their wishes. We were now the ideal subjects, willing and able to carry out orders of the greatest complexity for long periods of time under less than beneficent conditions. All of this was made possible by means of a simple injection given on a regular basis.

"As you might imagine, this was a very difficult time for the Madrelli. On the one hand, we had made huge leaps in intelligence, come further in a short period of time than we would have in several millennium of a more natural order. We were now fully thinking, sentient beings, enjoying the same emotions that you yourselves experience.

"But in gaining this intelligence, this gamut of emotion, we had lost our freedom, the right to govern ourselves; we had become little more than the slaves of others. Should we offend them, refuse to do their bidding, they had but to withhold the miracle of the serum and we would become as we had been, mere animals with one foot on the lowest rung of the ladder of life.

"We served our masters well for many long generations, dying in their stead in many instances, where the deeds were too dangerous to support even our poor, expendable lives. We served them faithfully on many planets, on many worlds, some sterile and barren and hostile to all life, others that were mere machines rotating in the cold darkness of empty space, but nowhere did we find a world like this one, a world perhaps like that of our own, wherever in the universe that that might have been.

"And then some six generations ago, we were sent here, as always, to do the bidding of our masters, still dependent on them as we always had been for the serum. And then one day, we made a miraculous discovery, here on this planet, this world of great beauty, we found a bush that produced a berry, a small red berry that duplicated in nature the properties of the serum, and in it we found the promise of freedom."

"Now wait a minute, let me understand you. You're saying that there are other worlds, other people somewhere else?" Carn was sitting on the edge of his chair, his face screwed up in an expression of total disbelief. "What kind of story is this? You expect us to believe that you come from another world? Do you think we're stupid?"

"Carn, please, let him tell the story," said Keri, her eyes fixed on Uba Mintch. "Listen at least, until he is done."

Braldt's mind was in a turmoil. Other worlds? Who and what were their masters? How could this be, and yet a part of his mind stood back and wondered how it could be anything other than the truth, for there was too much here that he could not explain. "These masters," he asked slowly. "Tell us about them. Who are they? Where are they? Are they here?"

"I am sorry if our story upsets you, it is upsetting to us as well for it is we who have lived and died to make it so. I will do my best to answer all your questions, but allow me to finish, so that you may know the whole story."

The three of them exchanged uneasy glances and sat back silent, prepared to hear the old man out.

"We had asked for our freedom many times and had been punished for our efforts. We knew that there was no sense in asking again so we bided our time, waiting for the proper moment in which to seize control of our lives.

"As with any people there are different factions within our tribe. Many cautioned that we do nothing, that our masters were not overly harsh and it would be better to leave well enough alone. Others wished to seize their freedom immediately. There were many thoughts between the one extreme and the other and nobody agreed with anyone else.

"I do not know what we might have done, had we been given the time to decide, but we were not allowed that choice. Recently, we learned that the reason for our presence on this planet, a substance known as rhodium, precious and rare and impossible to duplicate outside of nature, had been depleted. We were to be removed from this world that we have come to love and taken who knows where. The planet was to be destroyed, blown to bits so that our masters might extract whatever amounts of rhodium that are contained in its heart. This would be done by machines, and our services would no longer be required."

"Destroy our world? This world!" Carn leaped to his feet, fists clenched. "Are you mad, the gods would not allow such a thing to happen. We're crazy to even listen to you! This can't be true, it's some kind of a trick, isn't it, old man. Some kind of trick you're playing to get us to do something!"

"It's no trick, I'm afraid. No, Keri, it's all right, I quite understand your brother's anger. We have felt it many times ourselves. It is not pleasant to find out that you and your world are but another's plaything.''

"The gods would not let anything happen to us!" shouted Carn, his face a dangerous shade of red. "Mother Moon . . ."

"There are no gods," Uba Mintch said quietly, "and your Mother Moon is but a dead, lifeless bit of rock that shines only on this world, reflecting the image of your own small sun. The moon cannot help you, no one can help you other than you, yourselves. You would be better served to believe in your own abilities than in some amorphous being that cannot be seen or touched."

"Father, it is too much, do not take everything from them at once," Sytha Trubal whispered in the shocked silence that followed. "You forget how hard it was for us in the beginning when we learned the truth."

"No, daughter, I do not forget," replied Uba Mintch, "but there is no kindness in half truths, they must learn the truth sometime and it is better that they learn it now."

Braldt's mind reeled under Uba Mintch's words even though he himself had had doubts and questions that he had not dared to ask of the priests, questions that appeared in the darkness of night and disappeared with the coming of the dawn. "What happened then?" he asked, more to keep the old man talking and to distract Carn from foolish action, than from any desire to learn more of the story.

"We talked long into the night, trying to decide what to do, but even though all of us knew that we did not wish to leave this world and wanted to be free to lead our own lives, we could not decide upon the means.

"In the end, it was decided that we would speak to the masters once more and plead with them for our freedom. We would promise them that we would search the world over, find other deposits of the mineral that they sought, and deliver it to them as payment for our freedom. My son was part of that delegation, even though he did not believe that there could be a peaceful solution. He was right." The old man fell silent then, the brilliant stripes on his muzzle fading, becoming muddy and drab as he sat, lost in thought and painful memory.

"They went to speak to the masters on a day when they had come to supervise the collection. But the masters laughed at our offer, laughed at us, told us to be ready to leave within six dawnings or we could stay behind and die along with the planet.

"The delegation returned and told us of our masters' words, and while the others were wasting their time arguing, talking as always, Arba Mintch gathered a small band of friends and returned under darkness of night. The masters had gone, leaving only the hard ones behind, the hard ones who have no thoughts of their own but carry out the masters' wishes in total obedience.

"Arba Mintch and the others destroyed the hard ones and threw the great switch that allowed the masters to come and go, masking their presence from you and others who might take exception to their presence on this world. They severed the bond that held us in their thrall; we were free at last." The old man fell silent, his muzzle resting on his chest, eyes shut tightly, gripped in some terrible emotion, unable to continue.

"Arba Mintch was killed in the doing," said Sytha Trubal, her voice no more than a whisper. "He and two others were killed when they threw the switch and brought down destruction on the great chamber. Only now has the river brought us their bodies. Batta Flor was among those who made the journey and he alone survived to tell what happened."

There was silence then in the great room as each of them in turn thought over the words that had been said and dealt with their own painful private thoughts.

"The God Lights, the colors in the night sky. . ." Keri asked softly. "They are not God Lights at all?"

"If you refer to the shimmering borealis in the eastern sky, no, that is no light of the gods," replied Sytha Trubal. "It is an electromagnetic masking device that the masters created to hide their comings and goings. Otherwise you would have seen the crafts landing and taking off. This machine was also destroyed by Arba Mintch."

"Why must these masters hide their comings and goings?" asked Braldt, his lips feeling numb and strange even as they formed the words.

"I do not know," said Sytha Trubal, "but it has always been so and they were most anxious to conceal their presence. We were forbidden to reveal our true selves to you as well, under pain of death. Some of us thought that we might form an alliance between our two peoples, but all of our attempts were met with violence and our ambassadors killed and stripped of their pelts. Some of our people responded with violence of their own; it is wrong, I know, but understandable."

"We saw many armed Madrelli on our journey," said Braldt. "Are they going to attack the Duroni?"

"No, it is yet another attempt to establish an alliance, but this time they go in force so that they are not slain before they are heard." The old man raised his head and spoke directly to Braldt.

"Once your people are heard to speak, they will come to no harm."

"Are you so certain that this is true?" asked Uba Mintch.

And considering the ordered nature of his adopted people, knowing their intense dislike for anything that was out of the norm, Braldt wavered, less than certain of his answer.

"Why did the priests give us the vision then?" Carn cried angrily. "Why did they give us the vision and send us to this place to fix that which is broken? If there are no gods, then how do you answer that?"

Uba Mintch turned to Braldt in puzzlement. "What is this vision he speaks of? What is your purpose here? Why indeed have you come?"

Braldt paused, wondering how much he dared to tell the old man. Sytha Trubal had saved their lives. They had been welcomed into their home and learned the darkest of their secrets, surely they had earned the right to be told of their mission.

But from the sound of it, Arba Mintch and his companions had been responsible for the destruction of the very thing that they were charged with repairing! Could it be that these mysterious masters were in communion with the priests? Could it be that they too were but pawns manipulated in the game larger than the world itself? It was a staggering and deeply disturbing thought.

"Don't tell him anything, Braldt! They're nothing but dirty karks! It's some kind of trick, don't tell them anything! C'mon, let's get out of here! Keri! Now!"

Keri stared at her brother in shock, horror and shame in her eyes. She buried her face in the infant's soft belly and said nothing, her silence an answer in itself.

"Sit down, Carn," Braldt said quietly. "This is no trick, at least I do not think so. What would the motive be, they cannot know anything of our mission."

"If you tell them they will know," argued Carn. "Have you forgotten Auslic? He could be dying while we sit here doing nothing!"

"You know that I have not forgotten Auslic, but even he would wish that we learn all that there is to know about this matter. Can you not see that it affects the Duroni as well as the Madrelli?"

"Are you saying that you believe them?"

"I don't know, but, yes, I think I do believe that it is so, or at least that they believe it is true. What reason would they have to tell us this story?"

"To keep us from pulling the lever and getting the box!"

"But, Carn, they don't know our mission, as you yourself have said. How could they have known?"

"What is this mission you speak of?" Uba Mintch looked from one man to the other and so noble did he seem in his grief that he brought Auslic strongly to mind. The two men, so different and yet so alike, Braldt knew that given the opportunity, they would be able to span the differences and find only that which they held in common. In that moment, he made his decision. Before Carn could object, he told Sytha Trubal and Uba Mintch of their mission and of the medicine box they sought.

For a moment there was silence and then Uba Mintch spoke. "Do you realize what this means? It means that your priests have knowledge of this place, knowledge of the destruction, of the lever, and of this box as well. It can only mean one thing, that they are in league with the hard ones and the masters as well."

"It doesn't have to mean that," Keri said, her face pale and drawn. "Couldn't it just mean that they have visions, visions that tell them things? After all, they are priests."

"I think not, child," Uba Mintch said kindly. "If it were just a vision it would have directed them to the medicine box and no more. But in directing Carn and Braldt to throw the switch, they have revealed themselves as minions of the masters. Why else would they want the lever thrown, it benefits no one but the masters."

"And us," Carn said defiantly, rising to his feet and standing before the old man. "The box will save our leader's life and nothing you can say will stop us."

"It is possible that the contents of the box might contain something that will aid his recovery, but I find it doubtful," Uba Mintch mused. "More than likely it is but a ruse to have you do their bidding. But the entire matter is out of our hands, there is no way that you can reach the lever or the box, for the chamber has been flooded and cannot be reached at all."

Even Carn was silenced by this bit of news, for they had never considered the possibility that their mission could not be carried out.

"You are certain of this?" Braldt asked in a whisper.

Uba Mintch bowed his head, his grief resting heavily on him. "Batta Flor has told us of the destruction of the chamber. He was the only one to escape with his life. The great river now flows through the chamber and only yesterday did it deliver up my son's body. There is no way that the chamber can be entered."

"But in the vision, there was no water. Perhaps..."
But whatever Carn had been about to suggest remained
unknown, for at that moment the door burst open and
crashed against the walls. The high, shrill voice of the
serving maid was heard protesting. Then, even as Uba
Mintch and Braldt rose to their feet and turned toward the
door, Batta Flor entered the room with the serving maid
following close behind.

Batta Flor was no longer the somber, controlled figure he
had been at the edge of the bluff. The wild-eyed creature who
stood before them with his pelt rough and ungroomed, reeking of
liquor, bore no resemblance to that proud leader. He started
toward Braldt with hatred brimming in his red-streaked eyes, the
stripes of his muzzle vivid red and angry purple. Braldt eyed the
creature with alarm, his hand creeping toward his sword, but
he made no overt move and did his best to conceal his concern.

Batta Flor stumbled then and might have fallen had
Sytha Trubal not caught him and stood between his swaying
form and that of Braldt.

"G'out of my way, Sytha... won't hurt him, yet.
Can't take him to mate... 's wrong... Arba Mintch my
best frien'... can't let you do this. Not right. Love you.
Always loved you... even 'fore Arba Mintch. Never told
you, 's all. Arba Mintch would unnerstan'... he would
want me to take care of you an' the little one. Sytha..." He
put out a trembling hand and touched her cheek gently.
"Don' do this thing."

"Batta Flor..." Braldt began, thinking that he could
make his feelings known, allow the man to see that Sytha
had only claimed him as mate to prevent their deaths.
Thinking perhaps that this was the proper moment to straight-
en things out. But he was not given that opportunity.

Batta Flor straightened and thrust Sytha Trubal aside at
the sound of Braldt's voice and closed the distance between
them. His small, dark eyes glittered like chips of the
shining, black stone and the air between them fairly vibrated
with hostile emanations.

Without taking his eyes off Braldt, Batta Flor reached
behind him and drew a blade that had hung unseen between

his shoulder blades. Carn shouted a warning, but before Braldt could react, Batta Flor flung the long knife between them where it stood quivering, its blade buried deep in the joint between two stones. Braldt heard Sytha Trubal's cry of dismay but dared not take his eyes from the man who stood before him.

"Challenge!" snarled Batta Flor. "I, Batta Flor, challenge you for the right to claim Sytha Trubal to mate."

"No, you cannot do this thing!" cried Sytha Trubal, and she clung to Batta Flor's arm, begging him to reconsider.

"Please," said Uba Mintch, his voice quivering with emotion. "We cannot lose you too!"

"It is my right to challenge all suitors," replied the Madrelli, suddenly sobered by his action. "Nor will I lose. It is the two-foot who must prepare to die. Sytha Trubal will be mine."

14

Batta Flor's words had caught them off guard and they stood there, frozen in place like a strange tableau as the Madrelli turned away and left the room, slamming the door behind him, the still-quivering blade a silent reminder of his angry words.

The sound of the door shuddering in its frame released them at last and they all spoke at once, their voices jumbled together until Uba Mintch raised his hand and silenced them.

"You must go to him, you must stop him!" Sytha Trubal said anxiously. "He will kill this one!"

"I am not so easily killed, Sytha Trubal," protested Braldt, all the while remembering the powerful shoulders and the long, sharp incisors that could slice through human flesh so easily. "What are the rules for this competition?"

Beast walked up to the upright blade and sniffed it curiously, his lips curling back to reveal snarling teeth, and he retreated, pressing himself against Braldt's leg, growling low in his throat, perhaps scenting the bitter hatred that clung to the weapon.

"There are no rules," Uba Mintch said heavily as he sank into his chair, cradling his head on his palm as though it were too heavy to remain erect without assistance.

"No rules? Why that's crazy, barbaric!" yelled Carn. "Are you saying they just face off and fight until one of them is killed?"

"Basically, that is the way it is done," replied Uba Mintch. "But no weapons are allowed, the fighting is hand-to-hand. Generally, the combatants are more evenly matched."

"This is no even match!" Carn said hotly, advancing toward Uba Mintch until he stood directly before the old man, shaking his hand under his nose. "That kark will kill Braldt, tear him apart with his bare hands! His arms are longer and more powerful. Braldt won't stand a chance, you have to stop this!"

"I cannot," Arba Mintch said in a low tone. "It is his right to demand the competition, it is the way of the Madrelli."

"But it is not our way, sir." Keri joined her brother, still holding the small infant who looked from one adult to the other with a doleful expression, sensing that something was amiss and trying to decide whether or not to cry. "You are the chief, surely you can stop this fight, the people will listen to you."

"No, it would only make matters worse." Sytha Trubal came forward and took the baby from Keri. "You don't understand. Uba Mintch is not chief. Arba Mintch was chief, and now with his death, the tribe is without a formal leader. I am regent only until I marry. The man I marry then becomes chief. Uba Mintch is a respected elder, a past leader, but he does not have the power to stop the fight."

"Well, then you stop it!" said Carn. "You picked Braldt to be your mate. Unless you put a halt to this, you'll have two dead mates."

"There is nothing I can do," said Sytha Trubal. "My title is in name only, I have the power to choose my mate, nothing more."

Braldt spoke then, interrupting the conversation. "Is it allowed to make wagers, add to the stakes so to speak?"

"Wagers are not unheard of," allowed Uba Mintch, "although competitions such as this are infrequent. Why do you ask?"

"I am not as certain as all of you that such a contest will end in my death. There is always the possibility that I will win."

"Unlikely, unlikely," said Uba Mintch. The stripes of his muzzle had now become a dull, uniform shade of brown and his eyes were dark and joyless. "What your companions say is true. Batta Flor is the very best among us, more powerful and cunning than any two Madrelli. You cannot hope to win.''

"Even better," muttered Braldt. "Then, surely he would not refuse an additional wager if he is as confident of his skills as you are."

Everyone looked at him, wondering what he had in mind.

"What I propose is this. If I win, Batta Flor will guide us to the cavern where the lever and the medicine box are to be found. If I lose, not only does he gain the right to take Sytha Trubal to mate, but all of our edged weapons as well."

His words were met by an immediate outcry.

"You're not pledging my weapons!" cried Carn, turning on Braldt, his hand clutching the hilt of his knife. "What happens to us if you die and we're stuck here with no way to protect ourselves? Forget that!"

"Braldt, think of what you're saying," Keri pleaded, her eyes large and full of fright.

"What you are proposing is madness," said Uba Mintch, shaking his head from side to side.

"But is it allowed?" Braldt persisted. "Am I within my rights to demand such conditions?"

The old Madrelli and Sytha Trubal exchanged glances. "Yes," Sytha Trubal answered reluctantly. "Yes, it can be done, conditions are often set by the combatants."

"Good, I thought as much," said Braldt, clearly wrapped in deep thought. "How can I make my conditions known to Batta Flor?"

"I will see that it is done," Uba Mintch said quietly, then added, "there is always the possibility of flight. Conceding the battle to Batta Flor without contest and retaining your life as well."

"But not my honor. No, that is not the way of the Duroni. Deliver the message and do not despair for it is I who will be the victor."

The silence that followed his words told him of their lack of confidence, but after a long moment of silence, Uba

Mintch said, "I will do as you ask and may your gods watch over you."

"Those same gods that you say do not exist," murmured Braldt, feeling more alone than ever before in his life.

■

Messages were exchanged between the various parties, and as Braldt had hoped, Batta Flor agreed to the terms of his challenge. The time and place were established as well, the arena at the far edge of town, two dawnings hence.

Keri and Carn did their best in the small amount of time allotted to them to change Braldt's mind, trying to convince him that there was no dishonor in slipping away under the cover of darkness and continuing their mission. Even Sytha Trubal added her voice to theirs and their despair and desperation weighed heavily on Braldt, but he stood fast and would not give in to their demands.

"We cannot run, do you not see that? It is useless. We do not even know the way to the cavern, whereas they know the way well. Should we attempt to flee, it would be but a simple matter to hunt us down and slay us like low-bellied cowardly snakes. They will find us no matter if we advance or retreat, it is their country, not ours, and if Uba Mintch is to be believed, we do not even have the protection of the gods to guide our steps. We cannot do anything but that which I have done. Don't you see, we need Batta Flor to take us to this cavern. He is our only hope."

"You are a fool, Braldt. You will get yourself killed by this kark and us too. How long do you think they will allow us to live once you are dead? We will be killed before the blood has drained from your body."

"I'm glad to see you have such confidence in me, brother. You, better than any other, know my skill at hand-to-hand combat, do you not think that I stand a chance?"

"A chance? Certainly you have a chance. For that matter, there is always a chance that Mother Moon will fail to rise or that Sun the Giver will fade from the sky and leave us in darkness. I believe your chances at defeating the kark to be equally real."

Carn would say nothing more and avoided Braldt from that moment on, taking his meals in silence and staying in his room whenever possible.

Keri had become close to Sytha Trubal, finding that they had more in common than differences. The baby drew them together, and strangely enough Beast had taken a liking to the small creature and allowed her to crawl back and forth over his body, flinching and whining but making no attempt to bite when she pulled his long, coarse fur in her tiny fists.

Through Keri, Braldt learned that taking Batta Flor to mate was not an unpleasant thought so far as Sytha Trubal was concerned. The three of them, Batta Flor, Arba Mintch, and Sytha Trubal, had been friends since childhood and Sytha had loved them both, choosing Arba Mintch because her parents had viewed the joining as an advantageous match.

"Sounds like my mother talking," Keri said with a smile, thinking back on her own parents' numerous urgings.

Although Sytha Trubal had barely had time to comprehend the fact of her mate's death, much less mourn him properly, it was to be assumed that Batta Flor would have been a logical choice for a mate after a decent period of mourning had elapsed. At least it had been an option before she had rescued Braldt.

Now, her emotions were in turmoil; her mate was dead, violently killed by the hard ones; she had rescued a hereditary enemy and claimed him for a mate before her period of mourning was even begun, offending propriety and bringing herself into conflict with her tribe by her strange actions.

Furthermore, there was the matter of the contest. There was no good solution to the conflict. If Braldt lost, he would die, and Keri and Carn would surely be slain as well, widening the hostilities between their two tribes. If Braldt won, which could not be imagined, the outcome would be even worse for Batta Flor would die. If he lost the match but survived, he would be required to take them to the cavern where Arba Mintch had been slain. Then, Braldt would obey the dictates of his mission that was to throw the lever, undoing all that the Madrelli had wrought and in a single motion turning Arba Mintch's death into one of useless futility and unleashing the anger and retribution of the hard ones and the masters on the Madrelli.

Braldt was filled with his own thoughts and kept to himself as well, emerging from his room only for meals and for occasional conversation with Uba Mintch where he asked pointed and somewhat obscure questions, all the while studying the old Madrelli's physical structure with a critical eye.

The giggling maidservant was politely but firmly ejected from Braldt's quarters, while attempting to deliver an armload of fresh towels. But before the door closed on her, she was able to see that all the furniture had been moved to one corner of the room and the floor spread with blankets and carpets. Furthermore, strange bumps and grunts were often heard coming from the room, especially if one pressed one's ear close to the wood. The maidservant thought it most peculiar but having been warned by Uba Mintch for just such an activity only two moons prior, the maidservant was forced to keep the curious information to herself.

■

The second dawn arrived over the edge of the darkened horizon in due time and as Sun the Giver rose above the peaks, shedding its rosy hues on the tiers of the cold stone arena, giving the appearance of warmth without benefit of the fact, it found the combatants in their appropriate corners, attended by their various supporters. It seemed that the entire population of the town supported Batta Flor, for there was no one seated in Braldt's end of the court save his own companions, Uba Mintch, and Sytha Trubal. And from their downcast expressions, it was easy to see that they had no confidence in his ability to defeat Batta Flor.

It was easy to see why Batta Flor was the odds on favorite, for in the clear light of the rising sun, he was a magnificent example of a Madrelli male in his prime. His head was large and well formed, the ears set close to the sides and rising to the top of his skull in slender, tapering points. His eyes were wide-set and bright with intelligence as well as hatred as he in turn considered Braldt. His muzzle was brightly striped in bands of crimson, blue, and green with thin white bands separating each of the colors that were bright and bold and showed no sign of sickness or doubt. His shoulders were massive, equally as broad as Braldt's, but thicker, more dense as though the muscles themselves were composed of heavier bands. The musculature could only be guessed at for the entire upper body was thickly pelted in a mat of coarse golden hair that glinted in the sunlight. Only his belly was bare of fur, and this was as dark as tanned leather and rippled with layers of hard muscle. The arms were overly long and powerfully made, ending in the curious fingers, long and slender and well suited to difficult, delicate tasks. Each of the fingers bore long nails that had obviously been honed to razor sharpness. Braldt studied his opponent's hands carefully, for if the Madrelli had a weakness, surely it was his hands, incongruous on a creature so obviously designed for power.

The lower half of the creature gave Braldt no reason for hope for the narrow, tapering waist and hips flared again into massive thighs, the short, clipped fur giving definition to the long-exaggerated muscles. The legs were short and slightly bowed, but thicker still, ending in short, wide feet with six toes—the first, opposable, like that of a thumb—and each tipped with a single sharp, clawlike nail.

The two combatants studied each other while Uba Mintch and another official, both draped in long folds of white cloth to keep off the chill dawn, spoke quietly in the center of the small dirt-floored arena. The audience was not so well mannered and yelled encouragement to Batta Flor who ignored them as though they did not exist, staring with unblinking attention at Braldt. The spectators called out to Braldt as well, cursing him and jeering with undisguised hostility, wishing him a lingering and agonizing death. They called out bets also, but there were few takers who cared to wager on Braldt's chances and soon those voices were stilled.

Braldt had taken what precautions he was able to utilize. He had honed his knife and trimmed his hair as close to his skull as possible, so as to give the Madrelli nothing to seize.

He had also shed his clothing, after deciding that it would offer him little or no protection, and slicked his body with animal fat that he used to keep his boots supple. He had asked the maidservant for a fresh supply but her reply was more of the same unending giggles. But she had passed his request on to Uba Mintch, evidently she was capable of speech, who explained to Braldt that the Madrelli did not eat the flesh of others and were themselves total vegetarians. This fact should have been obvious to Braldt for their meals, while hot and tastefully prepared, had been comprised of root vegetables, several types of cooked grains, and much greenery accompanied by a variety of breads and cheeses. Braldt had turned down Uba Mintch's offer of vegetable oil, sensing that it would not prove as slippery nor as offensive to his opponent.

And now the time had come for the two older Madrelli parted, each to one of the contestants and spoke to them in unison in voices that could be clearly heard by all of the spectators, even those who had arrived late and been forced to climb the broad stone steps to the highest level.

"It is begun," intoned the two old men, each facing the fighters, holding their gaze and commanding their full attention. "That which is begun may be ended, by death or by default. There is no dishonor in default, nor is death necessary. Either may call for a halt to the contest at any time. No weapons may be used save those of strategy and strength. He is the winner who is left standing at the end of the contest. The contest is over when it is done. I ask you now, do you wish to withdraw your challenge? Do you wish to withdraw your reply?" Both queries were met by silence although it seemed to Braldt that Uba Mintch was silently urging him to withdraw now, before the contest was begun. When Braldt did not respond, the old Madrelli's shoulders sagged and his muzzle took on a tinge of grey, the bands of color all but overcome by his distress.

"It is begun," he said in a dull voice and turned aside,

unable to look at Braldt again, already consigning him to the death that had so recently robbed him of his only son.

The two old men had scarcely left the arena before Braldt and Batta Flor rose to their feet and began to circle, arms held apart from their bodies, eyes probing, searching for the first sign of weakness, for a mistake, a fatal opening that would allow them to dispatch their opponent quickly and with ease.

Braldt, being the taller of the two, was at a disadvantage so far as protecting his midsection, for no matter how far he hunched, Batta Flor was still able to come inside with his longer reach and shorter body. And it was there that he made his first move, a lightning slash that was finished before Braldt even sensed the movement, leaving a welter of crimson stripes across his belly, the razor-sharp nails slicing through his skin as easily as a hot knife passes through butter.

Braldt was stunned at the rapidity with which his opponent had struck. He danced backward on the balls of his feet, avoiding Batta Flor, which was not necessary for the Madrelli stood still, watching Braldt to see if the shedding of his blood was enough to convince him to concede the match.

Braldt glanced downward and ran his fingers over the bleeding furrows. He felt the burning ache of the torn flesh, realizing that it was but a simple flesh wound and also knowing that Batta Flor could just as easily have opened him from side to side, ending the contest then and there. But he had not done so, why? Perhaps because killing Braldt would only have widened the gap between himself and Sytha Trubal, perhaps even making such a union an impossibility. It was humiliation he was after as well as defeat, a living Braldt who would grovel and beg for mercy, thus demonstrating his unworthiness as Sytha's mate.

All of this flashed through Braldt's mind in an instant and he knew what it was that he had to do. Somehow he had to keep out of Batta Flor's reach and win the match without killing or demeaning his opponent, for Batta Flor would rather die than lessen himself in Sytha Trubal's eyes.

Braldt wiped the blood from his hands, smearing it across his chest, feeling the rough scar tissue bequeathed to him by the lupebeast, and tightened his lips, determined that he would have no new scars to remind him of this day's battle.

Once again they began to circle, only this time Braldt was careful to keep a greater distance between himself and his opponent. If Batta Flor attempted such a move again, he would be forced to cross a greater distance, thus signaling his intent and allowing Braldt a slight advantage. They continued to circle, each wary of the other, allowing the other no edge, until the audience grew weary at the lack of action and began to hiss, signaling their discontent.

It was Braldt who made the first move. Bouncing on the balls of his feet, he hurled himself into the air, exposing the entire length of his torso for one very long moment until he touched the ground with his hands and pushed off, springing into the air once again before the astonished Batta Flor could react, his body arcing over to land on his feet behind his opponent.

The audience was silent, dumbfounded, staring at him with wide eyes for they had never seen such a display of gymnastics that was but one of the skills all would-be Duroni warriors were taught early on in their training for it was said to quicken the mind and coordinate the body. As well as surprise the enemy.

Before Batta Flor could react, Braldt slipped in close behind him and brought his hands up in front of the Madrelli's arms and linked his hands behind the creature's neck, exerting a steady downward pressure. This was a time-honored hold, one that was all but certain to win contests in Duroni arenas, but Braldt was not dealing with one of his own kind. Locked in such a hold, one had but to flex the hands to snap the neck of one's opponent as well as dislocating the shoulders from their sockets.

But Braldt had badly misjudged the musculature and body structure of the Madrelli. The deadly hold did not even faze Batta Flor who turned his head to look at Braldt as though wondering if he had lost his mind. Then, with one casual shrug of his shoulders, he began to slip from Braldt's grasp.

Braldt attempted to tighten his hold, to force the massive shoulders out of their sockets, to press the head forward, for in that moment he was not so concerned with strategy as he was with survival. But the Madrelli's body was far more flexible than that of the Duroni and the shoulders drew inward till they nearly touched and still the Madrelli showed no sign of discomfort. At the same time he allowed his head to be pressed forward until the tip of his muzzle was touching his chest, and still there was no sound of cracking bones. The Madrelli slipped free of Braldt's would-be fatal hold with laughable ease.

Before the stunned Braldt could recover, attempt to think of another ploy, Batta Flor turned to face Braldt and gathered him up in an embrace, hugging him tightly to his chest. Realizing nearly too late what was about to happen, Braldt managed to bring his arms up, to wedge them between Batta Flor and himself. But it was not enough, it merely meant that his arms would break before his chest and spine.

The powerful vice tightened and Braldt felt his breath burning in his chest as he struggled to breathe. Spots appeared before his eyes, fogging his vision and blurring Batta Flor's grimace of hatred. He felt his feet leave the ground, saw Batta Flor's face whirl beneath him, heard a bone snap in his arm, and knew that his death was fast approaching. Dimly he heard Keri's voice crying his name and Beast's high, shrill bleat of alarm.

Using his last bit of strength, forcing himself to act through the red fog of agony that wrapped itself around his body, Braldt brought his knee up between the legs of the Madrelli and smashed it into Batta Flor's genitals. Then, even as he gave himself up to the blackness that crowded in on all sides, he felt himself falling and he welcomed the darkness and the release from pain.

Consciousness returned accompanied by a rush of pain as well as wonder that he was still alive. Dimly he sensed the presence of another and then as the roar of voices crashed down upon him, all of them calling Batta Flor's name and urging him to rise, he realized that he had brought himself a short respite.

He staggered to his feet, clutching his throbbing arm, taking note of Batta Flor writhing on the ground in even more intense pain, and wondering how it was that the Madrelli had allowed himself to be taken unaware by such an old trick. But there was no time for such thoughts, even now Batta Flor appeared to be struggling to his feet!

Braldt flung himself on the prone figure of the Madrelli and using all of his strength pinned Batta Flor's shoulders to the ground. Had he been unhurt, Batta Flor would simply have needed to wrap his legs around Braldt in a scissor hold to free himself, but fortunately the Madrelli was in too much pain to use the lower half of his body.

Braldt dragged himself upward, ignoring the pain of his own injured arm, trying to block out the sound of the broken bones grating against each other, and looked into Batta Flor's face. "Let us stop this," he whispered. "I have no wish to kill you or die in this place. Let us be comrades!"

Batta Flor's brightly striped muzzle had faded to muddy brown tinged with yellowish grey and his eyes were streaked with lines of red, yet still they blazed with hatred as he returned Braldt's gaze. His only reply was a loud grunt as he hurled himself over, pinning Braldt beneath him, allowing his massive weight to hold his opponent helpless, while he struggled to regain his strength.

Braldt knew now that he could never win out against the Madrelli in sheer physical combat, for the other was far too powerful and agile. He had not counted on the creature possessing such speed, thinking that one so powerfully built must be slow as well. It had been a near-fatal mistake. Even now, as he struggled to slither out from beneath the immense bulk, he realized that the Madrelli did not need to do anything else, he would die if they remained like this, squashed like a bug beneath a boulder.

But Batta Flor was not content to let it end in such a manner and he rose to his feet slowly, dragging Braldt with him, gripping him in one hand, his fingers closed in an iron band around his neck. Braldt pried at Batta Flor's fingers but he could not loosen even one digit despite the fact that they had appeared to be so delicate.

He grew desperate, knowing that Batta Flor intended to finish him off, and without thinking used a technique he had developed as a boy when he was smaller and thinner than most of his companions. Wrapping his arms around Batta Flor's own arm, using it like a horizontal tree branch, he climbed the Madrelli's body with his feet and then wrapped his legs around Batta Flor's neck. The Madrelli attempted to hold on, but the very surprise of the strange move, as well as the awkward angle, forced him to let go and Braldt rose atop his shoulders, legs firmly wrapped around his neck, like some odd totem.

Batta Flor and the crowd roared in anger. Batta Flor spun about, pulling at Braldt's legs and punching at them, but the angle was wrong and his blows did not carry the necessary force although they were painful enough. Braldt seized Batta Flor's ears and hung on as he had done as a child, knowing that if he let go, he was as good as dead. The cartilage of the ear was thin and fragile and Braldt realized that this was the vulnerable point he had sought, the chink in the Madrelli's defense.

Braldt thought swiftly, he did not want to cripple the creature or do him irreparable damage for he still hoped to convince him to help them. But he could not allow himself to be killed. He folded the tapered points of the Madrelli's ears between his fingers and pinched down as hard as he could and was instantly rewarded by a high shriek of pain. Batta Flor's hands fell away from Braldt's legs and began groping for his hands but they were blocked from his reach. Braldt squeezed again and Batta Flor sagged to his knees, dropping to the ground like a felled tree.

Braldt straddled Batta Flor's neck, never for the moment releasing his grip on the Madrelli's ears. Tears of pain poured down Batta Flor's face and his hands reached for Braldt. Braldt quickly jumped behind the agonized creature and his every attempt to seize him was met with yet another painful ear pinch. Braldt had heard the cartilage crack and felt the brittle stuff snap beneath his fingers; he could only imagine the pain he must be causing.

At last Batta Flor lay silent, unresisting, his huge chest heaving as Braldt knelt at his side. The roar of the crowd fell to a whisper and it was apparent that they thought that he was about to end Batta Flor's life. He could feel their hatred surrounding him like a living thing.

Batta Flor's eyes were open, fogged now with pain, his muzzle a sickly greenish brown. He watched Braldt without moving, resigned to his fate.

"Will you help us, Batta Flor?" whispered Braldt. "I have no wish to take your life. Take Sytha Trubal to mate and rule the Madrelli as is your right. I ask only that you do not play us false and guide us in our mission."

Batta Flor looked up at Braldt through pain-fogged eyes, baffled by the words that he was hearing, clearly wondering if they were a trap.

"I speak the truth," said Braldt, releasing his hold on the Madrelli's ears and rising to his feet, wondering if it were the last mistake he would ever make. The crowd seemed to hold its breath collectively. There was not a single sound from the hundreds who gathered there as Braldt extended his hand to their champion. A blackwing beat its way across the chill grey sky, its shrill cry the only sound to be heard as it winged homeward. Then, as Batta Flor reached up and took Braldt's hand in his own, climbing slowly to his feet, the silence was broken by the soft sound of a hundred sorrowful sighs.

15

"**You do not fight according to the rules,**" Uba Mintch observed as he bound Braldt's arm with strips of tightly woven cloth, winding it back and forth time and again until the pulse pounded within like a savage drum.

"You said there were no rules," Braldt replied through gritted teeth, trying hard to ignore the pain of the binding that was easily as bad as that of the injury.

"There are no rules in the broad sense, but there are the unspoken rules of civilized people everywhere. It is not civilized to kick one's opponent in such a place."

"I was not trying to be civilized," replied Braldt. "You seem to forget that I was fighting for my life."

"Batta Flor would not have killed you. The most he would have done was subdue you. Batta Flor is no killer."

"You said nothing of the sort before the match," Braldt said angrily. "Why did you not see fit to share this information with me then?"

"Would you have believed me?" Uba Mintch asked calmly as he continued to bind Braldt's arm. "Would you have fought differently?"

Braldt realized that the old Madrelli was right. He would not have believed him, nor was he certain even now that it was so. He had fought in the only way he had known in order to win.

"How is he?" Braldt asked gruffly, studying his arm, avoiding the old man's eyes as the last bit of bandage was tucked away. "Is he all right?"

"He will be stiff and in pain for several days," replied Uba Mintch as he rolled up what was left of the bandage and placed it in a small pouch. "His ears are another matter, they will need much attention if they are not to be damaged for life. How did you know about Madrelli ears? I did not suspect that you Duroni knew so much about us."

"What are you talking about?" Braldt looked up, curiously. "What is there to know?"

Uba Mintch put down the pouch and he and Braldt regarded each other, searching each other closely.

"You really didn't know, did you?" Uba Mintch said softly.

"Know what?" Braldt replied.

Uba Mintch shook his head, a small, dry chuckle escaping his thin lips. "Look you here," he said, turning sideways so that Braldt might study his own fragile, tapered ears, which were so transparent with age that it was possible to see the very movement of the blood as it flowed through the single red artery. Clustered along the edges of the ear under the translucent skin were clumps of what appeared to be whitish crystals.

"Do you see?" asked Uba Mintch.

"I see, but I do not know what it is that I see," replied Braldt.

"Our masters were not content to alter us through generations of breeding, nor even through the use of the serum, but have made it possible to reconstruct, change, alter our behavior by means of these tiny implants. Here, Sytha, give me Arlin."

Sytha Trubal willingly gave the small Madrelli into the hands of her grandfather, her arms and legs flailing wildly as usual. "You see here, look at her ears. Arlin was one of the first born after we discovered the bush." Uba Mintch placed the small wriggling bundle into Braldt's arms.

The small one twisted and turned until she could look up into his eyes and she fell silent, perhaps overwhelmed by his strangeness. Popping a thumb into her mouth she began to suck noisily, turning her head to watch him as he in turn studied her tiny ear. There was the same red line of blood, clearly visible along the rim and the peak of the tiny ear, but nowhere could he see the crystals that bulged under the surface of Uba Mintch's ear.

"What are they?" he asked, holding out a finger for the baby to grasp. "What are they and how did they get there?"

"They are sensors that relay the hard ones' wishes to us for they are silent and have no voice. They are also the method by which the hard ones dispense their punishment if we dare to displease them."

"I do not understand," said Braldt. "How can this be so. If they cannot speak, how can they relay their wishes much less inflict pain. And if they are defeated, why do you not remove these things from your bodies?"

Uba Mintch sighed again and stroked his ear in contemplation of Braldt's words. "It is a complicated matter and one that we do not fully comprehend ourselves, but I will do my best to answer you. First, the hard ones communicated through silent pictures that appeared inside our heads, although how this is done, we have never determined.

"The pain is delivered in much the same way as the pictures, like a thought, I believe. It begins at the edges of the ears and radiates inward, piercing one's mind and nearly melting one's bones with its intensity. There is none among us who has ever been strong enough to resist it. It can even kill. Several in Arba Mintch's party were slain in such a manner by the hard ones, but there were but a few of them and they were overwhelmed before they could kill the rest.

"As to why we do not remove them, quite simply, we do not know how. The hard ones implanted them shortly after the birth of our young and none of us were ever allowed to witness the operation. We have studied the matter, but have as yet to attempt their removal. It is quite possible that their removal will cause our death."

"I can't believe that," said Braldt, peering closely at the tiny clusters, noticing for the first time what appeared to be slender silver filaments trailing out of the crystals and tunneling into the darkness of the eardrum. "Why would it kill you?"

"Why would it not?" asked Uba Mintch. "If such a thing were implanted in your body, would you wish to take the risk? Would you volunteer yourself for the good and knowledge of the community?"

Braldt nodded, seeing what the old one was saying. "So, it is possible to cause pain with these things even though I am not a hard one and did not know what I was doing."

"I'd say that it worked well enough," Uba Mintch said dryly. "But there is another thing that we have learned, a thing of value. We cannot be controlled from a distance; it is necessary to be close or the crystals do not work. Were it otherwise, the masters could have elected to take their own action in safety from afar. At least we are spared that concern. So long as we can prevent their landing, we cannot be controlled."

"But do you not fear that they will give up the thought of bringing you under control once more and simply destroy the planet as was their original plan?" asked Braldt.

"I do not think that they will chance such a thing for there is the matter of the Grand Council. They would not risk their censure for we are a registered people and there are guidelines that even the masters must observe. They cannot eradicate us without facing the consequences."

"But what about us?" asked Keri who had come into the room silently and unseen. "Would this council not object to the eradication of our people?"

"I do not know," replied Uba Mintch, exchanging a troubled glance with Sytha Trubal. "There are many peoples on many planets, some more civilized than others. Some barely above the level of plants. There are rules for everything, this I know, but little more, for the hard ones and the masters did not share such knowledge with us. It was not in their best interests," he added dryly. "Ahh, here are our cups, drink, everyone, drink."

Braldt and Keri took the sturdy earthenware mugs from the serving girl's tray and sipped at the tart red tea, a daily tradition that was closely observed, even on a day such as this filled with pain and confusion. As he drank the pleasantly sour brew, Braldt was struck with a sudden realization. "This, this is the berry you were speaking of! This is the stuff that freed you from the masters!"

Uba Mintch nodded. Then he spoke, his voice oddly troubled. "Forgive me if I speak in rudeness, but there is a question I must ask of you, you are unlike the Duroni and do not appear to be of their kind. How is this? Who are your people?"

Braldt was startled by the question and could not help but notice how closely Uba Mintch and Sytha Trubal waited for his reply. He was puzzled by their interest but could not think of any reason to tell them anything but the truth.

"Odd, most odd," murmured Uba Mintch after a quick exchange of glances with Sytha Trubal. "Please forgive the curiosity of an old man," he said with a smile, denying the importance of his own question. "Strange thoughts just come into my mind and bother me till I have the answer. Think of it no more.

"Well, that will be Batta Flor, I imagine," he said, rising quickly at the first sound of knuckles on the door, and, without waiting for the serving girl, hurried to answer the door himself. Braldt thought the old man's behavior to be most peculiar, and that question . . . why would he wonder about Braldt's parentage? But there was no time for that now for the sound of footsteps echoed from the long hall and Braldt rose to his feet as Batta Flor entered the room.

Braldt was shocked at his appearance. The Madrelli's eyes were ringed with dark black circles that extended from the bridge of his nose to his ears, which were delicately bound up in thin bandages and fixed in place with sticking plaster. The whites of his eyes were awash with burst blood vessels and the colors of his muzzle were faded and dull. But his posture was proud and erect, even though he paced forward on stiff legs. Braldt knew that he must be in extreme pain, but he also knew that it had been necessary.

"I have been telling Batta Flor that there was no reason

for him to have come so soon. He should be home, gathering his strength," said Uba Mintch, "but he will not listen to me."

"I am glad that you have come," said Braldt as he crossed the room to greet his former opponent, extending his hand in a greeting as he would have done to one of his own comrades. Beast detached himself from Sytha's side and trotted forward on stiff legs, hair standing up along the ridge of his spine, and sniffed at Batta Flor's legs, then turned away with disinterest, all sign of animosity gone.

After a moment of hesitation, Batta Flor took Braldt's hand and clasped it in his own. His grip was powerful, and large as Braldt's hand was, it vanished in the Madrelli's grip. Once again he realized his good fortune in winning the contest.

"Did you mean what you said," Batta Flor asked abruptly, without any exchange of pleasantries.

"Yes," replied Braldt, his hand still buried within the Madrelli's firm grip. "I wish nothing but your friendship."

"And for me to take you to the cavern," added Batta Flor.

"That too," admitted Braldt, meeting the Madrelli's gaze.

"And you give up all claim to Sytha Trubal for now and all time?" asked Batta Flor.

"I do," Braldt replied levelly, hearing the soft gasp that came from Keri and Sytha Trubal, "if such a thing is agreeable to Sytha Trubal as well. Her wishes must also be considered in this matter."

"Sytha Trubal, will you have me to mate," Batta Flor asked softly, his red-rimmed eyes staring directly into hers.

"I will accept your proposal," replied Sytha Trubal, "for the good of the tribe."

"And for no other reason?" asked Batta Flor, dropping Braldt's hand and turning away from him as though he did not exist.

A crimson flush suffused Sytha's muzzle and she lowered

her head, her reaction all the answer that was required. Gently, Batta Flor gathered her into his immense arms and she rested her head on his chest. They stayed like that for a moment and no one spoke. Finally, Batta Flor said, "I will do this thing that I have promised. I will take these two-foots to the cavern and let them see for themselves that it is impossible to enter. Then I will return for you and we will be mated."

He turned to Braldt. "We leave at first dawning. Be ready."

"But, but . . . neither of you are ready to travel!" protested Sytha Trubal. "Both of you are hurt and need to rest!"

"Surely it would be better if you waited a day or two," said Uba Mintch.

"No good can come of waiting, waiting is for women, unless the two-foots want to wait," said Batta Flor, his lips drawn back in a sneer.

"This two-foot sees no reason to wait," said Braldt, even though his arm was aching badly. If the Madrelli could think of traveling with his injuries, then he would go as well.

"We leave at dawn, be ready," said Batta Flor, punctuating his words with a stabbing finger, and then he was gone.

▪

The serving girl, her giggles stilled for once, roused them before dawn, and as they assembled in the great room before the blazing fireplace and took the steaming mugs of sour berry tea and the hot, buttered grain patties from the silver tray, they saw that Uba Mintch was already seated, his old bones soaking up the welcome heat.

"I will not wish you well on your mission, for if you succeed, you will bring ruin upon us all. But I will pray that no harm befalls you."

"To whom or what do you pray, Uba Mintch, if as you say, Mother Moon is naught but a lifeless bit of rock and all our gods are but a sham?" Carn asked bitterly.

"We Madrelli have traveled to many worlds, seen

many strange sights. If we were to tell you of our experiences, you would not believe us. This world, beautiful as it is, is but a small dot in the universe that stretches beyond. Despite the cold words of the masters, to whom everything is but a part of the plan, I believe that there is something more, something that cannot be explained, something too big for even the masters to comprehend. It does not have a name, the word *god* will serve as well as any other. It is to that greater power that I utter my small prayers."

The old Madrelli uttered these words while staring into the blazing fire and almost seemed to be speaking to himself. Now, he turned and looked directly at Braldt, and almost for the first time, Braldt realized how old Uba Mintch must be, saw the grey fuzz spreading out from the base of the muzzle, saw that his hands trembled slightly even when in repose, saw the haze that clouded his eyes and knew that his end was drawing near.

Uba Mintch nodded once, as though confirming Braldt's insights, and spoke with a great calmness. "You take with you on this mission a heavy burden, for you carry with you the fate of your people as well as mine. Think carefully before you act, act cautiously and without haste or anger, for what you do will affect us all. May you travel in safety and return in health."

These words were spoken as a benediction, and turning, Braldt saw that Carn and Keri and Batta Flor, who had arrived without their notice, had taken it as such for all were subdued and silent. Somehow, as they gathered up their packs and filed out of the home with Uba Mintch, Sytha Trubal, and the little one waving their good-byes from the doorstep, he knew that none of them would ever see Uba Mintch again.

■

The valley of the Madrelli was soon left behind as the morning mists closed in around them, growing thicker as they climbed. The elevation rose steeply and they were forced to follow hard on Batta Flor's footsteps or risk being lost on the mountain. Batta Flor remained silent and they all found themselves wondering whether it was his intention to lose them, slipping away in the dense fog.

He called a halt by midmorning and it was a welcome relief for their legs were aching with fatigue and their hearts were pounding. They collapsed where they stood, hiding their exhaustion as best they were able, for none of them were willing to admit that they could not keep up with a Madrelli.

Batta Flor set about lighting a small fire with a cube of compressed wood chips, impregnated with a waxy substance. It lit instantly and soon the blessed warmth of the tart berry tea radiated through their bellies, restoring them.

Braldt stood up to stretch his aching muscles and saw that the fog had burned off the lower elevations and was astonished at how far they had come, the valley appeared to be no more than a child's plaything far below them. Batta Flor joined him and together they stared down at the peaceful scene below.

"I did not realize that we would climb so high," Braldt said, hoping to engage the Madrelli in conversation.

"This high and higher still," replied Batta Flor, his eyes still on the village. "If you can keep up."

"Do not worry about us," said Carn, "we can follow wherever you lead."

Batta Flor turned to contemplate Carn, the black circles under his inflamed eyes giving him a brutish and malignant appearance. "This is no game, two-foot. The way to the cavern will be difficult and dangerous. I do not even know if it can be done. I have given my word to take you to the cavern and I will do it if I can. But I will take no stupid risks, nor will I be badgered. I am the leader here, you are but the followers, and my word is law."

Carn smarted visibly under the Madrelli's words and he stepped forward, invading that personal space immediately in front of the Madrelli, stepping so close as to present a challenge that could not go unanswered.

Anxious to avoid a confrontation, Braldt took Batta Flor by the elbow and turned him aside. "Tell me, if you were working regularly in this cavern, surely it must be close by. Why is it necessary for us to travel so far and why will the going be so difficult?''

Batta Flor did not answer, glaring back at Carn over his shoulder, but Braldt continued walking and asking his quiet questions and after a moment Batta Flor allowed himself to be distracted.

"We flooded the chamber, this I have already told you. It is impossible to enter the chamber from below for the river runs through the cavern. The only way it can be approached is from above, the way we ourselves entered. I do not understand what good you think will come of this expedition. There is nothing to see but an empty riverbed and a fall of rock.''

"I do not know myself, but I must see it for myself for the life of my chief depends upon retrieving the box with the red mark upon its lid.''

"Then your chief must die for there is no way to enter the cavern and live. Don't you understand, it's flooded! Surely the box you speak of has been torn away by the waters, but even if it still remains, its contents will have been destroyed by the water!''

Braldt looked into Batta Flor's eyes and saw that the Madrelli was speaking the truth, or what he thought to be the truth, and for the first time he felt his hope dwindle within him as he contemplated the thought of failure, tried to visualize a life without the presence of Auslic. "Please,'' he said quietly, "please just take us there so that I may see this place for myself. I must know that I have done everything within my power.'' The two men stared at each other, linked by their promises, and seemed to see each other for the first time. Batta Flor nodded and some of the anger seemed to leave him.

He returned to the fire, poured the rest of the hot tea into a leather pouch that he slung over his shoulder, then kicked stones and dust over the small blaze, extinguishing it instantly. It seemed colder and more lonely without the tiny blaze. Picking up his spear and ignoring Carn completely, Batta Flor stepped onto the trail once more without looking back to see if the rest of the party was following him.

Keri stepped into place behind him, striding along easily, seemingly untired by the morning's work, adjusting the straps of her pack and admonishing Beast who snapped at her heels with her every step.

Braldt grabbed Carn just as he was about to join Keri and swung him around with some force. "Just what is it that you are trying to do?" he asked in an angry whisper. "This one is the only hope we have of reaching that cavern and finding a way in. The only hope we have of saving Auslic. Why are you trying to start a fight. Do you really think that you could win such a fight?"

"I would do better than you, brother," Carn said with a sneer. "You fought like a child, kicking him in the privates and pinching his ears. I'm surprised you didn't try biting. Why didn't you kill him and show these animals what fighting really is?"

"Carn," Braldt said, taking a deep breath and trying to calm himself. "I did not want to kill him; I wanted him to live so that he could take us to the cavern so we can find the box and bring it to Auslic."

"You want to be chief and nothing more," said Carn. "There was no water in our vision, the chamber was dry. This whole story is nothing but a kark trick. This journey is but an excuse to kill us off one at a time; I cannot understand why you do not see it. Or maybe you're part of it. Maybe this is all some plan that you and that old kark brewed up during one of your little fireside chats. Well, you may have fooled Keri, but not me, brother. I will be watching you, you and that kark, all of the time. Remember that and remember too that I cannot be tricked by foul blows and childish tricks. When you fight me, you will lose."

Braldt listened to Carn's words and heard the hatred in them. He wondered how long those feelings had been hidden. Had it always been so? Where was the brother he had loved, what had become of the bond that had joined them. And most of all, he wondered who would win, if ever they were forced to fight.

The last of the fog burned off by midday and Braldt almost wished that it had remained for it had hidden the great heights to which they had climbed. The mountain they were ascending rose high above them, its peak concealed by a swirl of heavy clouds. All around them were a multitude of lower peaks, barren and lifeless, shining in the cold, clear air.

The trail, if it could be called that, was a mere thread that picked its way from one narrow ledge to the next with nothing but empty space awaiting the incautious step. Braldt found himself wondering what or who had made such a trail, for he had seen no signs of life since beginning their climb. A cold wind blew across the mountain, plucking at their clothes and chilling them to the bone.

They were clambering around a tricky bit of rock that was cracked and fissured, above, below, and through the trail itself, with no other route available to them, when Braldt heard Beast's high shrill bark of alarm, then Keri cried out in fright. Batta Flor uttered a curse and scrambled forward, pressing Keri hard against the crumbling rock face with a hurried command to stay and not move. Brandishing his spear before him, he lunged forward and disappeared from sight.

Braldt could not see what it was that had alarmed them so, nor could he pass Keri and Carn who stood on the trail before him. But Keri was not one who took orders well, and ignoring Batta Flor's command, she followed swiftly on his heels, drawing her own blade as she ran. Carn, of course, was not one to be left behind and he drew his short sword and his dagger and joined the fray that was now a mixed cacophony of hissing and high-pitched barks, as well as yells and loud cries. Leaping forward over the last bit of crumbling rock, Braldt turned the corner and was confronted by such creatures as he had never before seen or imagined in all his life.

They were lizards of a sort, but large, standing as high as his knee, their heads rising even higher, with powerful tails, twice the length of their bodies and massive, high-domed heads. Their heads were long and slender as were their jaws, which were filled with long, sharp teeth. There were three of them, the largest nearly as long as Braldt himself. The second was a lighter shade of blue and Braldt guessed it to be a female. The third was a smaller version of the adults, but no less dangerous from the look of its wildly thrashing tail and the deep, bellowing grunts that rose from its throat. They stood on short, stocky bowed legs, tipped with six long, curved claws and a seventh claw located at the rear of each paw that served as an anchor, holding them securely to the rock at near-vertical angles.

Beast did not seem to recognize his danger for he danced forward and back, nipping at the lizards' legs, unmindful of their powerful jaws that could easily sever his head from his neck. Batta Flor struck out with his spear at the smallest of the lizards that stood nearest them and Beast seized his opportunity and darted forward, grabbing the lizard's leg and yanking hard. The lizard did not even move and his leg slid out of Beast's mouth with a sound like two sword points clashing. Beast tumbled back and would have fallen off the edge of the trail had he not rolled against Batta Flor's leg. He shook his head as though stunned and whined with distress. The lizard's leg showed not the slightest mark of Beast's teeth.

It soon became apparent to Braldt that Batta Flor was not making any real attempt to strike the lizard, but merely brandished his spear in its face and yelled loudly. The lizards swung their heavy heads from side to side, hissing and grunting out their deep bellows. But they did not move.

Then, the largest of the three creatures advanced on them, pacing slowly and deliberately forward, its head bobbing and weaving, its long forked tongue, an even deeper shade of blue, flicking back and forth as though tasting the air. The lizard's eyes were quite small and were located high up on either side of its head. It could not see them straight on and was forced to turn its head to one side in order to keep them in sight.

Batta Flor backed up slowly, the others forced in turn to step back as well, but retreat was not to be one of their options for as Braldt's heel came down upon the fault-riven ledge, it broke beneath his weight with a loud crack and the entire shelf plunged into the cold abyss.

They were trapped. The lizards were advancing on them with a slow, calm sense of assurance, the slope of the mountain was far too steep for them to ascend, and there was nothing behind or beside them but empty air. Batta Flor stood his ground and struck out with his spear, but to little avail. The lead lizard looked up and, almost as an afterthought, hooked the spear with one of its claws and sent it clattering over the edge.

Braldt thought rapidly as the others picked up rocks and threw them at the lizards. It was only an act of futile desperation and the rocks merely bounced off the tough skin with no effect. Batta Flor fumbled with the pouch that he had slung over his shoulder and pulled the stopper out, sending a jet of hot, steaming tea arcing into the lizard's gaping maw. The hot liquid struck the soft tissue that lined the lizard's mouth and it bellowed and jerked back, swinging its head from side to side in obvious pain.

Encouraged by his success, Batta turned the odd weapon on the other two, scalding the smaller creature's eyes and missing the third completely as the last bit of the hot fluid fell short of its target. But Batta Flor's effort had given Braldt an idea, and rummaging in his pouch, his fingers closed on a handful of the wax-impregnated pellets. Striving for the necessary calm, he struck his fire-starting stones together and ignited the pellets. Closing his mind to the pain of the flames, he picked them up and tossed them into the open mouths of the lizards.

His plan, devised in haste, succeeded far better than he could have imagined. Two of the pellets missed their mark entirely, but the third landed in the maw of the male and the tiny flames, fanned by the rush of air, leaped high, curling around the lizard's jaws, burning the soft tissue that lined its throat and incinerating its tongue. The melting wax aided the spread of the flames and the furious thrashing of the creature's head and its agonized bellows served only to increase the conflagration. Soon, the entire body of the lizard was wrapped in flames and its eyes had been seared by the heat. The air was filled with the stink of roasting flesh, and with a final convolution of pain, the lizard's struggles brought it to the edge of the path and it fell over the edge still screaming in agony.

The remaining lizards seemed confused by the peculiar turn of events and stood on the path with their heads and tails thrashing back and forth in indecision. Of the remaining pellets, two had rolled over the edge, harming nothing, but the last lay on the trail between the hideous creatures and themselves, the tiny flame flickering uncertainly. Then, fanned by a vagrant breeze, it caught hold and flared up brightly, the wax burning with an intense heat. This was all the incentive that the lizards needed and they backed away from the fire, their booming voices echoing distress as they scuttled across the face of the cliff and disappeared from sight.

The four of them stood and watched as the lizards vanished, praying that they would not return. Keri seemed to have frozen in place, still clutching her sword, eyes wide with terror. Braldt, knowing of her childhood fear of lizards and snakes and other such creatures, could only imagine how terrified she must have been. He squeezed her shoulder to comfort her, feeling his own heart beating hard within his chest. He suffered from no such fears, but the lizard things were unlike anything he had ever known before and he counted himself lucky to have escaped with nothing more than a bad fright.

Strangely enough, Carn had nothing to say, nor had he made any attempt to attack the beasts even though he had stood second behind Batta Flor. His face was beaded with sweat and he was still staring at the charred spot where the lizard had fallen from the trail. When he looked up, he did not seem to recognize Braldt and his eyes were glazed and full of fear. It seemed for a moment that he was going to run, but then Braldt put his hand on his shoulder and the touch seemed to break the spell. Carn shot Braldt a look of panic that settled into the now-familiar hatred. And Braldt knew that Carn would find it hard to forget that his fear had been seen.

"Hurry," whispered Batta Flor, taking Keri by the arm and urging her forward. "Where there are three there will surely be more. We must get to a place of safety where we can defend ourselves for they will be upon us soon!"

16

"More of them?" Keri asked, her eyes growing large in her pale face. "But what will we do?"

"Come," Batta Flor said persuasively, "let us get off this ledge and find a more sheltered spot and I will tell you about them. Please."

Keri looked about nervously, as if she expected the lizards to return at any moment, and even Braldt found himself resisting an urge to do the same. Carn was definitely spooked and, taking Keri's arm, hurried her forward, nearly pushing her in his haste to be gone. Keri looked back as though intending to upbraid him, but one look at his face convinced her to hold her tongue.

They found what they sought a short time later, a wide place in the trail where the mountain folded in upon itself, with a small bit of grassy ground lying between. The sun was shining full on the rock walls, and protected from the bite of the wind, it offered them a safe respite. Gladly they shrugged the heavy packs from their shoulders and sank down on the warm grass.

Only Batta Flor remained alert, prowling the perimeter of the enclosure, scanning the rocky walls carefully. Apparently he did not find what he sought and this seemed to please him, for only when his inspection was finished, did he join the others.

"What were those things?" demanded Carn.

"You said there would be more," Keri added, her statement sounding more like a question.

"Yes, many more," Batta Flor said with a sigh, "although I did not think to meet them so soon. We were lucky to have escaped without harm. My people call them shadows because they have the ability to change color at will, blending in with their surroundings so that they are nearly invisible. They are very dangerous and hard to kill. Their skin cannot be penetrated by any but the very sharpest of spears and their teeth and claws can easily kill an adult Madrelli."

"How can they be killed?" asked Braldt, more interested in knowing what would dispatch them than what would not.

"There are not many ways to hurt them," Batta Flor admitted reluctantly. "Fire is effective as is trickery for they are not very smart. Also speed, for as they do not think fast, it is sometimes possible to flee before they decide to follow."

"What do they eat?" asked Keri, beginning to regain a little of her color. "We've not seen another living creature on this mountain and there's hardly any grass or foliage for them to graze."

"They are not interested in grasses or foliage," Batta Flor replied with a grim smile. "They are meat eaters; they prey on the flesh of living beings. They climb the cliffs in search of nesting birds; they are very fond of eggs. But mostly they hunt the Madrelli, and when all else fails, each other."

Keri shivered and fell silent.

"And you say that we will encounter more of them," pondered Braldt. "Is there any way that we can avoid them?"

"No," said Batta Flor, "for our course will take us into the heart of their territory, inside the mountain itself."

His words were met with silence as Braldt, Keri, and Carn stared at him in disbelief. "In . . . inside the mountain?" said Keri as though hoping she had misunderstood him.

"I think that it is time that you told us the whole story," Braldt said grimly. "There is too much here that is unknown. If there are any more surprises such as these shadows, I would prefer to know before I encounter them."

For once Carn did not have anything disagreeable to add and placed his arm around his sister's shoulders to lend her strength, for he too was well aware of her weakness. He and Braldt had often played upon those fears when they were children, putting insects and small, harmless snakes in her bed and making frightening sounds in the middle of the night, but this was a time for strength and courage, not fears, and even Carn had the sense to realize it.

"This mountain," began Batta Flor, "as well as many of the smaller peaks you see, were formed during the birth of the world, or so the hard ones have said. Deep within the earth at the heart of the world is a great fire, hot enough to melt rock. I know that such a thing is hard to believe, but I have seen proof of it with my own eyes and so will you. When the fire burned very hot, sometimes, as with a pot atop a fire, it boiled over. Thus were our mountains formed, the hot rock inside the earth heaved upward and poured over the edges.

"This happened many, many times, and each time the flow stopped and the rock cooled, the mountain grew taller and taller. But the boiling rock did not always follow the same course, sometimes the pressure was not so great and the flow did not rise to the top. Other times, the hardened rock above formed too hard a cap to penetrate and the flow found other points of escape.

"As you have seen, the rock is brittle and porous." Batta Flor drove the point of his dagger into the ground and dug out a chunk of the grey rock that he crumbled between his fingers to demonstrate his words.

"So what does this have to do with us and the shadows?" demanded Carn.

"What it means is that the mountain is honeycombed with tunnels and passageways, the hollow tubes formed by the flow of molten rock that remained and hardened in place after each eruption. These passageways are now home to the shadows and many other such creatures; they are also the only way that remains to approach the flooded chamber.

"Here, I will show you." Batta Flor scraped the ground before them smooth with the edge of his hand, then drew the outline of the mountain. "Here, at the base, is the entrance to the chamber, where the river now flows. The river has its source here at the peak," and as he spoke, Batta Flor drew a circle on the top of the mountain.

"How can there be a river at the top of a mountain?" Carn asked in obvious disbelief.

"At some point in the past, during more violent times, the entire peak disappeared, destroyed in some eruption, I would imagine. Since that time, the hollow that remained has filled with rainwater and the runoff from the yearly melting of the snows that accumulate on Rouen Dor, its sister peak. We have long suspected that there is an underground river that flows through the mountain as well. All of these waters find their way down through the inner passages and it was their power that turned the huge machines that extracted the rhodium from the water for the masters."

"Please explain about these machines," said Braldt as he studied the drawing. "And tell us what you did to disrupt the flow of the water."

"It was simple, really," said Batta Flor. "Everything was controlled from the chamber, everything. We waited for the end of suntime, when the flow of water was lowest, when the snow was all but gone from the peaks. There was only one of us Madrelli on duty, one called Rutha Shan, and he was one who most believed in what we were attempting; we could not have done it without him." Batta Flor's voice sank to a whisper and he regarded the ground in silence. After a time he regained his composure and continued.

"There were many hard ones as usual, monitoring the machines and the gauges, weighing the rhodium and overseeing its packing. Rutha Shan let us into the control room. At first the hard ones did not seem alarmed, but then as we began shutting down the machines one after the other, they realized what we were doing and tried to stop us."

"What did they do? Are they good with swords?" asked Carn.

"The hard ones?" Batta Flor smiled at the thought. "No, they have no knowledge of weapons, they are but machines themselves. They sought to bring us under control by means of touch. There is a plate embedded in their hand with which they maintain contact with the masters. This plate, in fact any part of their hand, is able to deliver a paralyzing blow that is capable of killing. It stops the heart with a single touch. Even the slightest touch can bring a full-grown Madrelli to his knees. We knew this and were on our guard and still they managed to kill more than half of us, Rutha Shan included, before Arba Mintch opened the flood gates.''

"I do not understand," said Braldt.

"The control room monitored the flow of water," explained Batta Flor. "Here, in the passage outside of the control room, the water descended from above. The machines could only take so much pressure; if it was exceeded, they would turn too fast and destroy themselves. We did not want such a thing to happen for we thought that we might use the machines as a bargaining chip, a way of dealing with the masters. If the machines were destroyed, we had nothing to bargain with.

"But Arba Mintch realized that the hard ones would win out, they had already killed more than half of us and had succeeded in sending out an alarm to those others who were in their quarters. He knew that if they joined the fight, our efforts would be doomed and we would never get another chance to win our freedom. He did the only thing left, he opened the flood gates that allowed the water to flow as fast as it wished. Even at the peak of suntime, the flow was too great for the machines and they drove themselves into a tangle of twisted metal. The hard ones were upon us by then and all around me, Madrelli, friends and loved ones, were dying. Arba Mintch and I were the only ones left and the hard ones were closing in on us.

"Arba Mintch told me to run, to grab onto the ladder that led to the access tunnel above the control chamber. He told me it was our only chance. I thought that he was behind me, I did not realize until it was too late . . .''

"He stayed behind," said Keri, guessing what was to come.

"He stayed behind," Batta Flor said, still looking at the ground. "I leaped onto the ladder and it was only when I reached the top and looked back that I realized that he was not with me. He had returned to the controls and was smashing them to pieces. The hard ones were all around him and he was beating them off as well. Only when I had reached the top of the ladder and called his name did he reach for that last lever, the one that controlled the flow of water through the flood gates, that channel that ran through the control room itself and was only used to avert disaster.

"He smiled at me then, a smile that I will take to my death, and he pulled the lever all the way down. The hard ones were on him then, for they knew as well as I that it would spell their death, if machines can be said to die. A number of them reached him, I know, for I saw the sparks shoot from their hands into his body. I believe that he was dead before the water rose. But even in death he did not release his grip on the lever and the waters rose swiftly, the color of blood, covering Arba Mintch and the hard ones and the machines, stilling their noise until there was nothing left to see but the rising water lapping at my heels.

"I left then, finding my way out through the labyrinth of passages in utter darkness. I have no idea how I did so, nor do I know if I can repeat the journey, for the water accompanied me as I went and there were many times when I did not believe that I would survive. I have never been so frightened in all my life. If there are gods such as you two-foots believe, they must have been with me that night.

"I knew that we had succeeded when I emerged from the side of the mountain and saw that the borealis was gone from the sky, those flickering lights that had masked the night skies and hidden their true beauty for longer than any of us had lived."

"The God Lights," Keri said sadly, wrapping her arms around Beast and hugging him tight. Beast flattened his ears against his skull and looked at her through slitted eyes but made no attempt to bite her, much to Braldt's surprise. "I cannot believe that they were as you say. I wish it were not true. They were so very beautiful and it was good to think that the gods had given them to us as a sign of their love."

"It was exactly what the masters wanted you to believe," Batta Flor said bitterly. "Listen to yourself, doesn't it make you angry to think that you have been fooled, betrayed, used by another? Tell me, would you have dared to enter these grounds, dared to visit these God Lights as you call them, this symbol of your gods' love, had you not been ordered to do so by your priests?''

"No, of course not, it was forbidden!" replied Keri, stung by the Madrelli's words.

"Why was it forbidden if it was a sign of their love?" asked Batta Flor, his voice quivering with barely suppressed anger.

"Well, parents forbid you many things that they know will hurt you, especially if it's for your own good! You don't know everything! How do we know it's like you say?''

"It wasn't for your own good, you fool, it was for their own good that you were forbidden to enter these lands. How long could they have controlled you if you had discovered their secrets? How long would they have been able to rape and plunder your planet if you knew what they were doing? Would you consent to being blown up so that they might extract the very last bit of their precious metal? And as to proof, well, you shall see for yourself that I have spoken the truth. If there is a way to reach that chamber, I will take you there, and then you will see that it is as I have said."

"How do we go?" asked Braldt, speaking quickly to cut off the words that rose to Keri's and Carn's lips, for he knew that they would not take kindly to the Madrelli's words.

"I do not know that I can find the passage from which I escaped," said Batta Flor, turning his attention to Braldt. "But I do not think that it matters, one passage is as good a choice as another. They all look the same from outside and have equal chances of ending somewhere near the chamber."

"I do not like this," said Carn as he fingered his sword and glared at the Madrelli. "How do we know it's not a trap? He can lure us inside the mountain and then kill us off one at a time."

There was some degree of truth to Carn's words but Keri answered before Braldt. "Don't be stupid, Carn. We asked him to take us here. Can't you see that he likes it no more than we do?'' It appeared to be so for Batta Flor looked extremely uneasy at the thought of entering the mountain.

"How do we guard against these shadows and against the danger of becoming lost in these passageways?'' asked Braldt, anxious to keep his companions busy with real problems rather than dwelling on their dislike for one another.

Batta Flor appeared grateful for the question. Reaching into his pack, he withdrew a handful of sticks, none longer than the length of an arm, as well as a large clump of yellow chalk.

"Uba Mintch prepared these for us himself. They are branches from the Yuba tree that burn steadily but slowly. They will light our way down to the chamber and, if we are lucky, light our return. This chalk glows in darkness and can be used to mark our passage so that we do not become confused. The fire should keep the shadows away, although with shadows it is hard to know. They are not always predictable.''

"Where do we go?'' asked Keri, looking around her as though she expected to see a passage open before her.

"The nearest of the openings is yet some distance above us, we must climb farther to reach it. I would like to do so before darkness falls. Can you go on?''

"Of course,'' said Keri as she rose to her feet, for despite the Madrelli's kindness, she did not wish to give Braldt or Carn the satisfaction of thinking her too frail, too girllike, to continue. She was determined to hold her own.

"Good,'' said Batta Flor, reluctant approval for this female two-foot clearly visible in his eyes as he handed her a torch. Their fingers touched and they smiled at each other, for each of them knew that their fears were shared and understood. It was a silent bond between them.

Once more they began their ascent of the mountain, and now that they knew what they were looking for, it was easy to see places where the hot rock had flowed, bleeding out the side of the mountain. The sites of the flows were clearly marked by spills of the smooth, glassy rock identical to the plateau where Keri and Carn had nearly gone to their deaths. In most instances the rock was shiny black in color, darker than any night sky. But in other places, the smooth flows were red as blood and sometimes streaked with white or yellow.

Some of the flows emerged from openings in the mountain and others were closed by the stony cascades. But in every instance where entry was possible, Batta Flor deemed it unacceptable for one reason or another. They found what they sought, shortly before night fell, Sun the Giver, an immense crimson ball, immersing himself behind the dark peaks, slowly, reluctantly, as though unwilling to plunge them into darkness. His bright rays fingered the dark opening of the cavern mouth, staining it like blood without lifting the darkness that lay beyond as they lit their torches.

Batta Flor entered first, then Carn and Keri, who turned at the last moment and found the slim sickle of Mother Moon rising over the edge of the pale horizon and touched her head and her heart in a sign of obeisance before following after her brother. Braldt entered last with a whining Beast following close on his heels, wondering if and when they would ever see sun and moon again.

17

It was not as quiet within the mountain as Braldt had thought it would be. He was conscious of the great weight that surrounded him, the masses of rock that could snuff out their lives with one twitch of the rocky flank into which they burrowed.

There was no sign of the shadows although there were sounds aplenty, whispered rustlings just beyond the circle of their light and a multitude of creaks and groans and rumblings that emanated from the mountain itself. There was also the constant sound of water dripping from a hundred different points, the falling water creating a multikeyed backdrop to their every step. Into this strange world crept the small band, feeling their way forward and banishing the darkness with their torches.

The passage was wide and smooth and tall enough so that they were able to walk side by side. Their torches illuminated the tunnel, reflecting off the dark, glassy surfaces and holding back the darkness. The light refracted and splintered off every angled edge and filled their eyes with a dazzling glare.

The tunnel appeared to plunge directly into the heart of the mountain without even the slightest downward angle and it was this that concerned them most. "Are you sure we're going the right way?" asked Carn, carefully marking the wall beside him with a string of arrows to indicate the way they were traveling.

"All tubes go down sooner or later," replied Batta Flor. "They cannot do otherwise for they were born in the very heart of the mountain."

"What if a tunnel collapsed in on itself, we could be following a path to nowhere!" Carn persisted.

"Then we will turn around and go back, following your excellent trail of arrows, and find another tube," answered Batta Flor. "But this tube appears to be well formed, I do not think that it will end."

Carn muttered beneath his breath but said no more. Keri kept close to his side and trod on his heels several times, but even though he threw her an exasperated look, he did not chastise her, which was most unusual.

Beast appeared to be the most nervous among them and it was clearly evident that he did not like the close confines. He trotted forward to the edge of the circle of light and then halted abruptly, his ears plastered flat against his skull, teeth bared in a throaty growl, and eyes glowing in the torchlight. He allowed the others to overtake him and then hung back at Braldt's feet, all but tripping him up in his desire to remain close. Numerous times he rose up on his hind legs and scratched Braldt, begging to be picked up, whining low in his throat. But Beast had grown quickly and was no longer the tiny pup he had once been. It would have been an added burden to carry the pup and Braldt refused, ordering him down with a harshly whispered word. Thereafter, Beast slunk behind him, his belly nearly scraping the ground, tail tucked between his legs and whining nervously all the while.

It was the Madrelli who next sensed what Beast alone could hear, holding up his hand to stop them. And then they could hear it as well, a soughing sound, like wind gently drifting through the branches of a forest, stirring the leaves with its passage. But there was no wind in this place. And then it seemed that they could smell the presence of another as well, a scent like musty leaves left to crumble and rot. The sound came again, this time closer, almost daring to edge past the circle of light, and Beast began to bark, high and sharp, clearly the sound of alarm. The sound swelled in the narrow enclosure until it beat upon their eardrums and shut out all other sounds.

Then Braldt saw it. A long, thin, segmented body,

nearly the length and thickness of his arm bearing aloft two immense pincers. It was pure white in color, or perhaps merely no color at all, and was propelled into the circle of their torchlight by a multitude of swiftly moving legs. The rear portion of its body carried no appendages and was lifted above the ground and arched forward ending in a third and even more deadly looking pincer that opened and shut with a continuous rattling clack.

Braldt could see no eyes on the horrid creature, but it seemed quite able to track them, moving when they did, stopping and changing direction as they did themselves. Hesitant at first, it grew bolder after a short time and advanced toward them on its scuttling blur of legs, headed straight for Keri, singling her out as though it could sense her fear.

Keri screamed and the thing moved even faster, a gaping maw opening in the bulbous segment that was its head. Keri screamed again and brought her spear down with all the strength she could muster, plunging the point into the hideous head, skewering it like a fish in the water.

None of them were prepared for Keri's move. Braldt and Carn had raised their own spears only to have Keri strike the first blow. No one was prepared for what followed. Either the thing did not have a brain or it was situated elsewhere for the blow did not kill it. Instead, it flung itself about madly, thrashing and flapping wildly, the strength of its gyrations so strong that it pulled the spear from Keri's grasp. Dragging the spear along, the wound spewing a pale greenish ichor, the thing flung itself at Keri, all of its pincers opening and shutting in a frenzied manner, turning head over heels, the base of the spear clacking against the ground and the walls as the creature backed toward Keri, the third and largest of the pincers reaching for her legs.

Keri retreated from the awful creature until she bumped into the walls of the tunnel and could go on farther. She looked down on the thing, her eyes wide with terror, and even though she gripped her sword in her hand, she seemed frozen with fear, unable to think, much less act.

Braldt had no such problem, stepping on the base of

the spear as it clattered along the ground. He brought the creature to a halt and with two well-aimed strokes severed the monster into sections. But still it did not stop, each section continuing on, writhing forward as though each contained a mind of its own. The tail continued toward Keri while the midsection wandered off the way they had come and the head minced its way toward Braldt.

Braldt's action seemed to have freed Keri from her trance and she yelled aloud and attacked the thing, sword swinging until it was reduced to numerous small bits, and still she continued hacking at the remains until they were little more than a pool of gore. Only then did she stop and rest upon her sword, breathing heavily.

Braldt, Batta Flor, and Carn made short work of the remaining sections and soon there was nothing left that could harm them. Only Beast was not satisfied with their efforts, continuing to circle the various bits that still twitched and writhed upon the ground, even after death, growling and slavering though he would not venture close enough to touch them. Finally, he too slunk away from the grisly remains though he watched them constantly as if afraid that they might resurrect if he relaxed his vigil.

"What was that thing?" Keri asked as they hurried on, all of them anxious to leave it behind them.

"Some sort of stinger, grown large," said Batta Flor. "We have seen them in the control chamber, but they are small things, smaller than my little finger. Their bite is painful but not deadly. I would not care to test the venom of one so large."

Keri shuddered at the thought and held her spear away from her body and shook it to remove the last of the creature's pale blood. "I do not like them," she said firmly, and the manner in which she uttered the words caused them all to laugh, for none of them had liked the ugly thing any more than she.

"It was brave of you to move so swiftly," Batta Flor said softly as though uncertain how Keri would receive such words from one who was not of her tribe. To his relief, she grinned broadly and seemed to relax. "Yeah, it was kinda brave, wasn't it. You know, you men could move a little bit faster next time and not leave all the work to me." And smiling at their astonished expressions, she held her torch high and led the way forward.

They met many such stingers in the time that followed, although none so large as the first. Keri seemed to have overcome her fear of them, although not her dislike, and she took great pleasure in cutting them to bits or smashing them beneath the heel of her boot.

They saw other things as well, some which they could put a name to and others for which there were no names. There were rats, ranging in size from the tiniest mouse to those large enough to carry Beast off in its jaws. There was an abundance of bloodwings and numerous giant slugs and centipedes, most of which fled at the first sight of their torches.

There were others for which the flames appeared to hold no fear. Among these were the shadows that blended in with the rock and sometimes were not seen until after they had passed, and these attacked with all the stealth their limited brains were able to command. Fortunately, Beast had an uncanny knack of sensing the lizards and his loud alarms gave them adequate warning.

It was Beast himself who discovered the most deadly of the dangers that were to confront them, all the more dangerous because of its very innocuousness. They were in a portion of tunnel that was broken and shattered and filled with bits of fallen rock. Water dripped from the ceiling and lay in shallow pools and Beast bent forward to lap from one of them, treading on a large patch of what appeared to be moss or fungus. Instantly Beast leaped into the air, shrieking with pain and jumping up again and again, each time landing on the moss. No one could comprehend what had happened until the lupebeast pup managed to leap clear of the harmless-looking stuff and began licking his paws and crying piteously.

Braldt bent down and examined the pup's feet that had already broken out in a huge mass of watery blisters, some of which burst under the ministrations of the pup's tongue, revealing the angry red flesh beneath. Beast whimpered and looked up at Braldt with pleading eyes.

Carn crouched down and examined the moss, careful to touch it with the point of his spear, keeping it well away from contact with his skin. "Look," he said, severing a tiny bit of the plant and raising it for all to see. "Look there, on the end of each little bit of foliage there's a tiny bubble. If they are broken the fluid contained within is released."

"Obviously, it is capable of burning the skin," said Braldt. "Look what it has done to Beast's feet and they are thick and toughened with travel." Beast began to cry again and Braldt saw that blisters were forming on his tongue as well which had begun to swell inside his mouth.

Braldt realized that if the pup's tongue swelled much farther, it would inhibit his breathing, perhaps fatally. At the very least, it would send the young creature into hysterics and a hysterical Beast was not something they needed. Thinking swiftly, he pawed through the contents of his pouch until he found what he was looking for, a horn of the healing ointment. He knew it would work on the pup's feet, but he had no idea if it would be effective on his tongue or if the pup would even tolerate being ministered to.

"I'll need help here," he said taking his robe from his shoulder and swaddling the pup tightly, immobilizing him before he realized what had happened, leaving only his feet and his head exposed. Batta Flor moved to his side instantly and held the pup firmly, clasping his swathed body between his powerful thighs and holding muzzle and paws in his hands. Beast whined and thrashed in protest, but there was nothing he could do and Braldt suspected that his resistance was only token.

It was a simple matter to apply the thick ointment to the pup's paws and Beast's plaintive whines quieted with the application. It was cool and instantly soothing. But opening his mouth was another matter for the pup had closed it firmly and locked his jaws. Knowing the strength contained in those formidable mandibles, Braldt did not think it likely that he could open them against the pup's wishes.

Realizing Braldt's predicament, Keri came forward. "Here, let me try, I think I can help," she said.

"Why are we spending so much time on a stupid animal?" Carn asked impatiently. "It's not like he helps us out or even likes us! Let the cursed thing go, leave him here to fend for himself. We don't need him, he'll only slow us down!"

A look passed between Keri and Braldt and Batta Flor, Carn's words binding them more closely in that single instant than anything that had gone before. It was not necessary to respond to his words, each of them determined to help the small animal despite anything Carn might say.

Keri leaned over Beast as Batta Flor cradled him in his arms and crooned to him softly as a mother would sing to a child. Carn turned away in disgust and sat down against the wall, well clear of the carpet of stinging moss. Keri continued to croon to the pup and, after a moment, began stroking the underside of his jaw, stroking downward from the point of his muzzle to the base of his throat and then beginning again, the pressure soft but steady, blending in with the subtle song and becoming part of it. The song and the stroke had a hypnotic effect and even Batta Flor was forced to look away. Braldt yawned widely. Beast's jaw sagged open.

Keri continued to stroke the pup's throat, maintaining eye contact and singing her wordless lullaby as Braldt daubed a thick coating of the ointment on the pup's tongue and the roof of his mouth. The pup gagged and struggled briefly, but made no real attempt to bite as the cool, soothing effect of the gel eased his pain. Nor did Keri cease her song even when Braldt was finished, but waited until the pup sighed deeply and closed his eyes, falling into a peaceful sleep.

"There, that should keep him for a while," she said quietly.

"That was amazing," said Batta Flor, looking at her with admiration. "How did you do that? Where did you learn?"

"I learned it from Braldt," she replied, her cheeks flushing red. "He taught me how to do it to lizards that we caught as children. But it works on most animals. Since I am not mated, I am called on often to help with the infants and children of others. I tried it on them in order to keep my sanity and it works on children as well as beasts!"

"Please understand that I mean no offense," said Batta Flor as he cocked his head to one side and studied Keri intently. "Although you are missing too much fur to be truly attractive to a Madrelli, I think that by two-foot standards, you must surely be regarded as handsome. And surely you are well into the prime of your child-bearing years. How is it then that you are acting as a warrior and not as a mate?"

Batta Flor's words had a startling effect on Keri. Her cheeks flushed an intense shade of red that spread in all directions and her eyes glittered with tears. She opened her mouth as though to speak, but no words came out, and she glared at Batta Flor as though he had flung some foul curse at her. Then her gaze turned upon Braldt and he too felt the blaze of her fury. Stunned, he took a step backward. Glaring angrily at both of them, Keri's hands opened and shut in fists, and dashing her tears away with the backs of her hands, she picked up her torch, leaped over the deadly bit of moss, and strode off down the dark tunnel.

"Good work," Carn said with a chuckle as he rose to his feet and started after Keri, pausing only to stare at the astonished Braldt and Batta Flor. "This could prove interesting. And by the way, 'brother,' how do you explain why Keri isn't mated yet?"

18

They continued their journey into the heart of the mountain with Batta Flor leading the way and Carn trailing behind, marking the walls with his chunk of chalk. There was no more talk of mates or mating. In fact there was little or no talk and there was a new sense of tension in the air that had nothing to do with the dangerous quest.

The tunnel had begun to branch. First there was an intersection on the left that presented no new choices for it slanted upward and they could see daylight shining in the distance. Nor was the second branching a valid option for it had collapsed in upon itself and the sound of running water could be clearly heard. But the third choice was not so clear-cut. This tunnel was equally as wide as the one they traveled and slanted downward. There was no sign of instability nor was there the sound of running water.

"What shall we do?" Keri looked at the new tunnel with troubled eyes. "How can we know where it goes?"

Carn advanced into the mouth of the new opening and examined it with his torch. "Look how it slants down. The angle is far more steep than the path we have traveled thus far. Perhaps it will take us to our goal more swiftly."

"And perhaps it will lead us to our death," mused Batta Flor. "If it curves downward at such a steep angle now, while still high on the mountain's flank, it may plunge into the depths abruptly. We cannot descend at such a sharp angle; we would fall to our deaths. I suggest that we continue on the way we are traveling. It is better to be slow and safe than fast and dead."

"I thought you were so brave," sneered Carn. "Where is your manhood?"

"Bravery is one thing, stupidity is another," replied Batta Flor. "I have no wish to make this journey at all. I want nothing more than to fulfill my promise and return to Sytha Trubal. I cannot do that if I am dead."

Carn took a quick step forward and Braldt stepped between him and the Madrelli, placing his hands on Carn's shoulders and gently but firmly turning him aside. "The Madrelli has no reason to direct us falsely, brother," he said in a low tone that could be heard by no one other than Carn. "It is as he says. It is to his advantage to lead us to the chamber so that he may take his leave of us. You are allowing your temper to rule your tongue. I ask you to consider your words before you speak. Much depends upon the successful completion of this journey. We need this Madrelli as a friend, not an enemy. Can you not put your personal feelings aside until our mission is done? Do you forget that Auslic's very life depends upon us?"

"I have not forgotten," Carn said hotly, making no attempt to soften his words. "But how can you trust this kark? You are treating him as a friend, instead of the animal he is. So he talks pretty and he lives in a house. That doesn't change anything, he's still an animal and he's no friend of ours no matter what he promised. I think he'd gladly lead us to our deaths so as to get back all the quicker to that ugly she-kark he wishes to bed!"

Carn's voice rose until he was all but shouting at Batta Flor whose face tightened, the small, dark eyes glittering with anger and the red stripes flaring crimson. Keri took his arm before he could act and tugged him back, away from Carn, pulling on his hand and arm insistently, until she succeeded in drawing them apart. He was breathing heavily and Keri could feel him trembling beneath her hands.

"Do not listen to him," she whispered urgently. "Do not allow him to provoke you into a fight. It is just what he wants. He is my brother and I know him well. He is hot-tempered and slow to reason when the rage is upon him."

"But why does he say such things," asked Batta Flor. "I have given my word. Is a man's word not a thing of value among your people? Once given, a Madrelli does not break his promise. It is not a thing that is done."

"A man's word is sacred among our people as well," Keri said as she searched for the words to make Batta Flor understand. "It is just that, well, you know how badly you felt when you thought that Sytha Trubal had taken Braldt to mate?" Batta Flor nodded. "Well, Carn feels that strongly about this mission. Braldt is our brother, but he is different from us and sometimes things come easier to him than they do to Carn. No, not sometimes, always. Carn has always lived in Braldt's shadow. It would mean everything to him to succeed in this mission, for the success to be his and his alone."

The Madrelli cocked his head to one side; his intelligent eyes studied her carefully. "But wanting alone cannot make a thing happen; there must also be thought and careful planning."

"Sometimes a man's desire can be so great, there is no room for anything else."

"Or a woman's desires," he said softly, stroking her cheek with a single finger as a blush spread rapidly across her face. "I understand, little two-foot. I will try hard not to allow your brother's words to anger me. I will shut them out of my mind, but speaking honestly, I hope that the future of your tribe does not depend upon your brother."

Keri's cheeks flushed again, this time in response to Batta Flor's harsh judgment of Carn. But even as she opened her mouth to speak, she stopped, knowing in her heart that he was right.

Carn had all the makings of a good leader, intelligence, compassion, and moral strength. But all too often he was governed by anger and spite and jealousy. And always because of Braldt. All their lives they had been matched and compared against each other simply because they were brothers. Carn was a superior example of the very best Duroni qualities. It was not his fault that Braldt was even better.

But the constant competition, constant struggle, and constant loss to Braldt had taken its toll on Carn. Nor was the blow softened by Braldt's attitude, for winning truly did not seem to matter to him and his words of consolation or congratulations stung like salt in a wound. Over the years, watching Auslic's eyes light up at the mere sight of Braldt had caused the simmering jealousy to grow until it had become a full-blown hatred that seethed and fed upon itself until all love or liking for Braldt had been burned away. Unbeknownst to Keri, Carn was determined that there would be but one winner in this game they played and only one of them would return, successful. And it would not be Braldt.

Calm words and logic prevailed at last and Carn bowed to Batta Flor's decision to continue following the main flume, although two spots of color remained high on his cheeks and his eyes burned with a feverish intensity.

Beast had been wakened by the loud exchange of words and he wriggled inside Braldt's robe. The argument was put aside as they discussed what should be done with the pup for he was too large and too heavy to be carried, and his feet were still blistered and tender. At last they decided upon a course of action. Slathering the pup's feet with more healing ointment, they wrapped each foot in a piece of heavy leather and tied it firmly at the ankle.

"There, I'll bet that's the best pair of lupebeast boots ever made," Braldt said, struggling not to laugh as the pup turned in circles trying to catch his hind feet, snarling and barking at the strange appurtenances.

"I'll go you one better," chuckled Keri. "I'll bet you it's the *only* pair of lupebeast boots ever made!"

Beast sat down and began to gnaw on the foot coverings and Braldt clamped down on his muzzle. "Best be on our way or he'll have them off in no time."

They traveled swiftly then with Beast forced to lope after them or chance being left behind in the darkness. They were swiftly becoming accustomed to their new world and easily avoided the ever-present patches of moss, beat back the hissing advances of the shadows with their flaring torches, and crushed the biting, stinging creatures beneath their boots without a second thought.

Exhaustion and failing torches brought them to a halt

after a time, and they judged it to be nightfall on the world outside the mountain. Carn was in favor of continuing, but their empty, rumbling bellies demanded to be fed. Then suddenly the walls of the tunnel fell away without warning and they found themselves on the edge of a vast, black body of water that stretched away on all sides as far as they could see.

"I knew we should have taken that other tunnel," Carn said bitterly, and no one could deny that perhaps he had been right after all.

■

They camped there on the edge of the dark lake for they were tired and hungry and too dispirited to retrace their steps. There was a small expanse of finely grained black sand at the mouth of the tunnel several feet above the reach of the water and dry as well as oddly warm.

They placed new cubes of fuel in the ends of the torches and stuck them upright in the sand and in the crevices in the walls. As their eyes became accustomed to their surroundings, they were able to discern features that had escaped them at first. The roof was high above them and curved inward, and at the very center of the roof there fell a curtain of water. It was no torrent such as one might expect to find in a waterfall plummeting from such a height, but it was constant and it created such a din that it was necessary to speak loudly in order to be heard.

"The lake must be directly above us," Batta Flor said in a troubled tone, and all of them looked up, suddenly imagining the weight of the lake pressing down on them, held back by a mere layer of rock that might give way at the next twitch of the volatile mountain. It was not a comforting thought.

The far sides of the lake had come into view as their eyes adjusted to the dim light. The lake was not as large as they had thought at first and a number of openings could be seen along the edges, some lying nearly beneath the level of the water, others like their own at surface level, and still others opening far up on the shining walls. There appeared to be a narrow thread of sand and stone circling the lake, but where it would lead was the question.

Only Beast seemed unconcerned as he picked his way down to the water's edge, crouched, and leaned his head forward to lap. At the first touch of tongue to water, he let out a shrill yelp and sprang back, snapping his jaws and growling in fear and pain.

Braldt approached the dark water cautiously, wondering what new danger lurked beneath the surface. But there was nothing to be seen. He touched the water carefully with the point of his sword and, when nothing happened, brought it close to his face so that he might smell it. Water streamed down the length of the blade and puddled on his hand. Too late he noticed the steam rising from the blade, too late he realized what it meant, and he dropped the sword and clutched his hand to his chest, cursing loudly.

"It's hot!" he said in amazement.

"Surely you are mistaken," scoffed Carn, but as they joined him at the water's edge, Keri examining his hand with sounds of concern, it was all too easy to spot the trails of vapor rising from the dark surface.

"The fires of the mountain must lie directly below us," Batta Flor said quietly, "there is no other explanation."

They made a somber camp, eating their meager meal and curling up on the warm sand to sleep. They posted no guard for it seemed unlikely that anything could live in water that hot and Beast would alert them against the approach of shadows. But sleep would not come to any of them and they lay with open eyes and worried hearts, wondering what the morrow would bring.

Keri slept at last only to be pursued down the dark tunnels of her dreams by nameless horrors with writhing legs and clacking pincers that reached out for her flesh. It seemed that she spent the entire night in flight, and when she wrenched herself free of the nightmare and wakened to see the bright flare of the torch, her heart was pounding and she was more tired than when she had first lain down to rest.

The others were sprawled in poses of sleep, and as she

busied herself with the preparation of a meal, falling back on familiar routines to calm herself, she studied their faces, unguarded in sleep.

There was Carn, tucked into a tight ball, protecting himself even in slumber. But his face was smooth and untroubled and it was easy to see the boy he had once been before jealousy and envy had begun to eat at him from within.

Braldt lay beside Beast. He was lying on his side with one hand gripping the hilt of his sword and the other draped lightly over Beast who had fit himself into the curl of Braldt's body.

Keri allowed her eyes to rest on Braldt to drink in the sight of him as she would never do, could never do, if he were awake. She admired the long, square line of his jaw and the lean sweep of his muscular body. She tried to imagine what it would feel like to lie next to that body, to feel his arms close about her, to hold her close as a loved one, as a joined mate.

She could feel the old familiar ache begin somewhere deep inside her and not for the first time she wondered if it were possible to die of unrequited love. She had loved Braldt since she was a child tottering after the two older boys, trying even then to keep up. Braldt's blue eyes, the color of the sky, and his hair, so yellow as to be nearly white, drew her like no toy or doll and she had run her fingers through his hair, stroking it gently as if it might turn dull Duroni brown beneath her touch if she were not careful.

But his hair had not turned brown in the years that passed, if anything it was bleached even lighter by Sun the Giver, and his eyes had taken on the hue of the sky at dusk, a dark, intense shade of blue, clear and guileless as was his nature.

Her love had intensified as well. She was no longer the child she had been and she knew, despite all the arguments to the contrary, that she would never love another.

Her mother and father had talked with her, reasoned with her, and then spoken more forcefully, for it was against nature not to take a mate. They ignored her claims of love for Braldt, dismissed them out of hand, for were they not brother and sister? Such a mating was impossible.

In vain did she argue that Braldt was no issue of their joining, in vain did she point out the fact that there was no shared blood between them. Braldt was of their clan. He had been joined with them and under Duroni law he was her brother no matter what she might choose to think or say. It was forbidden. But they did not force her to choose a mate as some other parents might have done and allowed her time to see the error of her ways for they loved her greatly.

Keri knew that she would never choose another. If she could not have Braldt, she would have no one else despite the pain and silent censure such an act might cause her parents.

She had set about pleasing Braldt from her youngest days, doing the things that she thought would please him. The rough and tumble games of their childhood took on a more military air once Braldt and Carn entered the Hall of the Warriors. Whenever they were allowed leave to return home, she begged Braldt to teach her what he had learned. Thus, over the years, she had become adept at sword and knife play, throwing stick and snapstone. She would never be as good as the boys, but she was better than any other girl.

She had also learned to live and travel in the wild lands that surrounded the city-state, trapping small animals for food and finding safe water even in the dry times. She had struggled against her fears of the darkness, and fears of the tiny unseen insects that crawled in the night. And done it all in the name of love.

But all of her efforts had been for naught. Braldt refused to see her in any light other than sister, friend, and boon companion. Thanks to her efforts, she was accepted as a close friend, one whom he would choose to spend time with. But there was still a difference, she could never be as close to him as his men friends, nor would he ever think to lay hands on her body with thoughts of joining, for just as she was not a true warrior, neither, in his eyes, was she viewed as a true maiden.

Keri wondered what would happen if she told Braldt how she felt, confessed her love for him. But even as she brooded, she knew the answer; it would destroy any hopes she might have. It all seemed so hopeless. Then, without warning, tears began to roll down her cheeks and she pressed a hand to her heart, almost unable to bear the pain.

Suddenly there were arms around her and a hand that stroked her brow, wiping away the tears and whispering quiet sounds that eased her pain. Blindly she raised her face, and blinking back the tears, she started as she found herself looking into the dark eyes of Batta Flor. Startled, she tried to pull away, but Batta Flor held her easily and drew her against his chest, cradling her head in one hand and patting her back with the other while rocking her gently to and fro. "It is all right, little two-foot. I know how you feel for I have shared your pain. I am your friend and your secret is safe with me. Shhhhh."

Keri knew that Carn would not approve, knew that she should be strong enough to stand alone. But it was so good to have a friend, someone who knew and did not disapprove, and it was comforting to be held by one who cared. And so she allowed the tears to fall and they sat there side by side, Duroni and Madrelli locked in the heart of the dark mountain, hostages of love and circumstance.

19

Batta Flor crouched on the warm black sand and ate the meal of flat grain cakes and hard cheese, and finished with a handful of the precious red berries, savoring the tart, sour taste upon his tongue. He had no wish for the hot bitter-tasting brew that Keri had offered him, but he did not wish to hurt her feelings and accepted with a smile. She blushed and lowered her eyes, perhaps embarrassed by the memory of the moment they had shared.

These two-foots seemed uncomfortable with such displays of emotion, with the notable exception of anger. Anger and rage seemed entirely acceptable to two-foots, but none of the softer feelings. Batta Flor sighed. It was most odd, but still, being a warrior nation had allowed the Duroni to remain free of oppression while the gentle, peace-loving Madrelli had been enslaved for many long generations past. Who was to say that the two-foots were wrong.

But even as Batta Flor contemplated such thoughts, he knew that it was not so. The two-foots were living on borrowed time, and they and their warrior state existed only so long as the masters chose to allow them freedom.

That time of freedom was nearly over, whether the two-foots believed it or not. The world as they knew it was about to end. Batta Flor felt a moment's compassion for the Duroni but he shrugged it away. Why should he pity them, a hostile, ignorant, self-deceived tribe who hunted and killed those of his own tribe whenever possible with little or no provocation. They were a tribe who refused to believe the truth, even when it was carefully explained to them, and their only hope of survival lay in an alliance with the

Madrelli. If Carn was any example of what to expect, however, both tribes and the world they shared were doomed.

A strange idea began to take shape in Batta Flor's mind and he allowed his gaze to rest on Keri as she made certain that Carn, Braldt, and even the lupebeast had eaten their fill. It was an odd thought, but it held merit. He would think upon it at a later time, if and when the cursed mission was completed and he himself returned to Sytha Trubal's side.

And yet, Batta Flor wondered if such a thing were possible. It seemed most unlikely that the mission could succeed for their goals were completely opposed. The two-foots sought to enter the flooded chamber and throw the lever that would allow the ships of the masters to land.

Batta Flor had been instructed to take the two-foots to the chamber, but he had also been told to prevent the lever from being thrown. The words themselves were so simple, mere sounds. "Don't let it happen." But how was he to prevent it? The two-foots were very persistent and willing to fight at the drop of a feather.

The best he could hope for was that it would be impossible to enter the chamber, and, to the best of his knowledge, it was indeed impossible. Had he himself not turned the great wheel that controlled the flow of water? Had he himself not heard the machines attempt to compete with the flood and twist themselves into a tangled mass of contorted metal? The flow could not be reversed. So far as he knew, there was no way to drain the chamber. So long as it remained flooded, their world was safe from the return of the masters, even if the two-foots could not understand or believe such a thing.

What could be Braldt's game? Why was he with the Duroni? That was the real question. Uba Mintch had questioned him closely, heard the odd tale he told of being found in the desert, being raised by the Duroni. Was it possible that such a thing was true? How could it be so? He appeared to be far more honorable, intelligent, and trustworthy than the one he called "brother."

Batta Flor found himself liking the man, wanting to call him friend. Yet every time he looked into those blue eyes, saw the pale hair the color of the sun, his heart clenched inside his chest, and he felt the old fear settle upon him and knew that they could never be friends. Why was he living among the Duroni and calling himself one of them? Was it possible that he did not know the truth? How could he have known the Madrellis' weakness, the ears? No, such a thing was impossible. Braldt would have to be watched closely and he himself would have to guard against his own inclinations.

Carn was far easier to understand. He was Duroni through and through, quick to act without thought, violent, and unpredictable. He could be managed, but it would mean keeping a close rein on his own emotions and refusing to be baited. It would be hard, but it could be done. For the love of Sytha Trubal, he would have been willing to endure much, much more.

Braldt rose to his feet and slipped into his pack, signaling that the day was about to begin.

"Do you not think that we might try to circle the lake?" said Batta Flor, careful to phrase the thought in the form of a question, thus appealing to the two-foots' own sense of importance. "There appears to be a narrow band around the edges where we might safely travel. Our path must surely lie in one of those caverns on the far side."

His companions turned their attention to the path he had indicated. Carn was the first to speak.

"Never," he said flatly. "It's too dangerous. How do we know that it goes all the way around. It could stop halfway. And even if it does go all the way, the rock may be unstable and we'd fall into the lake and be cooked. I say we go back and take the other tunnel, the one that went down. At least we know it's going in the right direction."

"But, Carn, we're here," Keri said hesitantly. "I hate to go back all that way. Why don't we try doing what Batta Flor says. We can test the path with our spears and if it's not stable or ends, we can always come back and try the tunnel."

"You'd side with him?" Carn said with a hateful look. "I should have known. You should have stayed behind, you've been nothing but trouble from the first." Keri's face turned red, and staring down at the black sand, she bit back an angry reply.

"I am tempted to give this plan of yours a try," mused Braldt, breaking into the exchange. "But we cannot be certain that the path will continue or that any of those tunnels will lead to anything but dead ends. Whereas we know that the tunnel we passed is both clear and leads downward. I think that we should return and see where it leads. It is not so far that we cannot change our minds."

Rather than provoke further angry words from Carn, Keri and Batta Flor gave in and the small group began to retrace the previous day's steps. Beast seemed to think that they were returning to the surface and he bounded along, turning and barking at them if their steps flagged. The downward slope that had led them to the lake had seemed gentle during their descent, but returning was another matter and their aching muscles were a vivid reminder that whether inside or out, they were indeed climbing a mountain.

They reached their destination about midmorning, using the known burn time of the waxy cubes as a gauge. There had been an attack of shadows to keep them alert. The scaly creatures had chosen to attack at a turn in the tunnel where there was no forewarning. Beast had not scented them for some reason and Keri had sustained a painful scrape all along the length of one arm before the lizards were beaten back by the flames.

They turned into the new tunnel with a sense of relief and high expectations, with the exception of Batta Flor who became increasingly nervous as time passed. He examined his feelings but could place no name to them, but he was nervous and started at every unexpected noise and he felt anxious as though awaiting some unknown dreaded event. Several times he opened his mouth to speak, to share his fears with his companions. But each time he remained silent, knowing that the two-foots would not accept unsubstantiated fears as valid grounds for retreat. Carn would be certain to call him a coward, which would only make matters worse.

The farther they advanced, the more loudly Batta Flor's senses screamed of danger, yet there was no sign of anything wrong. The tunnel was both wide and smooth, and after the initial steep descent, it settled into an easy, gradual slope. Nor were shadows or the stinging moss in evidence. What's more, occasional glimpses of dim daylight filtered down through cracks in the roof above them. These outward signs of normalcy seemed to greatly pacify the two-foots even as Batta Flor's own senses warned him of imminent danger.

The tunnel suddenly took a precipitous plunge downward and the walls and roof above them splintered into a mass of fractured stone, the various layers twisted and broken as though rent by some great pressure. Threads of hot vapor rose from the fissured stone and the smell of rotten eggs hung heavy on the air. From time to time their torches flared up brightly as though they fed upon the very air itself.

"I think we should go back," urged Batta Flor, no longer caring whether his manhood was called into question for the feeling of disaster clung to him like a second skin.

"Look, we can get down easy, it's just like climbing steps," said Carn as he stepped down onto a great slab of tilted rock. "And there's still enough daylight to light the way, we probably don't even need these torches. Come on, let's not quit just yet. I think we're going the right way." To demonstrate his faith in his own judgment, Carn snuffed out the torch and, stowing it in his pack, began to descend the broken rock.

"No, wait!" cried Batta Flor, but the two-foots did not heed his warning and before he could stop them, Keri and Braldt had slipped over the edge and begun to follow Carn. Only the lupebeast pup remained on the edge of the break, whining nervously and trotting back and forth in indecision, even though he could easily have jumped to the next ledge.

"You feel it too, don't you," whispered Batta Flor, knowing with certainty that something was dreadfully wrong. Beast sat down on his haunches and, throwing his muzzle back, howled, an eerie sound that echoed throughout the tunnel, magnifying itself and returning over and over again. It was the sound of death.

Batta Flor could see them still, they had descended swiftly and now appeared to be resting some distance below him. Oddly enough, they did not seem to respond to the sound of Beast's cries. Batta Flor would have expected Braldt to call to the pup, reassuring him and urging him to follow. But there was no call from Braldt who appeared to be leaning back against a rock as though catching his breath. Nor was there any comment from Carn who would surely have welcomed the opportunity to heap scorn on Batta Flor's lack of courage. He had gone the farthest of the three and was lying on his belly, peering over the edge at what lay below. Keri was nearly hidden from sight, wedged in a narrow crack on a small ledge holding her head in her hands. Why were they resting, the descent was not that difficult?

Batta Flor gently wrapped his hand around Beast's muzzle, as he had seen Braldt do, urging the pup to be silent. The pup turned worried eyes to him and whimpered. "Yes, little one, I feel it too, something is wrong, but howling will not help. Listen now. What can be heard?" But there was nothing to be heard but a steady sibilant hiss and the crackling of his torch as it flared brightly.

Batta Flor placed his head on one side and then the other, listening, trying to place the sound, trying to remember . . . And then he had it! Bad air, poisoned air! Once, in the control chamber, such air had accumulated without warning, killing six Madrelli before the hard ones realized the cause. It had been necessary to drive ventilation shafts into the chamber from the surface, installing blowers that sucked the bad air out before it was safe to return. It had happened long before his own birth, but the tale was still told by the elders.

Batta Flor thought swiftly. What could be done? Were the two-foots already dead? How fast did the bad air work? His first thought was to run away, to leave the place as quickly as possible before he too fell victim to the poisonous gas . . . but then he looked down at Keri's still form and remembered the moment they had shared. How could he leave her to die; she did not deserve to perish. But if he rescued her, would he not have to rescue the one called Braldt as well? Keri would not thank him for saving her life while allowing Braldt to die. And if he rescued the two of them, how could he leave the hateful Carn behind? But if he did nothing at all, they would all die and he could return to the tribe and Sytha Trubal. He had warned them not to go and they had not listened. Their deaths would not be on his hands for they had willingly chosen their own course.

But despite all of his arguments, Batta Flor knew in an instant that he could not leave them to their fate. Sytha Trubal would know with but a single glance, and what was more, he would know as well, and it would always be between them. To leave the two-foots to perish was a thing without honor. It was not the way of the Madrelli.

The pup looked up at him and whined. "I will do my best, little one, but if I do not return, you must find your way back alone. You must save yourself if I fail."

Batta Flor fastened one end of his rope to the end of a rocky spire, tugging on it to see if it would hold his weight. Then, thinking of all that might go wrong, he wedged a bit of leather in between the rock and the rope so that its sharp edges would not sever the rope. There did not seem to be anything else he could do, and muttering loudly, cursing the Madrelli sense of honor, he began his descent, wishing not for the first time that it were possible to believe in the things the Duroni called gods.

His agility and the Madrellis' ability to use their feet with as much dexterity as their hands allowed him to descend quickly. Keri was the closest. He found her slumped across a fold of rock, eyelids fluttering, her color sickly, teetering on the edge of consciousness. Batta Flor debated taking her up first, but reasoned against it for although she was obviously not well, she was still alive. The others might need him more.

Holding his breath against the unseen poisonous air, Batta Flor fairly skipped down the rock face passing Braldt until he reached Carn. There was a high-pitched ringing in his ears and he felt dizzy, although whether it was from holding his breath or absorption of the gases, he did not know. Without pausing to see if Carn was alive or dead, he picked him up, threw him over his shoulder, and began the long climb to safety.

It was harder than he had thought it would be. Carn did not weigh half as much as he, but as he struggled up the fractured rocks, searching for handholds and footholds, Carn grew heavier and heavier. His vision blurred and his lungs burned and begged for air. He could not hold his breath any longer and breathed shallowly through his mouth. They passed the sprawled figure of Braldt, oddly stilled, like a child's toy with the stuffing removed, his face tinged with blue.

Batta Flor resisted the temptation to rest, knowing that he might not have the strength to return, seized Braldt by the wrist, and dragged him along, staggering now under the extra burden. His strength was great and his powerful shoulders capable of bearing great loads, but he was not performing under favorable conditions.

He was panting now, the breath searing all along the length of his throat, burning a line down the center of his chest. He could hear Beast barking but the sound rolled around inside his head, echoing loudly, over and over without end, and he wished he could make it stop.

Now he could hear his own breath as well, harsh, rasping gasps that were an auditory reflection of his pain. He could not feel his feet and looked down to discover them gripping stone and climbing as though with a mind of their own. One toe was bleeding badly from a long, deep gash, but it was as though it had happened to someone else for he could not feel the pain.

Keri was on the ledge where he had left her, mumbling to herself, and for some reason this struck him as humorous and he began to laugh, but laughing made him dizzy and he stumbled and fell to his knees, nearly letting go of Braldt. With great difficulty, he pulled the dead weight that was Braldt onto the ledge and he sucked in great breaths of air into anguished lungs. The world swung around him like a giant pendulum and he blinked his eyes and tried to stabilize. It only made things worse. Spittle was coating his cheek, clotting the fur, and he drew away in distaste for he was fastidious about his person.

He knew that he was in great danger. He would never see Sytha Trubal again if he did not rise, and this thought more than any other enabled him to fight off the desire to rest, to close his eyes for just one moment, to not have to climb with fingers that could no longer feel. He knelt beside Keri and knotted the rope around her chest. She stared at him with eyes that held no sign of recognition and he saw the faint blue tinge beginning to color her skin.

Beast's cries became louder and louder and then, even as he sought for another handhold on the smooth rock, he felt Beast's teeth close on his pelt and pull, hard enough to hurt. He cursed the pup for ignoring his command to stay. Why had it not been smart enough to remain where it was safe?

He raised his hand to continue, but there were no more handholds, the rock rose smooth and unbroken above him. There were no holds at all. They were on a ledge, a broad ledge, one that went back and back and back into darkness. Slowly, Batta Flor sank to his knees. He could do no more and Beast would not release his hold, which was becoming painful as well as bothersome. He had tried but he had failed. Tears came to his eyes as he thought of Sytha Trubal, the way the sun shone on her fur, the way her stripes flared when she was angry. The way she looked when she was in love, a look that would never be bestowed on him. Holding her vision to him, he allowed the darkness to take him.

It was Beast who brought him back, barking over and over in his ear and licking his muzzle and his eyelids, urging, no, demanding, that he waken. Lupebeast spittle coated his muzzle and stuck to his lashes and Batta Flor swatted at the small animal, cursing him as he sat up with a groan. His head ached as though he had been drinking fermented silverwood sap. There was a bad taste in his mouth and his blood flowed too loudly inside his head. He wished that he were at home in his own bed. Why had he come? For a moment he could not remember where he was or why.

And then he remembered. Keri! With barely a look at the crumpled figures beside him, he pulled on the rope, feeling the dead weight dangling on the other end, wondering, hoping, that she was still alive. How long had he been unconscious? He cursed himself for the lazy kark that he was, hoping, praying to the gods of the Duroni that the girl had not died. His arms trembled like those of a child and he felt as though he would be sick, but he worked at the rope, feeling it inch its way upward, fearing what he would find on the other end.

Keri's head came into sight, lolling back at an awkward angle, deeply tinged with the ominous blue, her eyes rolled back in their sockets. She did not seem to be breathing. Batta Flor pulled her over the edge onto the floor of the tunnel and loosened the rope from her chest, seeing the deep indentations left by the coarse fiber. He dragged her to one of the slender cracks in the rock, noting that darkness had all but arrived and placing her facedown, he began pressing on her back and then releasing it in a semblance of breathing. Nothing happened. Batta Flor's fingers were shaking when he turned her over; grasping her chin in one hand and her nose in the other, he began breathing into her mouth as he had been taught to do. Hot tears filled his eyes and dropped on her face. He continued his efforts long after he had reason to believe that he might succeed, simply because to cease was to release her unto death. This he could not bring himself to do.

"Please, please don't die," he whispered. A bright silvery shape came into view through the slender crack in the stone and even as he breathed into the girl's mouth, he composed a prayer to the orb whom the Duroni believed to be their god. Batta Flor had always been taught that there were no such things as divine beings, that everything in the universe had a cause and an explanation, but at that moment, the lack of a greater being in whom one might place one's fate meant that there was no one and nothing who could help Keri but he himself. And, he feared, that was not enough.

"Mother Moon, I speak to you as a Madrelli. I am not one of those who worship you, but this two-foot is. She is dying, Mother Moon, and she deserves to live. For the sake of this Duroni who believes in you, please grant her life."

No sooner had he thought the wish than he felt Keri stir beneath his hands. She turned her head to cough and the coughing led to vomiting. Batta Flor held her head over the edge of the precipice and wiped her face clean with tears of joy streaming down his muzzle. He did not know what it meant, and for the moment it was enough that she lived. But Batta Flor could not ignore the fact that his prayers had indeed been answered.

20

Batta Flor could scarcely remember the journey back to the dark lake. His head throbbed with pain and his eyes burned. His lungs felt as though they were afire, blazing anew with every inhalation, and he was overcome with nausea on numerous occasions. But he suffered far less than his companions, all of whom had stumbled and staggered along behind him, bound together with the rope tied around their waists.

It had been necessary to carry Carn a good portion of the way for he kept falling and bringing the others down with him since he had descended the farthest and thus breathed in more of the bad air. Even now he lay still on the black sands, unmoving, his skin an unnatural shade of grey, and Batta Flor wondered if he would survive. He would not miss the two-foot if he died and he would have the satisfaction of knowing that he had done all that was possible to save the man.

Keri crouched beside the fire, shivering even though the air was warm and close, and brewed more of the bitter brew that the Duroni seemed so fond of. Batta Flor took his own portion from her shaking fingers and was surprised to find that while it warmed his insides it also seemed to ease the pain in his chest. He drank the rest without argument and felt greatly revived, as the tight bands loosened their painful grip on his head.

Braldt was sitting up now, sipping the steaming brew from a gourd. His color was not good but at least he was alive. "You saved our lives," he said, looking Batta Flor directly in the eye. Batta Flor said nothing.

"You could have left us there and returned to your

197

people," added Keri. "Why did you come after us, does the bad air not affect the Madrelli?"

"Madrelli die just as easily as Duroni if the air is bad. But to have left you would have been a thing without honor. It is not the Madrelli way."

"It is not the Duroni way, either," said Braldt, "despite what you have come to know of us. I'm afraid you and your people have seen only the worst of us. But from this day forward, you will be as a brother to us."

"I accept the honor," Batta Flor said gravely, then nodded at Carn's still figure. "I assume that you are speaking for yourselves. This one will never welcome me as kin."

"You saved his life too," Keri said passionately. "Not even Carn can ignore such a thing!"

Batta Flor looked at Carn dubiously, doubting that the man would be pleased to find himself beholden to a Madrelli, but seeing Keri's distress, he held his silence.

"Do . . . do you think he'll be all right?" Keri asked tearfully. "He will not open his eyes and his heart is beating strangely; it flutters inside his chest like a trapped bird."

"I cannot say," replied Batta Flor. "My knowledge of such things is limited. But it would seem that when the torches flare and spit as they did, then we are entering an area of poisonous air. We should take careful note of this if it happens again."

"Do you think that we can circle the lake?" Braldt stared at the far shore, wondering what dangers awaited them there.

"It is our only hope. If such a thing is not possible, then we must abandon this mission and return. Perhaps we have already risked enough, my friend. We are all of us sick and this one is gravely ill and may die without attention. We have tried our best, there will be no dishonor in admitting failure. Let us return to the world of light."

Keri and Braldt looked at each other and then down at Carn's still figure. Keri's face was full of fear and her wishes were all too obvious. Braldt looked into her face and then uttered a single word, "Auslic," and she lowered her eyes and nodded although her face reflected her sorrow.

"We cannot return, my friend," Braldt said quietly, "even though we might wish it. Our wishes account for little; there are matters of far greater importance at work here."

"I only wish that our goals were alike," Batta Flor said sadly. "Can you not see that if you succeed in your mission, it will be the death of all of us? The hard ones and the masters are not benevolent beings. They care for us only so long as we serve their needs. The Madrelli have dared to disobey them. They will crush us and return us to our former slavery. I can only guess what they will do to you."

"Why would they do anything to us? We have not hurt them in any way," said Keri.

"Why can you not see," Batta Flor said in exasperation. "They have gone to great lengths to conceal their presence from you. Their very existence has been cloaked with mystery and mysticism to prevent you from learning about them. Mother Moon, the God Fires, the Forbidden Lands, and all the various myths and legends that abound, all created with but one purpose in mind, to keep themselves a secret. Now they need you to unravel the damage we have done, reverse the process so that they may land once again. Once that is done, your knowledge of their existence will not be tolerated. You will be eliminated!"

"Eliminated?" Keri said in a whisper.

"Killed. Made dead. Without life," Batta Flor said flatly. "They cannot risk allowing you to live, to return to the tribe to report what you have seen."

"But that would mean that you suspect some sort of communication between these hard ones and their masters and someone in our tribe," Braldt said slowly. "For how else would they have known what was needed."

"Now, at last, you begin to see," cried Batta Flor.

"How could that be!" asked Keri. "No one in the tribe would do such a thing. What would be the purpose?"

"I cannot tell you what the reason is," replied Batta

Flor. "But it must be so. How else would these priests of yours know about the chamber?"

"The priests! You think that the priests . . . !" Keri was aghast at the very thought.

"Yes, it must be so," Braldt said slowly. "Think, Keri! Think about what he is saying. It was the priests who told us to go."

"No, Braldt, it was . . . !" argued Keri.

"We are still doing the priest's bidding," said Braldt, brushing aside Keri's words. "It was their idea that we come. It was they who put the picture of the chamber in our heads, told us what to do. The priests must be in league with these hard ones and the masters. It's all some kind of game and we have served as their pawns for years." Braldt's tone was bitter as he contemplated the fact of the priests' duplicity.

"You cannot think that this is so!" cried Keri. "Mother Moon would not let . . ."

"Mother Moon is nothing but a dead rock, just as the Madrelli have said all along," Braldt interrupted harshly. "What better way to keep us in line than to wrap us up in a religion crafted to meet their needs. They have been very clever, these masters. But surely they did not plan for their slaves and their loyal pawns to piece the puzzle together. But it has now happened and we will have a chance at determining our own future. Now, we will make our own decisions."

Batta Flor was astonished at the two-foot's massive leap in deduction, his ability to understand and believe that which literally spelled the destruction of his religion as well as his way of life. But there was still another matter to be considered. One far more important than personal feelings.

"Then you agree that the lever must not be thrown. If we can somehow enter the chamber and retrieve this metal box, which you believe will save the life of your chief, there is no need to pull the lever as well."

"We will have to think on this matter and discuss it further," said Braldt. "At a later time," holding up his hand as Batta Flor opened his mouth to speak. "You have given me more than enough to think on for one day. You have my word that we will discuss this again.'' And even Batta Flor could see that Braldt could be pushed no further.

Keri was sitting wide-eyed and pale before the fire, clutching a gourd of the hot drink to her chest with unfeeling fingers. Batta Flor could feel her pain and knew that in destroying her religion, he had dealt her a cruel blow as well. But he also knew that there were no words that he could offer that would comfort her.

They made no effort to move and spent the remainder of that day and night resting at the edge of the dark shore, exploring the dangerous and disturbing new thoughts. As though by mutual agreement, there was no further talk on any but the most general of topics.

Batta Flor repacked their pouches more efficiently and treated their various wounds. Even Beast allowed him to change the dressing on his feet with no more than a token growl.

Keri tended to Carn who appeared to have fallen into a more natural sleep. She prepared their meals mechanically, without thought.

Braldt scouted along the edge of the lake and reported that it appeared possible to circumvent the entire lake in safety. What he did not report was that it appeared to be a trail that was well used and well maintained . . . and not by lizards.

Carn wakened on the following morning with a ravenous hunger and a terrible headache. He took in his surroundings with surprise and ate his meal with downcast eyes, pausing only briefly when told of Batta Flor's role in their heroic rescue.

Much to Batta Flor's surprise, Carn wiped his hands on his robe and extended his hand in the curious two-foot manner of greeting. Batta Flor took the proffered hand and held it, not knowing what was expected of him. Carn smiled and raised and lowered his hand twice.

"Look, I know what you think of me. And you're right. I've acted badly. But I am not so stupid as to not know the value of my own life. I would not have attempted to rescue you, had you fallen instead of me. I have been wrong.''

Total silence followed Carn's words as the others stared at him in disbelief. It was the Madrelli who recovered first. ''It would please me greatly to call you friend.'' Reaching out, he offered Carn his hand and when it was grasped, awkwardly raised and lowered it several times, Duroni fashion, in some manner sealing the words. Everyone smiled at everyone else and for the first time since they had been thrown into one another's company, they felt a fragile semblance of unity and friendship.

Carn, it appeared, had suffered no lasting effects from breathing the bad air, and proclaimed himself willing and ready to travel. He seemed to have attained a greater sense of teamwork as well as humility during his loss of consciousness and listened to Braldt and Batta Flor outline the plan to circle the lake without a comment. Braldt and Batta Flor exchanged astonished glances as Carn struggled into his backpack, then shared grins at the unexpected scope of their luck. ''Perhaps we should find a way to keep some of that bad air,'' murmured Batta Flor. ''Just in case he reverts.''

It was decided that they would circle along the left-hand side of the lake for that was the side closest to the outer world. It could do them no good, nor did there appear to be any cracks in the walls such as they had seen in the deep tunnel, but still the thought that only a thickness of rock separated them from the world they knew, a world of sunshine and free-flowing wind, comforted them in this black of stifling darkness.

Once more Beast took the lead, prancing along on his leather-shod paws as though it were merely some pleasurable afternoon jaunt. The trail was wide enough for two people to travel side by side and was flat, smooth, and free of broken rock. Braldt could only wonder at the fact that none of the others seemed to notice that it had not been created by a flow of molten rock as had the tunnels, but had been chiseled and worked by clever hands. Surely Batta Flor would notice, but no, the Madrelli appeared to be unaware of the difference even though he had dropped to all fours and was loping along at a comfortable pace, something he rarely did in the sight of the Duroni as though he feared that traveling in such a manner might somehow make him more animallike in their eyes.

Braldt studied the powerful build of the Madrelli and marveled at the strength contained in that body. Had it not been for the Madrelli, they would all be dead now.

Allowing Beast and Batta Flor to take the lead, Braldt allowed his thoughts to wander, wondering what they would do when and if they were able to reach the chamber. Could it be true, all that Batta Flor had told them? Braldt had never been much of a believer and while he had bent his knee to the Moon Mother a part of him had always remained apart. But now, to learn that all of it was a hoax perpetrated by beings from another world . . . it was hard, even for him.

Braldt began to wonder what else might not be true, what else they had always taken for granted that might not be as it had seemed. It was a disconcerting thought. Why did Batta Flor stare at him so when he thought that Braldt was not looking? He would have had to have been blind not to have noticed the way that many of the Madrelli reacted to him, staring at him as though they had seen some nightmare appear in the waking world. And then, after they had gotten over the first shock, they seemed to study him, to watch him as though expecting him to do or say something, he knew not what. And yet he knew without asking that they would have denied it had he confronted them.

Occupied with his own thoughts, Braldt did not at first notice that the others had come to a halt and were crouched at the edge of the trail, peering into the dark water.

"What's the matter, is there a problem?"

Keri turned worried eyes upon him. "Batta Flor thinks that he saw something move in the water, something alive."

"Couldn't be," Braldt replied. "That water's too hot for anything to live. It's just imagination."

"Perhaps," replied Batta Flor, his tone troubled as he stared down at the silent lake. "But I would have sworn that

I saw something move. Look here, Braldt, this is no sign of an overactive imagination!''

Moving to his side, Braldt stared at the ledge where Batta Flor's shaking finger pointed. There, from the very edge trailing down into the water was a silvery slick much like that which a land snail leaves behind to mark its progress.

"Look, look over here!" called Carn, his voice pitched high with excitement. He was on his hands and knees leaning out over the water at a place where the ledge had crumbled or broken away, leaving a small inlet. Carn turned toward them, holding something out on the palm of his hand. They rose to go to him and then, out of the dark gloom, a long, slender object rose up behind Carn and wavered for a moment as though hesitant. The three of them stood in shocked amazement, unable to speak or move. Then, even as the thing descended with lightning-fast speed, they began to scream and run toward Carn, drawing their swords and daggers. But it was already too late.

Even as Carn cocked his head to one side and peered at them in bewilderment, the thing was upon him. It was a coil, a living fleshy coil, although to what or whom it belonged was impossible to know. It wrapped itself around Carn, pinning his arms to his body, and then before he could react, or they could reach him, he was jerked off the ledge and dragged beneath the surface of the dark lake. Huge bubbles erupted and foamed on the surface as the waters heaved and lapped over the rocky trail. And then, slowly, the turbulence subsided and though the waters still rocked and a tiny trail of bubbles burst upward, there was nothing more to be seen.

Keri's screams echoed off the stony walls as she clutched her head and called out her brother's name again and again. Batta Flor and Braldt brandished their swords and strode back and forth on the narrow ledge searching the dark waters for a sign, a hint of the attacker. But there was nothing to be seen; the beast, whatever it was, had come and gone and taken Carn with it.

21

Scarcely had they left the beach behind when the dark water exploded in a flurry of white froth and rising high above the surface was a writhing welter of tentacles that darted down toward them with the speed of a striking snake. Keri cried out as the tip of a tentacle struck her a painful blow on the shoulder. She wrenched free even as the flexible tip coiled around her arm, tightening perceptibly in the instant it had her in its grip. Multitudes of fingerlike protrusions wriggled and reached toward her all along the grey-black length and she pressed herself against the wall, shrinking back from its reach.

Braldt and Batta Flor responded instantly, striking out with their swords, hacking at the thrashing coils that flailed the air on all sides. The flesh was hard and resisted the bite of the blades, causing them to rebound with an impact that shivered up through the muscles of their arms. Luck and desperation taught them swiftly that glancing blows were deflected, and that only direct, blade-on blows were able to penetrate the tough flesh. Again and again they struck at the creature, cursing when it grabbed hold of arms or legs or bits of their bodies and defending each other and Keri as well. Keri recovered quickly and, seizing the opportunity to avenge her brother's death, attacked with a fury that even Braldt did not know that she possessed.

One, two, and then four and more of the limbs were severed from the body and fell into the water, still wriggling as though they had a separate life of their own until they sank beneath the turbulent water. The creature began to shriek then, a piercing, mind-numbing wail that all but drove them to their knees. Unable to bear the terrible sound, they pressed their hands against their ears, swords clattering to the ledge or drooping from nerveless fingers.

Fortunately, the beast was suffering torments of its own and could not take advantage of their helpless state. Two heads were clearly visible, snakelike with fleshy protuberances like those of land snails bobbing from the front of a formless, bloblike head. Both mouths were stretched wide, emitting the terrible noise as the heads to which they belonged hurled themselves back and forth and side to side, keening with pain. Suddenly one of the heads uttered a terrible cry of rage and lunged forward, mouth agape, straight for Keri. The jaws closed around her body, engulfing her from shoulder to knee, and then jerked her roughly from the ledge.

Keri screamed and twisted within the creature's grip, attempting to free herself. Still holding her short sword, she began stabbing at the beast's mouth, penetrating the upper palate with her blade. The beast bellowed with pain and outrage, never for a moment releasing its grip on her body, but shifting her about in its mouth as though trying to find a hold that would not hurt quite so much.

Braldt seized the opportunity, the only one he would have, and jumped onto the creature's head, wrapping his legs around its neck and holding on to one of the fleshy antennae. Surprisingly, the beast was covered in a layer of slime that made it all the more difficult for Braldt to keep his hold. The creature did not seem to notice that Braldt had climbed upon its body, perhaps distracted by its pain and the difficulty of holding on to its prickly prey.

Viewed from such close proximity, Braldt was able to see that the thing was covered with lumpy, warty flesh, greyish black in color. Tiny openings located atop each lump secreted a constant ooze of mucus that Braldt suspected protected it in some way from the heat of the water. There were two eyes, tiny and insignificant, buried deep in the warty flesh. Clamping the slippery antenna tightly between arm and forearm he leaned forward and slashed at the creature's eyes, and was immediately rewarded by an agonized bellow of pain. The mouth opened wide, streaming blood, and Keri plunged into the water only to be seized by Batta Flor and dragged back onto the narrow ledge of rock.

Beast leaped up and down in a perfect frenzy of gnashing teeth and rolling eyes, threatening at any moment to fall into the water himself as he attempted to bite the monster. A tip of a tentacle thwacked the ledge next to him and he was on it in an instant, seizing it in his sharp teeth and ravaging it from side to side. Although not a serious threat, perhaps it served as a momentary distraction, which was good, for Braldt was hanging from the monster's head, dangling from the slimy antenna, more than twenty feet above the water.

It seemed as though the two heads were independent of each other, for even though the first head was streaming with rivulets of blood, the second head did not seem to notice but appeared to be far more interested in locating the source of its pain. Even now it was snaking down on Beast, mouth opened wide, ready to snatch him from the ledge when Batta Flor, choosing his moment carefully, stepped forward and brought his blade down across both pairs of the tiny eyes, blinding it as thoroughly as Braldt had maimed the first head.

The thing screeched aloud in double agony and flung itself backward into the water. Braldt was shaken loose from his precarious hold and hurtled into the watery maelstrom, still gripping his sword.

The water churned violently as the beast rolled about in agony, its many limbs crashing about, flailing both air and water. The water was whipped into whitened froth and heaved about like storm-tossed waves, and those clustered on the narrow ledge were unable to catch any glimpse of Braldt who had disappeared from sight. Just as they were growing desperate, Braldt's head broke the surface of the water and a hand groped for the edge of the rock.

Batta Flor and Keri reached for him with glad cries and dragged him out onto the rocky walk where they all drew back and watched as the last of the creature slid beneath the water leaving behind a swirl of mucus and blood.

They remained on the ledge for some time, too shaken

by their near demise to either continue or retreat. Nor were either of their options comforting. If they retreated, there was really nowhere to go, other than back the way they had come. But to advance was to advance into the unknown. It was quite possible that they would encounter other monsters of the same sort and that the next time they would not be so lucky. Or it was possible that they would find even worse things waiting for them.

In the end, they went on for they could not go back, too much was depending upon them. Despite the shrinking number of wax cubes left in their pouches, all three torches were lit to hold back the oppressive darkness, and they plunged ahead resolutely, walking at a swift pace, forcing themselves on along the narrow ledge, deeper and deeper into the heart of the mountain, farther and farther away from the light of day.

Eventually, the ledge grew wider and more irregular and it soon became apparent that it was now a natural formation and the ledge that had brought them so far had been carved out of the rock, enhancing the natural passage, although they did not know to whom or what it allowed access. Was it a well-traveled path, and if so, whose feet had trod it last? Was it possible that the hard ones had made it or were there still others whose presence could only be guessed at?

It was an unsettling thought and one that for the time would remain unanswered. Then, just as they were growing too weary to continue on, the wall opened wide before them, revealing a huge hollow bulge on the mountain's flank. The stone ledge gave way to mounds of the fine black sand that cushioned their weary limbs as they collapsed as far from the dark water as it was posssible to get.

It was soon discovered that Carn had carried a goodly portion of their foodstuffs as well as the torch cubes and now both supplies were running dangerously low. They made a rough camp and ate their brief meal in silence, too exhausted and dispirited to speak. They posted a guard and took turns sleeping, although whether it was night or day they could not have said, nor did it matter, for locked inside the eternal darkness of the mountain, time had become an all-but-meaningless measure.

When the last of them had wakened from their sleep they refreshed themselves with another small meal and warm water cautiously drawn from the lake. It was Keri who discovered the tunnel. Taking the pouch of warm water and a cleaning cloth, she availed herself of the privacy offered by a veil of rock that hung from the wall at the far edge of the rocky clearing. Staking her torch into the soft sand, she was startled to discover a cleanly cut opening concealed directly behind the rock. She probed its opening with the torch and was astounded to see a series of markings painted on the wall with bright colors. There were a number of glyphs that she could not decipher and two handprints, one pointed toward the lake, the other pointing into the dark maw of the tunnel.

"Braldt! Batta Flor!" she called their names excitedly, and fearing another attack they wasted no time in arriving at her side. Braldt studied the glyphs in puzzlement, but it was immediately apparent that Batta Flor had seen their like before for he studied them closely and his small, dark eyes glittered with excitement.

"We have found the way," he said, pointing to the strange marks. "It is the writing of the hard ones. It is old, strange . . . unlike that which I am familiar with, but I can read it."

"What does it say?" Braldt asked impatiently. Batta Flor studied it for a moment before he replied. " 'Beware the creatures of the water.' Good warning, too bad there was not such a warning where we entered."

"What does the rest of it say?" asked Braldt. "Surely there is more."

"Fourth level, down to minus level, that is what it says."

"What is minus level?" asked Keri.

"A level that is below the control chamber," answered Batta Flor. "It gives access to the ships when they land so that the fuel pods may be exchanged. There are also a number of work bays for maintenance and storage.''

''Is there a way to reach the outside from these lower chambers?''

''Yes!'' cried Batta Flor, excitement growing in his voice as he stared at Braldt, immediately grasping what it was he had in mind.

''Well, if they can be reached from the outside, why did we have to enter the mountain to get to them?'' Keri demanded angrily. ''Why did we have to go through all of this if we could have gotten there from the outside?''

''No, it's not like that.'' Batta Flor turned to her. ''They are small openings with heavy grates fitted over them, much too small for the Madrelli to fit through. We could not have entered that way, they are for drainage, for runoff, nothing more.''

''But they could be used to drain away the waters that have built up inside the chamber,'' muttered Braldt. ''Do the chambers connect?''

''There is access,'' Batta Flor admitted, ''but how would one escape the rising waters once the way was opened?''

''That is a thing I cannot answer until I see the place,'' replied Braldt. ''You can tell me about it as we go. Come, my friends, the sooner we are started, the sooner we are done. Let us be gone.''

The walls of the tunnel were smoothly carved from the surrounding rock. There was no question that this was a man-made passageway, man-made or whatever the hard ones were. But Batta Flor insisted that it had been driven by those of his own kind, and upon reflection, it seemed likely that he was right.

They lost no more time in searching out or arguing about the origins of the tunnel but, instead, packed up their few remaining supplies and set off at a swift pace. The tunnel descended smoothly in a series of gentle switchbacks. There was a deeply channeled groove running along one side of the tunnel and this they ascertained was to bring additional water from the lake, although why it had been needed was anyone's guess.

There were other tunnels as well, intersecting on both sides, some rising higher and others descending at steep angles. There were few if any indications where these tunnels went or what their purpose was, for when they were marked at all, it was with cryptic signs such as a pointing hand, either up or down, designating the direction of the tunnel and followed by a series of letters and numbers such as "A 1 b4," or "L 2 ac1."

While most of the tunnels were smoothly cut and gently graded as was the one they were following, others were cracked and fissured with chunks of rock littering the ground. The air was most often foul in these broken passageways and remembering their frightening experience with the poisonous air, they hurried past, making no effort to enter or explore.

After a time, they ceased to explore even those tunnels that appeared to be in perfect condition, for it seemed most likely that the main tunnel would take them where they wanted to go.

It was Keri who made the next discovery, literally falling over it as she followed behind Batta Flor. Although the torches illuminated much of the way if they were held high to show the way ahead, much of the floor was left in semidarkness. As their tunnel had been spared most of the damage noted in smaller passages, this was not deemed to be a problem. And such was the case, until Keri stubbed her foot hard against solid, unmoving rock and dropped her torch, cursing colorfully and holding her toe.

Hopping up and down, she lost her balance and sat down abruptly, which gave much humor to her companions who began to laugh, releasing some of the strain of the past few days. Their humor at her expense did nothing to assuage Keri's anger and she cursed them as well as the rock that had caused her such discomfort.

She groped around in the semidarkness, searching for the stone so that she might throw it at them, but instead of a rock fallen from the ceiling, her questing fingers encountered the smooth-cut angles of a long square object. Finding her torch, she brought it to bear on the object and found that it was the edge of a door that fitted flush against the wall and opened onto the tunnel. It was the leading edge of this door, which had come ajar, that her toe had met with such painful results.

Seeing no reason to say anything to Batta Flor and Braldt who were still choking with laughter and comparing her ungraceful posture to that of a bottom-heavy infant, she opened the door to its fullest extent and peered inside, wondering what she would find for it was the first such aperture they had encountered.

It was dark inside the door, a thick black clinging darkness that the flames of her torch did little to dispel. She blinked to clear her eyes and stepped forward. Too late she realized that there was nothing underfoot. She screamed aloud and flung out her hands to grab onto something, anything, to break her fall, but there was nothing, and with a rising sickness, she shrieked and fell into deep and utter darkness.

22

Carn stumbled along the sandy path, picking his way through large chunks of broken rock that had fallen from the ceiling and walls that surrounded him, lighting the way with one of the few torches he still possessed. In some places, the path disappeared completely, buried beneath massive falls of rock, and he despaired of finding the way again. The thought of ending his days entombed within the bowels of the mountain, never to breathe clean air or feel the touch of Sun the Giver upon his skin, however, gave him the strength to continue.

He prayed aloud to Mother Moon, uttering all the prayers he knew, even those that were reserved for the high elders. Part of his mind mocked him for saying the words that Batta Flor had all but convinced him were naught but trickery on the part of the masters. Yet another part of his mind refused to acknowledge the argument. What was faith if not a belief in that which required faith itself for its very existence? Some things were beyond logic, beyond explanation, beyond cold reason, and Carn found that once he had made such a decision, his heart was eased. Somehow, the reaffirmation of his faith made him stronger and that was what was needed if he were to survive.

The passage was filled with noises, the scamper of tiny feet, the click of claws, and the snick of teeth. There was the whisper of scales dragging over rock and shrill chitters that sounded like rats. The sound of dripping water was a constant, and in some places water could clearly be heard rushing past although there was no sign of a stream.

Most disconcerting of all was the sound of air or gas escaping under pressure, hissing loudly, and occasionally all but squealing in a high-pitched eerie wail. The sound raised the hair on the back of his neck and all along his arms and he held his breath and hurried through these places as swiftly as he was able. He suffered no ill effects from the passage and gave thanks to Mother Moon for watching over him, vowing to honor her always.

The way twisted and turned in all directions, first left, then right, first up, then down, snaking back on itself like a live thing, and it grew increasingly apparent that no hand of Madrelli or hard one had ever smoothed its way.

After a time Carn became aware of another fact, the rock and, indeed, the very air he breathed was becoming hotter. It was necessary for him to open his mouth to breathe and his air came in short, animallike pants. His lips were rough and cracked and the hair inside his nostrils were stiff and crackled with each inhalation. His tongue lay heavy and dry on the floor of his mouth and he fought against the urge to drain the water pouch dry.

He put out a hand to steady himself and quickly snatched his hand back even as the skin rose in instant blisters on his palm. The wall of the passage was burning hot! Carn fought down the panic that rose in his breast, and fought off the desire to turn and run back the way he had come, knowing that there was no hope to be had in that direction. His only hope was to continue on.

He stumbled over an unseen rock and dropped his torch. The flame was extinguished and instantly he was engulfed in darkness. Yet it was not the total darkness that he had expected. To his amazement, he saw that the wall on his right seemed to glow with a dull golden orange light, like Sun the Giver viewed through a parchment at midday.

Carn stared at the ominous sight with stricken eyes, wondering what it was that he was seeing, wondering what it could mean. Slowly he became aware of another sound, a sound that he had been hearing for some time. It was the sound of swift passage, as though something was flowing just beyond the glowing wall, something heavy but smooth surging along, scraping the walls with a constant murmur, bumping and thumping from time to time as though some heavier object had struck the rock.

Sweat beaded on Carn's forehead only to evaporate as soon as it had formed, but Carn did not notice. He stared at the glowing rock, working things out in his mind. Something flowed beyond the wall. Something hot, so hot that it was able to bring the rock itself to a red-hot glow. As he watched, wisps of steam curled away from the rock, reaching for him lazily, as though content to wait.

Carn forced himself to think. It could not be water behind the wall, for water was often heated in clay pots over fires and never did the clay pots turn such a color. If the fire were too hot, the pot simply broke, shattering under the extreme temperature.

No, it was not water, and with growing certainty and horror, Carn knew that what flowed beyond the wall of glowing rock was more rock, heated to the point where it melted and flowed like a flaming river of molten stone. Only the thin partition of rock separated Carn from certain death and the partition itself was all but liquid. How long had it held? How much longer would it hold? Centuries? Lifetimes? Hours or merely minutes? Those were questions to which Carn had no answers and he stared at the wall transfixed, unable to move, certain now that he was going to die.

After a time, he slumped forward, eyes closed, unable to maintain his horrified vigil. He was filled with fear. He wanted to cry, to bury his head in his mother's lap, but these actions would not save him. Then a vision began to form in his mind, a vision of Mother Moon red-orange, the same color as the glowing wall, rising above the red cliffs of home, rising out of the black night sky. Carn raised his head and stared at the fiery wall, wondering if it was an omen. The wall rock seemed to throb as he looked at it, always pulsing as though it were a living thing. It had the same heavy, gravid feel of Mother Moon at the peak of the Harvest Cycle.

Mother Moon would not have brought him this far only to kill him; there had to be a reason for all that had happened, there just had to be! Either the glowing wall was an omen from Mother Moon or—or his whole life was without meaning! Carn got to his feet and staggered on, determined to succeed. If Mother Moon, may she live in brightness, sent him a sign in this his darkest hour, then he would not betray her trust!

Others, like Braldt, might fail to honor her, might even believe the false words of animals, but those who were true believers would never be swayed from their faith so easily.

It was up to him, Carn, to save Auslic and the tribe and his sister as well from the danger of outsiders, all outsiders, whether Madrelli or these masters. Carn was not even sure that he believed in the masters and the so-called hard ones, but nothing, certainly no words from the mouth of an animal, would ever succeed in swaying him from his faith again. Mother Moon had seen fit to send him a sign in his hour of darkness; he had but to believe in her, to remain firm in his faith, and she would show him the way. Fevered and impassioned, Carn rose to his feet and set off down the fiery tunnel in search of salvation and glory.

■

Keri fell for what seemed to be a very long time, but in truth she fell no more than twenty feet before she landed atop a hard, unmoving object. She struck hard, but fortune was with her for she fell flat and as a result suffered no broken bones, although the breath was driven from her body. She took an experimental breath and was relieved when everything seemed to work. She wriggled her fingers and toes and then sat up gingerly, holding her head in both hands and blinking her eyes to shut out the disconcerting vision of the blinking lights.

She heard her name called aloud and was gratified to hear the degree of concern echoed in Braldt's voice. "Here!" she called weakly and after a moment Braldt's torch waved in the darkness above her. "I'm down here, be careful, it's a sheer drop!"

Outlined against the darkness of the doorway by the flare of his torch, Keri watched carefully as Braldt circled the opening with the flaming brand, searching for a way down.

"There!" Keri's voice rose as she pointed toward an object that Braldt could not see. "There, to the side, no, the other way! Isn't that a ladder?"

Braldt held his torch to the side, against the inner wall, and there, just as Keri had said, was a slender ladder attached to the wall with gleaming spikes the color of silver, the same color as the silver insets in the Temple of the Moon and the Council chambers.

Braldt's sword and dagger were forged of bronze, a soft metal that was quite adequate under most circumstances and certainly better than anything possessed by any of the other tribes or the slavers, but it could not compare to the hard edge of the silver metal that belonged to the priests and the priests alone. Braldt had often wondered what it would be like to possess a blade made of such a metal. It was easy to work, malleable and obedient under heat, forming itself into whatever shape was required, but nearly as hard as stone when cooled.

Braldt had always wanted a sword made of the bright shining metal, but the priests had decreed that it was for their use alone, and while the bronze was dug from the red cliffs and smelted on the hearths, the priests supplied the silver metal from sources that they never divulged. Now, here, right in front of him, was enough silver metal to forge a score of swords and daggers, a lifetime of shining weaponry!

"Braldt, do you see it?" Keri's voice rose from beneath him and he became aware of Batta Flor shaking him by the shoulder, concern in his voice.

"What? Yes, yes I see it. Are you all right? I'll be there in a moment." Holding on to the edge of the doorway, Braldt swung himself over, gripping the cold metal with hand and foot. It seemed steady, holding his weight with little difficulty even though it was apparent that the ladder had been constructed for something other than creatures of his size. The back of the handhold was a smooth slot and it seemed likely that whatever had climbed it last had clamped onto it and risen smoothly.

The crossbars that Braldt had at first taken for steps were affixed in such a manner as to allow unbroken access to the groove and provided a means of attaching the ladder to the wall. Whatever the purpose, it provided him with a means of reaching Keri, and he descended the ladder swiftly until he stood on the platform that had broken her fall, and without thinking, his arm circled her waist.

She leaned her head against his shoulder and sighed.

Braldt could see that they stood on a small square, no more than six feet in all directions and were enclosed on all sides by solid walls. Above them there appeared the outline of a door, like the one Keri had fallen through, but this door was closed and fitted flush with the wall. The surface they stood on was some sort of dull, unfinished metal and in the very center there was the outline of a smaller square. Around the edges of this smaller square were lights that blinked red and blue and white over and over again in sequence. Never had he seen anything like it. So much metal, his for the taking!

"Braldt, have you got her? Come back up!" Batta Flor's voice boomed down through the narrow opening and echoed in the small space.

"No, not yet, I want to see what's here first," Braldt replied as he knelt beside the small square.

The square was fitted with a latch that came open under his fingers and lifted easily although uttering screechy protest. Instantly the small chamber was flooded with brilliant light that all but blinded Braldt, blue, red, white, blue, red, white, the lights blinked over and over in an urgent sequence that seemed to be demanding some form of action. Braldt shielded his eyes and leaned forward, peering into the square framed by the blinking lights. At first he could see nothing, his vision blurred by the incredible intensity of the lights after the length of time they had spent in nearly total darkness. Braldt felt the platform dip as Batta Flor joined them and heard the scrabble of claws as Beast scrambled to find his footing on the metallic surface. But all of his attention was focused on the bright opening; closing his eyes against the glare, he knelt and ducked his head inside the lighted square.

In a moment he realized what he was seeing, to put words to it, but even then, it made little sense. It was an even smaller enclosure fitted with a tiny sliding door to match the one Keri had fallen through. Next to this door was a panel of sorts with smoothly carved knobs set into the surface and inscribed with more of the curious glyphs. The walls and floor were constructed of a material that Braldt did not recognize. It was not wood, nor was it metal. It was like nothing he had ever seen before. What was this thing they had found? It appeared to be no more than a large empty box fitted inside of a vertical tunnel of its own. It was very puzzling.

Batta Flor looked at him for a moment and then dropped to all fours and, grasping the edge of the opening, did a somersault and swung down into the cubicle before Braldt realized what he was going to do. Keri gasped and huddled beside Braldt, wondering what would happen to Batta Flor.

"It is as I suspected. It is naught but a lifter," said Batta Flor after a quick glance. "Come down, there is nothing to fear and perhaps it will still function and take us where we want to go."

He seemed completely at ease and opened the small panel, revealing a number of brightly colored coils attached to the back of the smoothly carved knobs where they came through the panel of the door. "Come down," Batta Flor urged, "I think it is still working, perhaps it had a power source of its own." He continued to murmur to himself as he fiddled with the brightly colored threads, screwing them more firmly to their fittings. Satisfied, he swung the panel shut and placed a finger on one of the knobs.

Keri threw Braldt a dubious glance and then slid through the opening into Batta Flor's waiting arms. Beast yipped as though fearing being left behind and he jumped through the small opening without a moment's hesitation. There was nothing left to do but join them.

Batta Flor waited until Braldt's feet touched the floor before he actually pressed the knob. This simple action was instantly followed by a throbbing vibration that filled the small box that contained them. There was a slight lurch and then the flashing lights ceased their manic action and a pale glow took their place shining down on them from the small square in the ceiling. They were like priest lights, but different, and Braldt would gladly have given up some time to examine them but he could not do so for immediately following the small lurch and the change of lights, the small enclosure began to fall! Keri screamed and scrambled to reach the escape hatch, but Batta Flor merely chuckled and held her loosely in his arm. "Do not worry, my friend, this is a good happening and nothing to fear."

"Tell that to Beast," shouted Braldt over the desperate keening of the terrified lupebeast who flung himself from one wall to the other, seeking escape. Braldt felt like doing much the same thing himself and it took every bit of his control to stand there, matching Batta Flor's calm air.

Batta Flor waited for his moment, waited until Beast struck the wall nearest him, feet desperately digging at the ungiving surface before he reached out and pinched the pup on either side of its neck with thumb and forefinger. Beast struggled for a moment longer and then sagged in Batta Flor's grasp as he was gently lowered to the floor.

Braldt stepped forward, anger growing in his eyes, for Beast and for himself and Keri as well. Who was this Madrelli and how well did he know the secrets contained in this mountain? Was he leading them into some trap, some manner of death from which only he would emerge?

Braldt's hand tightened on the hilt of his sword and he opened his mouth to speak just as the room came to a silent halt and the door slid back into the wall, revealing a corridor beyond. The corridor was unlike any other they had traveled, for it was paved with cream-colored stone and walls the color of the sky and all along the ceiling were rows of muted lights burning steadily. A soft humming could be heard in the distance, and in the hush there was the feeling of anticipation, a feeling of patient waiting.

Keri stepped free of the small enclosure with a glad cry. Batta Flor followed her and gestured toward Braldt with a crook of his shaggy eyebrow. Beast raised his head groggily and staggered out without a second glance, and Braldt could do nothing but follow suit, feeling slightly more than foolish for it was obvious that they had come to no harm. The door to the room slid shut behind him, but no sooner had it done so than the quiet of the corridor was broken by an odd metallic voice, jarringly strange in the utter calm. "Interference in the control room, danger in the compound! Repeat. Danger! Security has been breeched. Secure all positions! Danger! Danger!"

23

Carn had almost reached the end of his endurance. His skin was blistered from the heat and his sword had become too hot to hold. He had placed both sword and dagger in the folds of his pouch and robe, for it was too hot to wear and the ring clasp had burned his flesh. His feet were somewhat protected by his heavy leather traveling boots, but even so the soles of his feet had become painfully tender.

The wall continued to glow, a deep fiery color that was like looking into the heart of a smithy's forge. It was hypnotic, mesmerizing and constantly changing, going from red to scarlet to gold to white. Here and there droplets oozed from the wall and trickled down the sides, puddling at the base. Carn had to fight back the desire to thrust his sword into the wall, allowing the molten material on the other side to flow free. He knew it was madness, and could mean his death, but still, it was a thing that wanted doing.

Another factor had entered the already frightening picture, one that scared him even more. Deprived of an adequate supply of oxygen and laboring under demanding physical conditions, Carn had entered a hypnotic trance state and was highly influenced by the visions, primarily religious in nature, that his fevered mind created.

This hallucinogenic state permitted him to continue on, long after others would have lain down and died. He no longer recognized the constant shuddering of the earth for what it was, reason for great alarm and swift exodus.

The tunnel that he had been following suddenly branched; one tube, open and free of fallen debris, turning off to the left, away from the molten wall, and rising; the second tunnel swung sharply to the right, and if anything, the wall glowed even more brightly. Fixated as he was, Carn swung blindly to the right rather than choosing the path that would lead him to the surface and to safety.

The new tunnel was taller and broader than the original path he had followed, but the heat was even more intense. Without thinking, he dropped his pouch. It had become simply too much trouble to hold. He soon shed everything other than his small body pouch and his boots, but still he felt burdened. There was nothing left to leave behind.

The air at the top of the tunnel had become too hot to breathe and after a moment's thought Carn returned to his discarded possessions and retrieved his robe. Using his dagger, he ripped and sliced at the tightly woven fabric until he had reduced it to a number of broad strips. He wrapped several strips around his hands and up the length of his arm as far as the elbow. He did the same to his knees, cushioning them with folded thicknesses of fabric wrapped with additional strips and tied firmly behind the knee. Now he was able to crawl along the floor of the passage, scuttling like one of the shadows. The air was cooler there, although still hot enough to feel his body hair shriveling wherever it was exposed. He warily drank the last of his water and the empty pouch was left behind as he continued on toward the ultimate goal.

The end came sooner than he had anticipated, although his muddled mind had not truly formulated what it was that he thought he would find. The passage began to rise, gently at first and then more steeply, until he was forced to use hands and feet to climb rather than crawl. The fiery wall faded to a dull angry orange and then suddenly vanished, leaving Carn in darkness, or near darkness, for there was a shimmering edge of brightness somewhere above him. He missed a step as a chunk of rock broke away beneath the weight of his body and for a moment he hung free, feeling the black emptiness yawning beneath him as he desperately sought to regain his footing.

Heart pounding against his ribs, he rested his head against the rough rock for a moment, closing his eyes to shut out both the ever-present darkness as well as the awful glow that trembled above him at the edge of his vision.

With his ear pressed against the rock he felt and heard the pulse of the mountain, not the silence of dead rock, but the throbbing heartbeat of a living entity. The streaming rush of superheated rock had become a deep, pulsating, rhythmic turbulence, a feeling calling to him, drawing him onward like the pull of Mother Moon as she called to the waters at the height of her cycle.

Carn pressed his forehead against the hot rock and wept, the tears channeling through the grime on his cheeks. Somehow he knew in his heart that Mother Moon, the mother of them all, had allowed him and him alone to hear her heartbeat. He had been chosen above all others. He had been blessed, chosen for some special deed. He knew it was so.

Carn began to climb again, ignoring the pain in shoulders and hands and the deep, burning ache of his lungs. The great Mother was calling to him and he was hers to command. The bright, shimmering light drew ever nearer as he climbed with renewed fervor, feet and hands unerringly finding their way to safe holds. The higher he rose, the hotter it became, until he was breathing with open mouth, deep, rasping breaths that made him dizzy with each inhalation.

He had climbed as far as he could go, the rock tapering in toward the bright cloud that hung in the air, ending in a large flat rock. He took a short breath and doubled over, choking as burning air filled his chest, singeing his nostrils and throat. Collapsing forward, he rested the top half of his body on the rock, feeling the heat of it burning through the layers of cloth that protected his arms.

The sound was louder now, easily heard without pressing his ear against the rock, a deep, growling sound that vibrated through his body until he felt that it was a part of him, an audible extension of his physical being.

A bright, glowing iridescence lit the air around him, a shining corolla too hot to touch or breathe, a symbol of Mother Moon close enough to touch, drawing him on. It was close now, whatever it was that he had come so far to see. Closer, dragging himself forward, the cloth smoking where it touched the scorched rock. Carn shielded his eyes against the heat and the ever-increasing brilliance, his heart pounding inside his chest from anticipation rather than fear, somehow certain that he was about to see that which no man had ever been allowed to see before.

Then it was there before him, so dazzling, so huge, so impossible that it was all he could do to bear it, to comprehend what he was seeing. He knew without a doubt that he was looking into the very heart of Mother Moon. She was not a cold, dead rock circling in a lifeless void, existing only to reflect Sun the Giver as the lying karks had said. Here, here was all the proof he needed to refute that lie, to prove to Keri and Braldt that Mother Moon was alive, here on their world, a part of them that could not be denied.

The Duroni had never been able to answer the question of where Mother Moon went when Sun the Giver returned to claim the sky, or how she renewed herself after she sacrificed herself each cycle. Now he knew. He alone had been permitted to learn the truth, in order to save them in their time of crisis. It was a test. The gods were testing them to see if they were true believers. They had been given this task to see if they were worthy of their gods. The karks and their lies had been placed in their path to separate the true believers from those of little faith. Keri and Braldt had faltered. Only he, Carn, had remained true. The fate of the tribe and their very world depended on his actions.

Carn felt the tears rise up again and burn away before they could fall as he stared upon the glorious sight. He knew in some dim portion of his mind that he should look away, that this was not a sight that mortal eyes could comprehend for more than a brief moment, but he could not turn aside and might not have done so had an especially violent tremor not thrown him sideways, breaking the dangerous hold.

Still the vision remained imprinted on his mind and once again he saw the swirling vortex in shades of light and brilliance rather than color. Below him was a giant cauldron, larger, much, much larger than the dark lake, and as the lake had been dark as death, here was all the light in the world, surely the source of all power, for there was a sense of primal might rising from the sea of light that exceeded anything Carn had ever known before.

The seething, churning molten mass lay far below him, circling round and round in a slow spiral. A layer of darkened slag streaked the bright surface. Bits and pieces of this dark crust merged to form dark islands only to break apart and float away to rejoin elsewhere or be dragged beneath the surface and integrated into the whole once more.

It was not a static scene, but one filled with sudden violence that illustrated the strength of the gods. Huge geysers of molten stone were periodically hurled up out of the molten sea, spurting great gouts of liquid rock high into the air where they hung until falling back into the swirling sea.

All along the outer edges of the flaming sea, tall waves flung themselves against the walls that contained them, sizzling and hissing with a frightening violence. The imprint of their attack was clearly visible for in many places it had hardened on contact, thickening the walls, while elsewhere it had succeeded in ripping out immense chunks of rock, enlarging its area as well as consuming that which it had acquired. As the gods consumed and destroyed those who did not believe in them.

And the noise. The noise alone would have convinced Carn of the presence of the gods had he had any doubts, for it was a sound unlike anything he had ever heard before. It was very nearly beyond sound, a different dimension, for even as he felt it quivering in his bones, he heard it echoing inside his head, and saw it trembling in the air, and tasted and smelled the scorched stink of it as well. After a time, Carn ceased to hear it for the deep soul-grinding rumbling had become a part of him.

Carn never knew how long he remained there, for time ceased to have any meaning. Was it not enough that he was in the presence of the gods? But after a while, he knew that he must go. The gods were telling him so, for the earth was now shuddering constantly; some of the more violent spasms were easily capable of throwing him into the flaming pit. And while he did not believe that Mother Moon would take his life, after revealing unto him her secret, he knew that he must leave in order to fulfill her dictates.

He did not remember the long, difficult retreat down the face of the steep cliff, nor did he have any memory of retrieving his water sack and the pouch that held his possessions. Nor did he ever recall retracing his footsteps and seeking out the tunnel that led toward the surface.

Somehow, perhaps aided by his gods, he ate, slept, found water, and avoided the many dangers that lurked within the dark mountain. When he wakened, racked with the pain of burned and sloughing skin, his flesh reddened and too tender to bear even the slightest touch of his tattered robes, he did not know where he was. Somehow he had taken a wrong turn. Cool air no longer blew upon his face and the tunnel that sheltered him appeared to lead down rather than up.

His face was bloated and swollen, his eyelids twice their normal size, allowing him only a narrow band of sight. His lips were blistered and deeply fissured, rolled back upon themselves exposing the cracked enamel of his teeth. His eyebrows were gone, as was his hair, which had shriveled and frizzed with the stink of burning feathers. His scalp and his face, having endured the worst of the heat, were a deep purple-red beneath the puckered welter of blisters. He would bear the scars of his divine vision for the rest of his life . . . but none of it mattered, for he alone had been chosen by the gods.

Carn staggered to his feet, grimacing with pain, filled with the need to find his companions. Somehow he managed to light a torch cube and fitted it onto the end of his sword. He could but pray that he met no more dangers during the course of his search. His faith sustained him for he could not believe that Mother Moon would take him so far only to allow him to be killed by a shadow or one of the creeping stingers.

He wandered through dark tunnels, eating when his

body required fuel, sleeping when it demanded rest. He sang snippets of prayers and hymns sometimes, even though it hurt and his voice emerged a hoarse croak, the vocal cords forever damaged by the intense heat that had seared his throat.

His eyes had suffered permanent injury as well, the tender flesh at the outer corners of his eyes scarring, the new skin fusing so that his lids appeared thickened and hooded, giving him a brooding, ominous air.

The blisters on his head, face, and body broke, scabbed, and peeled, revealing a patchwork of thickened crimson flesh, twisted and distorted in places, permanent testimony to the anguish his tortured flesh had endured.

Carn had no mirror but he was aware of the changes that had transformed him from a handsome young man to a thing of horror. Never again would a maiden look upon him with favor. Never again would the quirk of his lips invite a gentle stolen kiss. Never again would the sight of him cause hearts to beat fast beneath gentle bosoms. But such matters did not cause him despair, if he even thought of them, for he had gladly suffered his stigmata for the greater glory of his god.

24

"**Danger! Danger!**" **The metallic voice continued to** blare out its message as Keri and Braldt crouched back-to-back, holding their swords at the ready, searching for the bodies that went with the voice. But no one appeared even though the message was repeated over and over and over, and after a short time Braldt began to wonder if they would. Perhaps it was but one sentry who was giving the alarm but dared not attack on his own. But how did he make his voice so loud and why did the words sound exactly the same each time they were spoken? And why did they sound so strange as though they were being spoken through a brass tube? Braldt looked around him, rising from his battle stance, wondering where the enemy could be hiding.

Following his lead, Keri rose too. To her amazement, she saw Batta Flor casually walking down the corridor, apparently unconcerned by the dire warnings. Reaching up, he opened a panel high on the wall, and after a brief examination of its contents, his nimble fingers tapped out a short sequence, the lights flickered, returned to full strength, and the metallic voice stopped in midword.

"Canned message, a tape," said Batta Flor, uttering the strange foreign words with a wide grin. "Scared you, huh?"

Braldt did not reply, merely watched the Madrelli carefully as though suspecting that he might have some further mischief to perform.

"What do you mean, 'canned message, a tape'?" Keri asked as she lowered her sword, feeling somewhat foolish in light of Batta Flor's nonchalant attitude.

"Of course, no way you could know," Batta Flor said

229

more to himself than to his companions. "It's a message that was prepared in anticipation of an attack and set to go off under certain circumstances."

"What circumstances?" Keri demanded suspiciously, wondering if Batta Flor could be making it all up. "How can a message be made in advance and where is the speaker?"

"You don't understand," Batta Flor said with a patient smile that did nothing to make Keri feel better. "There is no speaker, the message is played by a machine." He held his hand up quickly as Keri opened her mouth. "Wait, just wait and I will show you machines. They are things made by the masters and the hard ones to carry out the masters' orders in their absence. They do work that Madrelli and Duroni would otherwise have to do themselves. Please wait and I will show you. You have already met one such machine, the lifter."

Braldt and Keri exchanged a quick glance before Braldt nodded curtly to Batta Flor. The lifter had not been a pleasant experience. Braldt had faced many enemies, many dangers in his life. He knew how to fight off savage animals, how to defend himself against the slavers and members of the more primitive, violent tribes, and could even deal with such creatures as shadows and the monster of the lake. But there was something frightening about spaces that moved and voices that spoke without benefit of bodies. And machines that were not Duroni or Madrelli but something that had never enjoyed life. How did one deal with such things?

"The tape was probably triggered by our destruction of the control chamber," mused Batta Flor, combing his cheek fur with his long, slender fingers. "It's probably been playing over and over ever since. It's a good sign really. It means that some things are still operational. The lights are still on here and the ventilators are still working. Maybe there is a way to divert the water and get into the chamber after all."

Just then, Beast began to run back and forth in an agitated manner and throwing back his head he let loose a loud howl that reverberated within the narrow walls of the corridor until their ears rang with the eerie sound.

Braldt reached out to Beast intending to wrap his hand around the pup's muzzle but before he could touch it, the entire corridor seemed to shiver and the walls and floor and ceiling lurched sharply sideways, throwing all of them to the ground where they lay, stunned. The lights faded, returned briefly, and then died, and with them died the faint attendant hum that had been felt rather than heard.

Keri cried out and Beast began to whimper. Braldt had smacked his head hard against the wall with the first movement and the darkness spun around him, lighted by numerous bursts of color behind his eyes. Just as the dizziness receded, the floor seemed to heave upward as though a giant fist had punched the ground from below. The corridor swayed, rocked by a series of fierce jolts, and Braldt could hear the clang of metal and falling objects raining down around them. Batta Flor called out once loudly and then was still.

A deep growling noise began as though the earth itself were in pain. This was followed by a loud rumbling, so loud that Braldt pressed his hands against his ears to shut out the terrible noise. Then came a screeching, tearing sound, coupled with the thunderous growl, even louder than before. The corridor jerked violently from side to side and never had Braldt been more aware of the great mass of mountain resting above his head. He wondered if it would all come crushing down upon them.

Braldt tried to get to his feet and the floor heaved once more and then buckled, dropping several feet, causing Braldt to fall to his knees heavily. His sword fell from his hand and he cursed, hearing it dance away from him across the still-shuddering floor.

Then it stopped as suddenly as it had begun. Keri was crying softly somewhere to the right and Beast was whimpering beside him. Braldt climbed to his feet hesitantly, wondering if it would begin again. Reaching out with his hands, he found that the wall tilted inward at an awkward angle. He began to move forward slowly on shuffling feet, following the sound of Keri's crying, and banged his head a second time against a dangling section of the ceiling. Beast pressed tightly against his legs as though fearing to be separated.

Coils of rope made of the smooth, slick stuff that was not metal looped down from the open ceiling like the tentacles of the monster of the lake. Braldt became entangled in them, and fought down the panic that enveloped him, pushing his way free. He found that his upper body was coated with a slippery fluid that dripped from the severed ends of the coils.

He reached Keri and put his arms around her. Then, almost as though it had delayed until he found her, Braldt was all but overwhelmed by a dizzy sickness that whirled around his head and rose up, filling his throat with the bitter taste of bile. He sank to the floor, his legs unable to support the weight of his body.

Keri could not seem to stop crying, the sobs shaking her slender frame. As much as he wanted to comfort her, Braldt could not raise his head. It felt as though there were a heavy weight resting on the back of his skull and his ears were ringing. It was all that he could do to pat Keri on the shoulder. Keri leaned against him, her tears slowly trailing off into a hiccuping silence. After a while Braldt's dizziness began to pass, although the coppery taste of bile was still strong and his stomach roiled uneasily.

Braldt whispered Beast's name, placing his hand atop the pup's head. The frightened whimpering turned to glad barks as the pup burrowed his cold, damp nose under Braldt's arm, burying his head in his armpit while attempting to climb into Braldt's lap, which he had never done, not even when he was a round-bellied infant.

Batta Flor called to them and his voice echoed strangely. Braldt did not reply for the least effort brought back the awful sickness. Batta Flor called out again and as he did so the lights flickered and came back on with a subdued hum, startling them and driving back the oppressive darkness. Keri cried out with joy and Beast withdrew his head for a quick look, his eyes huge and full of fear. Braldt had never been so glad to see anything as he was to see the return of light, and he uttered a silent prayer of thanks.

The lights were dim, glimmering here and there in the ruins of the corridor like stars in a cloudy sky, but their presence, no matter how faint, gave them the courage to continue. Batta Flor called out once more and this time Braldt croaked out a reply. Keri pulled herself up on a ceiling panel that had fallen free. Another handspan and it would have fallen upon her, crushing her beneath its weight or cutting into her flesh with its sharp edges. Braldt helped her rise and felt the weakness in his knees and the unsteadiness in his legs and wondered if he had injured himself somehow.

"I feel awful," Keri said as she pressed her palms against her forehead. Turning to one side, she vomited and then sagged against the wall, crying softly.

Braldt could do nothing to comfort her but pat her gently on the shoulder. Beast whined in distress and butted her leg with his head. "I think it is a reaction to whatever it was that happened here. We are unharmed, but our bodies are distressed. I believe that it will pass in time."

"I hope that you are right," Keri said as she rinsed her mouth with water and wiped it on the hem of her shirt. "My legs feel as shaky as those of an infant. What happened here, Braldt? I thought we were going to die."

Braldt cupped his hand under her elbow and together they began to pick their way through the debris that littered the corridor. Whole panels had fallen from the ceiling and walls, exposing the inner workings that lay behind them. Here and there, sparks were fizzing at the ends of the brightly colored coils. Braldt was careful to avoid them. Fluid dripped and oozed from other coils, clear and clean as water, and amber and oily as the substance that still clung to Braldt's skin. The sound of hissing could be heard in the distance and Braldt worried that poisonous gas was being released into the corridor. And still there was no sign of Batta Flor. Nor did he answer when his name was called.

"The earth moved," Braldt said in answer to Keri's

question. "I do not know how or why. I only hope that it does not do so again."

"Oh, Braldt, perhaps the gods are angry with us," Keri said earnestly. "I know what the Madrelli said and maybe they're right about these masters and the hard ones. But could they not be wrong about the gods? How could Mother Moon not be real? Braldt, we can see her every night. She has watched over us all of our lives. What are we to worship if not Mother Moon? How can we be all alone with nothing to believe in but ourselves? Does that not frighten you? Maybe the gods have moved the earth to punish us for ceasing to have faith in them. I think it must be so." Her voice sank to a whisper.

She looked so frightened, so vulnerable, that Braldt folded her in his arms and hugged her gently, stroking her hair to calm her trembling. Her body felt good against him. She fitted herself to him like a glove and he felt his body stir in a way that was not proper with one's own sister. He started to pull away and Keri clung to him even tighter. His arms tightened around her without conscious thought and she looked up at him, her eyes large and luminous in the dim light and her lips parted. He bent down, perhaps to hear what she was going to say, but there were no words. Her lips, softer than the down of fledglings, pressed gently against his own and he felt himself drawn down in a dizzy spiral, impossible to stop even had he wanted to do so. When they parted, Braldt felt as though he had forgotten to breathe and took in great gulps of air to clear his spinning head. How could he have done such a thing! Keri was his sister!

"I'm not your little sister," Keri whispered as though able to read his thoughts. "Oh, Braldt, I've loved you forever, don't you know that? And I'm not your sister. We share no common blood and you know that is true. We are free to pledge our joining. Please say that you love me too."

"I am a warrior," Braldt said huskily.

"You are a man and I am a woman," Keri said angrily. "That comes before being a warrior. There is no rule other than stupid male pride that says that warriors cannot join!

Surely you are not so stupid! And do not tell me that you do not care for me for I will not believe you. I will not let it be so, I have loved you too long!''

Braldt could not understand the logic in that argument, but strangely he felt no desire to argue with Keri or deny his feelings. In truth, what he wanted to do more than anything was to kiss her again, to feel her soft lips and body pressed against his. It was far more pleasant than arguing. Keri began to speak again, her hands bunched into angry fists, and Braldt grabbed her by the arms and kissed her hard, stifling her words with his lips. It felt amazingly good. What a superb way to stop her from talking, Braldt thought as her body became pliant and she slowly folded herself around him again.

They did not speak for a time and Braldt's mind whirled as it had when the ground shook and he felt as though he were going through some sort of personal cataclysm. Keri was right, they shared no common blood. But they had been raised as brother and sister. What would Auslic think or Jos and Otius, not to mention Carn. And what of his warrior vows? It was not unheard of for a warrior to join, but it was most unusual and frowned upon by the priests. But what of the priests? If Batta Flor was correct . . . Batta Flor! Braldt wrenched himself free from Keri and held her at arm's length breathing deeply.

"Keri, we've got to find Batta Flor. Something must be wrong, he's not here and he has not spoken in some time. Come! This has waited our whole life, it can wait a little while longer."

Keri looked up at him and knew that he was right. Batta Flor! How could they have forgotten him? She also saw the look in Braldt's eyes, a look that had never been there before. It was as though he were seeing her for the very first time and she knew that never would he look on her as a sister again. She picked up her sword and nodded toward the corridor. "Let us hurry," she said with shining eyes, "one must be there for one's friends."

They found Batta Flor crumpled beneath a large section of wall that had fallen, striking him on the side of his head.

There was a large discolored lump of bruised flesh rising just above his left ear and dark blood streamed from the wound, puddling beneath his head. The panel lay across his body, pinning him to the ground, but of more concern than the panel or the head wound was the fact that the panel had all but destroyed Batta Flor's ear.

The delicate shell had nearly been ripped from his skull and was hanging by mere threads of skin. The outer labyrinth—which contained the crystal tubes that controlled the Madrelli's sense of balance and, even more importantly, his sense of pain—had been crushed. A thin, clear fluid leaking from the fragmented crystals mixed with the thicker, heavier blood and dripped upon the ground.

Batta Flor's breathing was hoarse and ragged and rasped in his throat. His eyelids fluttered and nothing but the whites of his eyes could be seen. His chest rose and fell in an irregular pattern, and even as they strove to lift the panel from his chest, he gasped sharply as though inhaling, but he did not breathe out and then he simply ceased to breathe at all.

Braldt and Keri exchanged a brief, horrified glance and then Braldt fell upon Batta Flor, pushing up and down on his chest. Keri threw herself down next to Batta Flor and breathed into his mouth as one would do to an infant. There was no movement for a long moment and then they were rewarded by a quick heave of Batta Flor's immense chest. Another followed and another and then he was breathing almost regularly and whimpering softly.

Working together, they managed to shove the panel off of Batta Flor's body. It was large and ungainly more than it was heavy. Batta Flor could have moved it easily with a casual flick of his fingers under normal circumstances.

"We have to fix this ear somehow," Braldt whispered. "How can we do that? We could bind it to his head, but the crystals are shattered beyond repair."

"I do not know what to do. There is so much blood. Braldt, do you think he'll die?" Keri said in a troubled tone.

"Not if I can help it," Braldt replied grimly. He turned to his pack and rummaged in it, searching out the tubes and horns of healing unguents; fortunately, they were in his pack and not in Carn's. Braldt cleaned the terrible gaping wound and the torn edges of the ear itself with a stinging antiseptic that caused Batta Flor to gasp even in the depths of his restless sleep. Braldt could only hope that he would not waken and worked swiftly in the event that he did.

He chose a thick, gummy paste that contained many healing properties as well as a substance that reduced bleeding. It was not used as often as some of the other medicines for it was sticky and awkward to work with. In this instance it was perfect. Braldt spread an ample amount of the gooey mess on Batta Flor's torn skull and then carefully and gently pressed the ragged edges of the all-but-severed ear into the gummy stuff. Batta Flor moaned and then whimpered, a thin, childlike noise that hurt far more than any other sound he might have made.

"Will he be all right?" Keri asked, staring at the huge, unmoving form.

"I cannot say," Braldt replied helplessly. "There is nothing we can do now, except keep him warm and pray."

"Pray?" said Keri. "Yes, we will pray, and if there is a god, his or ours or any other in that greater world he speaks of, he will know that this is one who deserves to live."

25

Carn wandered through the dark tunnels without any knowledge of where they were taking him. Not that it mattered. He had no alternative but to continue on or lay down and die. The choice was clear. At times he crawled and clawed his way up steep slopes with the walls closing in on him on all sides. At other times, he all but tumbled down equally steep slopes doing further damage to his ravaged body. He lost his pack on one of those falls and, despite a desperate search, was unable to find it.

After a time, the last torch cube burned itself out. He was on his own, forced to find his way through the labyrinth of tunnels by touch alone. He could easily have tumbled into one of the many deep cracks that fissured the ground, but he probed the way forward with a sliding, shuffling step that he hoped would detect such dangers before they found him.

Much to his surprise, he found that the darkness was comforting rather than oppressive or frightening, easier on his damaged eyes than the bright flames of the torch had been. Further, he discovered that many of the passages glowed with a soft luminosity that he could only guess was obliterated by the more powerful light of the torches. It was enough to help him find his way and was a comfort to him as well for he took it to be a sign that his gods had not abandoned him to wander alone in the darkness.

Hunger and thirst battled with pain but his physical body and its limitations were no longer of interest to Carn; it was merely an impediment, an irritating stumbling block to his goal, to that which he must achieve. The spirit would triumph over the physical in the end, but until then he would be forced to keep the shell that housed his spirit alive.

He abated his thirst by lapping water from places where it seeped from the walls. He stilled the demands of his growling belly by eating the pale blind salamanders that hid beneath rocks. He pinched the poisonous claws from the curled tails of stingers, crunched their hard bodies between his teeth, and devoured their sweet flesh. He even killed a small shadow, gripping it by the tail and bashing its head against a rock, but he could not penetrate the tough scaly skin and was forced to leave it behind.

He became a growling, snarling predator, capable of killing and consuming the killers much as they had sought to kill and consume him, in order that he might stay alive. Through it all, he never lost sight of his goal, to honor and protect Mother Moon against those who sought to discredit and disavow her; everything else paled before this objective.

After a while, it seemed that the tunnels began to drop, leading him deeper and deeper into the heart of the mountain. From time to time he passed deep crevasses and dark tunnels that released the hot stink of the fiery maelstrom, and he knew that despite the layers of rock that might separate them, the inferno was ever present, waiting. He had observed numerous dark openings all around the edges of the flaming pit and guessed that many of these tunnels would find their terminus there.

They drew him, those dark openings that carried the scent of Mother Moon's earthly lair, but he knew that he could not give himself up to her until he had found the others and told them of what he had learned. The revelation. He could picture their joy, envision their gladness at the news that their god was not dead as the lying karks had said.

Once, he thought he heard their voices echoing through the maze of tunnels. He had called our their names with the odd croaking voice that sounded strange even to his ears, but they did not reply. He ran, crying for them to stop, to wait, telling them that he was alive and had not perished.

But there was no answer other than the echoes of his own voice.

He had fallen then, tripping over a stone, and lay there, weeping. Only then did a snippet of reason return to his fevered brain and he realized with a rush of fear how very much he wanted to find the others, how very much he wanted not to be alone inside this dark and frightening mountain. But there was no one to hear his cries, and after a while he fell asleep, curled into a ball on the hard ground.

■

Consciousness returned slowly and he lay there, too exhausted to rise. For a time he thought about giving up, remaining there, allowing the shadows and stingers to find him and fight over his tormented flesh. It would be easier than going on. But then, even as he contemplated such an action, he felt the ground grow hot beneath him, searing hot, all in a single instant as though punishment for his traitorous thought. He sat up quickly, but before he could rise, the ground flung itself upward, howling him head over heels backward, slamming him into the wall. His head was filled with pain and it took a minute for him to realize that the deep, thunderous growl was not coming from inside his head but emanating from the earth itself! Mother Moon was speaking to him! Commanding him to rise, to continue on, to serve her greatest glory!

Carn staggered on, unmindful of the shaking earth, of the rocks falling all around him, some of which struck him, drawing blood. All that he could think of was that his god had revealed herself to him, answering his flagging spirit with words of her own. Carn was filled with terror at those words and filled with awe as well. How had he dared to consider death; was that not a form of disbelief? He knew now that he would continue on until he had succeeded or until he died; nothing else would stop him.

As though appeased by his new resolve, the earth stilled and then, echoing through the darkness, he heard the sound of voices; Batta Flor, the unbeliever, answered in turn by Braldt and Keri. He had found them. Turning toward the sound of their voices, he pressed close to the wall and nearly fell through a cracked section of rock. He staggered forward off balance, pushing through the wall itself that collapsed upon him, raining down with brutal force.

He was propelled forward by the outward thrust of the falling rock and to his surprise he discovered that he had broken through into another corridor, this one smooth and lined with a material that was unknown to him and dimly lit by lights similar to priest fire. Carn blinked, holding a hand before his eyes to shield them from the unaccustomed glare, and then he heard Braldt's and Keri's voices somewhere in the distance and the faint whimpers of the lupebeast. He had found them at last.

26

Batta Flor had regained consciousness, and lay staring at them without emotion. He did not speak. Keri and Braldt glanced at each other in dismay. "Can you hear me? Are you in much pain?" Braldt asked gently.

"No pain," said Batta Flor.

"Can you move?" Keri asked.

"Don't know."

"Here, take my hand." Braldt extended his hand for Batta Flor to grasp. Batta Flor merely stared into space as though he had not heard Braldt and made no effort to take his hand.

"What's the matter? Can you tell us what's wrong?" Keri laid a hand on his chest and leaned forward so that she could look into his yes. Batta Flor did not reply.

"Come on, you can't lie here forever, what if the earth shakes again. This is not a safe place to be; we need to be on our way." Still, Batta Flor made no answer to Braldt's comment and merely closed his eyes. After a while, his chest began to rise and fall with less agitation and his breathing fell into a smooth pattern. It was apparent to them both that the Madrelli had drifted into sleep.

"What do you think is the matter with him?" Keri asked as they leaned back against the wall, resigning themselves to the fact that they would not be going anywhere for the time being. There was no thought of moving him as they might have done with one of their own race, for the Madrelli was more than twice Braldt's weight and all of it solid muscle. He would move of his own volition or he would not move at all.

"I don't know," Braldt said thoughtfully as he opened

242

the pack and removed the last of the hard cheese rounds and a handful of dry biscuits, noting the fact that the Madrelli's supply of the sour red berries so necessary for his continued mental stability was growing dangerously short. "Perhaps he's merely disoriented by the pain; the shock to his system must have been significant. Remember that those crystals are their nerve center. A blow like that must have been a terrible overload for his body to handle. Rest is probably the best thing. All we can do now is let him sleep and hope that his body will heal itself."

"We can pray as well," Keri said firmly, her eyes glittering as though daring him to argue with her. He offered no argument, merely smiled down at her and touched her on the tip of her nose with his forefinger.

Keri smiled up at him and lay back against his chest, wrapping his arms around her waist, thinking how strange life was. Here they were buried deep within a mountain that threatened to fall down around their ears at any moment, surrounded by monsters and other horrors, and yet she was content. After all the years of futile yearnings, Braldt finally loved her or soon would if she had anything to say about it. It would have been nice if it had happened at home surrounded by nothing more threatening than the jealous looks of her friends, but Keri had waited long years for this moment and she was willing to take it wherever it came.

Braldt was still lost in the wonder of it all, the feel of her soft skin next to his, the clean scent of her hair as well as the subtle fragrance that was hers and hers alone. Had it always been like this? How could he have failed to notice for so many years? The thought was incomprehensible. His mind was filled with a whirlwind of thoughts as his arms tightened around her, holding her close. He would have to tell Auslic and then Jos and the rest of the tribe. And then the priests.

But that was another matter and Braldt's jaws clenched at the thought of them. How much of what Batta Flor and Uba Mintch had said was true? How much did the priests know about the hard ones and the masters and the myth that was their religion? How much of it was true? Braldt wished with all his heart that none of it were true, but he feared that it was.

For a time he had suspected some Madrelli scheme, some plan to defeat them from the inside by the destruction of their beliefs, but the more time he had spent with the old Madrelli and Sytha Trubal had all but convinced him that they were telling the truth, at least so far as they understood it. Batta Flor's courage and stalwart nobility had further convinced him, for Braldt knew in his heart that one such as Batta Flor would be incapable of deception or trickery. Batta Flor had behaved with honor and saved their lives on several occasions. They would remain here by his side for as long as it took for him to recover. He was their friend and the Duroni knew the meaning of honor too.

But what to do with the time? Braldt thought about scouting ahead, seeing if he could discover where the corridor led, maybe there was something important lying just around the corner. But then Keri turned in his arms and raised her face to his and all thought of leaving vanished from his mind. The corridor had been there waiting for a long time. He could see no harm in letting it wait just a little bit longer.

▪

As they slept beside Batta Flor, wrapped in each other's embrace, the tremors, which had never ceased completely, increased in strength and frequency. Beast, who had wedged himself firmly between them and refused to be ousted, wakened them with a litany of terrified whimpers as he tried to crawl farther under their bodies.

Braldt opened his eyes with a rude curse and was startled to find himself looking directly into Batta Flor's eyes. The Madrelli had regained consciousness. "How are you? How do you feel? Are you hurting?"

Braldt was concerned for all their sakes for he was worried about the constant movement of the earth. He was torn between the desire to fulfill his promise to Auslic and fear of the mountain. It seemed likely that the entire thing would soon collapse around them; Braldt knew without a doubt that they should be directing all their efforts at escape. They could do no good for anyone if they were dead.

"I am feeling nothing, no pain at all," Batta Flor said in a strange tone and his dark eyes appeared troubled. Braldt offered him a handful of the red berries, which the Madrelli scooped out of his palm and ate one by one with a distracted air.

"That's welcome news indeed, my friend! We did the best that we knew how. Do you think that it will heal correctly? How does it feel?"

"You don't understand," said Batta Flor, turning his gaze upon Braldt. "I feel nothing, nothing at all. No pain, no soreness, no aches. Nothing, nothing at all."

"How can that be!" Braldt exclaimed. "The ear was nearly separated from your head. The damage was significant. You must be feeling the shock of the wound. The medicine is good but not that good!"

"No, my friend, the medicine is not at fault. I'm sure you did your best and for that I thank you. It is something quite different. You might just as well have removed the ear while I was unconscious, or let me bleed to death for all the good it will do me now."

"What do you mean?" Braldt asked fearfully, disturbed by the Madrelli's calm air of resignation.

Batta Flor sighed and then spoke. "I told you once before, my friend, that we Madrelli are different from you Duroni. Our pain centers are located in our ear crystals. The crystals are fragile things, capable of being damaged and broken with the slightest blow. We are taught to protect them from our earliest days. But they are more than receptors for pain, they control all sensation, our balance and the flow of our sensuality as well."

"I—I don't understand," stammered Braldt.

"It is quite simple, really. I feel no pain at all. I am no longer capable of feeling anything, the touch of Sytha Trubal's lips upon my own, the little one's fingers grasping mine, or a sword thrust to the heart. They will all feel one and the same to me, nothing. Nor will I be able to sire children of my own. I am worthless to Sytha Trubal, to the tribe, to myself. I would be better off dead.''

"But you have two ears and the other ear is undamaged!" cried Braldt, seizing upon the only positive aspect he could think of, deeply shocked by the ramifications of his friend's injury.

"No, it doesn't work that way," relied Batta Flor, looking down at his fingers as though he had never seen them before. "It is a delicate balance of the fluids, an interchange between the two sets of crystals. If one is broken and the fluid lost, everything is lost."

"Surely they can be mended. Someone must know how!" cried Braldt. "I cannot believe that such a thing cannot be reversed!"

"Perhaps the masters know, since we are their creations. Probably they do. But since we have blocked their entry to our world the question is moot. Nor, should they somehow manage to reappear, do I envision them as falling over themselves in an effort to help me. After all, you forget that I was one of those responsible for the destruction of the chamber. No, there is nothing to be done. I am useless."

"Do you really think so?" asked Keri, startling both Braldt and Batta Flor for neither had realized that she was awake and listening to their conversation. She sat up and took one of Batta Flor's immense hands in her own.

"Do you think that if Braldt were injured, even as grievously as you have been hurt, that I would cease to love him, stop wanting him for my mate? Could my people do any better than take him for chief? The answer to all those questions is no. I would love him under any circumstances, no matter how badly he was injured. It is he I love, and not his looks or how many children he can sire. Nor could a better chief be found among all the Duroni.

"You put a cheaper price on your being than those who know and care for you," said Keri. "You also do Sytha Trubal and your people a grave injustice by making their choice for them and not doing them the honor of knowing that they would choose you above all others. Do you think that Sytha Trubal's love is so weak or so shallow that she could not love you in any state other than perfection? I am angry with you on her behalf! Shame!

"Braldt and I need you. Did we not follow you into this place? Have we not entrusted you with our lives? Furthermore, the life of our chief depends upon you and the future of this world as well. I'd say that was a fair amount of caring, my friend. Now, will you stop feeling sorry for yourself long enough to get us out of here? If you do not, then the entire mountain will probably collapse on top of us and far more than your ear and your feelings will be destroyed!"

Batta Flor looked at Keri with his mouth open, amazed at her sharp words, for Keri had always been the epitome of gentleness and tact. But her words, pointed as they were, had been right on target and Batta Flor was unable to stifle a rueful grin. He bowed his upper body toward Keri. "Well spoken, fair lady, you are right as always." He looked around him, seeming to notice the quaking mountain for the first time.

"It would seem that you are right about the mountain as well. It would be best to leave this place. I have hopes that this corridor will intersect with others that are better known to me and that we will be able to find a way out. Come, let us be on our way."

Braldt looked at Keri in amazement, astonished that she had been able to turn the Madrelli's fatalistic mood around so easily. Keri looked up at him and grinned as though she had read his thoughts. Slinging her pack over her shoulder, she stood there ready to leave, as though chiding them for moving so slowly.

Beast was more than anxious to be on his way and ran back and forth between them, dashing a short distance ahead and then returning, clearly unwilling to venture forth on his own. The ground continued its steady shaking, ceasing for a moment and then beginning anew. It was so constant that the infrequent lapses of inactivity and silence felt strange and unnatural.

As they continued it became apparent that they were entering an area that had been more severely affected by the movement of the mountain. Destruction was apparent on all sides. Panels had fallen from the walls and the ceiling and even the floor was dislodged in places. Footing was treacherous, the ground slick with oily viscous fluids dripping from the multitude of broken coils. Steam and noxious gases spewed into the air in numerous locations and Beast suffered a scorched back and singed tail when he did not heed their directions and rushed headlong through a dangerous stretch of corridor. The lights had been extinguished in many places and they were forced to depend on their torches, which burned fitfully in the bad air and added unwelcome clouds of noxious black smoke to the air.

They picked their way through the debris noting the strange glyphs inscribed on plaques where corridors intersected. Batta Flor studied them carefully and made his choices. It appeared that they were descending farther, rather than rising, a fact that did not reassure Braldt, but he held his silence for it would serve no purpose to express his doubts. Surely the Madrelli knew what he was doing.

"Is it my imagination or is it getting hot?" Keri asked as she set her pack down and wiped her face with the end of her skirt. "It's getting harder to breathe too."

"It is not your imagination." Batta Flor swung his own pack down from his shoulder and settled himself on a rock. The black skin that framed his features was dotted with beads of perspiration that he brushed away with the fur of his forearm. His ear jutted out at an unnatural angle, giving him a rakish air. It was as though a child had molded his head of clay and done it poorly.

Braldt wrenched his thoughts away from the Madrelli's ear and addressed the matter at hand. "Have you noticed the odd glow between the broken partitions? And the ground feels hot as well. I do not know what is the cause, but I do not like it. Are you certain that we are going in the right direction? Where is it that we are going? Do you recognize any of the glyphs?"

"Yes. I have noticed the heat and the glow as well," Batta Flor replied. "And yes, I think I know where we are. It is a section of corridors that I have never traveled before.

I do not know anyone who has. These are old corridors, driven by my ancestors, when the masters first came to this place. I did not know that they still existed or were still maintained. They serve no purpose but to get from one level to another. If I am reading the glyphs correctly, I believe that they will lead us to the level of the chamber that is the only exit I know other than the way by which we entered.''

"But how can we do that?" Keri asked in dismay. "That level is flooded. How will that do us any good? What about the entry to the launching pad? I thought we were going to try to reach that chamber?" For the first time since losing Carn, distress was clearly evident in her voice.

"The launching pad and the control chamber are side by side on the same level," Batta Flor explained in a calm tone, holding Keri's hand in his great paw and stroking it gently to calm her. "I do not know if the entire level is flooded. I only know what happened inside the chamber after the river broke through. We will have to see. It is our only hope unless you wish to return the way we came."

The mountain began to shake violently, rumbling and growling beneath their feet as though it were alive. The entire corridor shook spasmodically from side to side, shedding panels loose with the same ease that dogs shook water from their pelts. Keri shivered and shook her head. "No, I could not do it, could not go back the way we came. I don't want to see those things again. The monster . . . the place where Carn . . ." Her voice trembled and faded away.

"Good." Batta Flor smiled grimly. "Our only hope is to go forward. Come, we are not advancing ourselves by sitting here."

But before they could go any farther, it was necessary to fashion another pair of leather wraps for Beast's feet. He had long ago chewed the others free, and the floor of the chamber was too hot for him to go on without some form of protection.

Batta Flor led them to the next intersection of corridors and turned right once again. No sooner had he done so than the sound of running water was clearly heard. This new corridor was a ramp that led upward at a steep angle. The sound of the flow did not decrease as they climbed but grew steadily louder until it was impossible to be heard unless they shouted. Keri and Beast were clearly frightened and even Braldt had a difficult time keeping his fears in check. It was all too easy to envision the race of water pouring past them at a dizzying rate of speed, held back by only thin walls of rock and broken metal panels. Many of the walls glistened with water, almost appeared to be sweating. It was not in the least bit reassuring.

And then, suddenly, Batta Flor came to an abrupt halt. He raised his hand and pointed. They followed the direction of his finger and saw, glowing in the distance of the darkened corridor, a bright red light, shining at them like the single wicked eye of a predator gleaming from the depths of its dark lair. There was an unmistakable feeling of menace in the air.

Keri cried out and clutched Braldt's arm. He held her to him in a tight embrace and together they stared at the ominous red glow. Beast sat on Braldt's feet and whined, then rose up on his hind legs and scratched at Braldt's arm. He too wanted to be held. Braldt stroked the pup's head, knowing that his fear was justified. He turned to Batta Flor for an explanation. The space beside him was empty. Braldt looked behind him, wondering, but the Madrelli was not there, either. Braldt held his torch high and looked in all directions. But nowhere did he see anyone or anything. Hard as it was to believe, Batta Flor had disappeared.

■

Carn was desperate. He could hear Keri's and Braldt's voices and sometimes he even caught sight of them in the distance, but try as he might, he could not catch up with them. His voice, a rough raspy croak, would not carry more than a few yards. What if they disappeared and left him all alone! The thought lent speed to his feet and he hurried through the dark corridors, almost weeping with desperation. Then his vision blurred with tears of frustration and he slammed into a fallen panel. Reeling with pain, he staggered from one side of the corridor to the other. Blood coursed down his face and streamed into his eyes. He cursed and cried aloud, blinking his eyes and trying to stumble on, but the pain was too great and he sank to his knees and wept.

By the time the flow of blood was stemmed and his vision cleared, they were gone. He had known that it would be so and accepted it with a calm resignation, chiding himself. How had he dared to doubt? How could he have been so weak as to think that the gods would abandon him? Had they not given him the greatest gift of all? There must be a reason for this, even if he could not understand it. His faith had carried him through greater trials than this; he had only to place his trust in Mother Moon and she would show him the way.

He settled himself at the base of the fallen panel and waited calmly, absolutely certain now that his god would not desert him. After a while, he began to hear the murmur of voices. They were faint, distant, but they were unmistakably the sounds of his vanished companions. He had to listen closely to hear them above the constant mutter of the mountain, but they were there to be heard. He began to follow the thread of their voices, cautiously avoiding the many pitfalls that littered the broken corridor, certain now that he would find them.

■

There was a sick feeling in the pit of Braldt's stomach. Had the Madrelli betrayed them after all? It had always been a possibility, but after all they had gone through together, it was hard to believe. Still, there was no doubting the fact that he was gone. Keri had turned to one side and was now picking at what appeared to be a solid wall. She gave a small cry of amazement and called to Braldt. Just then, she took a step backward and Batta Flor rose up before her, appearing magically out of nowhere.

Braldt moved forward, angry words on his lips, but before he could speak, Batta Flor grabbed him by the wrist and began dragging him toward the narrow opening. "I've found it, found what we were looking for. Hurry, there may still be a chance!''

''Where were you and why did you slip away from us like that?'' Braldt said angrily, pulling free of Batta Flor's grasp, realizing then how completely they depended on him and how utterly lost they would be without him.

Batta Flor turned toward him with shining eyes, his excitement obvious. Seeing Braldt's glowering face, he faltered and the joyful look vanished, replaced by the somber, guarded expression that was the norm.

''I was gone for but a moment,'' he replied stiffly. ''I saw the cracked edge of the door and slipped inside to see if my suspicions were correct.''

He fell silent then and Braldt could do nothing but ask the question. ''And what did you find?''

''It was as I hoped, a stairway, with glyphs that have some meaning to me. They will lead us to the level above the chamber.''

''What good will that do?'' Keri asked.

''Don't you see.'' Batta Flor turned to her, his eyes bright with barely suppressed enthusiasm. ''This is a serviceway! It will give us access to the floor above the flooded chamber as well as the heating and cooling and fresh air ducts in the ceilings. It is possible that we can find an entry to the chamber or some way of shutting off the flow of water!''

''Do you really think so?'' Braldt asked, berating himself for suspecting the Madrelli of foul play.

''Yes,'' said Batta Flor. ''There is no doubt that it will lead to the right levels. whether we can enter safely is another matter entirely. Nor will we know the answer until we see with our own eyes. Come, let us go now. Sooner begun, soonest done!''

It was good to see Batta Flor in such good spirits and for the moment, he seemed to have forgotten about his injury. Keri noticed that the ear had come unstuck from the medicinal adhesive and was twisted forward at a strange angle. She raised her hand to press it back in place, but Batta Flor stopped her before she could touch it.

"No," he said softly. "Leave it, it does not matter anymore. It is a useless thing like a broken twig hanging from a tree." To her horror, he reached up and ripped the ear from his skull, tearing away the strip of flesh and fur that formed the fragile connection, and threw the severed ear down. It lay on the floor between them like the corpse of a small animal, rather than a portion of his living body.

Braldt gasped sharply and Keri bit back a cry and looked up at Batta Flor with wondering eyes. His own small, dark eyes glittered feverishly in the smooth, dark skin that framed his face. The thick fur seemed to crowd inward, compressing his features, making him appear more animallike, and Keri realized that it was because of the loss of the ear.

The ears had served to make his features more natural, more like a Duroni than an animal. She closed her eyes briefly and tried to remind herself that this was Batta Flor, her friend, with whom she had shared heartbreak, sorrow, and her most private thoughts. He was no animal but a stalwart and loyal friend.

"Don't you see," he said softly, taking her hands in his own and speaking directly to her. "It doesn't matter anymore. None of it. There is nothing left for me, I have no future, I cannot return. It would have been better if I had died back there, instead of dying in bits and pieces. No, please," he said, laying his fingers on her lips as she tried to speak. "Listen to me, our lives, our cultures, are different. I know what I am saying. I know what is best for me and for Sytha Trubal and the tribe."

"But you are giving up without even giving her the chance to speak for herself!" Keri said impatiently. "It's not fair, don't you see that! You men are always doing stupid things, making these dumb noble decisions when it is we women who must live a lifetime with the consequences. I will not let you do whatever it is that you are planning! I won't! And I speak for Sytha Trubal as well! Don't you dare go and do something dumb!"

"How like her you are," said Batta Flor with a sad smile.

"I don't know what either of you is talking about," said Braldt. "But don't you think that we should do whatever it is that needs to be done? We don't really have the time to stand around talking; the tremors are coming closer and closer together. We would do well to be away from this place if it is possible."

"The serviceway may have exterior outlets," Batta Flor replied and Braldt could not help but notice that the fur on his shoulder and chest was already matted with fresh blood.

Beast had slipped through the narrow crack and was whining softly. His huge scooped ears twitched back and forth as though catching sound from all directions and his muzzle quivered as well. He lifted his front paws, treading nervously as if there were water on the floor, and looked to Braldt for reassurance. Braldt ruffled the thick fur on the nape of his neck, and disturbed at the air of indecision that seemed to be affecting his companions, he opened the narrow door and stepped inside.

It took a moment for his eyes to adjust for the staircase was even more dimly lit than the corridor had been. Below him and off at an angle, a single light shed a pale cone of luminescence on a square bit of flooring. Even farther below in the distance there were other pricks of light like tiny white stars in a night sky. He could see nothing else.

Batta Flor and Keri appeared beside him; leaving the door open behind them to allow in as much light as possible, the three of them moved silently forward. Batta Flor moved into the lead, which Braldt did not contest. The wall was on their left and a slender waist-high rail ran along the right-hand edge of the stairs, which were both steep and narrow. Batta Flor dropped to all fours and moved more easily than his Duroni companions.

They reached the first light without incident and stood there for a moment waiting for their eyes to adjust to the deeper darkness, hoping to discern something of their surroundings. There was another of the now-familiar plaques affixed to the wall and Batta Flor stood up on his hind legs to inspect it, his keen eyes capable of reading in the near darkness.

"Two levels to go," he said in a soft tone.

"Is there another door here? Should we look and see what is to be found?" asked Keri, peering over Batta Flor's shoulder.

Batta Flor shrugged. "No reason to do so, a waste of time. I think that these were excavated when the place was first built, when they were still searching for the rhodium, exploratory shafts that they paneled over for safety when they were done. I don't think any of them really go anywhere. We were lucky to stumble on them the way we did or we'd still be wandering around back at the lake. No, this is the way we want to go."

"Shouldn't we light some torches?" Keri asked, looking out at the almost total darkness.

"No again. We won't be able to carry torches with us in the ducts, they're too narrow and the metal would hold the heat and burn us. It's best to become adjusted to the darkness now."

"You seem so certain of what we will find," Braldt said, wondering if it could really be so.

"I am sure," said Batta Flor. "These glyphs are known to me. We are on the right path." Braldt might have spoken again, questioned the Madrelli, but Batta Flor stepped forward into the darkness and began descending the next set of stairs in a smooth, swinging glide. Soon, he was lost to their sight. Beast whined and trotted down the stairs followed almost immediately by Keri. Braldt hesitated for a moment and then he too followed their lead.

They did not stop at the next landing, pausing only long enough for Batta Flor to run his fingertips over the glyph panel and grunt enigmatically. They plunged onward, taking the final set of steps with growing excitement, so caught up in their own rising hopes that they failed to notice the light dim three levels above them as a dark figure slipped through the doorway and stood there for a moment listening to their voices before it vanished in the darkness.

Beast yipped with nervous agitation and danced up and

down on his hind legs, easily divining the mood of his companions. The small band hurried down the final few steps and then came to an abrupt halt. Before them was an expanse of dark water that shone bleakly in the dim light from above and lapped at the foot of the stairs. They looked at one another, their eyes filled with dismay, knowing, now that the hope had been stripped from them, how very much they had counted on this avenue of escape. Their eyes returned to the sight of the dark water, felt the tremors beneath their feet, and knew that there was nowhere left to go.

27

Keri sank down on the lowest step and rested her head on her arms, unwilling to let the others see her tears that she could not hide. She was tired and hungry and afraid. She was tired of the overwhelming darkness and her heart still ached with the loss of Carn. More than anything she wanted to be home, to feel her mother's arms around her. Still, she could not complain, for she had won Braldt and that was reason enough for all that she had endured. Although nothing, not even Braldt, could ever make up for the loss of her brother.

She was still sitting there with her head bowed, trying to compose herself, when Batta Flor moved past her and stepped into the water. "What are you doing, where are you going?"

"Going to see what there is to see, girl," Batta Flor replied with a flash of white teeth. "That is, unless you feel like swimming and want to stay here for a while."

"Oh, no!" Keri cried, leaping to her feet. "It's just, I saw this water and—and I figured . . ."

"Figured you'd best give up," Batta Flor finished for her. "Well, we can give up or we can keep going. The water's not so high that we can't get through it. Come on, now, let's be on our way! Soonest begun . . ."

"Soonest done!" Keri finished with a short laugh, taking his hand and rising to her feet, her courage returning in the face of Batta Flor's equanimity.

Beast hesitated on the bottom step, whining and treading nervously for he had learned to fear water after their experiences at the lake. Braldt cupped the pup's rear in his hands and shoved him off the step before he realized what was happening. The pup yipped sharply and struck out, beating the water to a frenzied froth before he realized that it scarcely came halfway up his legs. He calmed quickly then and paced the narrow landing, sniffing at the dark water.

Braldt listened at the door and, hearing nothing ominous, opened it slowly. There was a slight eddying as water from the other side of the door flowed through, surging as it met the water of the flooded stairwell. There was light inside this corridor, a strange sort of light, pale and diffused as it wavered forth from beneath the foot of water that covered it. But still, it was light. They entered the corridor gratefully, glad to be free of the clinging darkness. Keri had looked over the rail before entering and saw the lights of the landings below, still shimmering up out of the dark depths like multiple reflections of Mother Moon. It was an oddly unsettling sight.

This corridor was clearly of a different nature than the ones they had traveled before. The walls served merely as dividers for the many rooms that lay beyond, all of which opened onto the long hallway. They entered the first of these rooms with some trepidation, feeling like intruders, for the room was imbued with the presence of those who had worked and occupied the space before the incident. It seemed quite likely that they might return at any moment.

This feeling was reinforced by the many articles that were strewn about the room, obviously discarded by their owners in a moment of extreme haste. A technical manual with numerous illustrations of brightly colored coils lay tossed in a corner atop a desk. Several chairs were overturned, their backs awash with water. A multitude of tools, some of which Braldt could only guess at their uses, lay scattered on a workbench with ghostly detached metallic hands lying beside them.

And there in a corner of the room propped up against the wall like a bit of discarded furniture was a man made entirely of a smooth, black material. He had no features at all, only the barest hint of sculpturing to indicate where eyes and nose might be. The mouth was another story, it was represented by a smooth bar of the bright silver metal punctured in a regular pattern with hundreds of tiny holes. It was complete, manlike, shorter than Braldt but whole in every way other than the hand that had been removed and was awaiting repair on the bench. Affixed in the very center of the man-thing's chest was another silver fixture, this one round and dotted with holes. It was identical to the one that Beast had found back at the sandy inlet.

Keri and Braldt eased around the dark figure, studying the strange thing with interest as well as caution as though fearing that it might come to life at any moment. Beast did not approach but viewed it from a safe distance, growling loudly and showing his double rows of sharp teeth.

"What, what is it?" Keri asked Batta Flor who exhibited no interest in the thing and was rummaging in a smaller storage area at the far side of the room.

"Hmm? Oh, that's a hard one," he replied, forgetting for the moment that Keri and Braldt had never seen one before. "Can't hurt us, though; it's switched off."

"What do you mean, 'switched off'? Can it be switched on?"

"Sure, I guess," Batta Flor said, puzzlement in his voice. "But why would we want to do that? This is the enemy."

"As I understand it, they are not creatures of their own will but obey the masters, am I right?" Batta Flor nodded. "Well, could we not make it do our bidding? Could we not command it to go where we cannot go and do the things that would be dangerous to us?"

"I do not know if such a thing is possible," Batta Flor said slowly. "I have never thought of this before, but maybe it could be done. They are complex machines, these hard ones. I do not know if they would function in water, perhaps they would short out, but maybe their wires are adequately sealed and mayhaps even the relays. It is worth a try."

"Don't! What if the masters are just waiting for such

a thing! Could they not take control and turn it against us!'' Keri was looking at the hard one with fear and distrust.

"Not if we can sever the connection first," Batta Flor assured her, and moving to the hard one's back, he flicked open a panel that revealed a complex array of wires and coils, all brightly colored and having their terminus in numerous small silver boxes. Batta Flor studied them carefully and then reached in with a pair of slender, long-nosed pincers and severed all the wires that led to the largest of the silver boxes.

He removed the box, placing it on the workbench with distaste, and then returned to the panel and studied it even more carefully. After a time his fingers rose to a series of small, flat buttons, each bearing a single glyph. His long, nimble fingers danced over the buttons, tapping out a sequence that had no meaning for Keri and Braldt who could make no sense of the glyphs in any case. They looked at each other and shrugged, hoping that Batta Flor knew what he was doing.

Suddenly the dark figure moved! It raised its single hand and turned its head almost completely around and looked at Batta Flor, or would have done so had it had eyes. Beast began to bark shrilly and darted forward to slash at the thing's legs, his teeth skidding off the hard surface leaving not the slightest trace of a mark. Beast danced up and down furiously and would have returned for a second attack, had Braldt not seized him and grabbed his muzzle. Even then, Beast continued to growl.

"Traitors!" The hard one spoke aloud, a peculiar, metallic voice similar to the voice in the corridor that had warned of danger, except that there was an added tone, one of arrogance. "Return to your positions immediately and there will be fewer reprisals!"

"We do not take your orders anymore," Batta Flor said coldly. "You are ours to command, you will do our bidding now."

The hard one did not answer but bending at the waist drove his single functioning hand down through the water and into the floor. The fingers wrapped around the silver strip of metal that served as some sort of support and ripped it free all in a single instant before any of them had even guessed at its intent. Rising, the hard one slashed out at them and they barely avoided being cut by the sharp edges. Braldt drew his sword and sliced downward, catching the silver strip and halting its return.

Braldt had expected to break the hard one's grip, to knock the strip of metal out of its hand, but he had totally underestimated its strength, which was equal to, if not greater than, his own. It was unnatural. The strip of metal pressed upward against the force of the sword and slid sideways with a grating screech of metal on metal. The hard one recovered almost before Braldt realized what was happening and swung the gleaming strip of metal in a vicious curve that would have cut Braldt in half had it landed. He leaped aside, feeling the first twinges of real concern over the spread of the hard one's reactions.

Braldt danced backward, giving himself time to think as the hard one moved forward, his movements unhindered by the calf-deep water. Batta Flor and Keri moved as well, intending to come to his rescue, but he waved them back, knowing that Keri could in no way stand up to the thing. Batta Flor was unwilling to stand and watch however, and ignoring Braldt's warning, he picked up a heavy chair and swung it at the hard one. The chair shattered on impact, breaking into a number of small pieces, and the hard one turned toward the Madrelli, the strip of metal held before it like a sword.

Almost faster than the eye could follow, the hard one lunged forward, thrusting its metal rod before it in a classic sword thrust. But fast as it was, the Madrelli was faster and he leaned to one side avoiding the thrust and grabbing the hard one's wrist and arm attempting to force it down.

The arm began to rise, barely slowed by the Madrelli's weight, and Braldt could see that the point of the metal strip was aimed for the Madrelli's throat. He hurled himself on the hard one's back, wrapping his arms around its neck, trying to force it backward, but to no avail for the thing was endowed with unbelievable strength.

The hard one's head turned toward him, turning farther than a head should turn, and looked at him with sightless eyes. "You too will die, all of you will die for daring to defy the masters." Braldt could see that the point of the metal strip was now touching Batta Flor's throat. The hard one's hand had twisted in the Madrelli's grip and imprisoned it in an unbreakable hold. Batta Flor pulled against the implacable grasp and Braldt could tell by the fear in his eyes that he could not free himself. The metal rod pressed against the dark fur at Batta Flor's throat.

"Well, maybe we are going to die, but it's not going to be anytime soon," said Braldt, and reaching into the open panel in the hard one's back, he began ripping out wires and their terminus boxes, not bothering to be selective but pulling out anything that would move. Sparks flew and a buzzing staticy sound filled the air. The hard one jerked violently, staggered forward, and then toppled face forward into the water where it lay unmoving like a dead thing.

Batta Flor, his hand pressed against his throat, which leaked a small amount of blood, felt behind him and found a desktop where he collapsed, breathing hard. Braldt crouched at his side, his hand on the Madrelli's shoulder, feeling his own heart still slamming against his ribs, and realized for the very first time what formidable enemies and taskmasters the hard ones had been. Such strength! It was terrifying to be so completely outmatched. Only then did he begin to appreciate the courage of the fallen Arba Mintch and his companions. It was nothing less than a miracle that Batta Flor had lived to tell the tale.

"Sorry," gasped the Madrelli. "I guess that was a mistake, but I really thought that I could do it, separate the machine from the masters."

Braldt looked at the Madrelli with concern, wondering at the tone of despair in his voice. "Do not worry yourself. It was a good idea, no harm done."

"You don't understand," Batta Flor said, raising his

head and looking at Braldt with an anguished expression. "That voice . . . the hard ones cannot speak for themselves. I thought that I could do it, separate the two. But it spoke. I was wrong."

"You mean that was the voice of the masters?" Braldt asked with growing certainty.

Batta Flor nodded. "And now they know that we are here."

"But what can they do?" asked Keri. "They can't do anything. Nothing has changed. If they had been able to do something, they'd have done it long ago. So they know we're here. So what. Let them worry for a while, they can't do anything to hurt us!"

Keri's impassioned words brought a smile to Braldt's and Batta Flor's faces and the tension seemed to lift from their shoulders. "She's right," Batta Flor said somewhat sheepishly. "I apologize for my fear, but we have suffered so much for so long . . . I—I . . ."

"No need to apologize, I was scared senseless myself. Tough opponent. Amazing power. We're lucky it had but the one hand or things might have ended differently."

"I know that Keri is right, the masters cannot hurt us, but still I feel that time is running out. I think that we must hurry, my friends. We must do what we have come for if it is possible and leave as quickly as possible. There is a feeling of wrongness in the air, a feeling of danger that has been with me since we entered this level. Call me foolish if you will, but let us leave this place as soon as we are able."

Keri and Braldt offered no argument for they too had felt the hostile emanations and were grateful to Batta Flor for speaking of them. They wasted no time in leaving the workroom, avoiding the dark figure that lay facedown, unmoving, in the water.

Batta Flor stuffed a few objects into a sack before they left, and as they walked swiftly down the corridor, barely glancing at the room that opened on either side, he handed Keri and Braldt long, slender tubes, no thicker than their thumb. He showed them how to depress a button at the base and chuckled at their cries of amazement when a bright beam of light shot out the far end.

And then they were there, a flat panel, no more than three feet square, screwed into the side of the wall. Batta Flor took a tool from the bag, fitted the metal tip into the grooved slot, and turned it quickly. In no time at all, the panel had been removed and beyond it they could see a smaller space, a shining hollow metal square. And close, very close, was the sound of running water.

"Leave everything behind except the light wands," Batta Flor directed. "It will be a closer fit and there will be no room for excess baggage."

"But what about our weapons, surely we should take those!"

"No, my brother, there is no danger other than the water and swords cannot protect us against that. If we are successful at stopping the flow, then we will be able to enter the chamber and retrieve the medicine box. We will also be able to leave the mountain and journey home. We will have no need of weapons. If we fail, well, weapons will be of no use to us if we are dead. Leave them, leave everything and let us be on our way."

It felt very odd to shed the various packs, pouches, swords, belts, and oddments that they had carried with them for so long, but they could clearly see that Batta Flor was right, the space was very small. It was hard to believe that one so large as Batta Flor would be able to fit, but he crouched low before the opening and, entering elbows first, disappeared into the silvery cube.

Braldt went next, wanting Keri at the rear should disaster befall them, allowing her a chance to escape, although where she would escape to was a question he could not have answered. Braldt could hear Beast whining in the distance and knew that the pup would not want to enter the strange hole. Nor would he want to be left behind. A short time later, Braldt heard the scrape of Beast's claws on the metal floor and knew that the pup had followed.

The metal enclosure was small, smaller than Braldt had

anticipated; there was scarcely room for his shoulders and only by hunching them inward was he able to move forward. Movement was an awkward business, achieved by punching down with one's elbows and then pushing off against the metal; the rest of one's body was dragged behind.

It was hot in the metal enclosure and it moved constantly, although whether it was from their efforts or the movement of the mountain, Braldt could not have said. It seemed sturdy enough and that was all that really concerned him. They crawled on and on, seemingly for hours, pausing from time to time as Batta Flor came to junctions and made decisions as to which way they should go. In this they were forced to depend on him completely for it was his knowledge of the mountain stronghold that they were relying on.

The metal enclosure widened into a space roughly four feet by four feet with room for all of them to squeeze together. Batta Flor was grinning widely. "We have done it," he chuckled. "We are directly above the control chamber." He was forced to speak loudly to be heard over the noise of rushing water. The small chamber was swaying back and forth, buffeted by a constant force that was extremely unnerving.

"What are we going to do now?" Keri asked, looking around nervously and hugging Beast tightly.

"*We* are not going to do anything. You are going to stay here and wait for me. I am going over there and place this charge against the wall. I'm going to try and bring the wall down, seal off the water."

"Where will it go if you seal the chamber," Braldt asked. "Can it push out through its old channel?"

"I don't think so," answered Batta Flor. "We did a good job of bringing the mountain down, but don't forget that there are many levels beneath this one. One level down is the launching pad with corridors hewn out of the bedrock. I think the water will channel itself there although where it will exit I cannot say. Wherever it goes, it will give us the time we need to retrieve the box and make our way out to safety. Now, stay here, I'll be back shortly."

However, Batta Flor's directive were issued too soon, for the duct that he had intended to follow was narrower than the one they had entered and no matter how hard he squirmed, it was impossible to fit his bulk through the small channel.

"Give it to me," said Braldt, reaching out his hand for the device that Batta Flor held so gingerly, "I will go."

"You cannot, you do not know what has to be done."

"Then explain it to me quickly, for it seems that I am our only hope." Batta Flor looked at Braldt and it was easy to read the indecision in his eyes. Just then a heavy tremor jolted the metal enclosure, one that shook the entire system, setting it to rattling all up and down its length. Somewhere in the distance, they could hear a great clanging as a section detached and fell, striking hard and bouncing again and again until they could hear it no longer. Wind whipped through the duct, hot and stinking of searing heat, burning their faces and stinging their nostrils.

Batta Flor handed Braldt the object, placing it gently in the center of his palm. "This is commandite. You must place it carefully, press it up against the wall directly above the flood so that it will bring the mass of rock down, shutting off the flow. Here, I will draw it out for you." He bent forward, crouching over the metal floor and picking up his dagger, and traced out the shape of the room that lay below them. It was six-sided. The water had entered on the right and punched a hole directly opposite. Batta Flor traced out the path of the metal duct, noting that it passed directly above the entry point of the water.

"You must break through the bottom of the duct and through the ceiling panels as well. This will help you in that task." He handed Braldt the slender tool he had used to open the duct panel in the hallway.

"How close to the ceiling is the water?" Keri asked, her face pale with fear.

"I have no way of knowing," replied Batta Flor. "From the sounds of it, I would say that it is quite close."

"Will the explosion not endanger us? If the water is so close, will the force of the blast not destroy the ducts or at the very least deafen us?" Braldt asked, fearful of the many flaws in the plan.

"It is quite possible that all of those things will happen," Batta Flor agreed. "But we will have to take that chance. We have always known that there were serious dangers involved. It is my hope that the concussion, the force of the explosion, will follow the outward thrust of the detonation, not implode inward." He did not share with them his fears that the explosion, blocked on either side by masses of water, would be driven upward, which would almost certainly mean their death. "You must set the device and then return to us as quickly as possible. You cannot remain, for you could not hope to live through the detonation at so close a distance."

"Have no worries on that score," said Braldt, "I too would like to grow old with my grandchildren. Now, show me what it is that I must do, how the device is activated." Batta Flor obliged, drawing his instructions on the soft metal and soon after, with only a single soft kiss as farewell, Braldt set off down the narrow metal channel.

Braldt soon began to suspect that the ceiling had been ripped away beneath him for the sound of rushing water was clearly audible, echoing loudly in the metal chamber. Furthermore, the duct was wracked by constant spasms that seemed to stress it to its limits. There was a steady metallic scream, thin and shrill, of metal pushed far beyond its normal limits. Braldt wondered if it would hold, for it seemed that the added weight of his body had introduced the final insult. He could feel the duct sagging beneath him and he moved as swiftly as possible, knowing that if the metal gave way, plunging him into the torrent that raged beneath him, he could not hope to survive, and with him would die the hopes and the future of the Duroni and the fate of the Madrelli.

He had counted the sections as Batta Flor had instructed him to do and came to a halt at the spot the Madrelli indicated would place him directly over the breached wall. If he had had any doubts, they were gone now for he could clearly hear the hissing roar of the water as it forced its way through the gap below him. The duct was vibrating wildly, and a high-pitched hum emanated from its fastenings, which did not appear to be holding very fast at all. Braldt could see spaces between the junctures as they shook on a continuous basis. It was not the least bit reassuring.

Braldt did not feel good about removing an entire panel. The entire structure was too weak as it was; if he removed a panel, it would weaken it even further. He was glad now that he had not given up his dagger. Pulling it free of his belt, he marked out a small square with the aid of the light beam and punched a small hole through the thin metal. Immediately he was wetted down by a spray of water. Hot water. It was as he had thought, the ceiling had been ripped from its moorings.

He continued working, sawing away at the soft metal, forcing the sharp edges down, away from the opening. More and more of the scene below was exposed and it was a terrifying picture, dark water rushing, no, hurtling past at a dizzying speed that he had never before seen in nature. It was an awesome as well as a stupefying vision, one that numbed his senses as eyes and brain tried to encompass what it was that he was seeing. But there was little time to be wasted on watching the water, it would serve no purpose other than to frighten him and that was something he didn't need.

He finished cutting out the square of metal and watched as it fell the several feet that separated him from the maelstrom and was instantly whipped away, sucked beneath the water and vanished from sight the instant it touched down. He swallowed a shiver of fear that inched up his spine and pressed himself flat against the opening before he could talk himself out of it, supporting himself with his hands braced against the sides. He lowered his head and looked not at the water but at the wall that was exactly where Batta Flor had said that it would be, no more than an arm's length away.

The water rushed through the opening that was beneath the surface and then thrust itself upward, impelled forward by the press of the water behind it. Occasional splashes struck the wall that was streaming with moisture and Braldt could only wonder if water would affect the performance of the explosive device. Such a thing was entirely beyond his comprehension and he had only Batta Flor's word that it would even work. It had been found in the workroom. Braldt wondered what they would have done had the device not been there. But such worries served no purpose and Braldt put them out of his head, concentrating on placing the device and activating it as per Batta Flor's instructions.

He leaned forward with the object in his hand, holding on as best he could with his free hand as well as bracing his legs against the sides of the duct. It was a greater distance than he had anticipated and he found that while he could touch the wall, he could not bring his weight to bear to press it into the wall. He would need to get closer. He inched himself forward, placing far more of his body than he would have liked over the gaping hole, but it could not be helped.

He stretched out his arm, reaching, reaching for the wall, and then, just as he touched it, the entire duct was struck by a powerful tremor that wrenched the metal chamber hard to one side, throwing Braldt off balance. He clung to the metal walls, feeling the thing shake and tremble beneath him like a living creature in torment. The shaking did not cease but went on and on, and Braldt knew with a sense of impending doom that whatever was wrong with the mountain was fast approaching crisis level. If this deed was to be done, it had to be done immediately.

Throwing caution to the wind, Braldt braced his thighs against the rough opening, ignoring the pain as the sharp edges cut into his flesh. He leaned his upper body forward parallel to the dizzying flux of water rushing just inches beneath his body and planted the device against the stone wall, pressing it firmly into place, feeling the sucking grip as it adhered to the damp stone, and knew that it would not pull loose. There was but one final thing to do; he pressed his thumb down atop the device and depressed a button that Batta Flor had already programmed to explode, giving Braldt only enough time for the return journey.

Then, disaster struck, just as he was pulling back, his upper body supported by nothing but his own strength, a crest of water rose up out of the darker mass and slapped him down as casually as he might have swatted at an annoying insect.

Braldt tried to save himself; he grabbed for the rough opening and missed. He dug in desperately, clinging to the smooth metal with his feet, but the water seized him then, slamming into him with a force that drove the breath out of his lungs. He reached for the open duct as the current grabbed him, but it vanished from sight as he was dragged beneath the surface of the water and sucked into the main force of the current. He had barely had time for a breath before he went under, and he tried to keep his wits about him as he was tumbled head over heels by the fierce flow. He would not have enough air to last until the explosion, and even though he was not versed in such things, he could imagine what would happen to him if he were in the water when the device went off.

Suddenly he was struck a heavy, glancing blow on the top of his shoulder, and looking up into the dark water, he felt rather than saw a large object falling past him, banging him on the knees and shins before it vanished. The duct! It too had fallen or been ripped from its place! Had Batta Flor and Keri fallen too? Desperation and fear battled inside him and he struggled against the burning in his lungs, the need for air, the need to open his mouth and breathe, sucking in only dark water as he was carried to his death.

The water bucked and heaved around him and for a moment he thought that the device had exploded, but it was too soon, and as darkness began to crowd in on his thoughts, he thought that it would be a wonderful bit of irony if the mountain self-destructed before the explosion went off.

He strained to remain conscious, to remain upright, but he had lost all sense of where he was and could not tell if he was even in a vertical position. The current had him in its grip as firmly as a lupebeast held its prey; there was no getting loose.

He felt himself blacking out, losing purpose, when suddenly he was slammed into something hard, something unmoving, and pinned there by the force of the water, unable to move. He fell slowly, pushed down the face of the wall where he had struck until he touched bottom, and then the current swept him up again and hurled him through a chaotic race of conflicting currents. He lost all hope then, as he was flung about, arms and legs, head and body, pulled in various directions as though the water would divide him up with a bit here and another bit there until he was torn completely asunder.

And then it was over as quickly as it had begun. His body floated upward, water trickling in through his nose and mouth, darkness fogging his mind. Then, suddenly, he bobbed to the surface and he breathed in air, glorious sweet air, instead of water. He bumped into an object floating atop the dark water and pulled himself aboard with the very last of his strength, his back rubbing against the rough surface of the ceiling that was no more than a foot above the water.

He could hear the rush of the torrent close by and could tell by the violent action of his rough raft that it was very near, but somehow it floated free of the main channel. A corner of the raft touched the greater turbulence and was flung sideways in a dizzying spin.

The raft careened across the water and bumped hard against a stone wall, nearly throwing Braldt from his precarious perch. His fingers tightened, determined not to be thrown into the dark water again. As he pressed himself against the wood surface of the unseen object, there was a dull *whumph* and the water punched upward, heaving Braldt and his raft against the ceiling before dropping them down hard atop the water. His ears rang as air was displaced by the force of the explosion and he felt his body compress, the air forced from his lungs as well. He clung to the raft, a sick feeling sweeping over him, and for the second time in as many minutes, he struggled to retain consciousness, but this time he did not succeed.

28

Braldt opened his eyes and stared around him, wondering if he was dead. He could see nothing, all was dark. But he was breathing and he hurt all over. That seemed to indicate that he was still alive. What had happened? He struggled to bring his thoughts into focus, to remember what had happened. The explosion! Braldt sat up, or tried to, a sharp pain at the base of his spine caught him up short and he doubled over, gasping with the unexpected shock of it. What had happened after the explosion? Where were Keri and Batta Flor and Beast? Had they been killed?

As though in answer to his fears, he heard excited cries nearby and raised his own voice in a shout, although he was surprised to hear that it was barely louder than a croak. Nonetheless, soon after he was rewarded by the wet snuffling of a questing snout and then a chorus of yips as though Beast had learned to speak. He was stroking the excited pup, praising it for its efforts when strobes of light swept across him and Batta Flor and Keri appeared at his side. Never had he been so glad to see anyone ever in his life.

Keri fell to her knees beside him, sobbing, and Batta Flor seemed equally overwhelmed, coughing and clearing his throat and patting him awkwardly on the shoulder. Beast butted him rudely with his head, so as not to be forgotten. It was a reason to laugh and everyone joined in to the pup's disgust, but the laughter after so much fear was cleansing and good.

Batta Flor ran his hands over Braldt's body and found no broken bones although much of his body had been deeply bruised and would feel the effects long after the

273

day's work was done. The Madrelli picked Braldt up and gently placed him on his feet, supporting him until the wave of dizziness and pain had passed.

They were standing in what little remained of a small room adjacent to the larger control chamber. The door had been unable to stand up to the force of the water that had channeled through shortly after the initial sabotage and had been widened by the needs of the river. The water had gone, all that remained were pools on the floor.

"Come," said Batta Flor, "we have waited long for this moment, let us go together." Supporting Braldt on one side, Keri on the other, the three of them passed through the shattered doorway and into the control room itself.

"I must have struck the wall here and then been spun through into the next room," Braldt said, staring at the wall in wonder, noting the many rough protrusions where blocks of equipment had been ripped away by the force of the water, knowing that if he had struck even one of them, he would not be alive at the moment.

The light beams revealed what remained of the room, and oddly enough, a goodly portion had survived the impact of the river. The center of the room had borne the brunt of the force and everything that had stood in the river's way had been swept away, the flooring and even the subflooring and all of the metal fittings scoured clean.

Batta Flor directed his beam against the wall where Braldt had set the charge. The wall had collapsed completely, bringing down the ceiling as well. Numerous threads of water still found its way through the mass of debris and the thunder of the river could be heard on the other side. It seemed likely that it would break through again, but for the moment they were safe.

Braldt saw that the duct he had traveled was completely gone, ripped from the ceiling. The rest of the duct work, including that portion that had held Batta Flor, Keri, and Beast, was attached only at its farthest point where they had entered, the rest of it lay slanted against the ground.

"The water ripped it loose, or maybe it was the explosion, I'm not sure, it happened so fast," Keri said, following his gaze. "I was scared to death. I thought we were going to die. I thought you were already dead. But as the level of the water dropped, so did we. We slid all the way down. It might have been fun if I hadn't been so afraid."

As the beam of light crossed her face, Braldt saw that she had not escaped entirely without harm. Streaks of blood stained her ears and neck and her nose had obviously bled. There was a long cut on one side of her forehead. Braldt took the beam from her fingers and shone it on the Madrelli. He too bore similar bloodstains and one of his wrists appeared to be dangling at an odd angle.

"It is nothing," said Batta Flor as he moved out of the light. "The force of the explosion concussed us slightly. We will suffer no lasting damage. Come now, let us do that which we have endured so much to achieve. Let us see if the medicine box has survived its immersion."

Batta Flor directed his light beam over the walls. Directly before them were panels of a clear material that looked outward onto another room, probably that of the water flumes where the rhodium had been extracted. Below the windows were banks of panels with knobs and levers and a myriad of fixtures that Braldt could in no way identify. Everything was coated with a layer of red silt that gritted underfoot as they made their way across the room. Here and there, crammed under bits of machinery or wrapped around fallen girders, were the remains of the hard ones. These they avoided even though it was clear that they were without life.

The lever that Braldt and Carn had seen in their vision was clearly visible. Braldt's and Batta Flor's eyes met and then, as though by mutual silent decision, they turned aside, the Madrelli sighing in quiet relief. Braldt knew then that Batta Flor had had his reservations about him, just as he too had doubted the Madrelli intentions to bring him to their goal.

The medicine box was exactly as it had been in the vision. It was white and in its center was a bright crimson cross. It was fixed firmly to the wall and only the fact that it was out of the direct line of the river's course had prevented it from being washed away. They had indeed been fortunate. Braldt reached up and, using the tool Batta Flor handed him, freed the box from the wall.

"We have done what we set out to accomplish," Batta Flor said with audible relief. "Let us leave this place for I do not feel that we were meant to escape so easily."

Keri and Braldt were in complete agreement and they followed Batta Flor as he led the way across the slippery floor, anxious now to be gone from this place that had cost them so dearly. They were halfway across the room when an odd, rasping voice shocked them into immobility.

"I should have known you were traitors," the voice said bitterly and Braldt's heart contracted sharply at the words. For a moment, he thought that one of the hard ones had somehow come back to life. But then something familiar in the tone caught his ear and he raised his light beam and swept it across the room.

There, not ten feet away, horribly disfigured, stood Carn! Keri screamed and then called his name and started to go to him.

"Stay," Carn said coldly. "You are a traitor too. I have heard everything. I have followed you, listened to you, watched you. I know everything. I know now that you have no intention of honoring Mother Moon, that our gods mean nothing to you, that you have swallowed this animal's dirty lies." Braldt stepped forward, but Carn raised his hand and in it was a strange object, unlike anything Braldt had ever seen before. Carn depressed a button and a stream of red light shot forth striking the floor next to Braldt, which erupted in a spray of rock chips leaving an enormous hole.

"Stay away from him," cried Batta Flor as he thrust himself in front of Keri and Braldt. "He has a stunner and it's set on high!" Braldt did not stop to ask what a stunner was, it scarcely mattered. What did matter was that Carn was alive and quite obviously mad.

"I'll take that," said Carn, holding out his hand for the medicine box. "No," he said, gesturing with the stunner. "Not you. Braldt, give it to Keri. I don't trust you."

Keri took the box and approached Carn with sideling steps. Whatever she had hoped to accomplish failed, for as soon as she was within reach, Carn's hand shot out and grabbed her arm, twisting it cruelly. He took the medicine box from her and then placed the stunner against her throat and walked her to the wall where the lever was.

"No, Carn, stop! Don't do it!" cried Braldt and Batta Flor, and Keri added her voice to theirs as well. But Carn did not listen. His hand was on the lever now and he turned toward them, savoring the moment, knowing that they would not attempt to rush him as long as he held Keri.

"You might want to know what I learned, before you die," he said smugly, a strange light glowing from what little could be seen of his eyes. "The karks were wrong about the gods. I have seen them myself. I have found where Mother Moon goes at night. I have found her earthly lair. I have looked on the face of the gods.

"I will return to the tribe. I will bring the box and save Auslic's life. I will be made chief. You will die. You and the kark and this one too for she is dirty. She has lain with you without the blessing of the priests. She is filth just like you. And the priests will honor me for I have done their bidding." And then, before they could stop him, Carn threw all of his weight behind the lever and it moved from top to bottom. The thing was done.

A tremendous rumbling filled the room, louder, far louder than anything they had heard before. The floor and walls and ceiling began to shake and the room was filled with hot droplets of steam. The earth quivered and tossed beneath them and Keri screamed and fell to the ground. Carn began to laugh, clutching the white box to his chest. "I've done it, I've done it!" he cried insanely and staggered across the room toward them, raising the stunner. Beast began to howl.

"But what has he done, that is the question," yelled Batta Flor as he moved backward. Suddenly he switched his light beam off, and realizing what it was that he was trying to do, Braldt quickly did the same. Carn screamed with rage and fired the stunner where they had stood, but both of his targets had moved and the stunner struck nothing but the ground.

The shaking had grown more violent and the noise was all but unbearable. Braldt found Batta Flor and they were crouched together in a huddle with Beast between them when suddenly the room was flooded with a brilliant icy blue light. Blinking their eyes against the glare, they looked up.

Braldt blinked again and his heart was nearly stilled with a tremendous shock for there before him was a man, no two, no three men who were as much like his image as only a reflection could be. Their hair was white-blond like his, their eyes, the color of a cold mountain lake, their build, tall and slender yet well developed. He could only look at them and wonder if he had gone mad, there was no other explanation. They were dressed in clothing such as he had never seen before, fabric unlike any the Duroni women knew how to weave, a deep rich blue with a gold and crimson design worked on the breast and tall black boots rising nearly to their knees.

"Protect us from the folly of fools!" cursed one of the men as they looked around them at the disaster of the room. "Listen to that, you know what they've done, don't you!"

"The river, it's pouring into the core. By all the stars, we're done for, we've got to get out of here before the whole thing goes up!"

Braldt was still frozen with the shock of what he was seeing. Some part of his mind registered the fact that Keri was on her knees, now on her feet, her hand reaching for the lever. Carn was staggering toward the men, pointing at Keri, gibbering, falling, and then rising again.

One of them noticed him and, turning, saw what Keri was about to do. He swore aloud and raised a weapon similar to the one that Carn held and pointed it at Keri.

"No!" screamed Braldt as he hurled himself at the man who could have been his brother. He heard Beast attack another of the men and Batta Flor, screaming out his hatred, tackled the third.

Braldt heard the metallic protest of the lever as it was raised and then just as the room vanished in a hideous rumbling of rock and steam he was seized by an invisible whirling, swirling whirlpool that seemed to suck him away down a long, dark tunnel that went on forever and ever and ever out of his world and time and away and gone.